SACRIFICED!

In hopeless horror, Regis watched his friends huddle together. Then the scene in the Taros hoop shifted from the lower levels of the guildhouse to a darker place, a place of smoke and shadows, of ghouls and demons.

A place where no sun shone.

"No!" the halfling cried out, realizing the wizard's intent. Seconds later, Regis saw his friends in their huddle again, this time in the swirling smoke of the dark plane.

Regis watched as his friends turned back to back in a pitiful attempt at defense. Already, dark shapes swooped about them or hovered over them—beings of great power and great evil.

Regis dropped his eyes, unable to watch.

FORGOTTEN REALMS

FORGOTTEN REALMS

THE HALFLING'S GEM

THE LEGEND OF DRIZZT
BOOK
VI

R. A. SALVATORE

Wizards
OF THE COAST

THE LEGEND OF DRIZZT
BOOK VI
THE HALFLING'S GEM

©1990 TSR, Inc.
©2005 Wizards of the Coast, Inc.

Cover art by Todd Lockwood
Map by Todd Gamble
This Edition First Printing: August 2007
Originally published as Book Three of the Icewind Dale Trilogy in January 1990.

9 8 7 6 5 4 3 2 1

ISBN: 978-0-7869-4289-3
620-95955740-001-EN

U.S., CANADA,
ASIA, PACIFIC, & LATIN AMERICA
Wizards of the Coast, Inc.
P.O. Box 707
Renton, WA 98057-0707
+1-800-324-6496

EUROPEAN HEADQUARTERS
Hasbro UK Ltd
Caswell Way
Newport, Gwent NP9 0YH
GREAT BRITAIN
Save this address for your records.

Visit our web site at www.wizards.com

TO MY SISTER SUSAN,
WHO'LL NEVER KNOW HOW
MUCH HER SUPPORT HAS MEANT
TO ME OVER THE LAST FEW YEARS

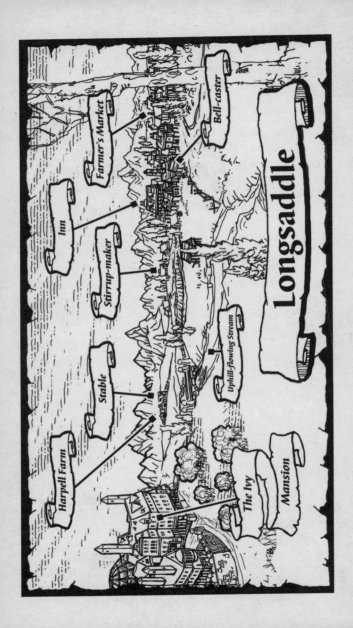

Longsaddle

Harpell Farm

Stable

Inn

Farmer's Market

Stirrup-maker

Bell-caster

Uphill-flowing Stream

The Ivy

Mansion

The wizard looked down upon the young woman with uncertainty. Her back was to him; he could see the thick mane of her auburn locks flowing around her shoulders, rich and vibrant. But the wizard knew, too, the sadness that was in her eyes. So young she was, barely more than a child, and so beautifully innocent.

PROLOGUE

Yet this beautiful child had put a sword through the heart of his beloved Sydney.

Harkle Harpell brushed away the unwanted memories of his dead love and started down the hill. "A fine day," he said cheerily when he reached the young woman.

"Do ye think they've made the tower?" Catti-brie asked him, her gaze never leaving the southern horizon.

Harkle shrugged. "Soon, if not yet." He studied Catti-brie and could find no anger against her for her actions. She had killed Sydney, it was true, but Harkle knew just by looking at her that necessity, not malice, had guided her sword arm. And now he could only pity her.

"How are you?" Harkle stammered, amazed at the courage she had shown in light of the terrible events that had befallen her and her friends.

Catti-brie nodded and turned to the wizard.

Surely there was sorrow edging her deep blue eyes, but mostly they burned with a stubborn resolve that chased away any hints of weakness. She had lost Bruenor, the dwarf who had adopted her and had reared her as his own since the earliest days of her childhood. And Catti-brie's other friends even now were caught in the middle of a desperate chase with an assassin across the southland.

"How quickly things have changed," Harkle whispered under his breath, feeling sympathy for the young woman. He remembered a time, just a few tendays earlier, when Bruenor Battlehammer and his small company had come through Longsaddle in their quest to find Mithral Hall, the dwarf's lost homeland. That had been a jovial meeting of tales exchanged and promises of future friendships with the Harpell clan. None of them could have known that a second party, led by an evil assassin, and by Harkle's own Sydney, held Catti-brie hostage and was gathering to pursue the company. Bruenor had found Mithral Hall, and had fallen there.

And Sydney, the female mage that Harkle had so dearly loved, had played a part in the dwarf's death.

Harkle took a deep breath to steady himself. "Bruenor will be avenged," he said with a grimace.

Catti-brie kissed him on the cheek and started back up the hill toward the Ivy Mansion.

She understood the wizard's sincere pain, and she truly admired his decision to help her fulfill her vow to return to Mithrall Hall and reclaim it for Clan Battlehammer.

But for Harkle, there had been no other choice. The Sydney that he had loved was a facade, a sugar coating to a power-crazed, unfeeling monster. And he himself had played a part in the disaster, unwittingly revealing to Sydney the whereabouts of Bruenor's party.

Harkle watched Catti-brie go, the weight of troubles slowing her stride. He could harbor no resentment toward her. Sydney had brought about the circumstances of her own death, and Catti-brie had no choice but to play them out. The wizard turned his gaze southward. He, too, wondered and worried for the drow elf and the huge barbarian lad. They had slumped back into Longsaddle just three days before, a sorrow-filled and weary band in desperate need of rest.

There could be no rest, though, not now, for the wicked assassin had escaped with the last of their group, Regis the halfling, in tow.

So much had happened in those few ten-days; Harkle's entire world had been turned upside down by an odd mixture of heroes from a distant, forlorn land called Icewind Dale, and by a beautiful young woman who could not be blamed.

And by the lie that was his deepest love.

Harkle fell back on the grass and watched

the puffy clouds of late summer meander across the sky.

⋈ ⋈ ⋈ ⋈ ⋈

Beyond the clouds, where the stars shone eternally, Guenhwyvar, the entity of the panther, paced excitedly. Many days had passed since the cat's master, the drow elf named Drizzt Do'Urden, had summoned it to the material plane. Guenhwyvar was sensitive to the onyx figurine that served as a link to its master and that other world; the panther could sense the tingle from that far-off place even when its master merely touched the statuette.

But Guenhwyvar hadn't felt that link to Drizzt in some time, and the cat was nervous now, somehow understanding in its otherworldly intelligence that the drow no longer possessed the figurine. Guenhwyvar remembered the time before Drizzt, when another drow, an evil drow, had been its master. Though in essence an animal, Guenhwyvar possessed dignity, a quality that its original master had stolen away.

Guenhwyvar remembered those times when it had been forced to perform cruel, cowardly acts against helpless foes for the sake of its master's pleasure.

But things had been very different since Drizzt Do'Urden came to possess the figurine.

Here was a being of conscience and integrity, and an honest bond of love had developed between Guenhwyvar and Drizzt.

The cat slumped against a star-trimmed tree and issued a low growl that observers to this astral spectacle might have taken as a resigned sigh.

Deeper still would the cat's sigh have been if it knew that Artemis Entreri, the killer, now possessed the figurine.

PART ONE

I am dying.

Every day, with every breath I draw, I am closer to the end of my life. For we are born with a finite number of breaths, and each one I take edges the sunlight that is my life toward the inevitable dusk.

HALFWAY TO EVERYWHERE

It is a difficult thing to remember, especially while we are in the health and strength of our youth, and yet, I have come to know that it is an important thing to keep in mind—not to complain or to make melancholy, but simply because only with the honest knowledge that one day I will die can I ever truly begin to live. Certainly I do not dwell on the reality of my own mortality, but I believe that a person cannot help but dwell, at least subconsciously, on that most imposing specter until he has come to understand, to truly understand and appreciate, that he will one day die. That he will one day be gone from this place, this life, this consciousness and existence, to whatever it is that awaits. For only when a person completely and honestly accepts the inevitability of death is he free of the fear of it.

So many people, it seems, stick themselves into the same routines, going through each day's rituals with almost religious precision. They become creatures of simple habit. Part of that is the comfort afforded by familiarity, but there is another aspect to it, a deep-rooted belief that as long as they keep everything the same, everything will remain the same. Such rituals are a way to control the world about them, but in truth, they cannot. For even if they follow the exact routine day after day after day, death will surely find them.

I have seen other people paralyze their entire existence around that greatest of mysteries, shaping their every movement, their every word, in a desperate attempt to find the answers to the unanswerable. They fool themselves, either through their interpretations of ancient texts or through some obscure sign from a natural event, into believing that they have found the ultimate truth, and thus, if they behave accordingly concerning that truth, they will surely be rewarded in the afterlife. This must be the greatest manifestation of that fear of death, the errant belief that we can somehow shape and decorate eternity itself, that we can curtain its windows and place its furniture in accordance with our own desperate desires. Along the road that led me to Icewind Dale, I came upon a group of followers of Ilmater, the god of suffering, who were so fanatical in their beliefs that they would beat each other senseless, and welcomed torment, even death itself, in some foolish belief that by doing so they would pay the highest tribute to their god.

I believe them to be wrong, though in truth, I cannot know anything for certain concerning what mystery lies beyond this mortal coil. And so I, too, am but a creature of faith and hope. I hope that Zaknafein has found eternal peace and joy, and pray with all my heart that when I cross over the threshold into the next existence, I will see him again.

Perhaps the greatest evil I see in this existence is when supposedly holy men prey upon the basic fears of death of the common folk to take from them. "Give to the church!" they cry. "Only then will you find salvation!" Even more subtle are the many religions that do not directly ask for a person's coin, but insist that anyone of goodly and godly heart who is destined for their particular description of heaven, would willingly give that coin over.

And of course, Toril is ripe with "doomsdayers," people who claim that the end of the world is at hand, and cry for repentance and for almost slavish dedication.

I can only look at it all and sigh, for as death is the greatest mystery, so it is the most personal of revelations. We will not know, none of us, until the moment it is upon us, and we cannot truly and in good conscience convince another of our beliefs.

It is a road we travel alone, but a road that I no longer fear, for in accepting the inevitable, I have freed myself from it. In coming to recognize my mortality, I have found the secret to enjoying those centuries, years, months, days, or even hours, that I have left to draw breath.

This is the existence I can control, and to throw away the precious hours over fear of the inevitable is a foolish thing indeed. And to subconsciously think ourselves immortal, and thus not appreciate those precious few hours that we all have, is equally foolish.

I cannot control the truth of death, whatever my desperation. I can only make certain that those moments of my life I have remaining are as rich as they can be.

—Drizzt Do'Urden

I

TOWER OF TWILIGHT

A day and more we have lost," the barbarian grumbled, reining in his horse and looking back over his shoulder. The lower rim of the sun had just dipped below the horizon. "The assassin moves away from us even now!"

"We do well to trust in Harkle's advice," replied Drizzt Do'Urden, the dark elf. "He would not have led us astray." With the sunshine fading, Drizzt dropped the cowl of his black cloak back onto his shoulders and shook free the locks of his stark white hair.

Wulfgar pointed to some tall pines. "That must be the grove Harkle Harpell spoke of," he said, "yet I see no tower, nor signs that any structure was ever built in this forsaken area."

His lavender eyes more at home in the deepening gloom, Drizzt peered ahead intently, trying to find some evidence to dispute his young friend. Surely this was the place that Harkle had indicated, for a short distance ahead of them lay the small pond, and beyond that the thick boughs of Neverwinter Wood. "Take heart," he reminded Wulfgar. "The wizard called patience the greatest aid in finding the home of Malchor. We have been here but an hour."

"The road grows ever longer," the barbarian mumbled, unaware that the drow's keen ears did not miss a word. There was merit in Wulfgar's complaints, Drizzt knew, for the tale of a farmer in Longsaddle—that of a dark, cloaked man and a halfling on a single horse—put the assassin fully ten days ahead of them, and moving swiftly.

But Drizzt had faced Entreri before and understood the enormity of the challenge before him. He wanted as much assistance as he could get in rescuing Regis from the deadly man's clutches. By the farmer's words, Regis was still alive, and Drizzt was certain that Entreri did not mean to harm the halfling before getting to Calimport.

Harkle Harpell would not have sent them to this place without good reason.

"Do we put up for the night?" asked Wulfgar. "By my word, we'd ride back to the road and to the south. Entreri's horse carries two and may have tired by now. We can gain on him if we ride through the night."

Drizzt smiled at his friend. "They have passed through the city of Waterdeep by now," he explained. "Entreri has acquired new horses, at the least." Drizzt let the issue drop at that, keeping his deeper fears, that the assassin had taken to the sea, to himself.

"Then to wait is even more folly!" Wulfgar was quick to argue.

But as the barbarian spoke, his horse, a horse raised by Harpells, snorted and moved to the small pond, pawing the air above the water as though searching for a place to step. A moment later, the last of the sun dipped under the western horizon and the

13

daylight faded away. And in the magical dimness of twilight, an enchanted tower phased into view before them on the little island in the pond, its every point twinkling like starlight, and its many twisting spires reaching up into the evening sky. Emerald green it was, and mystically inviting, as if sprites and faeries had lent a hand to its creation.

And across the water, right below the hoof of Wulfgar's horse, appeared a shining bridge of green light.

Drizzt slipped from his mount. "The Tower of Twilight," he said to Wulfgar, as though he had seen the obvious logic from the start. He swept his arm out toward the structure, inviting his friend to lead them in.

But Wulfgar was stunned at the appearance of the tower. He clutched the reins of his horse even tighter, causing the beast to rear up and flatten its ears against its head.

"I thought you had overcome your suspicions of magic," said Drizzt sarcastically. Truly Wulfgar, like all the barbarians of Icewind Dale, had been raised with the belief that wizards were weakling tricksters and not to be trusted. His people, proud warriors of the tundra, regarded strength of arm, not skill in the black arts of wizardry, as the measure of a true man. But in their many tendays on the road, Drizzt had seen Wulfgar overcome his upbringing and develop a tolerance, even a curiosity, for the practices of wizardry.

With a flex of his massive muscles, Wulfgar brought his horse under control. "I have," he answered through gritted teeth. He slid from his seat. "It is Harpells that worry me!"

Drizzt's smirk widened across his face as he suddenly came to understand his friend's trepidations. He himself, who had been raised amidst many of the most powerful and frightening sorcerers in all the Realms, had shaken his head in disbelief many times when they were guests of the eccentric family in Longsaddle. The

Harpells had a unique—and often disastrous—way of viewing the world, though no evil festered in their hearts, and they wove their magic in accord with their own perspectives—usually against the presumed logic of rational men.

"Malchor is unlike his kin," Drizzt assured Wulfgar. "He does not reside in the Ivy Mansion and has played advisor to kings of the northland."

"He is a Harpell," Wulfgar stated with a finality that Drizzt could not dispute. With another shake of his head and a deep breath to steady himself, Wulfgar grabbed his horse's bridle and started out across the bridge. Drizzt, still smiling, was quick to follow.

"Harpell," Wulfgar muttered again after they had crossed to the island and made a complete circuit of the structure.

The tower had no door.

"Patience," Drizzt reminded him.

They did not have to wait long, though, for a few seconds later they heard a bolt being thrown, and then the creak of a door opening. A moment later, a boy barely into his teens walked right through the green stone of the wall, like some translucent specter, and moved toward them.

Wulfgar grunted and brought Aegis-fang, his mighty war-hammer, down off his shoulder. Drizzt grasped the barbarian's arm to stay him, fearing that his weary friend might strike in sheer frustration before they could determine the lad's intentions.

When the boy reached them, they could see clearly that he was flesh and blood, not some otherworldly specter, and Wulfgar relaxed his grip. The youth bowed low to them and motioned for them to follow.

"Malchor?" asked Drizzt.

The boy did not answer, but he motioned again and started back toward the tower.

"I would have thought you to be older, if Malchor you be," Drizzt said, falling into step behind the boy.

"What of the horses?" Wulfgar asked.

Still the boy continued silently toward the tower.

Drizzt looked at Wulfgar and shrugged. "Bring them in, then, and let our mute friend worry about them," the dark elf said.

They found one section of the wall—at least—to be an illusion, masking a door that led them into a wide, circular chamber that was the tower's lowest level. Stalls lining one wall showed that they had done right in bringing the horses, and they tethered the beasts quickly and rushed to catch up to the youth. The boy had not slowed and had entered another doorway.

"Hold for us," Drizzt called, stepping through the portal, but he found no guide inside. He had entered a dimly lit corridor that rose gently and arced around as it rose, apparently tracing the circumference of the tower. "Only one way to go," he told Wulfgar, who came in behind him, and they started off.

Drizzt figured that they had done one complete circle and were up to the second level—ten feet at least—when they found the boy waiting for them beside a darkened side passage that fell back toward the center of the structure. The lad ignored this passage, though, and started off higher into the tower along the main arcing corridor.

Wulfgar had run out of patience for such cryptic games. His only concern was that Entreri and Regis were running farther away every second. He stepped by Drizzt and grabbed the boy's shoulder, spinning him about. "Are you Malchor?" he demanded bluntly.

The boy blanched at the giant man's gruff tone but did not reply.

"Leave him," Drizzt said. "He is not Malchor. I am sure. We

will find the master of the tower soon enough." He looked to the frightened boy. "True?"

The boy gave a quick nod and started off again.

"Soon," Drizzt reiterated to quiet Wulfgar's growl. He prudently stepped by the barbarian, putting himself between Wulfgar and the guide.

"Harpell," Wulfgar groaned at his back.

The incline grew steeper and the circles tighter, and both friends knew that they were nearing the top. Finally the boy stopped at a door, pushed it open, and motioned for them to enter.

Drizzt moved quickly to be the first inside the room, fearing that the angry barbarian might make less than a pleasant first impression with their wizard host.

Across the room, sitting atop a desk and apparently waiting for them, rested a tall and sturdy man with neatly trimmed salt-and-pepper hair. His arms were crossed on his chest. Drizzt began to utter a cordial greeting, but Wulfgar nearly bowled him over, bursting in from behind and striding right up to the desk.

The barbarian, with one hand on his hip and one holding Aegis-fang in a prominent display before him, eyed the man for a moment. "Are you the wizard named Malchor Harpell?" he demanded, his voice hinting at explosive anger. "And if not, where in the Nine Hells are we to find him?"

The man's laugh erupted straight from his belly. "Of course," he answered, and he sprang from the desk and clapped Wulfgar hard on the shoulder. "I prefer a guest who does not cover his feelings with rosy words!" he cried. He walked past the stunned barbarian toward the door—and the boy.

"Did you speak to them?" he demanded of the lad.

The boy blanched even more than before and shook his head emphatically.

"Not a single word?" Malchor yelled.

The boy trembled visibly and shook his head again.

"He said not a—" Drizzt began, but Malchor cut him off with an outstretched hand.

"If I find that you uttered even a single syllable . . ." he threatened. He turned back to the room and took a step away. Just when he figured that the boy might have relaxed a bit, he spun back on him, nearly causing him to jump from his shoes.

"Why are you still here?" Malchor demanded. "Be gone!"

The door slammed even before the wizard had finished the command. Malchor laughed again, and the tension eased from his muscles as he moved back to his desk. Drizzt came up beside Wulfgar, the two looking at each other in amazement.

"Let us be gone from this place," Wulfgar said to Drizzt, and the drow could see that his friend was fighting a desire to spring over the desk and throttle the arrogant wizard on the spot.

To a lesser degree, Drizzt shared those feelings, but he knew the tower and its occupants would be explained in time. "Our greetings, Malchor Harpell," he said, his lavender eyes boring into the man. "Your actions, though, do not fit the description your cousin Harkle mantled upon you."

"I assure you that I am as Harkle described," Malchor replied calmly. "And my welcome to you, Drizzt Do'Urden, and to you, Wulfgar, son of Beornegar. Rarely have I entertained such fine guests in my humble tower." He bowed low to them to complete his gracious and diplomatic—if not entirely accurate—greeting.

"The boy did nothing wrong," Wulfgar snarled at him.

"No, he has performed admirably," Malchor agreed. "Ah, you fear for him?" The wizard took his measure of the huge barbarian, Wulfgar's muscles still knotted in rage. "I assure you, the boy is treated well."

"Not by my eyes," retorted Wulfgar.

"He aspires to be a wizard," Malchor explained, not ruffled by the barbarian's scowl. "His father is a powerful land-owner and has employed me to guide the lad. The boy shows potential, a sharp mind, and a love for the arts. But understand, Wulfgar, that wizardry is not so very different from your own trade."

Wulfgar's smirk showed a difference of opinion.

"Discipline," Malchor continued, undaunted. "For whatever we do in our lives, discipline and control over our own actions ultimately measure the level of our success. The boy has high aspirations and hints of power he cannot yet begin to understand. But if he cannot keep his thoughts silent for a single month, then I shan't waste years of my time on him. Your companion understands."

Wulfgar looked to Drizzt, standing relaxed by his side.

"I do understand," Drizzt said to Wulfgar. "Malchor has put the youth on trial, a test of his abilities to follow commands and a revelation to the depth of his desires."

"I am forgiven?" the wizard asked them.

"It is not important," Wulfgar grunted. "We have not come to fight the battles of a boy."

"Of course," said Malchor. "Your business presses; Harkle has told me. Go back down to the stables and wash. The boy is setting supper. He shall come for you when it is time to eat."

"Does he have a name?" Wulfgar said with obvious sarcasm.

"None that he has yet earned," Malchor replied curtly.

⚔ ⚔ ⚔ ⚔

Though he was anxious to be back on the road, Wulfgar could not deny the splendor of the table of Malchor Harpell. He and Drizzt feasted well, knowing this to be, most probably, their last fine meal for many days.

"You shall spend the night," Malchor said to them after they had finished eating. "A soft bed would do you well," he argued against Wulfgar's disgruntled look. "And an early start, I promise."

"We will stay, and thank you," Drizzt replied. "Surely this tower will do us better than the hard ground outside."

"Excellent," said Malchor. "Come along, then, I have some items which should aid your quest." He led them out of the room and back down the decline of the corridor to the lower levels of the structure. As they walked, Malchor told his guests of the tower's formation and features. Finally they turned down one of the darkened side passages and passed through a heavy door.

Drizzt and Wulfgar had to pause at the entrance for a long moment to digest the wondrous sight before them, for they had come to Malchor's museum, a collection of the finest items, magical and otherwise, that the mage had found during the many years of his travels. Here were swords and full suits of polished armor, a shining mithral shield, and the crown of a long dead king. Ancient tapestries lined the walls, and a glass case of priceless gems and jewels glittered in the flicker of the room's torches.

Malchor had moved to a cabinet across the room, and by the time Wulfgar and Drizzt looked back to him, he was sitting atop the thing, casually juggling three horseshoes. He added a fourth as they watched, effortlessly guiding them through the rise and fall of the dance.

"I have placed an enchantment upon these that will make your steeds run swifter than any beasts in the land," he explained. "For a short time only, but long enough to get you to Waterdeep. That alone should be worth your delay in coming here"

"Two shoes to a horse?" Wulfgar asked, ever doubting.

"That would not do," Malchor came back at him, tolerant of the weary young barbarian. "Unless you wish your horse to rear up and run as a man!" He laughed, but the scowl did not leave Wulfgar's face.

"Not to fear," Malchor said, clearing his throat at the failed joke. "I have another set." He eyed Drizzt. "I have heard it spoken that few are as agile as the drow elves. And I have heard, as well, by those who have seen Drizzt Do'Urden at fight and at play, that he is brilliant even considering the standards of his dark kin." Without interrupting the rhythm of his juggling, he flipped one of the horseshoes to Drizzt.

Drizzt caught it easily and in the same motion put it into the air above him. Then came the second and third shoes, and Drizzt, without ever taking his eyes off Malchor, put them into motion with easy movements.

The fourth shoe came in low, causing Drizzt to bend to the ground to catch it. But Drizzt was up to the task, and he never missed a catch or a throw as he included the shoe in his juggling.

Wulfgar watched curiously and wondered at the motives of the wizard in testing the drow.

Malchor reached down into the cabinet and pulled out the other set of shoes. "A fifth," he warned, launching one at Drizzt. The drow remained unconcerned, catching the shoe deftly and tossing it in line.

"Discipline!" said Malchor emphatically, aiming his remark at Wulfgar. "Show me, drow!" he demanded, firing the sixth, seventh, and eighth at Drizzt in rapid succession.

Drizzt grimaced as they came at him, determined to meet the challenge. His hands moving in a blur, he quickly had all eight horseshoes spinning and dropping harmoniously. And as he settled into an easy rhythm, Drizzt began to understand the wizard's ploy.

Malchor walked over to Wulfgar and clapped him again on the shoulder. "Discipline," he said again. "Look at him, young warrior, for your dark-skinned friend is truly a master of his movements and thus, a master of his craft. You do not yet understand, but we two are not so different." He caught Wulfgar's eyes squarely with his own. "We three are not so different. Different methods, I agree. But to the same ends!"

Tiring of his game, Drizzt caught the shoes one by one as they fell and hooked them over his forearm, all the while eyeing Malchor with approval. Seeing his young friend slump back in thought, the drow wasn't sure which was the greater gift, the enchanted shoes or the lesson.

"But enough of this," Malchor said suddenly, bursting into motion. He crossed to a section of the wall that held dozens of swords and other weapons.

"I see that one of your scabbards is empty," he said to Drizzt. Malchor pulled a beautifully crafted scimitar from its mount. "Perhaps this will fill it properly."

Drizzt sensed the power of the weapon as he took it from the wizard, felt the care of its crafting and the perfection of its balance. A single, star-cut blue sapphire glittered in its pommel.

"Its name is Twinkle," Malchor said. "Forged by the elves of a past age."

"Twinkle," echoed Drizzt. Instantly a bluish light limned the weapon's blade. Drizzt felt a sudden surge within it, and somehow sensed a finer edge to its cut. He swung it a few times, trailing blue light with each motion. How easily it arced through the air; how easily it would cut down a foe! Drizzt slid it reverently into his empty scabbard.

"It was forged in the magic of the powers that all the surface elves hold dear," said Malchor. "Of the stars and the moon and the mysteries of their souls. You deserve it, Drizzt Do'Urden, and it will serve you well."

Drizzt could not answer the tribute, but Wulfgar, touched by the honor Malchor had paid to his oft-maligned friend, spoke for him. "Our thanks to you, Malchor Harpell," he said, biting back the cynicism that had dominated his actions of late. He bowed low.

"Keep to your heart, Wulfgar, son of Beornegar," Malchor answered him. "Pride can be a useful tool, or it can close your eyes to the truths about you. Go now and take your sleep. I shall awaken you early and set you back along your road."

⚔ ⚔ ⚔ ⚔ ⚔

Drizzt sat up in his bed and watched his friend after Wulfgar had settled into sleep. Drizzt was concerned for Wulfgar, so far from the empty tundra that had ever been his home. In their quest for Mithral Hall, they had trudged halfway across the northland, fighting every mile of the way. And in finding their goal, their trials had only begun, for they had then battled their way through the ancient dwarven complex. Wulfgar had lost his mentor there, and Drizzt his dearest friend, and truly they had dragged themselves back to the village of Longsaddle in need of a long rest.

But reality had allowed no breaks. Entreri had Regis in his clutches, and Drizzt and Wulfgar were their halfling friend's only hope. In Longsaddle, they had come to the end of one road but had found the beginning of an even longer one.

Drizzt could deal with his own weariness, but Wulfgar seemed cloaked in gloom, always running on the edge of danger. He was a young man out of Icewind Dale—the land that had been his only home—for the first time in his life. Now that sheltered strip of tundra, where the eternal wind blew, was far to the north.

But Calimport was much farther still, to the south.

Drizzt lay back on his pillow, reminding himself that Wulfgar had chosen to come along. Drizzt couldn't have stopped him, even if he had tried.

The drow closed his eyes. The best thing that he could do, for himself and for Wulfgar, was to sleep and be ready for whatever the next dawn would bring.

⚔ ⚔ ⚔ ⚔ ⚔

Malchor's student awakened them—silently—a few hours later and led them to the dining room, where the wizard waited. A fine breakfast was brought out before them.

"Your course is south, by my cousin's words," Malchor said to them. "Chasing a man who holds your friend, this halfling, Regis, captive."

"His name is Entreri," Drizzt replied, "and we will find him a hard catch, by my measure of him. He flies for Calimport."

"Harder still," Wulfgar added, "we had him placed on the road." He explained to Malchor, though Drizzt knew the words to be aimed at him, "Now we shall have to hope that he did not turn from its course."

"There was no secret to his path," argued Drizzt. "He made for Waterdeep, on the coast. He may have passed by there already."

"Then he is out to sea," reasoned Malchor.

Wulfgar nearly choked on his food. He hadn't even considered that possibility.

"That is my fear," said Drizzt. "And I had thought to do the same."

"It is a dangerous and costly course," said Malchor. "The pirates gather for the last runs to the south as the summer draws to an end, and if one has not made the proper arrangements . . ." He let the words hang ominously before them.

"But you have little choice," the wizard continued. "A horse cannot match the speed of a sailing ship, and the sea route is straighter than the road. So take to the sea, is my advice. Perhaps I can make some arrangements to speed your accommodations. My student has already set the enchanted shoes on your mounts, and with their aid, you may get to the great port in short days."

"And how long shall we sail?" Wulfgar asked, dismayed and hardly believing that Drizzt would go along with the wizard's suggestion.

"Your young friend does not understand the breadth of this journey," Malchor said to Drizzt. The wizard laid his fork on the table and another a few inches from it. "Here is Icewind Dale," he explained to Wulfgar, pointing to the first fork. "And this other, the Tower of Twilight, where you now sit. A distance of nearly four hundred miles lies between."

He tossed a third fork to Drizzt, who laid it out in front of him, about three feet from the fork representing their present position.

"It is a journey you would travel five times to equal the road ahead of you," Malchor told Wulfgar, "for that last fork is Calimport, two thousand miles and several kingdoms to the south."

"Then we are defeated," moaned Wulfgar, unable to comprehend such a distance.

"Not so," said Malchor. "For you shall ride with sails full of the northern wind, and beat the first snows of winter. You will find the land and the people more accommodating to the south."

"We shall see," said the dark elf, unconvinced. To Drizzt, people had ever spelled trouble.

"Ah," agreed Malchor, realizing the hardships a drow elf would surely find among the dwellers of the surface world. "But I have one more gift to give to you: a map to a treasure that you can recover this very day."

"Another delay," said Wulfgar.

"A small price to pay," replied Malchor, "and this short trip shall save you many days in the populated South, where a drow elf may walk only in the night. Of this I am certain."

Drizzt was intrigued that Malchor so clearly understood his dilemma and was apparently hinting at an alternative. Drizzt would not be welcome anywhere in the South. Cities that would grant the foul Entreri free passage would throw chains upon the dark elf if he tried to cross through, for the drow had long ago earned their reputation as ultimately evil and unspeakably vile. Few in all the Realms would be quick to recognize Drizzt Do'Urden as the exception to the rule.

"Just to the west of here, down a dark path in Neverwinter Wood and in a cave of trees, dwells a monster that the local farmers have named Agatha," said Malchor. "Once an elf, I believe, and a fair mage in her own right, according to legend, this wretched thing lives on after death and calls the night her time."

Drizzt knew the sinister legends of such creatures, and he knew their name. "A banshee?" he asked.

Malchor nodded. "To her lair you should go, if you are brave enough, for the banshee has collected a fair hoard of treasure, including one item that would prove invaluable to you, Drizzt Do'Urden."

He saw that he had the drow's full attention. Drizzt leaned forward over the table and weighed Malchor's every word.

"A mask," the wizard explained. "An enchanted mask that will allow you to hide your heritage and walk freely as a surface elf—or as a man, if that suits you."

Drizzt slumped back, a bit unnerved at the threat to his very identity.

"I understand your hesitancy," Malchor said to him. "It is not easy to hide from those who accuse you unjustly, to give credibility to their false perceptions. But think of your captive friend and know that I make this suggestion only for his sake. You may get through the southlands as you are, dark elf, but not unhindered."

Wulfgar bit his lip and said nothing, knowing this to be Drizzt's own decision. He knew that even his concerns about further delay could not weigh into such a personal discussion.

"We will go to this lair in the wood," Drizzt said at last, "and I shall wear such a mask if I must." He looked at Wulfgar. "Our only concern must be Regis."

⚔ ⚔ ⚔ ⚔ ⚔

Drizzt and Wulfgar sat atop their mounts outside the Tower of Twilight, with Malchor standing beside them.

"Be wary of the thing," Malchor said, handing Drizzt the map to the banshee's lair and another parchment that generally showed their course to the far South. "Her touch is deathly cold, and the legends say that to hear her keen is to die."

"Her keen?" asked Wulfgar.

"An unearthly wail too terrible for mortal ears to bear," said Malchor. "Take all care!"

"We shall," Drizzt assured him.

"We will not forget the hospitality or the gifts of Malchor Harpell," added Wulfgar.

"Nor the lesson, I hope," the wizard replied with a wink, drawing an embarrassed smile from Wulfgar.

Drizzt was pleased that his friend had shaken at least some of his surliness.

Dawn came upon them then, and the tower quickly faded into nothingness.

"The tower is gone, yet the wizard remains," remarked Wulfgar.

"The tower is gone, yet the door inside remains," Malchor corrected. He took a few steps back and stretched his arm out, his hand disappearing from sight.

Wulfgar jerked in bewilderment.

"For those who know how to find it," Malchor added. "For those who have trained their minds to the properties of magic." He stepped through the extradimensional portal and was gone from sight, but his voice came back to them one last time. "Discipline!" he called, and Wulfgar knew himself to be the target of Malchor's final statement.

Drizzt kicked his horse into motion, unrolling the map as he started away. "Harpell?" be asked over his shoulder, imitating Wulfgar's derisive tone of the previous night.

"Would that all of the Harpells were like Malchor!" Wulfgar replied. He sat staring at the emptiness that had been the Tower of Twilight, fully understanding that the wizard had taught him two valuable lessons in a single night: one of prejudice and one of humility.

✕ ✕ ✕ ✕ ✕

From inside the hidden dimension of his home, Malchor watched them go. He wished that he could join them, to travel along the road of adventure as he had so often in his youth, finding a just course and following it against any odds. Harkle had judged the principles of those two correctly, Malchor knew, and had been right in asking Malchor to help them.

The wizard leaned against the door to his home. Alas, his days of adventure, his days of carrying the crusade of justice on his shoulders, were fading behind him.

But Malchor took heart in the events of the last day. If the drow and his barbarian friend were any indication, he had just helped to pass the torch into able hands.

A Thousand Thousand Little Candles

The assassin, mesmerized, watched as the ruby turned slowly in the candlelight, catching the dance of the flame in a thousand thousand perfect miniatures—too many reflections; no gem could have facets so small and so flawless.

And yet the procession was there to be seen, a swirl of tiny candles drawing him deeper into the redness of the stone. No jeweler had cut it; its precision went beyond a level attainable with an instrument. This was an artifact of magic, a deliberate creation designed, he reminded himself cautiously, to pull a viewer into that descending swirl, into the serenity of the reddened depths of the stone.

A thousand thousand little candles

No wonder he had so easily duped the captain into giving him passage to Calimport. Suggestions that came from within the marvelous secrets of this gem could not easily be dismissed. Suggestions of serenity and peace, words spoken only by friends . . .

A smile cracked the usually grim set of his face. He could wander deep into the calm.

Entreri tore himself from the pull of the ruby and rubbed his eyes, amazed that even one as disciplined as he might be vulnerable to the gem's insistent tug. He glanced into the corner of the small cabin, where Regis sat huddled and thoroughly miserable.

"I can now understand your desperation in stealing this jewel," he said to the halfling.

Regis snapped out of his own meditation, surprised that Entreri had spoken to him—the first time since they had boarded the boat back in Waterdeep.

"And I know now why Pasha Pook is so desperate to get it back," Entreri continued, as much to himself as to Regis.

Regis cocked his head to watch the assassin. Could the ruby pendant take even Artemis Entreri into its hold? "Truly it is a beautiful gem," he offered hopefully, not quite knowing how to handle this uncharacteristic empathy from the cold assassin.

"Much more than a gemstone," Entreri said absently, his eyes falling irresistibly back into the mystical swirl of the deceptive facets.

Regis recognized the calm visage of the assassin, for he himself had worn such a look when he had first studied Pook's wonderful pendant. He had been a successful thief then, living a fine life in Calimport. But the promises of that magical stone outweighed the comforts of the thieves' guild. "Perhaps the pendant stole me," he suggested on a sudden impulse.

But he had underestimated the willpower of Entreri. The assassin snapped a cold look at him, with a smirk clearly revealing that he knew where Regis was leading.

But the halfling, grabbing at whatever hope he could find, pressed on anyway. "The power of that pendant overcame me, I think. There could be no crime; I had little choice—"

Entreri's sharp laugh cut him short. "You are a thief, or you are weak," he snarled. "Either way you shall find no mercy in my heart. Either way you deserve the wrath of Pook!" He snapped the pendant up into his hand from the end of its golden chain and dropped it into his pouch.

Then he took out the other object, an onyx statuette intricately carved into the likeness of a panther.

"Tell me of this," he instructed Regis.

Regis had wondered when Entreri would show some curiosity for the figurine. He had seen the assassin toying with it back at Garumn's Gorge in Mithral Hall, teasing Drizzt from across the chasm. But until this moment, that was the last Regis had seen of Guenhwyvar, the magical panther.

Regis shrugged helplessly.

"I'll not ask again," Entreri threatened, and that icy certainty of doom, the inescapable aura of dread that all of Artemis Entreri's victims came to know well, fell over Regis once more.

"It is the drow's," Regis stammered. "Its name is Guen—" Regis caught the word in his mouth as Entreri's free hand suddenly snapped out a jeweled dagger, readied for a throw.

"Calling an ally?" Entreri asked wickedly. He dropped the statuette back into his pocket. "I know the beast's name, halfling. And I assure you, by the time the cat arrived, you would be dead."

"You fear the cat?" Regis dared to ask.

"I take no chances," Entreri replied.

"But will you call the panther yourself?" Regis pressed, looking for some way to change the balance of power. "A companion for your lonely roads?"

Entreri's laugh mocked the very thought "Companion? Why would I desire a companion, little fool? What gain could I hope to make?"

"With numbers comes strength," Regis argued.

"Fool," repeated Entreri. "That is where you err. In the streets, companions bring dependence and doom! Look at yourself, friend of the drow. What strength do you bring to Drizzt Do'Urden now? He rushes blindly to your aid, to fulfill his responsibility as your companion." He spat the word out with obvious distaste. "To his ultimate demise!"

Regis hung his head and could not answer. Entreri's words rang true enough. His friends were coming into dangers they could not imagine, and all for his sake, all because of errors he had made before he had ever met them.

Entreri replaced the dagger in its sheath and leaped up in a rush. "Enjoy the night, little thief. Bask in the cold ocean wind; relish all the sensations of this trip as a man staring death in the face, for Calimport surely spells your doom—and the doom of your friends!" He swept out of the room, banging the door behind him.

He hadn't locked it, Regis noted. He never locked the door! But he didn't have to, Regis admitted in anger. Terror was the assassin's chain, as tangible as iron shackles. Nowhere to run; nowhere to hide.

Regis dropped his head into his hands. He became aware of the sway of the ship, of the rhythmic, monotonous creaking of old boards, his body irresistibly keeping time.

He felt his insides churning.

Halflings weren't normally fond of the sea, and Regis was timid even by the measures of his kind. Entreri could not have found a greater torment to Regis than passage south on a ship, on the Sea of Swords.

"Not again," Regis groaned, dragging himself to the small portal in the cabin. He pulled the window open and stuck his head out into the refreshing chill of the night air.

⚔ ⚔ ⚔ ⚔ ⚔

Entreri walked across the empty deck, his cloak tight about him. Above him, the sails swelled as they filled with wind; the early winter gales pushed the ship along its southern route. A billion stars dotted the sky, twinkling in the empty darkness to horizons bordered only by the flat line of the sea.

Entreri took out the ruby pendant again and let its magic catch the starlight. He watched it spin and studied its swirl, meaning to know it well before his journey's end.

Pasha Pook would be thrilled to get the pendant back. It had given him such power! More power, Entreri now realized, than others had assumed. With the pendant, Pook had made friends of enemies and slaves of friends.

"Even me?" Entreri mused, enthralled by the little stars in the red wash of the gem. "Have I been a victim? Or shall I be?" He wouldn't have believed that he, Artemis Entreri, could ever be caught by a magic charm, but the insistence of the ruby pendant was undeniable.

Entreri laughed aloud. The helmsman, the only other person on the deck, cast him a curious glance but thought no more about it.

"No," Entreri whispered to the ruby. "You shan't have me again. I know your tricks, and I'll learn them better still! I will run the path of your tempting descent and find my way back out again!" Laughing, he fastened the pendant's golden chain around his neck and tucked the ruby under his leather jerkin.

Then he felt in his pouch, grasped the figurine of the panther, and turned his gaze back to the north. "Are you watching, Drizzt Do'Urden?" he asked into the night.

He knew the answer. Somewhere far behind, in Waterdeep or

Longsaddle or somewhere in between, the drow's lavender eyes were turned southward.

They were destined to meet again; they both knew. They had battled once, in Mithral Hall, but neither could claim victory.

There had to be a winner.

Never before had Entreri encountered anyone with reflexes to match his own or as deadly with a blade as he, and memories of his clash with Drizzt Do'Urden haunted his every thought. They were so akin, their movements cut from the same dance. And yet, the drow, compassionate and caring, possessed a basic humanity that Entreri had long ago discarded. Such emotions, such weaknesses, had no place in the cold void of a pure fighter's heart, he believed.

Entreri's hands twitched with eagerness as he thought of the drow. His breath puffed out angrily in the chill air. "Come, Drizzt Do'Urden," he said through his clenched teeth. "Let us learn who is the stronger!"

His voice reflected deadly determination, with a subtle, almost imperceptive, hint of anxiety. This would be the truest challenge of both their lives, the test of the differing tenets that had guided their every actions. For Entreri, there could be no draw. He had sold his soul for his skill, and if Drizzt Do'Urden defeated him, or even proved his equal, the assassin's existence would be no more than a wasted lie.

But he didn't think like that.

Entreri lived to win.

⚔ ⚔ ⚔ ⚔ ⚔

Regis, too, was watching the night sky. The crisp air had settled his stomach, and the stars had sent his thoughts across the long miles to his friends. How often they had sat together on such nights in Icewind Dale, to share tales of adventure or just sit quietly in each others' company. Icewind Dale was a barren strip of frozen tundra, a land of brutal weather and brutal people, but the friends Regis had made there, Bruenor and Catti-brie, Drizzt and Wulfgar, had warmed the coldest of the winter nights and taken the sting out of the biting north wind.

In context, Icewind Dale had been but a short stopover for Regis on his extensive travels, where he had spent less than ten of his fifty years. But now, heading back to the southern kingdom where he had lived for the bulk of his life, Regis realized that Icewind Dale had truly been his home. And those friends he so often took for granted were the only family he would ever know.

He shook away his lament and forced himself to consider the path before him. Drizzt would come for him; probably Wulfgar and Catti-brie, too.

But not Bruenor.

Any relief that Regis had felt when Drizzt returned unharmed from the bowels of Mithral Hall had flown over Garumn's Gorge with the valiant dwarf. A dragon had them trapped while a host of evil gray dwarves had closed in from behind. But Bruenor, at the cost of his own life, had cleared the way, crashing down onto the dragon's back with a keg of burning oil, taking the beast—and himself—down into the deep gorge.

Regis couldn't bear to recall that terrible scene. For all of his gruffness and teasing, Bruenor Battlehammer had been the halfling's dearest companion.

A shooting star burned a trail across the night sky. The sway of the ship remained and the salty smell of the ocean sat thick in his nose, but here at the portal, in the sharpness of the clear night, Regis felt no sickness—only a sad serenity as he remembered all of those crazy times with the wild dwarf. Truly

Bruenor Battlehammer's flame had burned like a torch in the wind, leaping and dancing and fighting to the very end.

Regis's other friends had escaped, though. The halfling was certain of it—as certain as Entreri. And they would come for him. Drizzt would come for him and set things right.

Regis had to believe that.

And for his own part, the mission seemed obvious. Once in Calimport, Entreri would find allies among Pook's people. The assassin would then be on his own ground, where he knew every dark hole and held every advantage. Regis had to slow him down.

Finding strength in the narrow vision of a goal, Regis glanced about the cabin, looking for some clue. Again and again, he found his eyes drawn to the candle.

"The flame," he muttered to himself, a smile beginning to spread across his face. He moved to the table and plucked the candle from its holder. A small pool of liquid wax glittered at the base of the wick, promising pain.

But Regis didn't hesitate.

He hitched up one sleeve and dripped a series of wax droplets along the length of his arm, grimacing away the hot sting.

He had to slow Entreri down.

⚔ ⚔ ⚔ ⚔ ⚔

Regis made one of his rare appearances on the deck the next morning. Dawn had come bright and clear, and the halfling wanted to finish his business before the sun got too high in the sky and created that unpleasant mixture of hot rays in the cool spray. He stood at the rail, rehearsing his lines and mustering the courage to defy the unspoken threats of Entreri.

And then Entreri was beside him! Regis clutched the rail

tightly, fearing that the assassin had somehow guessed his plan.

"The shoreline," Entreri said to him.

Regis followed Entreri's gaze to the horizon and a distant line of land.

"Back in sight," Entreri continued, "and not too far." He glanced down at Regis and displayed his wicked smile once again for his prisoner's benefit.

Regis shrugged. "Too far."

"Perhaps," answered the assassin, "but you might make it, though your half-sized breed is not spoken of as the swimming sort. Have you weighed the odds?"

"I do not swim," Regis said flatly.

"A pity," laughed Entreri. "But if you do decide to try for the land, tell me first."

Regis stepped back, confused.

"I would allow you to make the attempt," Entreri assured him. "I would enjoy the show!"

The halfling's expression turned to anger. He knew that he was being mocked, but he couldn't figure the assassin's purpose.

"They have a strange fish in these waters," said Entreri, looking back to the water. "Smart fish. It follows the boats, waiting for someone to go over." He looked back to Regis to weigh the effect of his chiding.

"A pointed fin marks it," he continued, seeing that he had the halfling's full attention. "Cutting through the water like the prow of a ship. If you watch from the rail long enough, you will surely spy one."

"Why would I want to?"

"Sharks, these fish are called," Entreri went on, ignoring the question. He drew his dagger, putting its point against one of his fingers hard enough to draw a speck of blood. "Marvelous fish.

Rows of teeth as long as daggers, sharp and ridged, and a mouth that could *bite* a man in half." He looked Regis in the eye. "Or take a halfling whole."

"I do not swim!" Regis growled, not appreciating Entreri's macabre, but undeniably effective, methods.

"A pity," chuckled the assassin. "But do tell me if you change your mind." He swept away, his black cloak flowing behind him.

"Bastard," Regis mumbled under his breath. He started back toward the rail, but changed his mind as soon as he saw the deep water looming before him; he turned on his heel and sought the security of the middle of the deck.

Again the color left his face as the vast ocean seemed to close in over him and the interminable, nauseating sway of the ship . . .

"Ye seem ripe fer de rail, little one," came a cheery voice. Regis turned to see a short, bowlegged sailor with few teeth and eyes scrunched in a permanent squint. "Ain't to findin' yer sea legs yet?"

Regis shuddered through his dizziness and remembered his mission. "It is the other thing," he replied.

The sailor missed the subtlety of his statement. Still grinning through the dark tan and darker stubble of his dirty face, he started away.

"But thank you for your concern," Regis said emphatically. "And for all of your courage in taking us to Calimport."

The sailor stopped, perplexed. "Many a time, we's to taking ones to the south," he said, not understanding the reference to "courage."

"Yes, but considering the danger—though I am sure it is not great!" Regis added quickly, giving the impression that he was trying not to emphasize this unknown peril. "It is not important.

Calimport will bring our cure." Then under his breath but still loud enough for the sailor to hear, he said, "If we get there alive."

" 'Ere now, what do ye mean?" the sailor demanded, moving back over to Regis. The smile was gone.

Regis squeaked and grabbed his forearm suddenly as if in pain. He grimaced and pretended to battle against the agony, while deftly scratching the dried patch of wax, and the scab beneath it, away. A small trickle of blood rolled out from under his sleeve.

The sailor grabbed him on cue, pulling the sleeve up over Regis's elbow. He looked at the wound curiously. "Burn?"

"Do not touch it!" Regis cried in a harsh whisper. "That is how it spreads—I think."

The sailor pulled his hand away in terror, noticing several other scars. "I seen no fire! How'd ye git a burn?"

Regis shrugged helplessly. "They just happen. From the inside." Now it was the sailor's turn to pale. "But I will make it to Calimport," he stated unconvincingly. "It takes a few months to eat you away. And most of my wounds are recent." Regis looked down, then presented his scarred arm. "See?"

But when he looked back, the sailor was gone, rushing off toward the captain's quarters.

"Take that, Artemis Entreri," Regis whispered.

3

Conyberry's Pride

Those are the farms that Malchor spoke of," Wulfgar said as he and Drizzt came around a spur of trees on the great forest's border. In the distance to the south, a dozen or so houses sat in a cluster on the eastern edge of the forest, surrounded on the other three sides by wide, rolling fields.

Wulfgar started his horse forward, but Drizzt abruptly stopped him.

"These are a simple folk," the drow explained. "Farmers living in the webs of countless superstitions. They would not welcome a dark elf. Let us enter at night."

"Perhaps we can find the path without their aid," Wulfgar offered, not wanting to waste the remainder of yet another day.

"More likely we would get lost in the wood," Drizzt replied, dismounting. "Rest, my friend. This night promises adventure."

"Her time, the night," Wulfgar remarked, remembering Malchor's words about the banshee.

Drizzt's smile widened across his face. "Not this night," he whispered.

Wulfgar saw the familiar gleam in the drow's lavender eyes and obediently dropped from his saddle. Drizzt was already preparing himself for the imminent battle; already the drow's finely toned muscles twitched with excitement. But as confident as Wulfgar was in his companion's prowess, he could not stop the shudder running through his spine when he considered the undead monster that lay before them.

In the night.

⚔ ⚔ ⚔ ⚔ ⚔

They passed the day in peaceful slumber, enjoying the calls and dances of the birds and squirrels, already preparing for winter, and the wholesome atmosphere of the forest. But when dusk crept over the land, Neverwinter Wood took on a very different aura. Gloom settled all too comfortably under the wood's thick boughs, and a sudden hush descended on the trees, the uneasy quiet of poised danger.

Drizzt roused Walfgar and led him off to the south at once, not even pausing for a short meal. A few minutes later, they walked their horses to the nearest farmhouse. Luckily the night was moonless, and only a close inspection would reveal Drizzt's dark heritage.

"State yer business or be gone!" demanded a threatening voice from the low rooftops before they got close enough to knock on the house's door.

Drizzt had expected as much. "We have come to settle a score," he said without any hesitation.

"What enemies might the likes of yerselves have in Conyberry?" asked the voice.

"In your fair town?" Drizzt balked. "Nay, our fight is with a foe common to you."

Some shuffling came from above, and then two men, bows in hand, appeared at the corner of the farmhouse. Both Drizzt and Wulfgar knew that still more sets of eyes—and no doubt more bows—were trained upon them from the roof, and possibly from their flanks. For simple farmers, these folk were apparently well organized for defense.

"A common foe?" one of the men at the corner—the same who had spoken earlier from the roof—asked Drizzt. "Surely we've seen none of yer likes before, elf, nor of yer giant friend!"

Wulfgar brought Aegis-fang down from his shoulder, drawing some uneasy shuffling from the roof. "Never have we come through your fair town," he replied sternly, not thrilled with being called a giant.

Drizzt quickly interjected. "A friend of ours was slain near here, down a dark path in the wood. We were told that you could guide us."

Suddenly the door of the farmhouse burst open and a wrinkled old woman popped her head out. "Hey, then, what do ye want with the ghost in the wood?" she snapped angrily. "Not fer to both'ring those that leaves her to peace!"

Drizzt and Wulfgar glanced at each other, perplexed by the old woman's unexpected attitude. But the man at the corner apparently felt the same way.

"Yeah, leave Agatha be," he said.

"Go away!" added an unseen man from the roof.

Wulfgar, fearing that these people might be under some evil enchantment, gripped his warhammer more tightly, but Drizzt sensed something else in their voices.

"I had been told that the ghost, this Agatha, was an evil

spirit," Drizzt told them calmly. "Might I have heard wrong? For goodly folk defend her."

"Bah, evil! What be evil?" snapped the old woman, thrusting her wrinkled face and shell of a body closer to Wulfgar. The barbarian took a prudent step back, though the woman's bent frame barely reached his navel.

"The ghost defends her home," added the man at the corner. "And woe to those who go there!"

"Woe!" screamed the old woman, pushing closer still and poking a bony finger into Wulfgar's huge chest.

Wulfgar had heard enough. "Back!" he roared mightily at the woman. He slapped Aegis-fang across his free hand, a sudden rush of blood swelling his bulging arms and shoulders. The woman screamed and vanished into the house, slamming the door in terror.

"A pity," Drizzt whispered, fully understanding what Wulfgar had set into motion. The drow dived headlong to the side, turning into a roll, as an arrow from the roof cracked into the ground where he had been standing.

Wulfgar, too, started into motion, expecting an arrow. Instead, he saw the dark form of a man leaping down at him from the rooftop. With a single hand the mighty barbarian caught the would-be assailant in midair and held him at bay, his boots fully three feet off the ground.

At that same instant, Drizzt came out of his roll and into position in front of the two men at the corner, a scimitar poised at each of their throats. They hadn't even had time to draw their bowstrings back. To their further horror, they now recognized Drizzt for what he was, but even if his skin had been as pale as that of his surface cousins, the fire in his eyes would have taken their strength from them.

A few long seconds passed, the only movement being the

visible shaking of the three trapped farmers.

"An unfortunate misunderstanding," Drizzt said to the men. He stepped back and sheathed his scimitars. "Let him down," he said to Wulfgar. "Gently!" the dark elf added quickly.

Wulfgar eased the man to the ground, but the terrified farmer fell to the dirt anyway, looking up at the huge barbarian in awe and fear.

Wulfgar kept the grimace on his face—just to keep the farmer cowed.

The farmhouse door sprang open again, and the little old woman appeared, this time sheepishly. "Ye won't be killing poor Agatha, will ye?" she pleaded.

"Sure that she's no harm beyond her own door," added the man at the corner, his voice quaking with each syllable.

Drizzt looked to Wulfgar. "Nay," the barbarian said. "We shall visit Agatha and settle our business with her. But be assured that we'll not harm her.

"Tell us the way," Drizzt asked.

The two men at the corner looked at each other and hesitated.

"Now!" Wulfgar roared at the man on the ground.

"To the tangle of birch!" the man replied immediately. "The path's right there, running back to the east! Twists and turns, it does, but clear of brush!"

"Farewell, Conyberry," Drizzt said politely, bowing low. "Would that we could remain a while and dispel your fears of us, but we have much to do and a long road ahead." He and Wulfgar hopped into their saddles and spun their mounts away.

"But wait!" the old woman called after them. Their mounts reared as Drizzt and Wulfgar looked back over their shoulders. "Tell us, ye fearless—or ye stupid—warriors," she implored them, "who might ye be?"

"Wulfgar, son of Beornegar!" the barbarian shouted back, trying to keep an air of humility, though his chest puffed out in pride. "And Drizzt Do'Urden!"

"Names I have heard!" one of the farmers cried out in sudden recognition.

"And names you shall hear again!" Wulfgar promised. He paused a moment as Drizzt moved on, then turned to catch his friend.

Drizzt wasn't sure that it was wise to be proclaiming their identities, and consequently revealing their location, with Artemis Entreri looking back for them. But when he saw the broad and proud smile on Wulfgar's face, he kept his concerns to himself and let Wulfgar have his fun.

⚔ ⚔ ⚔ ⚔ ⚔

Soon after the lights of Conyberry had faded to dots behind them, Wulfgar turned more serious "They did not seem evil," he said to Drizzt, "yet they protect the banshee, and have even named the thing! We may have left a darkness behind us!"

"Not a darkness," Drizzt replied. "Conyberry is as it appears: a humble farming village of good and honest folk."

"But Agatha," Wulfgar protested.

"A hundred similar villages line this countryside," Drizzt explained. "Many unnamed, and all unnoticed by the lords of the land. Yet all of the villages, and even the Lords of Waterdeep, I would guess, have heard of Conyberry and the ghost of Neverwinter Wood."

"Agatha brings them fame," Wulfgar concluded.

"And a measure of protection, no doubt," added Drizzt.

"For what bandit would lay out along the road to Conyberry with a ghost haunting the land?" Wulfgar laughed. "Still, it seems a strange marriage."

"But not our business," Drizzt said, stopping his horse. "The tangle the man spoke of." He pointed to a copse of twisted birch trees. Behind it, Neverwinter Wood loomed dark and mysterious.

Wulfgar's horse flattened its ears. "We are close," the barbarian said, slipping from the saddle. They tethered their mounts and started into the tangle, Drizzt as silent as a cat, but Wulfgar, too big for the tightness of the trees, crunching with every step.

"Do you mean to kill the thing?" he asked Drizzt.

"Only if we must," the drow replied. "We are here for the mask alone, and we have given our word to the people of Conyberry."

"I do not believe that Agatha will willingly hand us her treasures," Wulfgar reminded Drizzt. He broke through the last line of birch trees and stood beside the drow at the dark entrance to the thick oaks of the forest.

"Be silent now," Drizzt whispered. He drew Twinkle and let its quiet blue gleam lead them into the gloom.

The trees seemed to close in about them; the dead hush of the wood only made them more concerned with the resounding noise of their own footfalls. Even Drizzt, who had spent centuries in the deepest of caverns, felt the weight of this darkest corner of Neverwinter on his shoulders. Evil brooded here, and if either he or Wulfgar had any doubts about the legend of the banshee, they knew better now. Drizzt pulled a thin candle from his belt pouch and broke it in half, handing a piece to Wulfgar.

"Stuff your ears," he explained in a breathless whisper, reiterating Malchor's warning. "To hear her keen is to die."

The path was easy to follow, even in the deep darkness, for the aura of evil rolled down heavier on their shoulders with every step. A few hundred paces brought the light of a fire into sight. Instinctively they both dropped to a defensive crouch to survey the area.

Before them lay a dome of branches, a cave of trees that was the banshee's lair. Its single entrance was a small hole, barely large enough for a man to crawl through. The thought of going into the lighted area within while on their hands and knees did not thrill either of them. Wulfgar held Aegis-fang before him and indicated that he would open a bigger door. Boldly he strode toward the dome.

Drizzt crept up beside him, uncertain of the practicality of Wulfgar's idea. Drizzt had the feeling that a creature who had survived so successfully for so very long would be protected against such obvious tactics. But the drow didn't have any better ideas at the moment, so he dropped back a step as Wulfgar hoisted the warhammer above his head.

Wulfgar spread his feet wide for balance and took a steadying breath, then slammed Aegis-fang home with all his strength. The dome shuddered under the blow; wood splintered and went flying, but the drow's concerns soon came to light. For as the wooden shell broke away, Wulfgar's hammer drove down into a concealed mesh of netting. Before the barbarian could reverse the blow, Aegis-fang and his arms were fully entangled.

Drizzt saw a shadow move across the firelight inside, and recognizing his companion's vulnerability, he didn't hesitate. He dived through Wulfgar's legs and into the lair, his scimitars nipping and jabbing wildly as he came. Twinkle nicked into something for just a split second, something less than tangible, and Drizzt knew that he had hit the creature of the nether world. But dazed by the sudden intensity of the light as he came into the lair, Drizzt had trouble finding his footing. He kept his head well enough to discern that the banshee had scampered into the shadows off to the other side. He rolled up to a wall, put his back against it for support, and scrambled to his feet, deftly slicing through Wulfgar's bonds with Twinkle.

Then came the wail.

It cut through the feeble protection of the candle wax with bone-shivering intensity, sapping into Drizzt's and Wulfgar's strength and dropping a dizzying blackness over them. Drizzt slumped heavily against the wall, and Wulfgar, finally able to tug free of the stubborn netting, stumbled backward into the black night and toppled onto his back.

Drizzt, alone inside, knew that he was in deep trouble. He battled against the dizzying blur and the stinging pain in his head and tried to focus on the firelight.

But he saw two dozen fires dancing before his eyes, lights he could not shake away. He believed that he had come out of the keen's effects, and it took him a moment to realize the truth of the place.

A magical creature was Agatha, and magical protections, confusing illusions of mirror images, guarded her home. Suddenly Drizzt was confronted on more than twenty fronts by the twisted visage of a long-dead elven maiden, her skin withered and stretched along her hollowed face and her eyes bereft of color or any spark of life.

But those orbs could see more clearly than any other in this deceptive maze. And Drizzt understood that Agatha knew exactly where he was. She waved her arms in circular motions and smirked at her intended victim.

Drizzt recognized the banshee's movements as the beginnings of a spell. Still caught in the web of her illusions, the drow had only one chance. Calling on the innate abilities of his dark race—and desperately hoping that he had correctly guessed which was the real fire—he placed a globe of darkness over the flames. The inside of the tree cave went pitch black, and Drizzt fell to his belly.

A blue bolt of lightning cut through the darkness, thundering just above the lying drow and through the wall. The air sizzled around him; his stark white hair danced on its ends.

Bursting out into the dark forest, Agatha's ferocious bolt shook Wulfgar from his stupor. "Drizzt," he groaned, forcing himself to his feet. His friend was probably already dead, and beyond the entrance was a blackness too deep for human eyes. But fearlessly, without a thought for his own safety, Wulfgar stumbled back toward the dome.

Drizzt crept around the black perimeter, using the heat of the fire as his guide. He brought a scimitar to bear with every step, but caught nothing with his cuts but air and the side of the tree cave.

Then, suddenly, his darkness was no more, leaving him exposed along the middle of the wall to the left of the door. And the leering image of Agatha was all about him, already beginning yet another spell. Drizzt glanced around for an escape route, but realized that Agatha didn't seem to be looking at him.

Across the room, in what must have been a real mirror, Drizzt caught sight of another image: Wulfgar crawling in defenselessly through the low entrance.

Again Drizzt could not afford to hesitate. He was beginning to understand the layout of the illusion maze and could guess at the general direction of the banshee. He dropped to one knee and scooped up a handful of dirt, splaying it in a wide arc across the room.

All of the images reacted the same way, giving Drizzt no clue as to which was his foe. But the real Agatha, wherever she was, was spitting dirt; Drizzt had disrupted her spell.

Wulfgar regained his feet and immediately smashed his hammer through the wall to the right side of the door, then reversed his swing and heaved Aegis-fang at the image across from the door, directly over the fire. Again Aegis-fang crashed into the wall, knocking open a hole to the nighttime forest.

Drizzt, firing his dagger futilely at yet another image across the way, caught a telltale flicker in the area where he had seen the reflection of Wulfgar. As Aegis-fang magically returned to Wulfgar's hands, Drizzt sprinted for the back of the chamber. "Lead me!" he cried, hoping his voice was loud enough for Wulfgar to hear.

Wulfgar understood. Bellowing "Tempus!" to warn the drow of his throw, he launched Aegis-fang again.

Drizzt dived into a roll, and the hammer whistled over his back, exploding into the mirror. Half of the images in the room disappeared, and Agatha screamed in rage. But Drizzt didn't even slow. He sprang over the broken mirror stand and the remaining chunks of glass.

Right into Agatha's treasure room.

The banshee's scream became a keen, and the killing waves of sound dropped over Drizzt and Wulfgar once again. They had expected the blast this time, though, and they pushed its force away more easily. Drizzt scrambled to the treasure hoard, scooping baubles and gold into a sack. Wulfgar, enraged, stormed about the dome in a destructive frenzy. Soon kindling lined the area where walls had stood, and scratches dripping tiny streams of blood crisscrossed Wulfgar's huge forearms. But the barbarian felt no pain, only the savage fury.

His sack nearly full, Drizzt was about to turn and flee when one other item caught his eye: He had been almost relieved that he hadn't found it, and a big part of him wished that it wasn't here, that such an item did not exist. Yet here it lay, an unremarkable mask of bland features, with a single cord to hold it in place over a wearer's face. Drizzt knew that, as plain as it seemed, it must be the item Malchor had spoken of, and if he had any thoughts of ignoring it now, they were quickly gone. Regis needed him, and to get to Regis quickly, Drizzt needed the mask. Still, the drow could not belay his sigh when he lifted it from the treasure hoard, sensing its tingling power. Without another thought, he put it in his sack.

Agatha would not so easily surrender her treasures, and the specter that confronted Drizzt when he hopped back over the broken mirror was all too real. Twinkle gleamed wickedly as Drizzt parried away Agatha's frantic blows.

Wulfgar suspected that Drizzt needed him now, and he dismissed his savage fury, realizing that a clear head was necessary in this predicament. He scanned the room slowly, hoisting Aegis-fang for another throw. But the barbarian found that he had not yet sorted out the pattern of the illusionary spells, and the confusion of a dozen images, and the fear of hitting Drizzt, held him in check.

Effortlessly Drizzt danced around the crazed banshee and backed her up toward the treasure room. He could have struck her several times, but he had given his word to the farmers of Conyberry.

Then he had her in position. He thrust Twinkle out before him and waded in with two steps. Spitting and cursing, Agatha retreated, tripping over the broken mirror stand and falling back into the gloom. Drizzt spun toward the door.

Watching the real Agatha, and the other images, disappear from sight, Wulfgar followed the sound of her grunt and finally sorted out the layout of the dome. He readied Aegis-fang for the killing throw.

"Let it end!" Drizzt shouted at him as he passed, slapping

Wulfgar on the backside with the flat of Twinkle to remind him of their mission and their promise.

Wulfgar turned to look at him, but the agile drow was already out into the dark night. Wulfgar turned back to see Agatha, her teeth bared and hands clenched, rise up on her feet.

"Pardon our intrusion," he said politely, bowing low—low enough to follow his friend outside to safety. He sprinted along the dark path to catch up to Twinkle's blue glow.

Then came the banshee's third keen, chasing them down the path. Drizzt was beyond its painful range, but its sting caught up to Wulfgar and knocked him off balance. Blindly, with the smug smile suddenly wiped from his face, he stumbled forward.

Drizzt turned and tried to catch him, but the huge man bowled the drow over and continued on.

Face first into a tree.

Before Drizzt could get over to help, Wulfgar was up again and running, too scared and embarrassed, to even groan.

Behind them, Agatha wailed helplessly.

⚔ ⚔ ⚔ ⚔ ⚔

When the first of Agatha's keens wafted on the night winds the mile or so to Conyberry, the villagers knew that Drizzt and Wulfgar had found her lair. All of them, even the children, had gathered outside of their houses and listened intently as two more wails had rolled through the night air. And now, most perplexing, came the banshee's continual, mournful cries.

"So much fer them strangers," chuckled one man.

"Nah, ye're wrong," said the old woman, recognizing the subtle shift in Agatha's tones. "Them's wails of losing. They beat her! They did, and got away!"

The others sat quietly, studying Agatha's cries, and soon

realized the truth of the old woman's observations. They looked at each other incredulously.

"What'd they call themselves?" asked one man.

"Wulfgar," offered another. "And Drizzt Do'Urden. I heared o' them before."

4

THE CITY OF SPLENDORS

They were back to the main road before dawn, thundering to the west, to the coast and the city of Waterdeep. With the visit to Malchor and the business with Agatha out of the way, Drizzt and Wulfgar once again focused their thoughts on the road ahead, and they remembered the peril their halfling friend faced if they failed in the rescue. Their mounts, aided by Malchor's enchanted horseshoes, sped along at a tremendous clip. All the landscape seemed only a blur as it rolled by.

They did not break when dawn came behind them, nor did they stop for a meal as the sun climbed overhead.

"We will have all the rest we need when we board ship and sail to the south," Drizzt told Wulfgar.

The barbarian, determined that Regis would be saved, needed no prompting.

The dark of night came again, and the thunder of the hooves continued unbroken. Then, when the second morning found their backs, a salty breeze filled the air and the high towers of Waterdeep, the City of Splendors, appeared on the western horizon. The two riders stopped atop the high cliff that formed the fabulous settlement's eastern border. If Wulfgar had been stunned earlier that year when he had first looked upon Luskan, five hundred miles up the coast, he now was stricken dumb. For Waterdeep, the jewel of the North, the greatest port in all the Realms, was fully ten times the size of Luskan. Even within its high wall, it sprawled out lazily and endlessly down the coast, with towers and spires reaching high into the sea mist to the edges of the companions' vision.

"How many live here?" Wulfgar gasped at Drizzt.

"A hundred of your tribes could find shelter within the city," the drow explained. He noted Wulfgar's anxiety with concern of his own. Cities were beyond the experiences of the young man, and the time Wulfgar had ventured into Luskan had nearly ended in disaster. And now there was Waterdeep, with ten times the people, ten times the intrigue—and ten times the trouble.

Wulfgar settled back a bit, and Drizzt had no choice but to put his trust in the young warrior. The drow had his own dilemma, a personal battle that he now had to settle. Gingerly he took the magical mask out of his belt pouch.

Wulfgar understood the determination guiding the drow's hesitant motions, and he looked upon his friend with sincere pity. He did not know if he could be so brave—even with Regis's life hanging on his actions.

Drizzt turned the plain mask over in his hands, wondering at the limits of its magic. He could feel that this was no ordinary item; its power tingled to his sensitive touch. Would it simply rob him of his appearance? Or might it steal his very identity? He had heard of other, supposedly beneficial, magical items that could not be removed once worn.

"Perhaps they will accept you as you are," Wulfgar offered hopefully.

Drizzt sighed and smiled, his decision made. "No," he answered. "The soldiers of Waterdeep would not admit a drow elf, nor would any boat captain allow me passage to the south." Without any more delays, he placed the mask over his face.

For a moment, nothing happened, and Drizzt began to wonder if all of his concerns had been for naught, if the mask were really a fake. "Nothing," he chuckled uneasily after a few more seconds, tentative relief in his tone. "It does not—" Drizzt stopped in midsentence when he noticed Wulfgar's stunned expression.

Wulfgar fumbled in his pack and produced a shiny metal cup. "Look," he bade Drizzt and handed him the makeshift mirror.

Drizzt took the cup in trembling hands—hands that trembled more when Drizzt realized they were no longer black—and raised it to his face. The reflection was poor—even poorer in the morning light to the drow's night eyes—but Drizzt could not mistake the image before him. His features had not changed, but his black skin now held the golden hue of a surface elf. And his flowing hair, once stark white, showed lustrous yellow, as shiny as if it had caught the rays of the sun and held them fast.

Only Drizzt's eyes remained as they had been, deep pools of brilliant lavender. No magic could dim their gleam, and Drizzt felt some small measure of relief, at least, that his inner person had apparently remained untainted.

Yet he did not know how to react to this blatant alteration. Embarrassed, he looked to Wulfgar for approval.

Wulfgar's visage had turned sour. "By all the measures known to me, you appear as any other handsome elven warrior," he answered to Drizzt's inquiring gaze. "And surely a maiden or two will blush and turn her eyes when you stride by."

Drizzt looked to the ground and tried to hide his uneasiness with the assessment.

"But I like it not," Wulfgar continued sincerely. "Not at all." Drizzt looked back to him uncomfortably, almost sheepishly.

"And I like the look upon your face, the discomfort of your spirit, even less," Wulfgar continued, now apparently a bit perturbed. "I am a warrior who has faced giants and dragons without fear. But I would pale at the notion of battling Drizzt Do'Urden. Remember who you are, noble ranger."

A smile found its way onto Drizzt's face. "Thank you, my friend," he said. "Of all the challenges I have faced, this is perhaps the most trying."

"I prefer you without the thing," said Wulfgar.

"As do I," came another voice from behind them. They turned to see a middle-aged man, well muscled and tall, walking toward them. He seemed casual enough, wearing simple clothes and sporting a neatly trimmed black beard. His hair, too, was black, though speckles of silver edged it.

"Greetings, Wulfgar and Drizzt Do'Urden," he said with a graceful bow. "I am Khelben, an associate of Malchor. That most magnificent Harpell bade me to watch for your arrival."

"A wizard?" Wulfgar asked, not really meaning to speak his thoughts aloud.

Khelben shrugged. "A forester," he replied, "with a love for painting, though I daresay that I am not very good at it."

Drizzt studied Khelben, not believing either of his disclaimers. The man had an aura of distinction about him, a distinguished manner and confidence befitting a lord. By Drizzt's measure, Khelben was more likely Malchor's peer, at least. And if the man truly loved to paint, Drizzt had no doubt that he had perfected the art as well as any in the North. "A guide through Waterdeep?" Drizzt asked.

"A guide to a guide," Khelben answered. "I know of your quest and your needs. Passage on a ship is not an easy thing to come by this late in the year, unless you know where to inquire. Come, now, to the south gate, where we might find one who knows." He found his mount a short distance away and led them to the south at an easy trot.

They passed the sheer cliff that protected the city's eastern border, a hundred feet high at its peak. And where the cliff sloped down to sea level, they found another city wall. Khelben veered away from the city at this point, though the south gate was now in sight, and indicated a grassy knoll topped by a single willow.

A small man jumped down from the tree as they breached the knoll, his dark eyes darting nervously about. He was no pauper, by his dress, and his uneasiness when they approached only added to Drizzt's suspicions that Khelben was more than he had presumed.

"Ah, Orlpar, so good of you to come," Khelben said casually. Drizzt and Wulfgar exchanged knowing smiles; the man had been given no choice in the matter.

"Greetings," Orlpar said quickly, wanting to finish the business as expediently as possible. "The passage is secured. Have you the payment?"

"When?" Khelben asked.

"A tenday," replied Orlpar. "The *Coast Dancer* puts out in a tenday."

Khelben did not miss the worried looks that Drizzt and Wulfgar now exchanged. "That is too long," he told Orlpar. "Every sailor in port owes you a favor. My friends cannot wait."

"These arrangements take time!" Orlpar argued, his voice rising. But then, as if he suddenly remembered who he was addressing, he shrank back and dropped his eyes.

"Too long," Khelben reiterated calmly.

Orlpar stroked his face, searching for some solution. "Deudermont," he said, looking hopefully to Khelben. "Captain Deudermont takes the *Sea Sprite* out this very night. A fairer man you'll not find, but I do not know how far south he will venture. And the price will be high."

"Ah," Khelben smiled, "but fear not, my little friend. I have wondrous barter for you this day."

Orlpar looked at him suspiciously. "You said gold."

"Better than gold," Khelben replied. "Three days from Longsaddle my friends have come, but their mounts have not broken even a sweat."

"Horses?" balked Orlpar.

"Nay, not the steeds," said Khelben. "Their shoes. Magical shoes that can carry a horse like the wind itself!"

"My business is with sailors!" Orlpar protested as vigorously as he dared. "What use would I find with horseshoes?"

"Calm, calm, Orlpar," Khelben said softly with a wink. "Remember your brother's embarrassment? You will find some way to turn magical horseshoes into profit, I know."

Orlpar took a deep breath to blow away his anger. Khelben obviously had him cornered. "Have these two at the Mermaid's Arms," he said. "I will see what I can do." With that, he turned and trotted off down the hill toward the south gate.

"You handled him with ease," Drizzt remarked.

"I held every advantage," Khelben replied. "Orlpar's brother heads a noble house in the city. At times, this proves a great benefit to Orlpar. Yet, it is also a hindrance, for he must take care not to bring public embarrassment to his family.

"But enough of that business," Khelben continued. "You may leave the horses with me. Off with you, now, to the south gate. The guards there will guide you to Dock Street, and from there you will have little trouble finding the Mermaid's Arms."

"You are not to come with us?" asked Wulfgar, slipping down from his saddle.

"I have other business," Khelben explained. "It is better that you go alone. You will be safe enough; Orlpar would not cross me, and Captain Deudermont is known to me as an honest seaman. Strangers are common in Waterdeep, especially down in the Dock Ward."

"But strangers wandering beside Khelben, the painter, might draw attention," Drizzt reasoned with good-humored sarcasm.

Khelben smiled but did not answer.

Drizzt dropped from big saddle. "The horses are to be returned to Longsaddle?"

"Of course."

"Our thanks to you, Khelben," said Drizzt. "Surely you have aided our cause greatly." Drizzt thought for a moment, eyeing his horse. "You must know that the enchantment Malchor put on the shoes will not remain. Orlpar will not profit from the deal he made this day."

"Justice," chuckled Khelben. "That one has turned many an unfair deal, let me assure you. Perhaps this experience will teach him humility and the error of his ways."

"Perhaps," said Drizzt, and with a bow, he and Wulfgar started down the hill.

"Keep your guard, but keep your calm," Khelben called after them. "Ruffians are not unknown on the docks, but the police are ever-present. Many a stranger spends his first night in the city dungeons!" He watched the two of them descend the knoll and remembered, as Malchor had remembered, those long-ago days when it was he who followed the roads to distant adventures.

"He had the man cowed," Wulfgar remarked when he and Drizzi were out of Khelben's earshot. "A simple painter?"

"More likely a wizard—a powerful wizard," Drizzt replied. "And our thanks again are owed to Malchor, whose influence has eased our way. Mark my words, 'twas no simple painter that tamed the likes of Orlpar."

Wulfgar looked back to the knoll, but Khelben and the horses were nowhere to be seen. Even with his limited understanding of the black arts, Wulfgar realized that only magic could have moved Khelben and the three horses from the area so quickly. He smiled and shook his head, and marveled again at the eccentric characters the wide world kept showing him.

⚔ ⚔ ⚔ ⚔

Following the directions given to them by the guards at the south gate, Drizzt and Wulfgar were soon strolling down Dock Street, a long lane that ran the length of Waterdeep Harbor on the south side of the city. Fish smells and salty air filled their nostrils, gulls complained overhead, and sailors and mercenaries from every stretch of the Realms wandered about, some busy at work, but most ashore for their last rest before the long journey to points south.

Dock Street was well outfitted for such merrymaking; every corner held a tavern. But unlike the city of Luskan's dockside, which had been given over to the rabble by the lords of the city long ago, Dock Street in Waterdeep was not an evil place. Waterdeep was a city of laws, and members of the Watch, Waterdeep's famed city guard, seemed always in sight.

Hardy adventurers abounded here, battle-hardened warriors that carried their weapons with cool familiarity. Still, Drizzt and Wulfgar found many eyes focused upon them, with almost every head turning and watching as they passed. Drizzt felt for his mask, at first worrying that it had somehow slipped off and revealed his heritage to the amazed onlookers. A quick inspection dispelled his fears, for his hands still showed the golden luster of a surface elf.

And Drizzt nearly laughed aloud when he turned to ask Wulfgar for confirmation that the mask still disguised his facial features, for it was then the dark elf realized that he was not the object of the gawks. He had been so close to the young barbarian for the last few years that he was used to Wulfgar's physical stature. Nearly seven feet tall, with corded muscles that thickened every year, Wulfgar strode down Dock Street with the easy air of sincere confidence.

Aegis-fang bouncing casually on one shoulder. Even among the greatest warriors in the Realms, this young man would stand out.

"For once, it seems that I am not the target of the stares," said Drizzt.

"Take off the mask, drow," Wulfgar replied, his face reddening with a rush of blood. "And take their eyes from me!"

"I would, but for Regis," Drizzt answered with a wink.

The Mermaid's Arms was no different from any other of the multitude of taverns that laced this section of Waterdeep. Shouts and cheers drifted out of the place, on air heavily scented with cheap ale and wine. A group of rowdies, pushing and shoving each other and throwing curses to the men they called friends, had gathered in front of the door.

Drizzt looked at Wulfgar with concern. The only other time the young man had been in such a place—at the Cutlass in Luskan—Wulfgar had torn apart the tavern, and most of its patrons, in a brawl. Clinging to ideals of honor and courage, Wulfgar was out of place in the unprincipled world of city taverns.

Orlpar came out of the Mermaid's Arms then and sifted

adeptly through the rowdy crowd. "Deudermont is at the bar," he whispered out of the corner of his mouth. He passed Drizzt and Wulfgar and appeared to take no notice of them. "Tall; blue jacket and yellow beard," added Orlpar.

Wulfgar started to respond, but Drizzt kept him moving forward, understanding Orlpar's preference for secrecy.

The crowd parted as Drizzt and Wulfgar strode through, all their stares squarely on Wulfgar. "Bungo'll have 'im," one of them whispered when the two companions had moved into the bar.

"Be worth the watchin', though," chuckled another.

The drow's keen ears caught the conversation, and he looked again at his huge friend, noting how Wulfgar's size always seemed to single the barbarian out for such trouble.

The inside of the Mermaid's Arms offered no surprises. The air hung thick with the smoke of exotic weeds and the stench of stale ale. A few drunken sailors lay facedown on tables or sat propped against walls while others stumbled about, spilling their drinks—often on more sober patrons, who responded by shoving the offenders to the floor. Wulfgar wondered how many of these men had missed the sailing of their ships. Would they stagger about in here until their coin ran out, only then to be dropped into the street to face the coming winter penniless and without shelter?

"Twice I have seen the bowels of a city," Wulfgar whispered to Drizzt. "And both times I have been reminded of the pleasures of the open road!"

"The goblins and the dragons?" Drizzt retorted lightheartedly, leading Wulfgar to an empty table near the bar.

"A far lot better than this," Wulfgar remarked.

A serving wench was upon them before they had even sat down. "What's yer pleasure?" she asked absently, having long ago lost interest in the patrons she served.

"Water," Wulfgar answered gruffly.

"And wine," Drizzt quickly added, handing over a gold piece to dispel the woman's sudden scowl.

"That must be Deudermont," Wulfgar said, deflecting any forthcoming scolding concerning his treatment of the wench. He pointed to a tall man leaning over the bar rail.

Drizzt rose at once, thinking it prudent to be done with their business and out of the tavern as quickly as possible. "Hold the table," he told Wulfgar

Captain Deudermont was not the average patron of the Mermaid's Arms. Tall and straight, he was a refined man accustomed to dining with lords and ladies. But as with all of the ship captains who put into Waterdeep Harbor, especially on the day of their departures, Deudermont spent most of his time ashore, keeping a watchful eye on his valued crew and trying to prevent them from winding up in Waterdeep's overfilled jails.

Drizzt squeezed in next to the captain, brushing away the inquiring look of the barkeep. "We have a common friend," Drizzt said softly to Deudermont.

"I would hardly number Orlpar among my friends," the captain replied casually. "But I see that he did not exaggerate about the size and strength of your young friend."

Deudermont was not the only one who had noticed Wulfgar. As did every other tavern in this section of Waterdeep—and most bars across the Realms—the Mermaid's Arms had a champion. A bit farther down the bar rail, a massive, hulking slob named Bungo had eyed Wulfgar from the minute the young barbarian had walked through the door. Bungo didn't like the looks of this one, not in the least. Even more than the corded arms, Wulfgar's graceful stride and the easy way he carried his huge warhammer revealed a measure of experience beyond his age.

Bungo's supporters crowded around him in anticipation of

the coming brawl, their twisted smiles and beer-reeking breath spurring their champion to action. Normally confident, Bungo had to work to keep his anxiety under control. He had taken many hits in his seven-year reign at the tavern. His frame was bent now, and dozens of bones had been cracked and muscles torn. Looking at the awesome spectacle of Wulfgar, Bungo honestly wondered if he could have won this match even in his healthier youth.

But the regulars of the Mermaid's Arms looked up to him. This was their domain, and he their champion. They provided his free meals and drinks—Bungo could not let them down.

He quaffed his full mug in a single gulp and pushed himself off the rail. With a final growl to reassure his supporters, and callously tossing aside anyone in his way, Bungo made his way toward Wulfgar.

Wulfgar had seen the group coming before it had ever started moving. This scene was all too familiar to the young barbarian, and he fully expected that he would once again, as had happened at the Cutlass in Luskan, be singled out because of his size.

"What're ye fer?" Bungo said with a hiss as he towered, hands on hips, over the seated man. The other ruffians spread out around the table, putting Wulfgar squarely within their ring.

Wulfgar's instincts told him to stand and drop the pretentious slob where he stood. He had no fears about Bungo's eight friends. He considered them cowards who needed their leader to spur them on. If a single blow put Bungo down—and Wulfgar knew it would—the others would hesitate before striking, a delay that would cost them dearly against the likes of Wulfgar.

But over the last few months, Wulfgar had learned to temper his anger, and he had learned a broader definition of honor. He shrugged, making no move that resembled a threat. "A place to sit and a drink," he replied calmly. "And who might you be?"

"Name's Bungo," said the slob, spittle spraying with every word. He thrust his chest out proudly, as if his name should mean something to Wulfgar.

Again Wulfgar, wiping Bungo's spray from his face, had to resist his fighting instincts. He and Drizzt had more important business, he reminded himself.

"Who said ye could come to my bar?" Bungo growled, thinking—hoping—that he had put Wijlfgar on the defensive. He looked around at his friends, who leaned closer over Wulfgar, heightening the intimidation.

Surely Drizzt would understand the necessity to put this one down, Wulfgar reasoned, his fists tightening at his sides. "One shot," he muttered silently, looking around at the wretched group—a group that would look better sprawled out unconscious in the corners of the floor.

Wulfgar summoned an image of Regis to ward off his welling rage, but he could not ignore the fact that his hands were now clenched on the rim of the table so tightly that his knuckles had whitened for lack of blood.

✕ ✕ ✕ ✕ ✕

"The arrangements?" Drizzt asked.

"Secured," replied Deudermont. "I've room on the *Sea Sprite* for you, and I welcome the added hands—and blades—especially of such veteran adventurers. But I've a suspicion that you might be missing our sailing." He grasped Drizzt's shoulder to turn him toward the trouble brewing at Wulfgar's table.

"Tavern champion and his cronies," Deudermont explained, "though my bet would be with your friend."

"Coin well placed," Drizzt replied, "but we have no time. . ."

Deudermont guided Drizzt's gaze across to a shadowy corner of the tavern and to four men sitting calmly watching the growing tumult with interest. "The Watch," Deudermont said. "A fight will cost your friend a night in the dungeons. I cannot hold port!"

Drizzt searched the tavern, looking for some out. All eyes seemed to be closing in on Wulfgar and the ruffians, eagerly anticipating the fight. The drow realized that if he went to the table now, he would probably ignite the whole thing.

⚔ ⚔ ⚔ ⚔

Bungo thrust his belly forward, inches from Wulfgar's face, to display a wide belt notched in a hundred places. "Fer every man I beat," he boasted. "Give me somethin' to do on my night in jail." He pointed at a large cut to the side of the buckle. "Killed that one there. Squashed 'is head real good. Cost me five nights."

Wulfgar eased his grip, not impressed, but wary now of the potential consequences of his actions. He had a ship to catch.

"Perhaps it was Bungo I came to see," he said, crossing his arms and leaning back in his chair.

"Get 'im, then?" growled one of the ruffians.

Bungo eyed Wulfgar wickedly. " Come lookin' fer a fight?"

"Nay, I think not," Wulfgar retorted. "A fight? Nay, I am but a boy out to see the wide world!"

Bungo could not hide his confusion. He looked around to his friends, who could only shrug in response.

"Sit," Wulfgar offered. Bungo made no move.

The ruffian behind Wulfgar poked him hard in the shoulder and growled, "What're ye fer?"

Wulfgar had to consciously catch his own hand before it shot across and squashed the ruffian's filthy fingers together. But he had control now. He leaned closer to the huge leader. "Not to fight; to watch," he said quietly. "One day, perhaps, I might deem myself worthy to challenge the likes of Bungo, and on that day I will return, for I have no doubt that you will still be the champion of this tavern. But that day is many years away, I fear. I have so much to learn."

"Then why've ye come?" Bungo demanded, his confidence brimming over. He leaned over Wulfgar, threateningly close.

"I have come to learn," Wulfgar replied. "To learn by watching the toughest fighter in Waterdeep. To see how Bungo presents himself and goes about his affairs."

Bungo straightened and looked around at his anxious friends, who were leaning nearly to the point of falling over the table. Bungo flashed his toothless grin, customary before he clobbered a challenger, and the ruffians tensed. But then their champion surprised them, slapping Wulfgar hard on the shoulder—the clap of a friend.

Audible groans issued throughout the tavern as Bungo pulled up a chair to share a drink with the impressive stranger.

"Get ye gone!" the slob roared at his companions. Their faces twisted in disappointment and confusion, but they did not dare disobey. The one behind Wulfgar poked him again for good measure, then followed the others back to the bar.

⚔ ⚔ ⚔ ⚔ ⚔

"A wise move," Deudermont remarked to Drizzt.

"For both of them," the drow replied, relaxing against the rail.

"You have other business in the city?" the captain asked.

Drizzt shook his head. "No. Get us to the ship," he said. "I fear that Waterdeep can bring only trouble."

✗ ✗ ✗ ✗

A million stars filled the sky that cloudless night. They reached down from the velvety canopy to join with the distant lights of Waterdeep, setting the northern horizon aglow. Wulfgar found Drizzt above decks, sitting quietly in the rolling serenity offered by the sea.

"I should like to return," Wulfgar said, following his friend's gaze to the now distant city.

"To settle a score with a drunken ruffian and his wretched friends," Drizzt concluded.

Wulfgar laughed but stopped abruptly when Drizzt wheeled on him.

"To what end?" Drizzt asked. "Would you then replace him as the champion of the Mermaid's Arms?"

"That is a life I do not envy," Wulfgar replied, chuckling again, though this time uncomfortably.

"Then leave it to Bungo," Drizzt said, turning back to the glow of the city.

Again Wulfgar's smile faded.

Seconds, minutes perhaps, slipped by, the only sound the slapping of the waves against the prow of the *Sea Sprite*. On an impulse, Drizzt slid Twinkle from its sheath. The crafted scimitar came to life in his hand, the blade glowing in the starlight that had given Twinkle its name and its enchantment.

"The weapon fits you well," Wulfgar remarked.

"A fine companion," Drizzt acknowledged, examining the intricate designs etched along the curving blade. He remembered another magical scimitar he had once possessed, a blade he had found in the lair of a dragon that he and Wulfgar had slain. That blade, too, had been a fine companion. Wrought of ice magic, the scimitar was forged as a bane to creatures of fire, impervious, along with its wielder, to their flames. It had served Drizzt well, even saving him from the certain and painful death of a demon's fire.

Drizzt cast his gaze back to Wulfgar. "I was thinking of our first dragon," he explained to the barbarian's questioning look. "You and I alone in the ice cave against the likes of Icingdeath, an able foe."

"He would have had us," Wulfgar added, "had it not been for the luck of that huge icicle hanging above the dragon's back."

"Luck?" Drizzt replied. "Perhaps. But more often, I dare to say, luck is simply the advantage a true warrior gains in executing the correct course of action."

Wulfgar took the compliment in stride; he had been the one to dislodge the pointed icicle, killing the dragon.

"A pity I do not have the scimitar I plundered from Icingdeath's lair to serve as a companion for Twinkle," Drizzt remarked.

"True enough," replied Wulfgar, smiling as he remembered his early adventures beside the drow. "But, alas, that one went over Garumn's Gorge with Bruenor."

Drizzt paused and blinked as if cold water had been thrown in his face. A sudden image flooded through his mind, its implications both hopeful and frightening. The image of Bruenor Battlehammer drifting slowly down into the depths of the gorge on the back of a burning dragon.

A burning dragon!

It was the first time Wulfgar had ever noted a tremble in the voice of his normally composed friend, when Drizzt rasped out, "Bruenor had my blade?"

ASHES

T he room was empty, the fire burning low. The figure knew
that there were gray dwarves, duergar, in the side chamber,
through the partly opened door, but he had to chance it. This
section of the complex was too full of the scum for him to continue along the tunnels without his disguise.

He slipped in from the main corridor and tiptoed past the
side door to get to the hearth. He knelt before it and laid his fine
mithral axe at his side The glow of the embers made him flinch
instinctively, though he felt no pain as he dipped his finger into
the ash.

He heard the side door swing open a few seconds later and
rubbed a final handful of the ash over his face, hoping that he
had properly covered his telltale red beard and the pale flesh of
his long nose ail the length to its tip.

"What ye be doin'?" came a croak behind him.

The ash-covered dwarf blew into the embers, and a small

flame came to life. "Bit o' chill," he answered. "Be needin' rest"
He rose and turned, lifting the mithral axe beside him.

Two gray dwarves walked across the room to stand before
him, their weapons securely sheathed. "Who ye be?" one asked.
"Not o' Clan McUduck, an' not belongin' in these tunnels!"

"Tooktook o' Clan Trilk," the dwarf lied, using the name
of a gray dwarf he had chopped down just the morning before.
"Been patrollin', and been lost! Glad I be to find a room with
a hearth!"

The two gray dwarves looked at each other, and then back
to the stranger suspiciously. They had heard the reports over
the last few tendays—since Shimmergloom, the shadow dragon
that had been their god-figure, had fallen—tales of slaughtered
duergar, often beheaded, found in the outer tunnels. And why
was this one alone? Where was the rest of his patrol? Surely
Clan Trilk knew enough to keep out of the tunnels of Clan
McUduck.

And, why, one of them noticed, was there a patch of red on
this one's beard?

The dwarf realized their suspicion immediately and knew
that he could not keep this charade going for long. "Lost two
o' me kin," he said. "To a drow." He smiled when he saw the
duergar's eyes go wide. The mere mention of a drow elf always
sent gray dwarves rocking back on their heels—and bought
the dwarf a few extra seconds. "But worth it, it were!" he proclaimed, holding the mithral axe up beside his head. "Found me
a wicked blade! See?"

Even as one of the duergar leaned forward, awed by the
shining weapon, the red-bearded dwarf gave him a closer look,
putting the cruel blade deep into his face. The other duergar just
managed to get a hand to his sword hilt when he got hit with a
backhand blow that drove the butt of the axe handle into his eye

He stumbled back, reeling, but knew through the blur of pain that he was finished a full second before the mithral axe sliced the side of his neck.

Two more duergar burst in from the anteroom, their weapons drawn. "Get help!" one of them screamed, leaping into the fight. The other bolted for the door.

Again, luck was with the red-bearded dwarf. He kicked hard at an object on the floor, launching it toward the fleeing duergar, while parrying the first blow of his newest opponent with his golden shield.

The fleeing duergar was only a couple of strides from the corridor when something rolled between his feet, tripping him up and sending him sprawling to the floor, He got back to his knees quickly but hesitated, fighting back a gush of bile, when he saw what he had stumbled over.

The head of his kin.

The red-bearded dwarf danced away from another strike, rushing across the room to shield-slam the now-kneeling duergar, smashing the unfortunate creature into the stone wall.

But the dwarf, overbalanced in the fury of his rush, was down on one knee when the remaining duergar caught up to him. The intruder swung his shield back above him to block a downward thrust of the duergar's sword, and countered with a low sweep of his axe, aiming for the knees.

The duergar sprang back just in time, taking a nick on one leg, and before he could fully recover and come back with a counter, the red-bearded dwarf was up and at the ready.

"Yer bones are for carrion-eaters!" the dwarf growled.

"Who ye be?" the duergar demanded. "Not o' me kin, fer sure!"

A white smile spread across the dwarf's ash-covered face. "Battlehammer's me name," he growled, displaying the standard emblazoned upon his shield—the foaming mug emblem of Clan Battlehammer. "Bruenor Battlehammer, rightful king of Mithral Hall!"

Bruenor chuckled softly to see the gray dwarf's face blanch to white. The duergar stumbled back toward the door of the anteroom, understanding now that he was no match for this mighty foe. In desperation, he spun and fled, trying to slam the door shut behind him.

But Bruenor guessed what the duergar had in mind, and he got his heavy boot through the door before it could close. The mighty dwarf slammed his shoulder into the hard wood, sending the duergar flying back into the small room and knocking aside a table and chair.

Bruenor strode in confidently, never fearing even odds.

With no escape, the gray dwarf rushed back at him wildly, his shield leading and his sword above his head. Bruenor easily blocked the downward thrust, then smashed his axe into the duergar's shield. It, too, was of mithral, and the axe could not cut into it. But so great was Bruenor's blow that the leather strappings snapped apart and the duergar's arm went numb and drooped helplessly. The duergar screamed in terror and brought his short sword across his chest to protect his opened flank

Bruenor followed the duergar's swordarm with a shield-rush, shoving into his opponent's elbow and causing the duergar to overbalance. In a lightning combination with his axe, Bruenor slipped the deadly blade over the duergar's dipped shoulder.

A second head dropped free to the floor.

Bruenor grunted at the job well done and moved back into the larger room. The duergar beside the door was just regaining consciousness when Bruenor came up to him and shield-slammed him back into the wall. "Twenty-two," he mumbled to himself, keeping count of the number of gray dwarves he had cut down during these last few tendays.

Bruenor peeked out into the dark corridor. All was clear. He closed the door softly and went back to the hearth to touch up his disguise.

Following the wild descent to the bottom of Garumn's Gorge on the back of a flaming dragon, Bruenor had lost consciousness. Truly he was amazed when he managed to open his eyes. He knew the dragon to be dead as soon as he looked around, but he couldn't understand why he, still lying atop the smoldering form, had not been burned.

The gorge had been quiet and dark around him; he could not begin to guess how long he had remained unconscious. He knew, though, that his friends, if they had escaped, would probably have made their way out through the back door, to the safety of the surface.

And Drizzt was alive! The image of the drow's lavender eyes staring at him from the wall of the gorge as the dragon had glided past in its descent remained firmly etched in Bruenor's mind. Even now, tendays later as far as he could figure, he used that image of the indomitable Drizzt Do'Urden as a litany against the hopelessness of his own situation. For Bruenor could not climb from the bottom of the gorge, where the walls rose straight and sheer. His only option had been to slip into the sole tunnel running off the chasm's base and make his way though the lower mines.

And through an army of gray dwarves—duergar even more alert, for the dragon Bruenor had killed, Shimmergloom, had been their leader.

He had come far, and each step he took brought him a little closer to the freedom of the surface. But each step also brought him closer to the main host of the duergar. Even now he could hear the thrumming of the furnaces of the great undercity, no doubt teeming with the gray scum. Bruenor knew that he had to pass through there to get to the tunnels connecting the higher levels.

But even here, in the darkness of the mines, his disguise could not hold out to close scrutiny. How would he fare in the glow of the undercity, with a thousand gray dwarves milling all about him?

Bruenor shook away the thought and rubbed more ash onto his face. No need to worry now; he'd find his way through. He gathered up his axe and shield and headed for the door.

He shook his head and smiled as he approached, for the stubborn duergar beside the door was awake again—barely—and struggling to find his feet.

Bruenor slammed him into the wall a third time and casually dropped the axe blade onto his head as he slumped, this time never to awaken. "Twenty-two," the mighty dwarf reiterated grimly as he stepped into the corridor.

The sound of the closing door echoed through the darkness, and when it died away, Bruenor heard again the thrumming of the furnaces.

The undercity, his only chance.

He steadied himself with a deep breath, then slapped his axe determinedly against his shield and started stomping along the corridor toward the beckoning sound.

It was time to get things done.

The corridor twisted and turned, finally ending in a low archway that opened into a brightly lit cavern.

For the first time in nearly two hundred years, Bruenor Battlehammer looked down upon the great undercity of Mithral Hall. Set in a huge chasm, with walls tiered into steps and lined with decorated doorways, this massive chamber had once housed

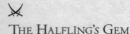

the entirety of Clan Battlehammer with many rooms to spare.

The place had remained exactly as the dwarf remembered it, and now, as in those distant years of his youth, many of the furnaces were bright with fire and the floor level teemed with the hunched forms of dwarven workers. How many times had young Bruenor and his friends looked down upon the magnificence of this place and heard the chiming of the smithies' hammers and the heavy sighing of the huge bellows? he wondered.

Bruenor spat away the pleasant memories when he reminded himself that these hunched workers were evil duergar, not his kin. He brought his mind back into the present and the task at hand. Somehow he had to get across the open floor and up the tiers on the far side, to a tunnel that would take him higher in the complex.

A shuffle of boots sent Bruenor back into the shadows of the tunnel. He gripped his axe tightly and didn't dare to breathe, wondering if the time of his last glory had finally caught up to him. A patrol of heavily armed duergar marched up to the archway then continued past, giving only a casual glance down the tunnel.

Bruenor sighed deeply and scolded himself for his delay. He could not afford to tarry; every moment he spent in this area was a dangerous gamble. Quickly he searched for options. He was about halfway up one wall, five tiers from the floor. One bridge, at the highest tier, traversed the chasm, but no doubt it would be heavily guarded. Walking alone up there, away from the bustle of the floor, would make him too conspicuous.

Across the busy floor seemed a better route. The tunnels halfway up the other wall, almost directly across from where he now stood, would lead him to the western end of the complex, back to the hall he had first entered on his return to Mithral Hall, and to the open valley of Keeper's Dale beyond. It was his best chance, by his estimation—if he could get across the open floor.

He peeked out under the archway for any signs of the returning patrol. Satisfied that all was clear, he reminded himself that he was a king, the rightful king of the complex, and boldly stepped out onto the tier. The closest steps down were to the right, but the patrol had headed that way and Bruenor thought it wise to keep clear of them.

His confidence grew with each step. He passed a couple of gray dwarves, answering their casual greetings with a quick nod and never slowing his stride.

He descended one tier and then another, and before he even had time to consider his progress, Bruenor found himself bathed in the bright light of the huge furnaces at the final descent, barely fifteen feet from the floor. He crouched instinctively at the glow of the light, but he realized on a rational level that the brightness was actually his ally. Duergar were creatures of the dark, not accustomed to, nor liking, the light. Those on the floor kept their hoods pulled low to shield their eyes, and Bruenor did likewise, only improving his disguise. With the apparently unorganized movements on the floor, he began to believe that the crossing would be easy.

He moved out slowly at first, gathering speed as he went, but staying in a crouch, the collar of his cloak pulled up tightly around his cheeks, and his battered, one-horned helmet dipped low over his brow. Trying to maintain an air of easiness, Bruenor kept his shield arm at his side, but his other hand rested comfortably on his belted axe. If it came to blows, Bruenor was determined to be ready.

He passed by the three central forges—and the cluster of duergar they attracted—without incident, then waited patiently as a small caravan of ore-filled wheelbarrows were carted by. Bruenor, trying to keep the easy, cordial atmosphere, nodded to the passing band, but bile rose in his throat as he saw the mithral load in the carts—and at the thought of the gray scum extracting the precious metals from the walls of his hallowed homeland.

"Ye'll be paid for yer troubles," he mumbled under his breath. He rubbed a sleeve over his brow. He had forgotten how very hot the bottom area of the undercity became when the furnaces were burning. As with everyone else there, streaks of sweat began to make their way down his face.

Bruenor thought nothing of the discomfort at first, but then the last of the passing miners gave him a curious side-long glance.

Bruenor hunched even lower and quickly stepped away, realizing the effect his sweating would have on his feeble disguise. By the time he reached the first stair on the other side of the chasm, his face was fully streaked and parts of his whiskers were showing their true hue.

Still, he thought he might make it. But halfway up the stair, disaster struck. Concentrating more on hiding his face, Bruenor stumbled and bumped into a duergar soldier standing two steps above him. Reflexively Bruenor looked up, and his eyes met with the duergar's.

The dumbfounded stare of the gray dwarf told Bruenor beyond any doubt that the ploy was over. The gray dwarf went for his sword, but Bruenor didn't have time for a pitched battle. He drove his head between the duergar's knees—shattering one kneecap with the remaining horn of his helmet—and heaved the duergar behind him and down the stairs

Bruenor glanced around. Few had noticed, and fights were commonplace among the duergar ranks. Casually he started again up the stairs.

But the soldier was still conscious after he crashed to the floor and still coherent enough to point a finger up to the tier and shout, "Stop 'im!"

Bruenor lost all hope of remaining inconspicuous. He pulled out his mithral axe and tore along the tier toward the next stair. Cries of alarm sprang up throughout the chasm. A general commotion of spilled wheelbarrows, the clanging of weapons being drawn, and the thumping of booted feet closed in around Bruenor. Just as he was about to turn onto the next stairway, two guards leaped down in front of him.

"What's the trouble?" one of them cried, confused and not understanding that the dwarf they now faced had been the cause of the commotion. In horror, the two guards recognized Bruenor for what he was just as his axe tore the face off one and he shoulder-blocked the other off the tier.

Then up the stairs he sprinted, only to reverse his tracks as a patrol appeared at the top. Hundreds of gray dwarves rushed all about the undercity, their focus increasing on Bruenor.

Bruenor found another stair and got to the second tier.

But he stopped there, trapped. A dozen duergar soldiers came at him from both directions, their weapons drawn.

Bruenor scanned the area desperately. The tumult had brought more than a hundred of the gray dwarves on the floor rushing over to, and up, the original stair he had climbed.

A broad smile found the dwarf's face as he considered a desperate plan. He looked again at the charging soldiers and knew that he had no choice. He saluted the groups, adjusted his helmet and dropped suddenly from the tier, crashing down into the crowd that had assembled on the tier below him. Without losing his momentum, Bruenor continued his roll to the ledge, dropping along with several unfortunate gray dwarves onto another group on the floor.

Bruenor was up in a flash, chopping his way through. The

surprised duergar in the crowd climbed over each other to get out of the way of the wild dwarf and his deadly axe, and in seconds, Bruenor was sprinting unhindered across the floor.

Bruenor stopped and looked all around. Where could he go now? Dozens of duergar stood between him and any of the exits from the undercity, and they grew more organized with every second.

One soldier charged him, only to be chopped down in a single blow. "Come on, then!" Bruenor shouted defiantly, figuring to take a fair share and more of the duergar down with him. "Come on, as many as will! Know the rage of the true king o' Mithral Hall!"

A crossbow quarrel clanked into his shield, taking a bit of the bluster out of his boastings. More on instinct than conscious thought, the dwarf darted suddenly for the single unguarded path—the roaring furnaces. He dropped the mithral axe into his belt loop and never slowed. Fire hadn't harmed him on the back of the falling dragon, and the warmth of the ashes he'd rubbed off his face never seemed to touch his skin.

And once again, standing in the center of the open furnace, Bruenor found himself impervious to the flames. He didn't have time to ponder this mystery and could only guess the protection from fire to be a property of the magical armor he had donned when he had first entered Mithral Hall.

But in truth, it was Drizzt's lost scimitar, neatly strapped under Bruenor's pack and almost forgotten by the dwarf, that had once again saved him.

The fire hissed in protest and started to burn low when the magical blade came in. But it roared back to life as Bruenor quickly started up the chimney. He heard the shouts of the astonished duergar behind him, along with cries to get the fire out. Then one voice rose above the others in a commanding tone. "Smoke 'im!" it cried.

Rags were wetted and thrown into the blaze, and great bursts of billowing gray smoke closed in around Bruenor. Soot filled his eyes and he could find no breath, still he had no choice but to continue his ascent. Blindly he searched for cracks into which he could wedge his stubby fingers and pulled himself along with all of his strength.

He knew that he would surely die if he inhaled, but he had no breath left, and his lungs cried out in pain.

Unexpectedly he found a hole in the wall and nearly fell in from his momentum. A side tunnel? he wondered, astonished. He then remembered that all of the chimneys of the undercity had been interconnected to aid in their cleaning.

Bruenor pulled himself away from the rush of smoke and curled up inside the new passage. He tried to wipe the soot from his eyes as his lungs mercifully took in a deep draft, but he only aggravated the sting with his soot-covered sleeve. He couldn't see the blood flowing over his hands, but could guess at the extent of his wounds from the sharp ache along his fingernails.

As exhausted as he was, he knew that he could afford no delays. He crawled along the little tunnel, hoping that the furnace below the next chimney he came to was not in use.

The floor dropped away in front of him, and Bruenor almost tumbled down another shaft. No smoke, he noted, and with a wall as broken and climbable as the first. He tightened down all of his equipment, adjusted his helmet one more time, and inched out, blindly seeking a handhold and ignoring the aches in his shoulders and fingers. Soon he was moving steadily again.

But seconds seemed like minutes, and minutes like hours, to the weary dwarf, and he found himself resting as much as climbing, his breaths coming in heavy labored gasps. During one such rest, Bruenor thought he heard a shuffle above him. He paused to consider the sound. These shafts should not connect to any higher side passages, or to the overcity, he thought. Their ascent is straight to the open air of the surface. Bruenor strained to look upward through his soot-filled eyes. He knew that he had heard a sound.

The riddle was solved suddenly, as a monstrous form shuffled down the shaft beside Bruenor's precarious perch and great, hairy legs began flailing at him. The dwarf knew his peril at once.

A giant spider.

Venom-dripping pincers tore a gash into Bruenor's forearm. He ignored the pain and the possible implications of the wound and reacted with matched fury. He drove himself up the shaft, butting his head into the bulbous body of the wretched thing, and pushed off from the walls with all his strength.

The spider locked its deadly pincers onto a heavy boot and flailed with as many legs as it could spare while holding its position.

Only one course of attack seemed feasible to the desperate dwarf: dislodge the spider. He grasped at the hairy legs, twisting himself to snap them as he caught them, or at least to pull them from their hold on the wall. His arm burned with the sting of poison, and his foot, though his boot had repelled the pincers, was twisted and probably broken.

But he had no time to think of the pain. With a growl, he grabbed another leg and snapped it apart.

Then they were falling.

The spider—stupid thing—curled up as best it could and released its hold on the dwarf. Bruenor felt the rush of air and the closeness of the wall as they sped along. He could only hope that the shaft was straight enough to keep them clear of any sharp edges. He climbed as far over the spider as he could, putting the bulk of its body between himself and the coming impact.

They landed in a great splat. The air blasted from Bruenor's lungs, but with the wet explosion of the spider beneath him, he sustained no serious wounds. He still could not see, but he realized that he must again be on the floor level of the under-city, though luckily—for he heard no cries of alarm—in a less busy section. Dazed but undaunted, the stubborn dwarf picked himself up and wiped the spider fluid from his hands.

"Sure to be a mother's mother of a rainstorm tomorrow," he muttered, remembering an old dwarven superstition against killing spiders. And he started back up the shaft, dismissing the pain in his hands, the ache in his ribs and foot, and the poisoned burn of his forearm.

And any thoughts of more spiders lurking up ahead.

He climbed for hours, stubbornly putting one hand over the other and pulling himself up. The insidious spider venom swept through him with waves of nausea and sapped the strength from his arms. But Bruenor was tougher than mountain stone. He might die from his wound, but he was determined that it would happen outside, in the free air, under the stars or the sun.

He would escape Mithral Hall.

A cold blast of wind shook the exhaustion from him. He looked up hopefully but still could not see—perhaps it was nighttime outside. He studied the whistle of the wind for a moment and knew that he was only yards from his goal. A burst of adrenaline carried him to the chimney's exit—and the iron grate that blocked it.

"Damn ye by Moradin's hammer!" Bruenor spat. He leaped from the walls and grasped the bars of the grate with his bloodied fingers. The bars bent under his weight but held fast.

"Wulfgar could break it," Bruenor said, half in exhausted delirium. "Lend me yer strength, me big friend," he called out to the darkness as he began tugging and twisting.

Hundreds of miles away, caught up in nightmares of his lost mentor, Bruenor, Wulfgar tossed uneasily in his bunk on the *Sea Sprite*. Perhaps the spirit of the young barbarian did come to Bruenor's aid at that desperate moment, but more likely the dwarf's unyielding stubbornness proved stronger than the iron. A bar of the grate bent low enough to slip out of the stone wall, and Bruenor held it free.

Hanging by one hand, Bruenor dropped the bar into the emptiness below him. With a wicked smile he hoped that some duergar scum might, at that instant, be at the bottom of the chimney, inspecting the dead spider and looking upward to find the cause.

Bruenor pulled himself halfway through the small hole he had opened, but had not the strength to squeeze his hips and belt through. Thoroughly drained, he accepted the perch, though his legs were dangling freely over a thousand-foot drop.

He put his head on the iron bars and knew no more.

6

BALDUR'S GATE

"To de rail! To de rail!" cried one voice.

"Toss 'em over!" agreed another. The mob of sailors crowded closer, brandishing curved swords and clubs.

Entreri stood calmly in the midst of the storm, Regis nervously beside him. The assassin did not understand the crew's sudden fit of anger, but he guessed that the sneaky halfling was somehow behind it. He hadn't drawn weapons; he knew he could have his saber and dagger readied whenever he needed them, and none of the sailors, for all their bluster and threats, had yet come within ten feet of him.

The captain of the ship, a squat, waddling man with stiff gray bristles, pearly white teeth, and eyes lightened in a perpetual squint, made his way out from his cabin to investigate the ruckus.

"To me, Redeye," he beckoned the grimy sailor who had first brought to his ears the rumor that the passengers were infected with a horrible disease—and who had obviously spread the tale to the other members of the crew. Redeye obeyed at once, following his captain through the parting mob to stand before Entreri and Regis.

The captain slowly took out his pipe and tamped down the weed, his eyes never releasing Entreri's from a penetrating gaze.

"Send 'em over!" came an occasional cry, but each time, the captain silenced the speaker with a wave of his hand. He wanted a full measure of these strangers before he acted, and he patiently let the moments pass as he lit the pipe and took a long drag.

Entreri never blinked and never looked away from the captain. He brought his cloak back behind the scabbards on his belt and crossed his arms, the calm and confident action conveniently putting each of his hands in position barely an inch from the hilts of his weapons.

"Ye should have told me, sir," the captain said at length.

"Your words are as unexpected as the actions of your crew," Entreri replied evenly.

"Indeed," the captain answered, drawing another puff.

Some of the crew were not as patient as their skipper. One barrel-chested man, his arms heavily muscled and tattooed, grew weary of the drama. He boldly stepped behind the assassin, meaning to toss him overboard and be done with him.

Just as the sailor started to reach out for the assassin's slender shoulders, Entreri exploded into motion, spinning and returning to his cross-armed pose so quickly that the sailors watching him tried to blink the sun out of their eyes and figure out whether he had moved at all.

The barrel-chested man slumped to his knees and fell facedown on the deck, for in that blink of an eye, a heel had smashed his kneecap, and even more insidious, a jeweled dagger had come out of its sheath, poked his heart, and returned to rest on the assassin's hip.

"Your reputation precedes you," the captain said, not flinching.

"I pray that I do it justice," Entreri replied with a sarcastic bow.

"Indeed," said the captain. He motioned to the fallen man. "Might his friends see to his aid?"

"He is already dead," Entreri assured the captain. "If any of his friends truly wish to go to him, let them, too, step forward."

"They are scared," the captain explained. "They have witnessed many terrible diseases in ports up and down the Sword Coast."

"Disease?" Entreri echoed.

"Your companion let on to it," said the captain.

A smile widened across Entreri's face as it all came clear to him. Lightning quick, he tore the cloak from Regis and caught the halfling's bare wrist, pulling him up off his feet and shooting a glare into the halfling's terror-filled eyes that promised a slow and painful death. Immediately Entreri noticed the scars on Regis's arm.

"Burns?" He gawked.

"Aye, that's how the little one says it happens," Redeye shouted, sinking back behind his captain when Entreri's glare settled upon him. "Burns from the inside, it does!"

"Burns from a candle, more likely," Entreri retorted. "Inspect the wounds for yourself," he said to the captain. "There is no disease here, just the desperate tricks of a cornered thief." He dropped Regis to the deck with a thud.

Regis lay very still, not even daring to breathe. The situation had not evolved quite as he had hoped.

"Toss 'em over!" cried an anonymous voice.

"Not fer chancin'!" yelled another

"How many do you need to sail your ship?" Entreri asked the captain. "How many can you afford to lose?"

The captain, having seen the assassin in action and knowing the man's reputation, did not for a moment consider the simple questions as idle threats. Furthermore, the stare Entreri now fixed upon him told him without doubt that he would be the initial target if his crew moved against the assassin.

"I will trust in your word," he said commandingly, silencing the grumbles of his nervous crew. "No need to inspect the wounds. but disease or no, our deal is ended." He looked pointedly to his dead crewman.

"I do not mean to swim to Calimport," Entreri said in a hiss.

"Indeed," replied the captain. "We put in at Baldur's Gate in two days. You shall find other passage there."

"And you shall repay me," Entreri said calmly, "every gold piece."

The captain drew another long drag from his pipe. This was not a battle he would choose to fight. "Indeed," he said with equal calm. He turned toward his cabin and ordered his crew back to their stations as he went.

⚔ ⚔ ⚔ ⚔

He remembered the lazy summer days on the banks of Maer Dualdon in Icewind Dale, How many hours he had spent there, fishing for the elusive knucklehead trout, or just basking in the rare warmth of Icewind Dale's summer sun. Looking back on his years in Ten-Towns, Regis could hardly believe the course fate had laid out for him.

He thought he had found his niche, a comfortable existence—

more comfortable still with the aid of the stolen ruby pendant—in a lucrative career as a scrimshander, carving the ivorylike bone of the knucklehead into marvelous little trinkets. But then came that fateful day, when Artemis Entreri showed up in Bryn Shander, the town Regis had come to call home, and sent the halfling scampering down the road to adventure with his friends.

But even Drizzt, Bruenor, Catti-brie, and Wulfgar had not been able to protect him from Entreri.

The memories provided small comfort to him as several grueling hours of solitude in the locked cabin slipped by. Regis would have liked to hide away in pleasant recollections of his past, but invariably his thoughts led back to the awful present, and he found himself wondering how he would be punished for his failed deception. Entreri had been composed, even amused, after the incident on the deck, leading Regis down to the cabin and then disappearing without a word.

Too composed, Regis thought.

But that was part of the assassin's mystique. No man knew Artemis Entreri well enough to call him friend, and no enemy could figure the man out well enough to gain an even footing against him.

Regis shrank back against the wall when Entreri at last arrived, sweeping through the door and over to the room's table without so much as a sidelong glance at the halfling. The assassin sat, brushing back his ink-black hair and eyeing the single candle burning on the table.

"A candle," he muttered, obviously amused. He looked at Regis. "You have a trick or two, halfling," he chuckled.

Regis was not smiling. No sudden warmth had come into Entreri's heart, he knew, and he'd be damned if he let the assassin's jovial facade take his guard down.

"A worthy ploy," Entreri continued. "And effective. It may

take us a tenday to gain passage south from Baldur's Gate. An extra tenday for your friends to close the distance. I had not expected you to be so daring."

The smile left his face suddenly, and his tone was noticeably more grim when he added, "I did not believe that you would be so ready to suffer the consequences."

Regis cocked his head to study the man's every movement. "Here it comes," he whispered under his breath.

"Of course there are consequences, little fool. I commend your attempt—I hope you will give me more excitement on this tedious journey! But I cannot belay punishment. Doing so would take the dare, and thus the excitement, out of your trickery."

He slipped up from his seat and started around the table. Regis sublimated his scream and closed his eyes; he knew that he had no escape.

The last thing he saw was the jeweled dagger turning over slowly in the assassin's hand.

✕ ✕ ✕ ✕ ✕

They made the River Chionthar the next afternoon and bucked the currents with a strong sea breeze filling their sails. By nightfall, the upper tiers of the city of Baldur's Gate lined the eastern horizon, and when the last hints of daylight disappeared from the sky, the lights of the great port marked their course as a beacon. But the city did not allow access to the docks after sunset, and the ship dropped anchor a half-mile out.

Regis, finding sleep impossible, heard Entreri stir much later that night. The halfling shut his eyes tightly and forced himself into a rhythm of slow, heavy breathing. He had no idea of Entreri's intent, but whatever the assassin was about, Regis didn't want him even suspecting that he was awake.

Entreri didn't give him a second thought. As silent as a cat—as silent as death—the assassin slipped through the cabin door. Twenty-five crewmen manned the ship, but after the long day's sail, and with Baldur's Gate awaiting the first light of dawn, only four of them would likely be awake.

The assassin slipped through the crew's barracks, following the light of a single candle at the rear of the ship. In the galley, the cook busily prepared the morning's breakfast of thick soup in a huge cauldron. Singing as he always did when he was at work, the cook paid no attention to his surroundings. But even if he had been quiet and alert, he probably would not have heard the slight footfalls behind him.

He died with his face in the soup.

Entreri moved back through the barracks, where twenty more died without a sound. Then he went up to the deck.

The moon hung full in the sky that night, but even a sliver of a shadow was sufficient for the skilled assassin, and Entreri knew well the routines of the watch. He had spent many nights studying the movements of the lookouts, preparing himself, as always, for the worst possible scenario. Timing the steps of the two watchmen on deck, he slithered up the mainmast, his jeweled dagger in his teeth.

An easy spring of his taut muscles brought him into the crow's nest.

Then there were two.

Back down on deck, Entreri moved calmly and openly to the rail. "A ship!" he called, pointing into the gloom. "Closing on us!"

Instinctively the two remaining watchmen rushed to the assassin's side and strained their eyes to see the peril in the dark —until the flash of a dagger told them of the deception.

Only the captain remained.

Entreri could easily have picked the lock on his cabin door and killed the man in his sleep, but the assassin wanted a more dramatic ending to his work; he wanted the captain to fully understand the doom that had befallen his ship that night. Entreri moved to the door, which opened onto the deck, and took out his tools and a length of fine wire.

A few minutes later, he was back at his own cabin, rousing Regis. "One sound, and I'll take your tongue," he warned the halfling.

Regis now understood what was happening. If the crew got to the docks at Baldur's Gate, they would no doubt spread the rumors of the deadly killer and his "diseased" friend, making Entreri's search for passage south impossible to fulfill.

The assassin wouldn't allow that at any cost, and Regis could not help but feel responsible for the carnage that night.

He moved quietly, helplessly, beside Entreri through the barracks, noting the absence of snores, and the quiet of the galley beyond. Surely the dawn was approaching; surely the cook would be hard at work preparing the morning meal. But no singing floated through the half-closed galley door.

The ship had stocked enough oil in Waterdeep to last the entire journey to Calimport, and kegs of the stuff still remained in the hold. Entreri pulled open the trap door and hoisted out two of the heavy barrels. He broke the seal on one and kicked it into a roll through the barracks, spewing oil as it went. Then he carried the other—and half-carried Regis, who was limp with fear and revulsion—topside, spreading the oil out more quietly and concentrating the spill in a tight arc around the captain's door.

"Get in," he told Regis, indicating the single rowboat hanging in a jigger off the starboard side of the ship. "And carry this." He handed the halfling a tiny pouch.

Bile rose in Regis's throat when he thought of what was inside the bag, but he took the pouch anyway and held it securely, knowing that if he lost it, Entreri would only get another.

The assassin sprang lightly across the deck, preparing a torch as he went. Regis watched him in horror, shuddering at the cold appearance of his shadowed face as he tossed the torch down the ladder to the oil-soaked barracks. Grimly satisfied as the flames roared to life, Entreri raced back across the deck to the captain's door.

"Good-bye!" was the only explanation he offered as he banged on the door. Two strides took him to the rowboat.

The captain leaped from his bed, fighting to orient himself. The ship was strangely calm, except for a telltale crackle and a wisp of smoke that slipped up through the floorboards.

Sword in hand, the captain threw the bolt back and pulled open the door. He looked around desperately and called for his crew. The flames had not reached the deck yet, but it was obvious to him—and should have been to his lookouts—that the ship was on fire. Beginning to suspect the awful truth, the captain rushed out, clad only in his nightshift.

He felt the tug of the trip-wire, then grimaced in further understanding as the wire noose bit deeply into his bare ankle. He sprawled face down, his sword dropping out in front of him. An aroma filled his nostrils, and he fully realized the deadly implications of the slick fluid drenching his nightshirt. He stretched out for his sword's hilt and clawed futilely at the wooden deck until his fingers bled.

A lick of flame jumped through the floorboards.

Sounds rolled eerily across the open expanse of water, especially in the empty dark of night. One sound filled the ears of Entreri and Regis as the assassin pulled the little rowboat against the currents of the Chionthar. It even cut through the din of the taverns lining the docks of Baldur's Gate, a half-mile away.

As if enhanced by the unspoken cries of protest of the dead crew—and by the dying ship itself—a singular, agonized voice screamed for all of them.

Then there was only the crackle of fire.

✠ ✠ ✠ ✠ ✠

Entreri and Regis entered Baldur's Gate on foot soon after daybreak. They had put the little rowboat into a cove a few hundred yards downriver, then sank the thing. Entreri wanted no evidence linking him to the disaster of the night before.

"It will be good to get home," the assassin chided Regis as they made their way along the extensive docks of the lower city. He led Regis's eye to a large merchant ship docked at one of the outer piers. "Do you remember the pennant?"

Regis looked to the flag flying atop the vessel, a gold field cut by slanted blue lines, the standard of Calimport. "Calimshan merchants never take passengers aboard," he reminded the assassin, hoping to diffuse Entreri's cocky attitude.

"They will make an exception," Entreri replied. He pulled the ruby pendant out from under his leather jacket and displayed it beside his wicked smile.

Regis fell silent once more. He knew well the power of the ruby and could not dispute the assassin's claim.

With sure and direct strides revealing that he had often before been in Baldur's Gate, Entreri led Regis to the harbor-master's office, a small shack just off the piers. Regis followed obediently, though his thoughts were hardly focused on the events of the present. He was still caught in the nightmare of the tragedy of the night before, trying to resolve his own part in the deaths of twenty-six men. He hardly noticed the harbormaster and didn't even catch the man's name.

But after only a few seconds of conversation, Regis realized that Entreri had fully captured the man under the hypnotic spell of the ruby pendant. The halfling faded out of the meeting altogether, disgusted with how well Entreri had mastered the powers of the pendant. His thoughts drifted again to his friends and his home, though now he looked back with lament, not hope. Had Drizzt and Wulfgar escaped the horrors of Mithral Hall, and were they now in pursuit? Watching Entreri in action and knowing that he would soon be back within the borders of Pook's realm, Regis almost hoped that they wouldn't come after him. How much more blood could stain his little hands?

Gradually Regis faded back in, half-listening to the words of the conversation and telling himself that there might be some important knowledge to be gained.

"When do they sail?" Entreri was saying.

Regis perked up his ears. Time was important. Perhaps his friends could get to him here, still a thousand miles from the stronghold of Pasha Pook.

"A tenday," replied the harbormaster, his eyes never blinking nor turning from the spectacle of the spinning gemstone.

"Too long," Entreri muttered under his breath. Then to the harbormaster, "I wish a meeting with the captain."

"Can be arranged."

"This very night . . . here."

The harbormaster shrugged his accord.

"And one more favor, my friend," Entreri said with a mock smile. "You track every ship that comes into port?"

"That is my job," said the dazed man.

"And surely you have eyes at the gates as well?" Entreri inquired with a wink.

I have many friends," the harbormaster replied. "Nothing

happens in Baldur's Gate without my knowledge."

Entreri looked to Regis. "Give it to him," he ordered,

Regis, not understanding, responded to the command with a blank stare.

"The pouch," the assassin explained, using the same light-hearted tone that had marked his casual conversation with the duped harbormaster.

Regis narrowed his eyes and did not move, as defiant an act as he had ever dared to show his captor.

"The pouch," Entreri reiterated, his tone now deadly serious. "Our gift for your friends." Regis hesitated for just a second, then threw the tiny pouch to the harbormaster.

"Enquire of every ship and every rider that comes through Baldur's Gate," Entreri explained to the harbormaster. "Seek out a band of travelers—two at the least, one an elf, likely to be cloaked in secrecy, and the other a giant, yellow-haired barbarian. Seek them out, my friend. Find the adventurer who calls himself Drizzt Do'Urden. That gift is for his eyes alone. Tell him that I await his arrival in Calimport." He sent a wicked glance over at Regis. "With more gifts."

The harbormaster slipped the tiny pouch into his pocket and gave Entreri his assurances that he would not fail the task.

"I must be going," Entreri said, pulling Regis to his feet. "We meet tonight," he reminded the harbormaster. "An hour after the sun is down."

⋇ ⋇ ⋇ ⋇ ⋇

Regis knew that Pasha Pook had connections in Baldur's Gate, but he was amazed at how well the assassin seemed to know his way around. In less than an hour, Entreri had secured their room and enlisted the services of two thugs to stand guard over Regis while the assassin went on some errands.

"Time for your second trick?" he asked Regis slyly just before leaving. He looked at the two thugs leaning against the far wall of the room, engrossed in some less-than-intellectual debate about the reputed virtues of a local "lady."

"You might get by them," Entreri whispered.

Regis turned away, not enjoying the assassin's macabre sense of humor.

"But, remember, my little thief, once outside, you are on the streets—in the shadow of the alleyways, where you will find no friends, and where I shall be waiting." He spun away with an evil chuckle and swept through the door.

Regis looked at the two thugs, now locked in a heated argument. He probably could have walked out the door at that very moment.

He dropped back on his bed with a resigned sigh and awkwardly locked his hands behind his head, the sting in one hand pointedly reminding him of the price of bravery.

⚔ ⚔ ⚔ ⚔ ⚔

Baldur's Gate was divided into two districts: the lower city of the docks and the upper city beyond the inner wall, where the more important citizens resided. The city had literally burst its bounds with the wild growth of trade along the Sword Coast. Its old wall set a convenient boundary between the transient sailors and adventurers who invariably made their way in and the long-standing houses of the land. "Halfway to everywhere" was a common phrase there, referring to the city's roughly equal proximity to Waterdeep in the North and Calimport in the South, the two greatest cities of the Sword Coast.

In light of the constant bustle and commotion that followed

such a title, Entreri attracted little attention as he slipped through the lanes toward the inner city. He had an ally, a powerful wizard named Oberon, there who was also an associate of Pasha Pook's. Oberon's true loyalty, Entreri knew, lay with Pook, and the wizard would no doubt promptly contact the guildmaster in Calimport with news of the recovered pendant, and of Entreri's imminent return.

But Entreri cared little whether Pook knew he was coming or not. His intent was behind him, to Drizzt Do'Urden, not in front, to Pook, and the wizard could prove of great value to him in learning more of the whereabouts of his pursuers.

After a meeting that lasted throughout the remainder of the day, Entreri left Oberon's tower and made his way back to the harbormaster's for the arranged rendezvous with the captain of the Calimport merchant ship. Entreri's visage had regained its determined confidence; he had put the unfortunate incident of the night before behind him, and everything was going smoothly again. He fingered the ruby pendant as he approached the shack.

A tenday was too long a delay.

⚔ ⚔ ⚔ ⚔ ⚔

Regis was hardly surprised later that night when Entreri returned to the room and announced that he had "persuaded" the captain of the Calimport vessel to change his schedule.

They would leave in three days.

EPILOGUE

Wulfgar heaved and strained on the ropes, trying to keep the mainsail full of the scant ocean wind as the crew of the *Sea Sprite* looked on in amazement. The currents of the Chionthar pushed against the ship, and a sensible captain would normally have dropped anchor to wait for a more favorable breeze to get them in. But Wulfgar, under the tutelage of an old sea dog named Mirky, was doing a masterful job. The individual docks of Baldur's Gate were in sight, and the *Sea Sprite*, to the cheers of several dozen sailors watching the monumental pull, would soon put in.

"I could use ten of him on my crew," Captain Deudermont remarked to Drizzt.

The drow smiled, ever amazed at the strength of his young friend. "He seems to be enjoying himself. I would never have put him as a sailor."

"Nor I," replied Deudermont. "I only hoped to profit from

his strength if we engaged with pirates. But Wulfgar found his sea legs early on."

"And he enjoys the challenge," Drizzt added. "The open ocean, the pull of the water, and of the wind, tests him in ways different than he has ever known."

"He does better than many," Deudermont replied. The experienced captain looked back downriver to where the open ocean waited. "You and your friend have been on but one short journey, skirting a coastline. You cannot yet appreciate the vastness and the power of the open sea."

Drizzt looked at Deudermont with sincere admiration and even a measure of envy. The captain was a proud man, but he tempered his pride with a practical rationale. Deudermont respected the sea and accepted it as his superior. And that acceptance, that profound understanding of his own place in the world, gave the captain as much of an advantage as any man could gain over the untamed ocean. Drizzt followed the captain's longing stare and wondered about this mysterious allure the open waters seemed to hold over so many.

He considered Deudermont's last words. "One day, perhaps," he said quietly.

They were close enough now, and Wulfgar released his hold and slumped, exhausted, to the deck. The crew worked furiously to complete the docking, but each stopped at least once to slap the huge barbarian across the shoulder. Wulfgar was too tired to even respond.

"We will be in for two days," Deudermont told Drizzt. "It was to be a tenday, but I am aware of your haste. I spoke with the crew last night, and they agreed—to a man—to put right back out again."

"Our thanks to them, and to you," Drizzt replied sincerely.

Just then, a wiry, finely dressed man hopped down to the

pier. "What ho, *Sea Sprite*?" he called. "Is Deudermont at your reins?"

"Pellman, the harbormaster," the captain explained to Drizzt. "He is!" he called to the man. "And glad to see Pellman, as well!"

"Well met, Captain," Pellman called. "And as fine a pull as I've ever seen! How long are you in port?"

"Two days," Deudermont replied. "Then off to the sea and the south."

The harbormaster paused for a moment, as if trying to remember something. Then he asked, as he had asked to every ship that had put in over the last few days, the question Entreri had planted in his mind. "I seek two adventurers," he called to Deudermont. "Might you have seen them?"

Deudermont looked to Drizzt, somehow guessing, as had the drow, that this inquiry was more than a coincidence.

"Drizzt Do'Urden and Wulfgar, by name," Pellman explained. "Though they may be using others. One's small and mysterious—elflike—and the other's a giant and as strong as any man alive!"

"Trouble?" Deudermont called.

"Not so," answered Pellman. "A message."

Wulfgar had moved up to Drizzt and heard the latter part of the conversation. Deudermont looked to Drizzt for instructions. "Your decision."

Drizzt didn't figure that Entreri would lay any serious traps for them; he knew that the assassin meant to fight with them, or at least with him, personally. "We will speak with the man," he answered.

"They are with me," Deudermont called to Pellman. " 'Twas Wulfgar," he looked at the barbarian and winked, then echoed Pellman's own description, "as strong as any man alive, who made the pull!"

Deudermont led them to the rail. "If there is trouble, I shall do what I can to retrieve you," he said quietly. "And we can wait in port for as long as two tendays if the need arises."

"Again, our thanks," Drizzt replied. "Surely Orlpar of Waterdeep set us aright."

"Leave that dog's name unspoken," Deudermont replied. "Rarely have I had such fortunate outcomes to my dealings with him! Farewell, then. You may take sleep on the ship if you desire."

Drizzt and Wulfgar moved cautiously toward the harbormaster, Wulfgar in the lead. Drizzt searched for any signs of ambush.

"We are the two you seek," Wulfgar said sternly, towering over the wiry man.

"Greetings," Pellman said with a disarming smile. He fished in his pocket. "I have met with an associate of yours," he explained, "a dark man with a halfling lackey."

Drizzt moved beside Wulfgar, and the two exchanged concerned glances.

"He left this," Pellman continued, handing the tiny pouch to Wulfgar. "And bade me to tell you that he will await your arrival in Calimport."

Wulfgar held the pouch tentatively, as if expecting it to explode in his face.

"Our thanks," Drizzt told Pellman. "We will tell our associate that you performed the task admirably."

Pellman nodded and bowed, turning away as he did so, to return to his duties. But first, he realized suddenly, he had another mission to complete, a subconscious command that he could not resist. Following Entreri's orders, the harbormaster moved from the docks and toward the upper level of the city.

Toward the house of Oberon.

Drizzt led Wulfgar off to the side, out of plain view. Seeing the barbarian's paling look, he took the tiny pouch and gingerly loosened the draw string, holding it as far away as possible. With a shrug to Wulfgar, who had moved a cautious step away, Drizzt brought the pouch down to his belt level and peeked in.

Wulfgar moved closer, curious and concerned when he saw Drizzt's shoulders droop. The drow looked to him in helpless resignation and inverted the pouch, revealing its contents.

A halfling's finger.

PART TWO

The world is full of ruffians. The world is full of people of good character. Both of these statements are true, I believe, because within most of the people I have known lies the beginning points of both seemingly disparate paths.

ALLIES

Some people are too timid to ever be ruffians, of course, and others too kindhearted, and similarly, some folk are too hard-tempered to ever let their good qualities show. But the emotional make-up of most people lies somewhere in the middle, a shade of gray that can be easily darkened or lightened by simple interaction. Race can certainly alter the shade—how well I have seen that since my road led me to the surface! An elf might noticeably flinch at the approach of a dwarf, while a dwarf might do likewise, or even spit upon the ground, if the situation is reversed.

Those initial impressions are sometimes difficult to overcome, and sometimes become lasting, but beyond race and appearance and other things that we cannot control, I have learned that there are definite decisions that I can make concerning which reaction I will edge someone else toward.

The key to it all, I believe, is respect.

When I was in Luskan with Wulfgar, we crossed through a tavern full of ruffians, men who used their fists and weapons on an almost daily basis. Yet, another friend of mine, Captain Deudermont of the Sea Sprite, often frequents such taverns, and rarely, very rarely, ever gets into so much as a verbal argument. Why is this? Why would a man such as Deudermont, obviously (as is shown by his dress and manner) a man of some wealth, and a man of respectable society, as well, not find himself immersed in brawls as regularly as the others? He often goes in alone, and stands quietly at the bar, but though he hardly says a word, he surely stands out among the more common patrons.

Is it fear that holds the ruffians from the man? Are they afraid that if they tangle with Deudermont, they will find retribution at the hands of his crew? Or has Deudermont simply brought with him such a reputation for ferocity as to scare off any potential challengers?

Neither, I say. Certainly the captain of the Sea Sprite must be a fine warrior, but that is no deterrent to the thugs of the taverns; indeed, the greatest fighting reputation only invites challenges among those folk. And though Deudermont's crew is formidable, by all accounts, more powerful and connected men than he have been found dead in the gutters of Luskan.

No, what keeps Captain Deudermont safe is his ability to show respect for anyone he meets. He is a man of charm, who holds well his personal pride. He grants respect at the outset of a meeting and continues that respect until the person forfeits it. This is very different than the way most people view the world. Most people insist that respect has to be earned, and with many, I have come to observe, earning it is no easy task! Many, and I include Bruenor and Wulfgar in this group, demand that anyone desiring their friendship first earn their respect, and I can understand their point of view, and once believed that I held one similar.

On my journey south on the Sea Sprite, Captain Deudermont taught me better, made me realize, without ever uttering a word on the subject, that demanding of another that he earns your respect is, in of itself, an act of arrogance, a way of self-elevation, implying by its very nature that your respect is worth earning.

Deudermont takes the opposite approach, one of acceptance and one lacking initial judgment. This may seem a subtle alternative, but it most certainly is not. Would that the man be anointed a king, I say, for he has learned the secret of peace. When Captain Deudermont, dressed in his finery, enters a tavern of common peasant thugs, most within the place, and society at large, would view him as superior. And yet, in his interactions with these people, there is no air of superiority about the man at all. In his eyes and in his heart, he is among peers, among other intelligent creatures whose paths have led them to a different—and not better or worse—place than his own. And when Deudermont grants respect to men who would think nothing of cutting his heart out, he disarms them, he takes away whatever reason they might have found to fight with him.

There is much more to it than that. Captain Deudermont is able to do this because he can honestly attempt to see the world through the eyes of another. He is a man of empathy, a man who revels in the differences of people rather than fearing those differences.

How rich is his life! How full of wonder and how wide of experience!

Captain Deudermont taught these things to me, by example. Respect is one of the most basic needs of reasoning creatures, particularly among men. An insult is just that because it is an assault upon respect, upon esteem, and upon that most dangerous of qualities: pride.

So when I meet people now, they do not have to earn my respect. I grant it, willingly and happily, expecting that in doing so I will come to learn even more about this beautiful world around me, that my experiences will widen.

Certainly some people will see this as weakness or cowardice, will misconstrue my intentions as sublimation, rather than an acceptance of equal worth. But it is not fear that guides my actions—I have seen far too much of battle to fear it any longer—it is hope.

The hope that I will find another Bruenor, or another Catti-brie, for I have come to know that I can never have too many friends.

So I offer you respect, and it will take much for you to lose it. But if you do, if you choose to see it as weakness and seize upon your perceived advantage, well . . .

Perhaps I'll then let you talk with Guenhwyvar.

—Drizzt Do'Urden

STIRRINGS

The first thing he noticed was the absence of the wind. He had lain long hour after hour on his perch at the top of the chimney, and through it all, even in his semiconscious state, there had been the unceasing presence of the wind. It had taken his mind back to Icewind Dale, his home for nearly two centuries. But Bruenor had felt no comfort in the gale's forlorn moan, a continual reminder of his predicament and the last sound he thought he would ever hear.

But it was no more. Only the crackle of a nearby fire broke the quiet stillness. Bruenor lifted a heavy eyelid and stared absently into the flames, trying to discern his condition and his whereabouts. He was warm and comfortable, with a heavy quilt pulled up tightly around his shoulders. And he was indoors—the flames burned in a hearth, not in the open pit of a campfire.

Bruenor's eye drifted to the side of the hearth and focused on a neatly stacked pile of equipment.

His equipment!

The one-horned helm, Drizzt's scimitar, the mithral armor, and his new battle-axe and shining shield. And he was stretched out under the quilt, wearing only a silken night-shirt.

Suddenly feeling very vulnerable, Bruenor pulled himself up to his elbows.

A wave of blackness rolled over him and sent his thoughts reeling in nauseous circles. He dropped heavily to his back.

His vision returned for just a moment, long enough to register the form of a tall and beautiful woman kneeling over him. Her long hair, gleaming silver in the firelight, brushed across his face.

"Spider's poison," she said softly. "Would have killed anything but a dwarf."

Then there was only the blackness.

Bruenor awoke again a few hours later, stronger and more alert. Trying not to stir and bring any attention, he half-opened one eye and surveyed the area, glancing at the pile first. Satisfied that all of his equipment was there, he slowly turned his head over.

He was in a small chamber, apparently a one-roomed structure, for the only door seemed to lead outside. The woman he had seen earlier—though Bruenor wasn't really sure until now if that image had been a dream—stood beside the door, staring out the room's single window to the night sky beyond. Her hair was indeed silver. Bruenor could see that its hue was no trick of the firelight. But not silver with the graying of age; this lustrous mane glowed with vibrant life.

"Yer pardon, fair lady," the dwarf croaked, his voice cracking on every syllable. The woman twirled and looked at him curiously.

"Might I be getting a bit o' food?" asked Bruenor, never one to mix up his priorities.

The woman floated across the room and helped Bruenor up

into a sitting position. Again a wave of blackness swirled over the dwarf, but he managed to shrug it away.

"Only a dwarf!" the woman muttered, astonished that Bruenor had come through his ordeal.

Bruenor cocked his head up at her. "I know ye, lady, though I cannot find yer name in me thoughts."

"It is not important," the woman replied. "You have come through much, Bruenor Battlehammer." Bruenor cocked his head further and leaned away at the mention of his name, but the woman steadied him and continued. "I attended to your wounds as best I could, though I feared that I had come upon you too late to mend the hurts of the spider's poison."

Bruenor looked down at his bandaged forearm, reliving those terrible moments when he had first encountered the giant spider. "How long?"

"How long you lay atop the broken grate, I do not know," the woman answered. "But here you have rested for three days and more—too long for your stomach's liking! I will prepare some food." She started to rise, but Bruenor caught her arm.

"Where is this place?"

The lady's smile eased his grip. "In a clearing not far from the grate. I feared to move you."

Bruenor didn't quite understand. "Yer home?"

"Oh, no," the woman laughed, standing. "A creation, and only temporary. It will be gone with the dawn's light if you feel able to travel."

The tie to magic flickered recognition. "Ye're the Lady of Silverymoon!" Bruenor spouted suddenly.

"Clearmoon Alustriel," the woman said with a polite bow. "My greetings, noble King."

"King?" Bruenor echoed in disgust. "Suren me halls are gone to the scum."

"We shall see," said Alustriel.

But Bruenor missed the words altogether. His thoughts were not on Mithral Hall, but on Drizzt and Wulfgar and Regis, and especially on Catti-brie, the joy of his life. "Me friends," he begged to the woman. "Do ye know o' me friends?"

"Rest easy," Alustriel answered. "They escaped the halls, each of them."

"Even the drow?"

Alustriel nodded. "Drizzt Do'Urden was not destined to die in the home of his dearest friend."

Alustriel's familiarity with Drizzt triggered another memory in the dwarf. "Ye met him before," he said, "on our road to Mithral Hall. Ye pointed the way for us. And that is how ye knew me name."

"And knew where to search for you," Alustriel added. "Your friends think you dead, to their ultimate grief. But I am a wizard of some talent and can speak to worlds that oft bring surprising revelations. When the specter of Morkai, an old associate who passed from this world a few years ago, imparted to me an image of a fallen dwarf, half out of a hole on the side of a mountain, I knew the truth of the fate of Bruenor Battlehammer. I only hoped that I would not be too late."

"Bah! Fit as ever!" Bruenor huffed, thumping a fist into his chest. As he shifted his weight, a stinging pain in his seat made him wince.

"A crossbow quarrel," Alustriel explained.

Bruenor thought for a moment. He had no recollection of being hit, though the memory of his flight from the undercity was perfectly clear. He shrugged and attributed it to the blindness of his battle-lust. "So one o' the gray scum got me," he started to say, but then he blushed and turned his eyes away at the thought of this woman plucking the quarrel from his backside.

Alustriel was kind enough to change the subject. "Dine and then rest," she instructed. "Your friends are safe . . . for the present."

"Where—"

Alustriel cut him off with an outstretched palm. "My knowledge in this matter is not sufficient," she explained. "You shall find your answers soon enough. In the morning, I will take you to Longsaddle and Catti-brie. She can tell you more than I."

Bruenor wished that he could go right now to the human girl he had plucked from the ruins of a goblin raid and reared as his daughter, that he could crush her against him in his arms and tell her that everything was all right. But he reminded himself that he had never truly expected to see Catti-brie again, and he could suffer through one more night.

Any fears he had of anxious restlessness were washed away in the serenity of exhausted sleep only minutes after he had finished the meal. Alustriel watched over him until contented snores resounded throughout the magical shelter.

Satisfied that only a healthy sleeper could roar so loudly, the Lady of Silverymoon leaned back against the wall and closed her eyes.

It had been a long three days.

⚔ ⚔ ⚔ ⚔ ⚔

Bruenor watched in amazement as the structure faded around him with the first light of dawn, as if the dark of night had somehow lent the place the tangible material for its construction. He turned to say something to Alustriel but saw her in the midst of casting a spell, facing the pinkening sky and reaching out as though trying to grab the rays of light.

She clenched her hands and brought them to her mouth, whispering the enchantment into them. Then she flung the captured light out before her, crying out the final words of the dweomer, "Equine aflame!" A glowing ball of red struck the stone and burst into a shower of fire, forming almost instantly into a flaming chariot and two horses. Their images danced with the fire that gave them shape, but they did not burn the ground.

"Gather your things," the lady instructed Bruenor. "It is time we leave."

Bruenor stood motionless a moment longer. He had never come to appreciate magic, only the magic that strengthened weapons and armor, but neither did he ever deny its usefulness. He collected his equipment, not bothering to don armor or shield, and joined Alustriel behind the chariot. He followed her onto it, somewhat reluctantly, but it did not burn and it felt as tangible as wood.

Alustriel took a fiery rein in her slender hand and called to the team. A single bound lifted them into the morning sky, and they shot away, west around the bulk of the mountain and then south.

The stunned dwarf dropped his equipment to his feet—his chin to his chest—and clutched the side of the chariot. Mountains rolled out below him; he noted the ruins of Settlestone, the ancient dwarven city, now far below, and only a second later, far behind. The chariot roared over the open grassland and skimmed westward along the northern edge of the Trollmoors. Bruenor had relaxed enough to spit a curse as they soared over the town of Nesme, remembering the less-than-hospitable treatment he and his friends had received at the hands of a patrol from the place. They passed over the Dessarin River network, a shining snake writhing through the fields, and Bruenor saw a large encampment of barbarians far to the north.

Alustriel swung the fiery chariot south again, and only a few minutes later, the famed Ivy Mansion of Harpell Hill, Longsaddle, came into view.

A crowd of curious wizards gathered atop the hill to watch the chariot's approach, cheering somberly—trying to maintain a distinguished air—as they always did when Lady Alustriel graced them with her presence. One face in the crowd blanched to white when the red beard, pointed nose, and one-horned helm of Bruenor Battlehammer came into view.

"But . . . you . . . uh . . . dead . . . fell," stammered Harkle Harpell as Bruenor jumped from the back of the chariot.

"Nice to see yerself, too," Bruenor replied, clad only in his nightshirt and helm. He scooped his equipment from the chariot and dropped the pile at Harkle's feet. "Where's me girl?"

"Yes, yes . . . the girl . . . Catti-brie . . . oh, where? Oh, there," he rambled, the fingers of one hand nervously bouncing on his lower lip. "Do come, yes do!" He grabbed Bruenor's hand and whisked the dwarf off to the Ivy Mansion.

They intercepted Catti-brie, barely out of bed and wearing a fluffy robe, shuffling down a long hall. The young woman's eyes popped wide when she spotted Bruenor rushing at her, and she dropped the towel she was holding, her arms falling limply to her side. Bruenor buried his face into her, hugging her around the waist so tightly that he forced the air from her lungs. As soon as she recovered from her shock, she returned the hug tenfold.

"Me prayers," she stammered, her voice quaking with sobs. "By the gods, I'd thought ye dead!"

Bruenor didn't answer, trying to hold himself steady. His tears were soaking the front of Catti-brie's robe, and he felt the eyes of a crowd of Harpells behind him. Embarrassed, he pushed open a door to his side, surprising a half-clad Harpell who stood naked to the waist.

"Excuse—" the wizard began, but Bruenor grabbed his shoulder and pulled him out into the hall, at the same time leading Catti-brie into the room. The door slammed in the wizard's face as he turned back to his chamber. He looked helplessly to his gathered kin, but their wide smiles and erupting laughter told him that they would be of no assistance. With a shrug, the wizard moved on about his morning business as though nothing unusual had happened.

It was the first time Catti-brie had ever seen the stoic dwarf truly cry. Bruenor didn't care and couldn't have done a thing to prevent the scene anyway. "Me prayers, too," he whispered to his beloved daughter, the human child he had taken in as his own more than a decade and a half before.

"If we'd have known," Catti-brie began, but Bruenor put a gentle finger to her lips to silence her. It was not important; Bruenor knew that Catti-brie and the others would never have left him if they had even suspected that he might be alive.

"Suren I know not why I lived," the dwarf replied. "None o' the fire found me skin." He shuddered at the memories of his tendays alone in the mines of Mithral Hall. "No more talk o' the place," he begged. " Behind me it is. Behind me to stay!"

Catti-brie, knowing of the approach of armies to reclaim the dwarven homeland, started to shake her head, but Bruenor didn't catch the motion.

"Me friends?" he asked the young woman. "Drow eyes I saw as I fell."

"Drizzt lives," Catti-brie answered, "as does the assassin that chased Regis. He came up to the ledge just as ye fell and carried the little one away."

"Rumblebelly?" Bruenor gasped.

"Aye, and the drow's cat as well."

"Not dead . . ."

"Nay, not to me guess," Catti-brie was quick to respond. "Not yet. Drizzt and Wulfgar have chased the fiend to the south, knowing his goal to be Calimport."

"A long run," Bruenor muttered. He looked to Catti-brie, confused. "But I'd have thought ye'd be with them."

"I have me own course," Catti-brie replied, her face suddenly stern. "A debt for repaying."

Bruenor understood at once. "Mithral Hall?" he choked out. "Ye figured to return, avengin' meself?"

Catti-brie nodded, unblinking.

"Ye're bats, girl!" Bruenor said. "And the drow would let ye go alone?"

"Alone?" Catti-brie echoed. It was time for the rightful king to know. "Nay, nor would I so foolishly end me life. A hundred kin make their way from the north and west," she explained. "And a fair number of Wulfgar's folk beside 'em."

"Not enough," Bruenor replied. "An army of duergar scum holds the halls."

"And eight thousand more from Citadel Adbar to the north and east," Catti-brie continued grimly, not slowing a beat. "King Harbromme of the dwarves of Adbar says he'll see the halls free again! Even the Harpells have promised their aid."

Bruenor drew a mental image of the approaching armies—wizards, barbarians, and a rolling wall of dwarves—and with Catti-brie at their lead. A thin smile cut the frown from his face. He looked upon his daughter with even more than the considerable respect he had always shown her, his eyes wet with tears once more.

"They wouldn't beat me," Catti-brie growled. "I meant to see yer face carved in the Hall of Kings, and meant to put yer name in its proper place o' glory!"

Bruenor grabbed her close and squeezed with all his strength.

Of all the mantles and laurels he had found in the years gone by, or might find in the years ahead, none fit as well or blessed him as much as "Father."

✂ ✂ ✂ ✂ ✂

Bruenor stood solemnly on the southern slope of Harpell Hill that evening, watching the last colors fade out of the western sky and the emptiness of the rolling plain to the south. His thoughts were on his friends, particularly Regis—Rumblebelly—the bothersome halfling that had undeniably found a soft corner in the dwarf's stone heart.

Drizzt would be all right—Drizzt was always all right—and with mighty Wulfgar walking beside him, it would take an army to bring them down.

But Regis.

Bruenor never had doubted that the halfling's carefree manner of living, stepping on toes with a half-apologetic and half-amused shrug, would eventually get him in mud too deep for his little legs to carry him through. Rumblebelly had been a fool to steal the guildmaster's ruby pendant.

But "just desserts" did nothing to dispel the dwarf's pity at his halfling friend's dilemma, nor Bruenor's anger at his own inability to help. By his station, his place was here, and he would lead the gathering armies to victory and glory, crushing the duergar and bringing a level of prosperity back to Mithral Hall. His new kingdom would be the envy of the North, with crafted items that rivaled the works of the ancient days flowing out into the trade routes all across the Realms.

It had been his dream, the goal of his life since that terrible day nearly two centuries before, when Clan Battlehammer had been nearly wiped out and those few who had survived, mostly children, had been chased out of their homeland to the meager mines of Icewind Dale.

Bruenor's lifelong dream was to return, but how hollow it seemed to him now, with his friends caught in a desperate chase across the southland.

The last light left the sky, and the stars blinked to life. Nighttime, Bruenor thought with a bit of comfort.

The time of the drow.

The first hints of his smile dissipated, though, as soon as they began, as Bruenor suddenly came to view the deepening gloom in a different perspective. "Nighttime," he whispered aloud.

The time of the assassin.

8

A PLAIN BROWN WRAPPER

The simple wooden structure at the end of Rogues Circle seemed understated even for the decrepit side of the sprawling southern city of Calimport. The building had few windows, all boarded or barred, and not a terrace or balcony to speak of. Similarly, no lettering identified the building, not even a number on the door to place it. But everyone in the city knew the house and marked it well, for beyond either of its iron-bound doors, the scene changed dramatically. Where the outside showed only the weathered brown of old wood, the inside displayed a myriad of bright colors and tapestries, thickly woven carpets, and statues of solid gold. This was the thieves' guild, rivaling the palace of Calimshan's ruler himself in riches and decor.

It rose three floors from the street level, with two more levels hidden below. The highest level was the finest, with five rooms—an octagonal central hall and four antechambers off it—all designed for the comfort and convenience of one man: Pasha Pook. He was the guildmaster, the architect of an intricate thieving network. And he made certain that he was the first to enjoy the spoils of his guild's handiwork.

Pook paced the highest level's central hall, his audience chamber, stopping every circuit to stroke the shining coat of the leopard that lay beside his great chair. An uncharacteristic anxiety was etched upon the guildmaster's round face, and he twiddled his fingers nervously when he was not petting his exotic pet.

His clothes were of the finest silk, but other than the brooch that fastened his wrappings, he wore none of the abundant jewelry customary among others of his station—though his teeth did gleam of solid gold. In truth, Pook seemed a half-sized version of one of the four hill giant eunuchs that lined the hall, an inconspicuous appearance for a silver-tongued guildmaster who had brought sultans to their knees and whose name sent the sturdiest of the ruffian street dwellers scurrying for dark holes.

Pook nearly jumped when a loud knock resounded off the room's main door, the one to the lower levels. He hesitated for a long moment, assuring himself that he would make the other man squirm for waiting—though he really needed the time to compose himself. Then he absently motioned to one of the eunuchs and moved to the overstuffed throne on the raised platform opposite the door and dropped a hand again to his pampered cat.

A lanky fighter entered, his thin rapier dancing to the swagger of his stride. He wore a black cape that floated behind him and was bunched at his neck. His thick brown hair curled into and around it. His clothes were dark and plain but crisscrossed by straps and belts, each with a pouch or sheathed dagger or some other unusual weapon hanging from it. His high leather boots, worn beyond any creases, made no sound other than the timed clump of his agile stride.

"Greetings, Pook," he said informally.

Pook's eyes narrowed immediately at the sight of the man. "Rassiter," he replied to the wererat.

Rassiter walked up to the throne and bowed halfheartedly, throwing the reclining leopard a distasteful glance. Flashing a rotted smile that revealed his lowly heritage, he put one foot upon the chair and bent low to let the guildmaster feel the heat of his breath.

Pook glanced at the dirty boot on his beautiful chair, then back at the man with a smile that even the uncouth Rassiter noticed was a bit too disarming. Figuring that he might be taking his familiarity with his partner a bit too far, Rassiter removed his foot from its perch and shuffled back a step.

Pook's smile faded, but he was satisfied. "It is done?" he asked the man.

Rassiter danced a circle and nearly laughed out loud. "Of course," he answered, and he pulled a pearl necklace from his pouch.

Pook frowned at the sight, just the expression the sly fighter had expected. "Must you kill them all?" the guildmaster said in a hiss.

Rassiter shrugged and replaced the necklace. "You said you wanted her removed. She is removed."

Pook's hands clutched the arms of the throne. "I said I wanted her taken from the streets until the job was completed!"

"She knew too much," Rassiter replied, examining his fingernails.

"She was a valuable wench," Pook said, back in control now. Few men could anger Pasha Pook as did Rassiter, and fewer still would have left the chamber alive.

"One of a thousand," chuckled the lanky fighter.

Another door opened, and an older man entered, his purple robes embroidered with golden stars and quarter-moons and a huge diamond fastening his high turban. "I must see——"

Pook cast him a sidelong glance. "Not now, LaValle."

"But Master——"

Pook's eyes went dangerously thin again, nearly matching the lines of his lipless grimace. The old man bowed apologetically and disappeared back through the door, closing it carefully and silently behind him.

Rassiter laughed at the spectacle. "Well done!"

"You should learn LaValle's manners," Pook said to him.

"Come, Pook, we are partners," Rassiter replied. He skipped over to one of the room's two windows, the one that looked south to the docks and the wide ocean. "The moon will be full tonight," he said excitedly, spinning back on Pook. "You should join us, Pasha! A grand feasting there will be!"

Pook shuddered to think of the macabre table that Rassiter and his fellow wererats planned to set. Perhaps the wench was not yet dead. . . .

He shook away such thoughts. I am afraid I must decline," he said quietly.

Rassiter understood—and had purposely enticed—Pook's disgust. He danced back over and put his foot on the throne, again showing Pook that foul smile. "You do not know what you are missing," he said. "But the choice is yours; that was our deal." He spun away and bowed low. "And you are the master."

"An arrangement that does well by you and yours," Pook reminded him.

Rassiter turned his palms out in concession, then clapped his hands together. "I cannot argue that my guild fares better since you brought us in." He bowed again. "Forgive my insolence, my dear friend, but I can hardly contain the mirth of my fortunes. And tonight the moon will be full!"

"Then go to your feast, Rassiter."

The lanky man bowed again, cast one more glare at the leopard, and skipped from the room.

When the door had closed, Pook ran his fingers over his brow and down through the stylishly matted remains of what once had been a thick tousle of black hair. Then he dropped his chin helplessly into a plump palm and chuckled at his own discomfort in dealing with Rassiter, the wererat.

He looked to the harem door, wondering if he might take his mind off his associate. But he remembered LaValle. The wizard would not have disturbed him, certainly not with Rassiter in the room, unless his news was important.

He gave his pet a final scratch on the chin and moved through the chamber's southeast door, into the wizard's dimly lit quarters. LaValle, staring intehtly into his crystal ball, did not notice him as he entered. Not wanting to disturb the wizard, Pook quietly took the seat across the small table and waited, amusing himself with the curious distortions of LaValle's scraggly gray beard through the crystal ball as the wizard moved this way and that.

Finally LaValle looked up. He could clearly see the lines of tension still on Pook's face, not unexpected after a visit from the wererat. "They have killed her, then?" he asked, already knowing the answer.

"I despise him," said Pook.

LaValle nodded in agreement. "But you cannot dismiss the power that Rassiter has brought you."

The wizard spoke the truth. In the two years since Pook had allied himself with the wererats, his guild had become the most prominent and powerful in the city. He could live well simply from the tithes that the dockside merchants paid him for protection—from his own guild. Even the captains of many of the visiting merchant ships knew enough not to turn away Pook's collector when he met them on the docks.

And those who didn't know better learned quickly.

No, Pook couldn't argue about the benefits of having Rassiter and his fellows around. But the guildmaster had no love for the wretched lycanthropes, human by day and something beastly, half rat and half man, by night. And he wasn't fond of the way they handled their business.

"Enough of him," Pook said, dropping his hands to the velvety black tablecloth. "I am certain that I shall need a dozen hours in the harem to get over our meeting!" His grin showed that the thought did not displease him. "But what did you want?"

A wide smile spread over the wizard's face. "I have spoken with Oberon in Baldur's Gate this day," he said with some pride. "I have learned of something that may make you forget all about your discussion with Rassiter."

Pook waited curiously, allowing LaValle to play out his dramatics. The wizard was a fine and loyal aide, the closest thing the guildmaster had to a friend.

"Your assassin returns!" LaValle proclaimed suddenly.

It took Pook a few moments to think through the meaning and implications of the wizard's words. But then it hit him, and he sprang up from the table. "Entreri?" he gasped, barely finding his breath.

LaValle nodded and nearly laughed out loud.

Pook ran his hand through his hair. Three years. Entreri, deadliest of the deadly, was returning to him after three long years. He looked curiously at the wizard.

"He has the halfling," LaValle answered to his unspoken question. Pook's face lit up in a broad smile. He leaned forward eagerly, his golden teeth shining in the candlelight.

Truly LaValle was glad to please his guildmaster, to give him the news he had waited so very long to hear. "And the ruby pendant!" the wizard proclaimed, banging a fist on the table.

"Yes!" Pook snarled, exploding into laughter. His gem, his most prized possession. With its hypnotic powers, he could rise to even greater heights of prosperity and power. Not only would he dominate all he met, but he would make them glad for the experience. "Ah, Rassiter," Pook muttered, suddenly thinking of the upper hand he could gain on his associate. "Our relationship is about to change, my rodent friend."

"How much will you still need him?" LaValle asked.

Pook shrugged and looked to the side of the room, to a small curtain.

The Taros Hoop.

LaValle blanched at the thought of the thing. The Taros Hoop was a mighty relic capable of displacing its owner, or his enemies, through the very planes of existence. But the power of this item was not without price. Thoroughly evil it was, and every one of the few times LaValle had used it, he had felt a part of himself drain away, as though the Taros Hoop gained its power by stealing his life force. LaValle hated Rassiter, but he hoped that the guildmaster would find a better solution than the Taros Hoop.

The wizard looked back to find Pook staring at him. "'Tell me more!" Pook insisted eagerly.

LaValle shrugged helplessly and put his hand on the crystal ball. "I have not been able to glimpse them myself," he said. "Ever has Artemis Entreri been able to dodge my scrying. But by Oberon's words, they are not too far. Sailing the waters north of Calimshan, if not already within the borders. And they fly on a swift wind, Master. A tenday or two, no more."

"And Regis is with him?" Pook asked.

"He is."

"Alive?"

"Very much alive," said the wizard.

"Good!" Pook sneered. How he longed to see the treacherous halfling again! To have his plump hands around Regis's little neck! The guild had fallen on tough times after Regis had run off with the magical pendant. In truth, the problems had come mostly from Pook's own insecurity in dealing with people without the gem, so long had he been using it, and from the guildmaster's obsessive—and expensive—hunt to find the halfling. But to Pook, the blame fell squarely upon Regis. He even blamed the halfling for the alliance with the wererats' guild, for certainly he wouldn't have needed Rassiter if he had had his pendant.

But now everything would work out for the best, Pook knew. Possessing the pendant and dominating the wererats, perhaps he could even think of expanding his power outside Calimport, with charmed associates and lycanthrope allies heading guilds throughout the southland.

LaValle seemed more serious when Pook looked back at him. "How do you believe Entreri will feel about our new associates?" he asked grimly.

"Ah, he does not know," said Pook, realizing the implications. "He has been gone too long." He thought for a moment then shrugged. "They are in the same business, after all. Entreri should accept them."

"Rassiter disturbs everyone he meets," the wizard reminded him. "Suppose that he crosses Entreri?"

Pook laughed at the thought. "I can assure you that Rassiter will cross Artemis Entreri only once, my friend."

"And then you shall make arrangements with the new head of the wererats," LaValle snickered.

Pook clapped him on the shoulder and headed for the door. "Learn what you can," he instructed the wizard. "If you can find them in your crystal ball, call to me. I cannot wait to glimpse the face of Regis the halfling again. So much I owe to that one."

"And you shall be?"

"In the harem," Pook answered with a wink. "Tension, you know."

LaValle slumped back in his chair when Pook had gone and considered again the return of his principal rival. He had gained much in the years since Entreri had left, even rising to this room on the third level as Pook's chief assistant.

This room, Entreri's room.

But the wizard never had any problems with the assassin. They had been comfortable associates, if not friends, and had helped each other many times in the past. LaValle couldn't count the number of times he had shown Entreri the quickest route to a target.

And there was that nasty situation with Mancas Tiveros, a fellow mage. "Mancas the Mighty," the other wizards of Calimport had called him, and they had pitied LaValle when he and Mancas fell into dispute concerning the origins of a particular spell. Both had claimed credit for the discovery, and everyone waited for an expected war of magic to erupt. But Mancas suddenly and inexplicably went away, leaving a note disclaiming his role in the spell's creation and giving full credit to LaValle. Mancas had never been seen again—in Calimport or anywhere else.

"Ah, well," LaValle sighed, turning back to his crystal ball. Artemis Entreri had his uses.

The door to the room opened, and Pook stuck his head

back in. "Send a messenger to the carpenter's guild," he said to LaValle. "Tell them that we shall need several skilled men immediately."

LaValle tilted his head in disbelief.

"The harem and treasury are to stay," Pook said emphatically, feigning frustration over his wizard's inability to see the logic. "And certainly I am not conceding my chamber!"

LaValle frowned as he thought he began to understand.

"Nor am I about to tell Artemis Entreri that he cannot have his own room back," said Pook. "Not after he has performed his mission so excellently!"

"I understand," said the wizard glumly, thinking himself relegated once again to the lower levels.

"So a sixth room must be built," laughed Pook, enjoying his little game. "Between Entreri's and the harem." He winked again at his valued assistant. "You may design it yourself, my dear LaValle. And spare no expense!" He shut the door and was gone.

The wizard wiped the moisture from his eyes. Pook always surprised him, but never disappointed him. "You are a generous master, my Pasha Pook," he whispered to the empty room.

And truly Pasha Pook was a masterful leader as well, for LaValle turned back to his crystal ball, his teeth gritted in determination. He would find Entreri and the halfling. He wouldn't disappoint his generous master.

9
FIERY RIDDLES

Now running with the currents of the Chionthar, and with the breeze at enough of an angle from the north for the sails to catch a bit of a push, the *Sea Sprite* cruised away from Baldur's Gate at a tremendous rate, spitting a white spray despite the concurrent movement of the water.

"The Sword Coast by midafternoon," Deudermont said to Drizzt and Wulfgar. "And off the coast, with no land in sight until we make Asavir's Channel. Then a southern journey around the edge of the world and back east to Calimport.

"Calimport," he said again, indicating a new pennant making its way up the mast of the *Sea Sprite*, a golden field crossed by slanted blue lines.

Drizzt looked at Deudermont suspiciously, knowing that this was not an ordinary practice of sailing vessels.

"We run Waterdeep's flag north of Baldur's Gate," the captain explained. "Calimport's south."

"An acceptable practice?" Drizzt asked.

"For those who know the price," chuckled Deudermont. "Waterdeep and Calimport are rivals, and stubborn in their feud. They desire trade with each other—they can only profit from it—but do not always allow ships flying the other's flag to dock in their harbors."

"A foolish pride," Wulfgar remarked, painfully reminded of some similar traditions his own clannish people had practiced only a few years before.

"Politics," Deudermont said with a shrug. "But the lords of both cities secretly desire the trade, and a few dozen ships have made the connections to keep business moving. The *Sea Sprite* has two ports to call home, and everyone profits from the arrangement."

"Two markets for Captain Deudermont," Drizzt remarked slyly. "Practical."

"And it makes good sailing sense as well," Deudermont continued, his smile still wide. "Pirates running the waters north of Baldur's Gate respect the banner of Waterdeep above all others, and those south of here take care not to rouse the anger of Calimport and her massive armada. The pirates along Asavir's Channel have many merchant ships to pick from in the straights, and they are more likely to raid one that carries a flag of less weight."

"And you are never bothered?" Wulfgar couldn't help but ask, his voice tentative and almost sarcastic, as though he hadn't yet figured out if he approved of the practice.

"Never?" echoed Deudermont. "Not 'never,' but rarely. And on those occasions that pirates come at us, we till our sails and run. Few ships can catch the *Sea Sprite* when her sails are full of wind."

"And if they do catch you?" asked Wulfgar.

"That is where you two can earn your passage," Deudermont laughed. "My guess is that those weapons you carry might soften a looting pirate's desire to continue the pursuit."

Wulfgar brought Aegis-fang up in front of him. "I pray that I have learned the movements of a ship well enough for such a battle," he said. "An errant swing might send me over the rail!"

"Then swim to the side of the pirate ship," Drizzt mused, "and tip her over!"

⋈ ⋈ ⋈ ⋈ ⋈

From a darkened chamber in his tower in Baldur's Gate, the wizard Oberon watched the *Sea Sprite* sail out. He probed deeper into the crystal ball to scry the elf and huge barbarian standing beside the ship's captain on the deck. They were not from these parts, the wizard knew. By his dress and his coloring, the barbarian was more likely from one of those distant tribes far to the north, beyond even Luskan and around the Spine of the World mountains, in that desolate stretch of land known as Icewind Dale. How far he was from home, and how unusual to see one of his kind sailing the open sea!

"What part could these two play in the return of Pasha Pook's gem?" Oberon wondered aloud, truly intrigued. Had Entreri gone all the way to that distant strip of tundra in search of the halfling? Were these two pursuing him south?

But it was not the wizard's affair. Oberon was just glad that Entreri had called in the debt with so easy a favor. The assassin had killed for Oberon—more than once—several years ago, and though Entreri had never mentioned the favors in his many visits to Oberon's tower, the wizard had always felt as if the assassin held a heavy chain around his neck. But this very night, the long-standing debt would be cleared in the puff of a simple signal.

Oberon's curiosity kept him tuned to the departing *Sea Sprite* a bit longer. He focused upon the elf—Drizzt Do'Urden, as Pellman, the harbormaster, had called him. To the wizard's experienced eye, something seemed amiss about this elf. Not out of place, as the barbarian seemed. Rather something in the way Drizzt carried himself or looked about with those unique, lavender orbs.

Those eyes just did not seem to fit the overall persona of that elf, Drizzt Do'Urden.

An enchantment, perhaps, Oberon guessed. Some magical disguise. The curious wizard wished that he had more information to report to Pasha Pook. He considered the possibilities of whisking himself away to the deck of the ship to investigate further, but he hadn't the proper spells prepared for such an undertaking. Besides, he reminded himself again, this was not his affair.

And he did not want to cross Artemis Entreri.

⚔ ⚔ ⚔ ⚔ ⚔

That same night, Oberon flew out of his tower and climbed into the night sky, a wand in hand. Hundreds of feet above the city, he loosed the proper sequence of fireballs.

⚔ ⚔ ⚔ ⚔ ⚔

Riding the decks of a Calimport ship named *Devil Dancer*, two hundred miles to the south, Artemis Entreri watched the display. "By sea," he muttered, noting the sequence of the bursts. He turned to the halfling standing beside him.

"Your friends pursue us by sea," he said. "And less than a tenday behind! They have done well."

Regis's eyes did not flicker in hope at the news. The climate change was very evident now, every day and every night. They had left the winter far behind, and the hot winds of the southern Realms had settled uneasily on the halfling's spirits. The trip to Calimport would not be interrupted by any other stops, and no ship—even one less than a tenday behind—could hope to catch the speedy *Devil Dancer*.

Regis wrestled against an inner dilemma, trying to come to terms with the inevitability of his meeting with his old guildmaster.

Pasha Pook was not a forgiving man. Regis had personally witnessed Pook dealing out severe punishments to those thieves who dared to steal from other members of the guild. And Regis had gone even a step further than that; he had stolen from the guildmaster himself. And the item he had plucked, the magical ruby pendant, was Pook's most treasured possession. Defeated and despairing, Regis put his head down and walked slowly back toward his cabin.

The halfling's somber mood did nothing to quell the tingle running through Entreri's spine. Pook would get the gem and the halfling, and Entreri would be paid well for the service. But in the assassin's mind, Pook's gold was not the true reward for his efforts.

Entreri wanted Drizzt Do'Urden.

※ ※ ※ ※ ※

Drizzt and Wulfgar also watched the fireworks over Baldur's Gate that night. Back in the open sea, but still more than a hundred and fifty miles north of the Devil Dancer, they could only guess at the display's significance.

"A wizard," Deudermont remarked, coming over to join the two. "Perhaps he does battle with some great aerial beast," the captain offered, trying to draw up some entertaining story. "A dragon or some other monster of the sky!"

Drizzt squinted to gain a closer look at the fiery bursts. He saw no dark forms weaving around the flares, nor any hint that they were aimed at a particular target. But possibly the *Sea Sprite* was simply too far away for him to discern such detail.

"Not a fight—a signal," Wulfgar blurted, recognizing a pattern to the explosions. "Three and one. Three and one.

"It seems a bit of trouble for a simple signal," Wulfgar added. "Would not a rider carrying a note serve better?"

"Unless it is meant as a signal to a ship," offered Deudermont.

Drizzt had already entertained that very thought, and he was becoming more than a little suspicious of the display's source, and of its purpose.

Deudermont studied the display a moment longer. "Perhaps it is a signal," he conceded, recognizing the accuracy of Wulfgar's observations of a pattern. "Many ships put in to and out of Baldur's Gate each day. A wizard greeting some friends or saying farewell in grand fashion."

"Or relaying information," Drizzt added, glancing up at Wulfgar. Wulfgar did not miss the drow's point; Drizzt could tell by the barbarian's scowl that Wulfgar was entertaining similar suspicions.

"But for us, a show and nothing more," Deudermont said, bidding them good night with a pat on the shoulder. "An amusement to be enjoyed."

Drizzt and Wulfgar looked at each other, seriously doubting Deudermont's assessment.

⊠ ⊠ ⊠ ⊠ ⊠

"What game does Artemis Entreri play?" Pook asked rhetorically, speaking his thoughts aloud.

Oberon, the wizard in the crystal ball, shrugged. "Never have I pretended to understand the motives of Artemis Entreri."

Pook nodded his accord and continued to pace behind LaValle's chair.

"Yet I would guess that these two have little to do with your pendant," said Oberon.

"Some personal vendetta Entreri acquired along his travels," agreed Pook.

"Friends of the halfling?" wondered Oberon. "Then why would Entreri lead them in the right direction?"

"Whoever they may be, they can only bring trouble," said LaValle, seated between his guildmaster and the scrying device.

"Perhaps Entreri plans to lay an ambush for them," Pook suggested to Oberon. "That would explain his need for your signal."

"Entreri instructed the harbormaster to tell them that he would meet them in Calimport," Oberon reminded Pook.

"To throw them off," said LaValle. "To make them believe that the way would be clear until they arrived in the southern port."

"That is not the way of Artemis Entreri," said Oberon, and Pook was thinking the same thing. "I have never known the assassin to use such obvious tricks to gain the upper hand in a contest. It is Entreri's deepest pleasure to meet and crush challengers face to face."

The two wizards and the guildmaster who had survived and thrived by his ability to react to such puzzles appropriately all held their thoughts for a moment to consider the possibilities. All that Pook cared about was the return of his precious pendant. With it he could expand his powers ten times, perhaps even gaining the favor of the ruling Pasha of Calimshan himself.

"I do not like this," Pook said at length. "I want no complications to the return of the halfling, or of my pendant."

He paused to consider the implications of his decided course, leaning over LaValle's back to get close to Oberon's image. "Do you still have contact with Pinochet?" he asked the wizard slyly.

Oberon guessed the guildmaster's meaning. "The pirate does not forget his friends," he answered in the same tone. "Pinochet contacts me every time he finds his way to Baldur's Gate. He inquires of you as well, hoping that all is well with his old friend."

"And is he now in the isles?"

"The winter trade is rolling down from Waterdeep," Oberon replied with a chuckle. "Where else would a successful pirate be?"

"Good," muttered Pook.

"Should I arrange a welcome for Entreri's pursuers?" Oberon asked eagerly, enjoying the intrigue and the opportunity to serve the guildmaster.

"Three ships—no chances," said Pook. "Nothing shall interfere with the halfling's return. He and I have so very much to discuss!"

Oberon considered the task for a moment. "A pity," he remarked. "The *Sea Sprite* was a fine vessel."

Pook echoed a single word for emphasis, making it absolutely clear that he would tolerate no mistakes.

"Was."

THE WEIGHT OF A KING'S MANTLE

The halfling hung by his ankles, suspended upside down with chains above a cauldron of boiling liquid. Not water, though, but something darker. A red hue, perhaps.

Blood, perhaps.

The crank creaked, and the halfling dropped an inch closer. His face was contorted, his mouth wide, as if in a scream.

But no screams could be heard. Just the groans of the crank and a sinister laugh from an unseen torturer.

The misty scene shifted, and the crank came into view, worked slowly by a single hand that seemed unattached to anything else.

There was a pause in the descent.

Then the evil voice laughed one final time. The hand jerked quickly, sending the crank spinning.

A scream resounded, piercing and cutting, a cry of agony—a cry of death.

⚔ ⚔ ⚔ ⚔ ⚔

Sweat stung Bruenor's eyes even before he had fully opened them. He wiped the wetness from his face and rolled his head, trying to shake away the terrible images and adjust his thoughts to his surroundings.

He was in the Ivy Mansion, in a comfortable bed in a comfortable room. The fresh candles that he had set out burned low. They hadn't helped; this night had been like the others: another nightmare.

Bruenor rolled over and sat up on the side of his bed. Everything was as it should be. The mithral armor and golden shield lay across a chair beside the room's single dresser. The axe that he had used to cut his way out of the duergar lair rested easily against the wall beside Drizzt's scimitar, and two helmets sat atop the dresser, the battered, one-horned helm that had carried the dwarf through the adventures of the last two centuries, and the crown of the king of Mithral Hall, ringed by a thousand glittering gemstones.

But to Bruenor's eyes, all was not as it should be. He looked to the window and the darkness of the night beyond. Alas, all he could see was the reflection of the candlelit room, the crown and armor of the king of Mithral Hall.

It had been a tough tenday for Bruenor. All the days had been filled with the excitement of the times, of talk of the armies coming from Citadel Adbar and Icewind Dale to reclaim Mithral Hall. The dwarf's shoulders ached from being patted so many times by Harpells and other visitors to the mansion, all anxious to congratulate him in advance for the impending return of his throne.

But Bruenor had wandered through the last few days absently, playing a role thrust upon him before he could truly appreciate it. It was time to prepare for the adventure Bruenor had fantasized about since his exile nearly two centuries before. His father's father had been king of Mithral Hall, his father before him, and back to the beginnings of Clan Battlehammer. Bruenor's birthright demanded that he lead the armies and retake Mithral Hall, that he sit in the throne he had been born to possess.

But it was in the very chambers of the ancient dwarven home-land that Bruenor Battlehammer had realized the truth of what was important to him. Over the course of the last decade, four very special companions had come into his life, not one of them a dwarf. The friendship the five had forged was bigger than a dwarven kingdom and more precious to Bruenor than all the mithral in the world. The realization of his fantasy conquest seemed empty to him.

The moments of the night now held Bruenor's heart and his concentration. The dreams, never the same but always with the same terrible conclusion, did not fade with the light of day.

"Another one?" came a soft call from the door. Bruenor looked over his shoulder to see Catti-brie peeking in on him. Bruenor knew that he didn't have to answer. He put his head down in one hand and rubbed his eyes.

"About Regis again?" asked Catti-brie, moving closer. Bruenor heard the door softly close.

"Rumblebelly," Bruenor softly corrected, using the nickname he had tagged on the halfling who had been his closest friend for nearly a decade.

Bruenor swung his legs back up on the bed. "I should be with him," he said gruffly, "or at least with the drow and Wulfgar, lookin' for him!"

"Yer kingdom awaits," Catti-brie reminded him, more to dispel his guilt than to soften his belief in where he truly belonged—a belief that the young woman wholeheartedly shared. "Yer kin from Icewind Dale'll be here in a month, the army from Adbar in two."

"Aye, but we can't be going to the halls till the winter's past."

Catti-brie looked around for some way to deflect the sinking conversation. "Ye'll wear it well," she said cheerfully, indicating the bejeweled crown.

"Which?" Bruenor retorted, a sharp edge to his tongue.

Catti-brie looked at the dented helm, pitiful beside the glorious one, and nearly snorted aloud. But she turned to Bruenor before she commented, and the stern look stamped upon the dwarf's face as he studied the old helmet told her that Bruenor had not asked in jest. At that moment, Catti-brie realized, Bruenor saw the one-horned helmet as infinitely more precious than the crown he was destined to wear.

"They're halfway to Calimport," Catti-brie remarked, sympathizing with the dwarf's desires. "Maybe more."

"Aye, and few boats'll be leaving Waterdeep with the winter coming on," Bruenor muttered grimly, echoing the same arguments Catti-brie had leveled on him during his second morning in the Ivy Mansion, when he had first mentioned his desire to go after his friends.

"We've a million preparations before us," said Catti-brie, stubbornly holding her cheerful tone. "Suren the winter'll pass quickly, and we'll get the halls in time for Drizzt and Wulfgar and Regis's return."

Bruenor's visage did not soften. His eyes locked on the broken helmet, but his mind wandered beyond the vision, back to the fateful scene at Garumn's Gorge. He had at least made peace with Regis before they were separated . . .

Bruenor's recollections blew away from him suddenly. He

snapped a wry glance upon Catti-brie. "Ye think they might be back in time for the fighting?"

Catti-brie shrugged "If they put right back out," she replied, curious at the question, for she knew that Bruenor had more in mind than fighting beside Drizzt and Wulfgar in the battle for Mithral Hall. "They can be coverin' many miles over the southland—even in the winter."

Bruenor bounced off the bed and rushed for the door, scooping up the one-horned helmet and fitting it to his head as he went.

"Middle o' the night?" Catti-brie gawked after him. She jumped up and followed him into the hall.

Bruenor never slowed. He marched straight to Harkle Harpell's door and banged on it loudly enough to wake everyone in that wing of the house. "Harkle!" he roared.

Catti-brie knew better than to even try to calm him. She just shrugged apologetically to each curious head that popped into the hall to take a look.

Finally, Harkle, clad only in a nightshirt and ball-tipped cap, and holding a candle, opened his door.

Bruenor shoved himself into the room, Catti-brie in tow. "Can ye make me a chariot?" the dwarf demanded.

"A what?" Harkle yawned, trying futilely to brush his sleep away. "A chariot?"

"A chariot!" Bruenor growled. "Of fire. Like the Lady Alustriel bringed me here in! A chariot of fire!"

"Well," Harkle stammered. "I have never—"

"Can ye do it?" Bruenor roared, having no patience now for unfocused blabbering.

"Yes . . . uh, maybe," Harkle proclaimed as confidently as he could. "Actually, that spell is Alustriel's specialty. No one here has ever . . ." He stopped, feeling Bruenor's frustrated glare boring into him. The dwarf stood straight-legged, one bare heel grinding into the floor, and his gnarled arms crossed over his chest, the stubby fingers of one hand tapping an impatient rhythm on his knotted biceps.

"I shall speak to the lady in the morning," Harkle assured him. "I am certain—"

"Alustriel's still here?" Bruenor interrupted

"Why, yes," Harkle replied. "She stayed on a few extra—"

"Where is she?" Bruenor demanded.

"Down the hall."

"Which room?"

"I shall take you to her in the morn—" Harkle began.

Bruenor grabbed the front of the wizard's nightshirt and brought him down to a dwarf's eye level. Bruenor proved the stronger even with his nose, for the long, pointy thing pressed Harkle's nose flat against one of his cheeks. Bruenor's eyes did not blink, and he spoke each word of his question slowly and distinctly, just the way he wanted the answer. "Which room?"

"Green door, beside the bannister." Harkle gulped.

Bruenor gave the wizard a goodhearted wink and let him go. The dwarf turned right past Catti-brie, returning her amused smile with a determined shake of his head, and burst into the hall.

"Oh, he should not disturb the Lady Alustriel at this late hour!" Harkle protested.

Catti-brie could not help but laugh. "So stop him yerself!

Harkle listened to the dwarf's heavy footsteps resounding down the hall; Bruenor's bare feet thudded on the wooden floor like bouncing stones. "No," Harkle answered her offer, his smile widening to match her own. "I think not."

Abruptly awakened in the night, the Lady Alustriel appeared

no less beautiful, her silvery mane somehow mystically connected to the soft glow of the evening. Bruenor composed himself when he saw the lady, remembering her station and his manners.

"Uh, begging the lady's pardon," he stammered, suddenly very embarrassed by his actions.

"It is late, good King Bruenor," Alustriel said politely, an amused smile on her face as she viewed the dwarf, dressed only in his nightshirt and broken helmet. "What might have brought you to my door at this hour?"

"What with all that's going on about, I did not even know ye were still in Longsaddle," Bruenor explained.

"I would have come to see you before I left," Alustriel replied, her tone still cordial. "No need to disturb your sleep—or mine."

"Me thoughts weren't for good-byes," Bruenor said. "I be needing a favor."

"Urgently?"

Bruenor nodded emphatically. "A favor I should've asked afore we e'er got here."

Alustriel led him into her room and closed the door behind them, realizing the seriousness of the dwarf's business.

"I need another one of them chariots," said Bruenor. "To take me to the south."

"You mean to catch your friends and aid in the search for the halfling," Alustriel reasoned.

"Aye, I know me place."

"But I cannot accompany you," Alustriel said. "I have a realm to rule; it is not my place to journey unannounced to other kingdoms."

"I wouldn't be askin' ye to go," replied Bruenor.

"Then who will drive the team? You have no experience with such magic."

Bruenor thought for just a moment. "Harkle'll take me!" he blurted.

Alustriel couldn't hide a smirk as she thought of the possibilities for disaster. Harkle, like so many of his Harpell kin, usually hurt himself when spellcasting. The lady knew that she would not sway the dwarf, but she felt it her duty to point out all of the weaknesses of his plan.

"Calimport is a long way indeed," she told him. "The trip there on the chariot will be speedy, but the return could take many months. Will not the true king of Mithral Hall lead the gathering armies in the fight for his throne?"

"He will," Bruenor replied, "if it be possible. But me place's with me friends. I owe them at least that!"

"You risk much."

"No more than they've risked for me—many the times."

Alustriel opened the door. "Very well," she said, "and my respect on your decision. You will prove a noble king, Bruenor Battlehammer."

The dwarf, for one of the few times in his life, blushed.

"Now go and rest," said Alustriel. "I will see what I may learn this night. Meet me on the south slope of Harpell Hill before the break of dawn."

Bruenor nodded eagerly and found his way back to his room. For the first time since he had come to Longsaddle, he slept peacefully.

⚔ ⚔ ⚔ ⚔ ⚔

Under the lightening sky of predawn, Bruenor and Harkle met Alustriel at the appointed spot. Harkle had eagerly agreed to the journey; he had always wanted a crack at driving one of Lady Alustriel's famed chariots. He seemed out of place next to the battle-charged dwarf, though, wearing his wizard's robe—tucked into leather hip boots—and an oddly shaped silver helmet with fluffy white fur wings and a visor that kept flopping down over his eyes.

Alustriel had not slept the rest of that night. She had been busy staring into the crystal ball the Harpells had provided her, probing distant planes in search of clues to the whereabouts of Bruenor's friends. She had learned much in that short time and had even made a connection to the dead mage Morkai in the spirit world to garner further information.

And what she had learned disturbed her more than a little.

She stood now, components in hand and awaiting the break of dawn, quietly facing the east. As the first rays of the sun peeked over the horizon, she swept them into her grasp and executed the spell. Minutes later, a flaming chariot and two fiery horses appeared on the hillside, magically suspended an inch from the ground. The licks of their flames sent tiny streams of smoke rising from the bedewed grass.

"To Calimport!" Harkle proclaimed, rushing over to the enchanted carriage.

"Nay," Alustriel corrected. Bruenor turned a confused glance on her.

"Your friends are not yet in the Empire of the Sands," the lady explained. "They are at sea and will find grave danger this day. Set your course to the southwest, to the sea, then true south with the coast in sight." She tossed a heart-shaped locket to Bruenor. The dwarf fumbled it open and found a picture of Drizzt Do'Urden inside.

"The locket will warm when you approach the ship that carries your friends," Alustriel said. "I created it many tendays ago, that I might have known if your group approached Silverymoon on your return from Mithral Hall." She avoided Bruenor's probing gaze, knowing the myriad of questions that must have been going through the dwarf's mind. Quietly, almost as if embarrassed, she added, "I should like it returned."

Bruenor kept his sly remarks to himself. He knew of the growing connection between Lady Alustriel and Drizzt. It became clearer and clearer every day. "Ye'll get it back," he assured her. He scooped the locket up in his fist and moved to join Harkle.

"Tarry not," Alustriel told them. "Their need is pressing this day!"

"Wait!" came a call from the hill. All three turned to see Catti-brie, fully outfitted for the road, with Taulmaril, the magical bow of Anariel that she had recovered from the ruins of Mithral Hall, slung easily over her shoulder. She ran down to the back of the chariot. "Ye weren't meaning to leave me so?" she asked Bruenor.

Bruenor couldn't look her in the eye. He had indeed meant to leave without so much as a good-bye to his daughter. "Bah!" he snorted. "Ye'd have only tried to stop me going!"

"Never I would!" Catti-brie growled right back at him. "Me thinkin's that yer doing right. But ye'd do righter if ye'd move over and make room for me!"

Bruenor shook his head emphatically.

"I've as much the right as yerself!" Catti-brie protested.

"Bah!" Bruenor snorted again. "Drizzt and Rumblebelly are me truest friends!"

"And mine!"

"And Wulfgar's been akin to a son to me!" Bruenor shot back, thinking he had won the round.

"And a mite bit more than that to me," Catti-brie retorted, "if he gets back from the South!" Catti-brie didn't even need to remind Bruenor that she had been the one who introduced him to Drizzt. She had defeated all of the dwarf's arguments. "Move aside, Bruenor Battlehammer, and make room! I've as much at stake as yerself, and I'm meaning to come along!"

"Who'll be seeing to the armies?" Bruenor asked.

"The Harpells'll put them up. They won't be marching to the halls until we're back, or until the spring at least."

"But if both of you go and do not return," Harkle interjected, letting the thought hang over them for a moment. "You are the only ones who know the way."

Bruenor saw Catti-brie's crestfallen look and realized how deeply she desired to join him on his quest. And he knew she was right in coming, for she had as much at stake in the chase across the southland as he. He thought for a moment, suddenly shifting to Catti-brie's side in the debate. "The lady knows the way," he said, indicating Alustriel.

Alustriel nodded. "I do," she replied. "And I would gladly show the armies to the halls. But the chariot will carry only two riders."

Bruenor's sigh was as loud as Catti-brie's. He shrugged helplessly at his daughter. "Better that ye stay," he said softly. "I'll bring'em back for ye."

Catti-brie wouldn't let it go so easily. "When the fighting starts," she said, "and suren it will, would ye rather ye had Harkle and his spells beside ye, or me and me bow?"

Bruenor glanced casually at Harkle and immediately saw the young woman's logic. The wizard stood at the reins of the chariot, trying to find some way to keep the visor of his helmet up on his brow. Finally Harkle gave up and just tilted his head back far enough so he could see under the visor.

"Here, ye dropped a piece of it," Bruenor said to him. "That's why it won't stay up!"

Harkle turned and saw Bruenor pointing to the ground off

the back of the chariot. He shuffled around beside Bruenor and bent over, trying to see what the dwarf was pointing at.

As Harkle bent to look, the weight of his silver helmet—which actually belonged to a cousin much larger than he—toppled him over and left him sprawled face down on the lawn. In the same moment, Bruenor swept Catti-brie into the chariot beside him.

"Oh, drats!" Harkle whined. "I would have so loved to go!"

"The lady'll make ye another one to fly," Bruenor said to comfort him. Harkle looked to Alustriel.

"Tomorrow morning," Alustriel agreed, quite amused by the whole scene. Then to Bruenor she asked, "Can you guide the chariot?"

"As well as he, by me guess!" the dwarf proclaimed, grabbing up the fiery reins. "Hold on, girl. We've half a world to cross!" He snapped the reins, and the chariot lifted into the morning sky, cutting a fiery streak across the blue-gray haze of dawn.

The wind rushed past them as they shot into the west, the chariot rocking wildly from side to side, up and down. Bruenor fought frantically to hold his course; Catti-brie fought frantically just to hold on. The sides wobbled, the back dipped and climbed, and once they even spun in a complete vertical circle, though it happened so fast—luckily—that neither of the riders had time to fall out!

A few minutes later, a single thundercloud loomed ahead of them. Bruenor saw it, and Catti-brie yelled a warning, but the dwarf hadn't mastered the subtleties of driving the chariot well enough to do anything about their course. They blew through the darkness, leaving a hissing steam tail in their wake, and rocketed out above the cloud.

And then Bruenor, his face glistening with wetness, found the measure of the reins. He leveled off the chariot's course and put the rising sun behind his right shoulder. Catti-brie, too, found her footing, though she still clung tightly to the chariot's rail with one hand, and to the dwarf's heavy cloak with the other.

✕ ✕ ✕ ✕ ✕

The silver dragon rolled over onto its back lazily, riding the morning winds with its legs—all four—crossed over it and its sleepy eyes half closed. The good dragon loved its morning glide, leaving the bustle of the world far below and catching the sun's untainted rays above the cloud level.

But the dragon's marvelous orbs popped open wide when it saw the fiery streak rushing at it from the east. Thinking the flames to be the forerunning fires of an evil red dragon, the silver swooped around into a high cloud and poised to ambush the thing. But the fury left the dragon's eyes when it recognized the strange craft, a fiery chariot, with just the helm of the driver, a one-horned contraption, sticking above the front of the carriage and a young human woman standing behind, her auburn locks flying back over her shoulders.

Its huge mouth agape, the silver dragon watched as the chariot sped past. Few things piqued the curiosity of this ancient creature, who had lived so very many years, but it seriously considered following this unlikely scene.

A cool breeze wafted in then and washed all other thoughts from the silver dragon's mind. "Peoples," it muttered, rolling again onto its back and shaking its head in disbelief.

✕ ✕ ✕ ✕ ✕

Catti-brie and Bruenor never even saw the dragon. Their eyes were fixed squarely ahead, where the wide sea was already in sight on the western horizon, blanketed by a heavy morning mist. A half-hour later, they saw the high towers of Waterdeep to the north and moved out from the Sword Coast and over the water. Bruenor, getting a better feel of the reins, swung the chariot to the south and dropped it low.

Too low.

Diving into the gray shroud of mist, they heard the lapping of the waves below them and the hiss of steam as the spray hit their fiery craft.

"Bring her up!" Catti-brie yelled. "Ye're too low!"

"Need to be low!" Bruenor gasped, fighting the reins. He tried to mask his incompetence, but he fully realized that they were indeed too close to the water. Struggling with all his might, he managed to bring the chariot up a few more feet and level it off. "There," he boasted. "Got it straight, and got it low."

He looked over his shoulder at Catti-brie. "Need to be low," he said again into her doubting expression. "We have to see the durn ship to find it!"

Catti-brie only shook her head.

But then they did see a ship. Not *the* ship, but a ship nonetheless, looming up in the mist barely thirty yards ahead.

Catti-brie screamed—Bruenor did, too—and the dwarf fell back with the reins, forcing the chariot upward at as steep an angle as possible. The ship's deck rolled out below them.

And the masts still towered above them!

If all the ghosts of every sailor who had ever died on the sea had risen from their watery graves and sought vengeance on this particular vessel, the lookout's face would not have held a truer expression of terror. Possibly he leaped from his perch—more likely he toppled in fright—but either way, he missed the deck and dropped safely into the water at the very last second before the chariot streaked past his crow's nest and nipped the top of the mainmast.

Catti-brie and Bruenor composed themselves and looked back to see the tip of the ship's mast burning like a single candle in the gray mist.

"Ye're too low," Catti-brie reiterated.

HOT WINDS

The *Sea Sprite* cruised easily under clear blue skies and the lazy warmth of the southern Realms. A strong trade wind kept its sails filled, and only six days after their departure from Baldur's Gate, the western tip of the Tethyr Peninsula was already in sight—a journey that normally took more than a tenday.

But a wizard's call traveled faster still.

Captain Deudermont took the *Sea Sprite* down the center of Asavir's Channel, trying to keep a safe distance from the peninsula's sheltered bays—bays that often held pirates poised for passing merchant vessels—and also cautious to keep a healthy gap of water between his ship and the islands on his west: the Nelanther, the infamous Pirate Isles. The captain felt safe enough in the crowded sea lane, with the banner of Calimport flying above his craft and the sails of several other merchant ships dotting the horizon every so often both in front of and behind the *Sea Sprite*.

Using a common merchant's trick, Deudermont closed in on a vessel and shadowed its course, keeping the *Sea Sprite* in its wake. Less maneuverable and slower than the *Sea Sprite* and flying the flag of Murann, a lesser city on the Sword Coast, this second ship would provide a much easier target to any pirates in the area.

Eighty feet above the water, taking a turn in the crow's nest, Wulfgar had the clearest view of the deck of the ship ahead. With his strength and agility, the barbarian was fast becoming quite a sailor, eagerly taking his turn at every job alongside the rest of the crew. His favorite duty was the crow's nest, though it was a tight fit for a man of his size. He was at peace in the warm breeze and solitude. He rested against the mast, using one hand to block out the daytime glare, and studied the crew's activities on the ship ahead.

He heard the front ship's lookout call something down, though he couldn't make out the words, then saw the crew rushing about frantically, most heading for the prow to watch the horizon. Wulfgar jolted upright and leaned over the nest, straining his eyes to the south.

⚔ ⚔ ⚔ ⚔ ⚔

"How do they feel, having us in tow?" Drizzt, standing beside Deudermont on the bridge, asked the captain. While Wulfgar had been building a rapport working beside the crew, Drizzt had struck a solid friendship with the captain. And realizing the value of the elf's opinions, Deudermont gladly shared his knowledge of his station, and of the sea, with Drizzt. "Do they understand their role as fodder?"

"They know our purpose in shadowing them, and their captain—if he is an experienced sailor—would do the same if our positions were reversed," Deudermont replied. "Yet we bring them an extra measure of safety as well. Just having a ship from Calimport in sight will deter many of the pirates."

"And perhaps they feel that we would come to their aid in the face of such an attack?" Drizzt was quick to ask.

Deudermont knew that Drizzt was interested in discovering if the *Sea Sprite* would indeed go to the other ship's aid. Drizzt had a strong streak of honor in him, Deudermont understood, and the captain, of similar morals, admired him for it. But Deudermont's responsibilities as the captain of a vessel were too involved for such a hypothetical situation. "Perhaps," he replied.

Drizzt let the line of questioning end, satisfied that Deudermont kept the scales of duty and morality in proper balance.

"Sails to the south!" came Wulfgar's call from above, bringing many of the *Sea Sprite's* crew to the forward rail.

Deudermont's eyes went to the horizon, then to Wulfgar. "How many?"

"Two ships!" Wulfgar called back. "Running north and even, and wide apart!"

"Port and starboard?" Deudermont asked.

Wulfgar took a close measure of the intercepting course, then affirmed the captain's suspicions. "We will pass between them!"

"Pirates?" Drizzt asked, knowing the answer.

"So it would seem," the captain replied. The distant sails came into view to the men on the deck.

"I see no flag," one of the sailors near the bridge called to the captain.

Drizzt pointed to the merchant ship ahead. "Are they the target?"

Deudermont nodded grimly. "So it would seem," he said again.

"Then let us close up with them," the drow said. "Two against two seems a fairer fight."

Deudermont stared into Drizzt's lavender eyes and was almost stunned by their sudden gleam. How could the captain hope to make this honorable warrior understand their place in the scenario? The *Sea Sprite* flew Calimport's flag, the other ship, Murann's. The two were hardly allies.

"The encounter may not come to blows," he told Drizzt. "The Murann vessel would be wise to surrender peacefully."

Drizzt began to see the reasoning. "So flying Calimport's flag holds responsibilities as well as benefits?"

Deudermont shrugged helplessly "Think of the thieves' guilds in the cities you have known," he explained. "Pirates are much the same—an unavoidable nuisance. If we sail in to fight, we would dispel any self-restraint the pirates hold upon themselves, most probably bringing more trouble than need be."

"And we would mark every ship under Calimport's flag sailing the Channel," Drizzt added, no longer looking at the captain, but watching the spectacle unfold before him. The light dropped from his eyes.

Deudermont, inspired by Drizzt's grasp of principles—a grip that would not allow such acceptance of rogues—put a hand on the elf's shoulder. "If the encounter comes to blows," the captain said, drawing Drizzt's gaze back to his own, "the *Sea Sprite* will join the battle."

Drizzt turned back to the horizon and clapped Deudermont's hand with his own. The eager fire returned to his eyes as Deudermont ordered the crew to stand ready.

The captain really didn't expect a fight. He had seen dozens of engagements such as this, and normally when the pirates outnumbered their intended victim, the looting was accomplished without bloodshed. But Deudermont, with so many years of experience on the sea, soon realized that something was strange this time. The pirate ships kept their course wide, passing too far abreast of the Murann ship to board it. At first, Deudermont thought the pirates meant to launch a distance strike—one of the pirate vessels had a catapult mounted to its afterdeck—to cripple their victim, though the act seemed unnecessary.

Then the captain understood the truth. The pirates had no interest in the Murann ship. The *Sea Sprite* was their target.

From his high perch, Wulfgar, too, realized that the pirates were sailing right by the lead ship. "Take up arms!" he cried to the crew. "They aim for us!"

"You may indeed get your fight," Deudermont said to Drizzt. "It seems that Calimport's flag will not protect us this time."

To Drizzt's nightattuned eyes, the distant ships appeared as no more than tiny black dots in the glare of the shining water, but the drow could make out what was happening well enough. He couldn't understand the logic of the pirates' choice, though, and he had a strange feeling that he and Wulfgar might be somehow connected to the unfolding events. "Why us?" he asked Deudermont.

The captain shrugged. "Perhaps they have heard a rumor that one of Calimport's ships will be laden with a valuable cargo."

The image of the fireballs exploding in the night sky over Baldur's Gate flashed in Drizz's mind. A signal? he wondered again. He couldn't yet put all of the pieces together, but his suspicions led him invariably to the theory that he and Wulfgar were somehow involved in the pirates' choice of ships.

"Do we fight?" he started to ask Deudermont, but he saw that the captain was already laying the plans.

"Starboard!" Deudermont told the helmsman. "Put us west to the Pirate Isles. Let us see if these dogs have a belly for the reefs!" He motioned another man to the crow's nest, wanting

Wulfgar's strength for the more important duties on the deck.

The *Sea Sprite* bit into the waves and bowed low in a sharp right turn. The pirate vessel on the east, now the farthest away, cut its angle to pursue directly while the other, the bulkier of the two, kept its course straight, each second bringing the *Sea Sprite* closer for a shot of its catapult.

Deudermont pointed to the largest of the few islands visible in the west. "Skim her close," he told the helmsman, "but ware the single reef. Tide's low, and she should be visible."

Wulfgar dropped to the deck beside the captain.

"On that line," Deudermont ordered him. "You've the mainmast. If I bid you to pull, then heave for all your strength! We shan't get a second chance."

Wulfgar took up the heavy rope with a grunt of determination, wrapping it tightly around his wrists and hands.

"Fire in the sky!" one of the crewmen yelled, pointing back to the south, toward the bulky pirate ship. A ball of flaming pitch soared through the air, splashing harmlessly into the ocean with a hiss of protest, many yards short of the *Sea Sprite*.

"A tracing shot," Deudermont explained, "to give them our range."

Deudermont estimated the distance and figured how much closer the pirates would get before the *Sea Sprite* put the island between them.

"We'll slip them if we make the channel between the reef and the island," he told Drizzt, nodding to indicate that he thought the prospects promising.

But even as the drow and the captain began to comfort themselves with thoughts of escape, the masts of a third vessel loomed before them in the west, slipping out of the very channel that Deudermont had hoped to enter. This ship had its sails furled and was prepared for boarding.

Deudermont's jaw dropped open. "They were lying for us," he said to Drizzt. He turned to the elf helplessly. "They were lying for us."

"But we've no cargo of particular value," the captain continued trying to reason through the unusual turn of events. "Why would pirates run three vessels in a strike against a single ship?"

Drizzt knew the answer.

⚔ ⚔ ⚔ ⚔ ⚔

The ride was easier for Bruenor and Catti-brie now. The dwarf had settled comfortably at the reins of the fiery chariot, and the morning haze had burned away. They cruised down the Sword Coast, amused by the ships they passed over and the astonished expressions of every sailor who turned his eyes heavenward.

Soon after, they crossed the entrance to the River Chionthar, the gateway to Baldur's Gate. Bruenor paused a moment to consider a sudden impulse, then veered the chariot away from the coast.

"The lady bid us to stay to the coast," said Catti-brie as soon as she realized the shift in course

Bruenor grabbed Alustriel's magical locket, which he had strung around his neck, and shrugged his shoulders. "It's tellin' me different," he replied.

⚔ ⚔ ⚔ ⚔ ⚔

A second load of burning pitch hit the water, this time dangerously close to the *Sea Sprite*.

"We can run by her," Drizzt said to Deudermont, for the third ship still had not raised its sails.

The experienced captain recognized the flaw in the reasoning. The primary purpose of the ship coming out from the island was to block the channel's entrance. The *Sea Sprite* could indeed sail past that ship, but Deudermont would have to take his ship outside the dangerous reef and back into open water. And by then, they would be well within the catapult's range.

Deudermont looked over his shoulder. The remaining pirate ship, the one farthest to the east, had its sails full of wind and was cutting the water even more swiftly than the *Sea Sprite*. If a ball of pitch came in on the mark and the *Sea Sprite* took any damage at all to its sails, it would be quickly overtaken.

And then a second problem dramatically grabbed the captain's attention. A bolt of lightning blasted across the *Sea Sprite's* deck, severing some lines and splintering off pieces of the mainmast. The structure leaned and groaned against the strain of the full sails. Wulfgar found a foothold and tugged against the pull with all his strength.

"Hold her!" Deudermont cheered him. "Keep us straight and strong!"

"They've a wizard," Drizzt remarked, realizing that the blast had come from the ship ahead of them.

"I feared as much," Deudermont replied grimly.

The seething fire in Drizzt's eyes told Deudermont that the elf had already decided upon his first task in the fight. Even in their obvious disadvantage, the captain felt a tug of pity for the wizard.

A sly expression came over Deudermont's face as the sight of Drizzt inspired a desperate plan of action. "Take us right up on her port," he told the helmsman. "Close enough to spit on them!"

"But, Captain," the sailor protested, "that'd put us in line for the reef!"

"Just what the dogs had hoped," Deudermont came back. "Let them think that we do not know these waters; let them think that the rocks will do their business for them!"

Drizzt felt comfortable with the security in the captain's tone. The wily old sailor had something in mind.

"Steady?" Deudermont called to Wulfgar.

The barbarian nodded.

"When I call for you, pull, man, as if your life depends on it!" Deudermont told him.

Next to the captain, Drizzt made a quiet observation. "It does."

⋊⋉ ⋊⋉ ⋊⋉ ⋊⋉ ⋊⋉

From the bridge of his flagship, the fast-flying vessel on the east, Pinochet the pirate watched the maneuvering of the *Sea Sprite* with concern. He knew Deudermont's reputation well enough to know that the captain would not be so foolish as to put his ship onto a reef under a bright midday sun at low tide. Deudermont meant to fight.

Pinochet looked to the bulky ship and measured the angle to the *Sea Sprite*. The catapult would get two more shots, maybe three, before their target ran alongside the blocking ship in the channel. Pinochet's own ship was still many minutes behind the action, and the pirate captain wondered how much damage Deudermont would inflict before he could aid his allies.

But Pinochet quickly put thoughts of the cost of this mission out of his mind. He was doing a personal favor for the guildmaster of the largest gang of thieves in all of Calimport. Whatever the price, Pasha Pook's payment would surely outweigh it!

⋊⋉ ⋊⋉ ⋊⋉ ⋊⋉ ⋊⋉

Catti-brie watched eagerly as each new ship came into view, but Bruenor, confident that the magical locket was leading him to the drow, paid them no heed. The dwarf snapped the reins, trying to urge the flaming horses on faster. Somehow—perhaps it was another property of the locket—Bruenor felt that Drizzt was in trouble and that speed was essential.

The dwarf then snapped a stubby finger in front of him. "There!" he cried as soon as the *Sea Sprite* came into view.

Catti-brie did not question his observation. She quickly surveyed the dramatic situation unfolding below her.

Another ball of pitch soared through the air, slapping into the tail of the *Sea Sprite* at water level but catching too little of the ship to do any real damage.

Catti-brie and Bruenor watched the catapult being pulled back for another shot; they watched the brutish crew of the ship in the channel, their swords in hand, awaiting the approach of the *Sea Sprite*; and they watched the third pirate ship, rushing in from behind to close the trap.

Bruenor veered the chariot to the south, toward the bulkiest of the ships. "First for the catapult!" the dwarf cried in rage.

Pinochet, as well as most of the crewmen on the back two pirate ships, watched the fiery craft cutting a streak down from the northern sky, but the captain and crew of the *Sea Sprite* and the other ship were too enmeshed in the desperation of their own situation to worry about events behind them. Drizzt did give the chariot a second look, though, noticing a glistening reflection that might have been a single horn of a broken helmet peeking above the flames, and a form in back of that with flowing hair that seemed more than vaguely familiar.

But perhaps it was just a trick of the light and Drizzt's own undying hopes. The chariot moved away into a fiery blur and Drizzt let it go, having no time now to give it further thought.

The *Sea Sprite*'s crew lined the foredeck, firing crossbows at the pirate ship, hoping, more than anything else, to keep the wizard too engaged to hit them again.

A second lightning bolt did roar in, but the *Sea Sprite* was rocking wildly in the breakers rolling off the reef, and the wizard's blast cut only a minor hole in the mainsail.

Deudermont looked hopefully to Wulfgar, tensed and ready for the command.

And then they were crossing beside the pirates, barely fifteen yards from the other ship, and apparently heading on a deadly course into the reef.

"Pull!" Deudermont cried, and Wulfgar heaved, every muscle in his huge body reddening with a sudden influx of blood and adrenaline.

The mainmast groaned in protest, beams creaked and cracked, and the wind-filled sails fought back as Wulfgar looped the rope over his shoulder and drove himself forward. The *Sea Sprite* verily pivoted in the water, its front end lifting over the roll of a wave and lurching at the pirate vessel. Deudermont's crew, though they had witnessed Wulfgar's power in the River Chionthar, grabbed desperately at the rail and held on, awestruck.

And the stunned pirates, never suspecting that a ship under full sail could possibly cut so tight a turn, reacted not at all. They watched in blank amazement as the prow of the *Sea Sprite* smashed into their port flank, entangling the two ships in a deadly embrace.

"Take it to them!" Deudermont cried. Grapples soared through the air, further securing the *Sea Sprite*'s hold, and boarding planks were thrown down and fastened into place.

Wulfgar scrambled to his feet and pulled Aegis-fang off his back. Drizzt drew his scimitars but made no immediate move, instead scanning the deck of the enemy ship. He quickly focused on one man, not dressed like a wizard, but unarmed as far as Drizzt could tell.

The man went through some motions, as if in spellcasting, and the telltale magical sprinkles dusted the air around him.

But Drizzt was quicker. Calling on the innate abilities of his heritage, the drow limned the wizard's form in harmless purplish flames. The wizard's corporeal body faded from sight as his invisibility spell took effect.

But the purple outline remained.

"Wizard, Wulfgar!" Drizzt called.

The barbarian rushed to the rail and surveyed the pirate ship, easily spotting the magical outline.

The wizard, realizing his predicament, dived behind some casks.

Wulfgar didn't hesitate. He sent Aegis-fang hurtling end over end. The mighty warhammer drove through the casks, sending wood and water exploding into the air, and then found its mark on the other side.

The hammer blasted the wizard's broken body—still visible only by the outline of the drow's faerie fire—into the air and over the far rail of the pirate ship.

Drizzt and Wulfgar nodded to each other, grimly satisfied. Deudermont slapped a hand across his unbelieving eyes.

Perhaps they did have a chance.

⚔ ⚔ ⚔ ⚔ ⚔

The pirates on the two back ships paused in their duties to consider the flying chariot. As Bruenor swung around the back of the bulky catapult ship and came in from behind, Catti-brie pulled the Taulmaril's bowstring tight.

"Think o' yer friends," Bruenor comforted her, seeing her hesitation. Only a few tendays earlier, Catti-brie had killed a human out of necessity, and the act had not set well with her. Now, as they closed on the ship from above, she could rain death among the exposed sailors.

She huffed a deep breath to steady herself and took a bead on a sailor, standing mouth agape, not even realizing that he was about to die.

There was another way.

Out of the corner of her eye, Catti-brie spotted a better target. She swung the bow toward the back of the ship and sent a silver arrow streaking down. It blasted into the arm of the catapult, cracking the wood, the arrow's magical energy scorching a black hole as the silver shaft ripped through.

"Taste me flames!" Bruenor cried, steering the chariot downward. The wild dwarf drove his flaming horses straight through the mainsail, leaving a tattered rag in his wake.

And Catti-brie's aim was perfect; again and again the silver arrows whistled into the catapult. As the chariot rushed past a second time, the ship's gunners tried to respond with a ball of burning pitch, but the catapult's wooden arm had taken too much damage to retain any strength, and the ball of pitch lobbed weakly, a few feet up and a few feet out.

And dropped onto the deck of its own ship!

"One more pass!" Bruenor growled, looking back over his shoulder at the fires now roaring on the mast and the deck.

But Catti-brie's eyes were forward, to where the *Sea Sprite* had just crashed onto one vessel, and where the second pirate ship would soon join the fray. "No time!" she yelled. "They be needin' us up ahead!"

✗ ✗ ✗ ✗ ✗

Steel rang against steel as the crew of the *Sea Sprite* locked against the pirates. One rogue, seeing Wulfgar launch the warhammer, crossed over to the *Sea Sprite* and made for the unarmed barbarian, thinking him easy prey. He rushed in, thrusting his sword ahead.

Wulfgar easily sidestepped the blow, caught the pirate by the wrist, and slapped his other hand into the man's crotch. Changing the pirate's direction slightly but not breaking his momentum, Wulfgar hoisted him into the air and heaved him over the back rail of the *Sea Sprite*. Two other pirates, having the same initial response to the unarmed barbarian as their unfortunate comrade, stopped in their tracks and sought out better armed, but less dangerous, opponents.

Then Aegis-fang magically returned to Wulfgar's waiting grasp, and it was his turn to charge.

Three of Deudermont's crew, trying to cross over, were cut down on the central boarding plank, and now the pirates came rushing back across the opening to flood the *Sea Sprite*'s deck.

Drizzt Do'Urden stemmed the tide. Scimitars in hand— Twinkle glowing an angry blue light—the elf sprang lightly onto the wide boarding plank.

The group of pirates, seeing only a single, slender enemy barring the way, expected to bowl right through.

Their momentum slowed considerably when the first rank of three stumbled down in a whirring blur of blades, grasping at slit throats and bellies.

Deudermont and the helmsman, rushing to support Drizzt, slowed and watched the display, Twinkle and its companion scimitar rose and dipped with blinding speed and deadly accuracy. Another pirate went down, and yet another had his sword struck from his hand, so he dived into the water to escape the terrible elven warrior.

The remaining five pirates froze as if paralyzed, their mouths hanging open in silent screams of terror.

Deudermont and the helmsman also jumped back in surprise and confusion, for with Drizzt absorbed in the concentration of battle, the magical mask had played a trick of its own. It had slipped from the drow's face, revealing his dark heritage to all around.

ᕮ ᕮ ᕮ ᕮ ᕮ

"Even if ye flame the sails, the ship'll get in," Catti-brie observed, noting the short distance between the remaining pirate ship and the tangled ships at the entrance to the channel.

"The sails?" Bruenor laughed. "Suren I mean to get more than that!"

Catti-brie stood back from the dwarf, digesting his meaning. "Ye're daft!" She gawked as Bruenor brought the chariot down to deck level.

"Bah! I'll stop the dogs! Hang on, girl!"

"The demons, I will!" Catti-brie shouted back. She patted Bruenor on the head and went with an alternate plan, dropping from the back of the chariot and into the water.

"Smart girl," Bruenor chuckled, watching her splash safely. Then his eyes went back to the pirates. The crew at the rear of the ship had seen him coming and were diving every which way to get clear.

Pinochet, at the front of the ship, looked back at the unexpected commotion just as Bruenor crashed in.

"Moradin!"

ᕮ ᕮ ᕮ ᕮ ᕮ

The dwarf's war cry resounded to the decks of the *Sea Sprite* and the third pirate vessel, above all the din of battle. Pirates and sailors alike on the embattled ships glanced back at the explosion on Pinochet's flagship, and Pinochet's crew answered Bruenor's cry with one of terror.

Wulfgar paused at the plea to the dwarven god, remembering a dear friend who used to shout such names at his enemies.

Drizzt only smiled.

⚔ ⚔ ⚔ ⚔ ⚔

As the chariot crashed to the deck, Bruenor rolled off the back and Alustriel's dweomer came apart, transforming the chariot into a rolling ball of destruction. Flames swept across the deck, licked at the masts, and caught the bottoms of the sails.

Bruenor regained his feet, his mithral axe poised in one hand and shining golden shield strapped across his other. But no one cared to challenge him at that moment. Those pirates who had escaped the initial devastation were concerned only with escape.

Bruenor spat at them and shrugged. And then, to the amazement of those few who saw him, the crazy dwarf walked straight into the flames, heading forward to see if any of the pirates up front wanted to play.

Pinochet knew at once that his ship was lost. Not the first time, and probably not the last, he consoled himself as he calmly motioned his closest officer to help him loose a small rowboat. Two of his other crewmen had the same idea and were already untying the little boat when Pinochet got there.

But in this disaster, it was every man for himself, and Pinochet stabbed one of them in the back and chased the other away.

Bruenor emerged, unbothered by the flames, to find the front of the ship nearly deserted. He grinned happily when he saw the little boat, and the pirate captain, touch down in the water. The other pirate was bent over the rail, untying the last of the lines.

And as the pirate hoisted one leg over the rail, Bruenor helped him along, putting a booted foot into his rear and launching him clear of the rail, and of the little rowboat.

"Turn yer back, will ye?" Bruenor grunted at the pirate captain as the dwarf dropped heavily into the rowboat. "I've a girl to pick out of the water!"

Pinochet gingerly slid his sword out of its sheath and peeked back over his shoulder.

"Will ye?" Bruenor asked again.

Pinochet swung about, chopping down viciously at the dwarf.

"Ye could've just said no," Bruenor taunted, blocking the blow with his shield and launching a counter at the man's knees.

⚔ ⚔ ⚔ ⚔ ⚔

Of all the disasters that had befallen the pirates that day, none horrified them more than when Wulfgar went on the attack. He had no need for a boarding plank; the mighty barbarian leaped the gap between the ships. He drove into the pirate ranks, scattering rogues with powerful sweeps of his warhammer.

From the central plank, Drizzt watched the spectacle. The drow had not noticed that his mask had slipped, and he wouldn't have had time to do anything about it anyway. Meaning to join his friend, he rushed the five remaining pirates on the plank. They parted willingly, preferring the water below to the killing blades of a drow elf.

Then the two heroes, the two friends, were together, cutting a swath of destruction across the deck of the pirate ship. Deudermont and his crew, trained fighters themselves, soon cleared the *Sea Sprite* of pirates and had won over every boarding plank. Now knowing victory to be at hand, they waited at the rail of the pirate ship, escorting the growing wave of willing prisoners back to the *Sea Sprite*'s hold while Drizzt and Wulfgar finished their task.

✕ ✕ ✕ ✕ ✕

"You will die, bearded dog!" Pinochet roared, slashing with his sword.

Bruenor, trying to settle his feet on the rocking boat, let the man keep the offensive, holding his own strikes for the best moments.

One came unexpectedly as the pirate Bruenor had booted from the burning ship caught up to the drifting rowboat. Bruenor watched his approach out of the corner of his eye.

The man grabbed the side of the little boat and hoisted himself up—only to be met with a blow to the top of the head by Bruenor's mithral axe.

The pirate dropped back down beside the rowboat, turning the water crimson.

"Friend o' yers?" Bruenor taunted.

Pinochet came on even more furiously, as Bruenor had hoped. The man missed a wild swing, overbalancing to Bruenor's right. The dwarf helped Pinochet along, shifting his weight to heighten the list of the boat and slamming his shield into the pirate captain's back.

"On yer life," Bruenor called as Pinochet bobbed back above the water a few feet away, "lose the sword!" The dwarf recognized the importance of the man, and he preferred to let someone else row.

With no options open to him, Pinochet complied and swam back to the little boat. Bruenor dragged him over the side and plopped him down between the oars. "Turn 'er back!" the dwarf roared. "And be pullin' hard!"

✖ ✖ ✖ ✖ ✖

"The mask is down," Wulfgar whispered to Drizzt when their business was finished. The drow slipped behind a mast and replaced the magical disguise.

"Do you think they saw?" Drizzt asked when he returned to Wulfgar's side. Even as he spoke, he noticed the *Sea Sprite*'s crew lining the deck of the pirate ship and eyeing him suspiciously, their weapons in hand.

"They saw," Wulfgar remarked. "Come," he bade Drizzt, heading back toward the boarding plank. "They will accept this!"

Drizzt wasn't so certain. He remembered other times when he had rescued men, only to have them turn on him when they saw under the cowl of his cloak and learned the true color of his skin.

But this was the price of his choice to forsake his own people and come to the surface world.

Drizzt grabbed Wulfgar by the shoulder and stepped by him, resolutely leading the way back to the *Sea Sprite*. Looking back at his young friend, he winked and pulled the mask off his face. He sheathed his scimitars and turned to confront the crew.

"Let them know Drizzt Do'Urden," Wulfgar growled softly behind him, lending Drizzt all the strength he would ever need.

12
COMRADES

B ruenor found Catti-brie treading water beyond the carnage of Pinochet's ship. Pinochet paid the young woman no attention, though. Far in the distance, the crew on his remaining ship, the bulky artillery vessel, had brought the fires under control, but had turned tail and sailed away with all the speed it could muster.

"I thought ye had forgot me," Catti-brie said as the rowboat approached.

"Ye should've stayed by me side," the dwarf laughed at her.

"I've not the kinship with fire as yerself," Catti-brie retorted with a bit of suspicion.

Bruenor shrugged. "Been that way since the halls," he replied. "Mighten be me father's father's armor."

Catti-brie grabbed the side of the low-riding boat and started up, then paused in a sudden realization as she noticed the scimitar strapped across Bruenor's back. "Ye've got the drow's blade!" she said, remembering the story Drizzt had told her of his battle with a fiery demon. The magic of the ice-forged scimitar had saved Drizzt from the fire that day. "Suren that's yer salvation!"

"Good blade," Bruenor muttered, looking at its hilt over his shoulder. "The elf should find it a name!"

"The boat will not hold the weight of three," Pinochet interrupted.

Bruenor turned an angry glare on him and snapped, "Then swim!"

Pinochet's face contorted, and he started to rise threateningly.

Bruenor recognized that he had taunted the proud pirate too far. Before the man could straighten, the dwarf slammed his forehead into Pinochet's chest, butting him over the back of the rowboat. Without missing a beat, the dwarf grabbed Catti-brie's wrist and hoisted her up by his side.

"Put yer bow on him, girl," he said loudly enough for Pinochet, once again bobbing in the water, to hear. He threw the pirate the end of a rope. "If he don't keep up, kill 'im!"

Catti-brie set a silver-shafted arrow to Taulmaril's string and took a bead on Pinochet, playing through the threat, though she had no intention of finishing off the helpless man. "They call me bow the Heartseeker," she warned "Suren ye'd be wise to swim."

The proud pirate pulled the rope around him and paddled.

⚔ ⚔ ⚔ ⚔ ⚔

"No drow's coming back to this ship!" one of Deudermont's crewmen growled at Drizzt.

The man took a slap on the back of the head for his words, and then sheepishly moved aside as Deudermont stepped up to the boarding plank. The captain studied the expressions of his crewmen as they surveyed the drow who had been their companion for tendays.

"What'll ye do with him?" one sailor dared to ask.

"We've men in the water," the captain replied, deflecting the pointed question. "Get them out and dry, and throw the pirates in chains." He waited a moment for his crewmen to disperse, but they held their positions, entranced by the drama of the dark elf.

"And get these ships untangled!" Deudermont roared.

He turned to face Drizzt and Wulfgar, now only a few feet from the plank. "Let us retire to my cabin," he said calmly. "We should talk."

Drizzt and Wulfgar did not answer. They went with the captain silently, absorbing the curious, fearful, and outraged stares that followed them.

Deudermont stopped halfway across the deck, joining a group of his crew as they looked to the south, past Pinochet's burning ship, to a small rowboat pulling hard in their direction.

"The driver of the fiery chariot that rushed across the sky," one of the crewman explained.

"He took down that ship!" another exclaimed, pointing to the wreckage of Pinochet's flagship, now listing badly and soon to sink. "And sent the third one running!"

"Then a friend of ours, he is indeed!" the captain replied.

"And of ours," Drizzt added, turning all eyes back upon him. Even Wulfgar looked curiously at his companion. He had heard the cry to Moradin, but had not dared to hope that it was indeed Bruenor Battlehammer rushing to their aid.

"A red-bearded dwarf, if my guess is correct," Drizzt continued. "And with him, a young woman."

Wulfgar's jaw dropped open. "Bruenor?" he managed to whisper. "Catti-brie?"

Drizzt shrugged. "That is my guess."

"We shall know soon enough," Deudermont assured them. He instructed his crewmen to bring the passengers of the rowboat to his cabin as soon as they came aboard, then he led Drizzt and Wulfgar away, knowing that on the deck the drow would prove a distraction to his crew. And at this time, with the ships fouled, they had important work to complete.

"What do you mean to do with us?" Wulfgar demanded when Deudermont shut the cabin door. "We fought for—"

Deudermont stopped the growing tirade with a calming smile. "You certainly did," he acknowledged. "I only wish that I had such mighty sailors on every voyage south. Surely then the pirates would flee whenever the *Sea Sprite* broke the horizon!"

Wulfgar eased back from his defensive posture.

"My deception was not intended to bring harm," Drizzt said somberly. "And only my appearance was a lie. I require passage to the south to rescue a friend—that much remains true."

Deudermont nodded, but before he could answer, a knock came on the door and a sailor peeked in. "Beggin' yer pardon," he began.

"What is it?" asked Deudermont.

"We follow yer every step, Captain, ye know that," the sailor stammered. "But we thought we should let ye know our feelings on the elf."

Deudermont considered the sailor, and then Drizzt, for a moment. He had always been proud of his crew; most of the men had been together for many years, but he seriously wondered how they would come through this dilemma.

"Go on," he prompted, stubbornly holding his trust in his men.

"Well, we know he's a drow," the sailor began, "and we know

what that means." He paused, weighing his next words carefully. Drizzt held his breath in anticipation; he had been down this route before.

"But them two, they pulled us through a bad jam there," the sailor blurted all of a sudden. "We wouldn't a gotten through without 'em!"

"So you want them to remain aboard?" Deudermont asked, a smile growing across his face. His crew had come through once again.

"Aye!" the sailor replied heartily. "To a man! And we're proud to have 'em!"

Another sailor, the one who had challenged Drizzt at the plank just a few minutes before, poked his head in. "I was scared, that's all," he apologized to Drizzt.

Overwhelmed, Drizzt hadn't found his breath yet. He nodded his acceptance of the apology.

"See ye on deck, then," said the second sailor, and he disappeared out the door.

"We just thought ye should know," the first sailor told Deudermont, and then he, too, was gone.

"They are a fine crew," Deudermont said to Drizzt and Wulfgar when the door had closed.

"And what are your thoughts?" Wulfgar had to ask.

"I judge a man—elf—by his character, not his appearance," Deudermont declared. "And on that subject, keep the mask off, Drizzt Do'Urden. You are a far handsomer sort without it!"

"Not many would share that observation," Drizzt replied.

"On the *Sea Sprite*, they would!" roared the captain. "Now, the battle is won, but there is much to be done. I suspect that your strength would be appreciated at the prow, mighty barbarian. We have to get these ships unfouled and moving before that third pirate comes back with more of his friends!

"And you," he said to Drizzt with a sneaky smile. "I would think that no one could keep a shipload of prisoners in line better than you."

Drizzt pulled the mask off his head and tucked it in his pack. "There are advantages to the color of my skin," he agreed, shaking the gnarls out of his white locks. He turned with Wulfgar to leave, but the door burst in before them.

"Nice blade, elf!" said Bruenor Battlehammer, standing in a puddle of seawater. He tossed the magical scimitar to Drizzt. "Find a name for it, will ye? Blade like that be needing a name. Good for a cook at a pig roastin'!"

"Or a dwarf hunting dragons," Drizzt remarked. He held the scimitar reverently, remembering again the first time he had seen it, lying in the dead dragon's horde. Then he gave it a new home in the scabbard that had held his normal blade, thinking his old one a fitting companion for Twinkle.

Bruenor walked up to his drow friend and clasped his wrist firmly. "When I saw yer eyes lookin' out at me from the gorge," the dwarf began softly, fighting back a choke that threatened to break his voice apart, "suren then I knew that me other friends would be safe!"

"But they are not," Drizzt replied. "Regis is in dire peril."

Bruenor winked. "We'll get him back, elf! No stinkin' assassin's going to put an end to Rumblebelly!" He clenched the drow's arm tightly one final time and turned to Wulfgar, the lad he had ushered into manhood.

Wulfgar wanted to speak but could find no path for the words beyond the lump in his throat. Unlike Drizzt, the barbarian had no idea that Bruenor might still be alive, and seeing his dear mentor, the dwarf who had become as a father to him, back from the grave and standing before him was simply too much for him to digest. He grabbed Bruenor by the shoulders just as the dwarf was about to say something, and hoisted him up, locking him in a great bear hug.

It took Bruenor a few seconds of wiggling to get loose enough to draw breath. "If ye'd squeezed the dragon like that," the dwarf coughed, "I wouldn't've had to ride it down the gorge!"

Catti-brie walked through the door, soaking wet, with her auburn hair matted to her neck and shoulders. Behind her came Pinochet, drenched and humbled.

Her eyes first found the gaze of Drizzt, locking the drow in a silent moment of emotion that went deeper than simple friendship. "Well met," she whispered. "Good it is to look upon Drizzt Do'Urden again. Me heart's been with ye all along."

Drizzt cast her a casual smile and turned his lavender eyes away. "Somehow I knew that you would join our quest before it was through," he said. "Well met, then, and welcome along."

Catti-brie's gaze drifted past the drow to Wulfgar. Twice she had been separated from the man, and both times when they again had met, Catti-brie was reminded how much she had come to love him.

Wulfgar saw her, too. Droplets of seawater sparkled on her face, but they paled next to the shine of her smile. The barbarian, his stare never leaving Catti-brie, eased Bruenor back to the floor.

Only the embarrassment of youthful love kept them apart at that moment, with Drizzt and Bruenor looking on.

"Captain Deudermont," said Drizzt, "I give you Bruenor Battlehammer and Catti-brie, two dear friends and fine allies."

"And we brought ye a present," Bruenor chuckled. "Seeing as we got no coin to pay ye for passage." Bruenor walked over, grabbed Pinochet by the sleeve, and pulled the man front and center. "Captain o' the ship I burned, by me guess."

"Welcome to both of you," Deudermont replied. "And I

assure you that you have more than earned your passage." The captain moved to confront Pinochet, suspecting the man's importance.

"Do you know who I am?" the pirate said in a huff, thinking that he now had a more reasonable person to deal with than the surly dwarf.

"You are a pirate," Deudermont replied calmly.

Pinochet cocked his head to study the captain. A sly smile crossed his face. "You have perhaps heard of Pinochet?"

Deudermont had thought, and feared, that he had recognized the man when Pinochet had first entered the cabin. The captain of the *Sea Sprite* had indeed heard of Pinochet—every merchant along the Sword Coast had heard of Pinochet.

"I demand that you release me and my men!" the pirate blustered.

"In time," Deudermont replied. Drizzt, Bruenor, Wulfgar, and Catti-brie, not understandingthe extent of the influence of the pirates, all looked at Deudermont in disbelief.

"I warn you that the consequences of your actions will be dire!" Pinochet continued, suddenly gaining the upper hand in the confrontation. "I am not a forgiving man, nor are my allies."

Drizzt, whose own people commonly bent the tenets of justice to fit rules of station, understood the captain's dilemma at once. "Let him go," he said. Both of his magical scimitars came out in his hands, Twinkle glowing dangerously. "Let him go and give him a blade. Neither am I forgiving."

Seeing the horrified look the pirate gave the drow, Bruenor was quick to join in. "Ayuh, Captain, let the dog free," the dwarf scowled. "I only kept his head on his shoulders to give ye a livin' gift. If ye don't want him . . ." Bruenor pulled his axe from his belt and swung it easily at the end of his arm.

Wulfgar didn't miss the point. "Bare hands and up the mast!" the barbarian roared, flexing his, muscles so they seemed they would burst. "The pirate and me! Let the winner know the glory of victory. And let the loser drop to his death!"

Pinochet looked at the three crazed warriors. Then, almost pleading for help, he turned back to Deudermont.

"Ah, ye're all missing the fun." Catti-brie grinned, not to be left out. "Where's the sport in one of ye tearin' the pirate apart? Give him the little boat and set him off." Her spritely face turned suddenly grim, and she cast a wicked glare at Pinochet. "Give him a boat," she reiterated, "and let him dodge me silver arrows!"

"Very well, Captain Pinochet," Deudermont began, barely hiding a chuckle. "I would not invoke the rage of the pirates. You are a free man and may go when you choose."

Pinochet snapped around, face to face with Deudermont.

"Or," continued the captain of the *Sea Sprite*, "you and your crew can remain in my hold, under my personal protection, until we reach port."

"You cannot control your crew?" the pirate spat.

"They are not my crew," Deudermont replied. "And if these four chose to kill you, I daresay that I could do little to deter them."

"It is not the way of my people to let our enemies live!" Drizzt interjected in a tone so callous that it sent shivers through the spines of even his closest friends. "Yet I need you, Captain Deudermont, and your ship." He sheathed his blades in a lightning-quick movement. "I will let the pirate live in exchange for the completion of our arrangements."

"The hold, Captain Pinochet?" Deudermont asked, waving two of his crewmen in to escort the pirate leader.

Pinochet's eyes were back on Drizzt. "If you ever sail this way again . . ." the stubborn pirate began ominously.

Bruenor kicked him in the behind. "Wag yer tongue again dog," the dwarf roared, "and suren I'll cut it out!"

Pinochet left quietly with Deudermont's crewmen.

✕ ✕ ✕ ✕ ✕

Later that day, while the crew of the *Sea Sprite* continued its repairs, the reunited friends retired to Drizzt and Wulfgar's cabin to hear of Bruenor's adventures in Mithral Hall. Stars twinkled in the evening sky and still the dwarf went on, talking of the riches he had seen, of the ancient and holy places he had come across in his homeland, of his many skirmishes with duergar patrols, and of his final, daring escape through the great undercity.

Catti-brie sat directly across from Bruenor, watching the dwarf through the swaying flame of the single candle burning on the table. She had heard his story before, but Bruenor could spin a tale as well as any, and she leaned forward in her chair, mesmerized once again. Wulfgar, with his long arms draped comfortably over her shoulders, had pulled his chair up behind her.

Drizzt stood by the window and gazed at the dreamy sky. How like the old times it all seemed, as if they had somehow brought a piece of Icewind Dale along with them. Many were the nights that the friends had gathered to swap tales of their pasts or to just enjoy the quiet of the evening together. Of course, a fifth member had been with the group then and always with an outlandish tale that outdid all the others.

Drizzt looked at his friends and then back to the night sky, thinking—hoping—of a day when the five friends would be rejoined.

A knock on the door made the three at the table jump, so

engrossed were they—even Bruenor—in the dwarf's story. Drizzt opened the door, and Captain Deudermont walked in.

"Greetings," he said politely. "I would not interrupt, but I have some news."

"Just getting to the good part," Bruenor grumbled, "but it'll get better with a bit o' waiting!"

"I have spoken with Pinochet once again," said Deudermont. "He is a very prominent man in this land, and it does not fit well that he set up three ships to stop us. He was after something."

"Us," Drizzt reasoned.

"He said nothing directly," replied Deudermont, "but I believe that to be the case. Please understand that I cannot press him too far."

"Bah! I'll get the dog a barkin'!" Bruenor buffed.

"No need," said Drizzt. "The pirates had to be looking for us."

"But how would they know?" Deudermont asked.

"Balls of fire over Baldur's Gate," Wulfgar reasoned.

Deudermont nodded, remembering the display. "It would seem that you have attracted some powerful foes."

"The man we seek knew that we would come into Baldur's Gate," said Drizzt. "He even left a message for us. It would not have been difficult for the likes of Artemis Entreri to arrange a signal detailing how and when we left."

"Or to arrange the ambush," Wulfgar said grimly.

"So it would seem," said Deudermont.

Drizzt kept quiet, but suspected differently. Why would Entreri lead them all this way, only to have them killed by pirates? Someone else had entered the picture, Drizzt knew, and he could only guess that that person was Pasha Pook himself.

"But there are other matters we must discuss," said Deudermont. "The *Sea Sprite* is seaworthy, but we have taken serious damage as has the pirate ship we have captured."

"Do you mean to sail both out of here?" Wulfgar asked.

"Aye," replied the captain. "We shall release Pinochet and his men when we get to port. They will take the vessel from there."

"Pirates deserve worse," Bruenor grumbled.

"And will this damage slow our journey?" Drizzt asked, more concerned with their mission.

"It will," Deudermont replied. "I am hoping to get us to the kingdom of Calimshan, to Memnon, just beyond the Tethyr border. Our flag will aid us in the desert kingdom. There, we may dock and repair."

"For how long?"

Deudermont shrugged. "A tenday, perhaps, maybe longer. We'll not know until we can properly assess the damage. And another tenday after that to sail around the horn to Calimport."

The four friends exchanged disheartened and worried glances. How many days did Regis have left to live? Could the halfling afford the delay?

"But there is another option," Deudermont told them. "The journey from Memnon to Calimport by ship, around the city of Teshburl and into the Shining Sea, is much longer than the straight land route. Caravans depart for Calimport nearly every day, and the journey, though a hard one through the Calim Desert, takes but a few days."

"We have little gold for passage," said Catti-brie.

Deudermont waved the problem away. "A minor cost," he said. "Any caravan heading through the desert would be glad to have you along as guards. And you have earned ample reward from me to get you through." He jiggled a bag of gold strapped to his belt. "Or, if you choose, you may remain with the *Sea Sprite* for as long as you wish."

"How long to Memnon?" Drizzt asked.

"It depends on how much wind our sails can hold," replied Deudermont. "Five days; perhaps a tenday."

"Tell us of this Calim Desert," said Wulfgar. "What is a desert?"

"A barren land," replied Deudermont grimly, not wanting to understate the challenge that would be before them if they chose that course. "An empty wasteland of blowing, stinging sands and hot winds. Where monsters rule over men, and many an unfortunate traveler has crawled to his death to be picked clean by vultures."

The four friends shrugged away the captain's grim description. Except for the temperature difference, it sounded like home.

13
PAYING THE PIPER

The docks rolled away beyond sight in either direction, the sails of a thousand ships speckled the pale blue waters of the Shining Sea, and it would take them hours to walk the breadth of the city before them, no matter which gate they sought.

Calimport, the largest city in all the Realms, was a sprawling conglomeration of shanties and massive temples, of tall towers springing from plains of low wooden houses. This was the hub of the southern coast, a vast marketplace several times the area of Waterdeep.

Entreri moved Regis off the docks and into the city. The half-ling offered no resistance; he was too caught up in the striking emotions that the unique smells, sights, and sounds of the city brought over him. Even his terror at the thought of facing Pasha Pook became buried in the jumble of memories invoked by his return to his former home.

He had spent his entire childhood here as an orphaned waif, sneaking meals on the streets and sleeping curled up beside the trash fires the other bums set in the alleys on chilly nights. But Regis had an advantage over the other vagabonds of Calimport. Even as a young lad, he had undeniable charm and a lucky streak that always seemed to land him on his feet. The grubby bunch he had run with just shook their heads knowingly on the day their halfling comrade was taken in by one of the many brothels of the city.

The "ladies" showed Regis much kindness, letting him do minor cleaning and cooking tasks in exchange for a high lifestyle that his old friends could only watch and envy. Recognizing the charismatic halfling's potential, the ladies even introduced Regis to the man who would become his mentor and who would mold him into one of the finest thieves the city had ever known: Pasha Pook.

The name came back to Regis like a slap in the face, reminding him of the terrible reality he now faced. He had been Pook's favorite little cutpurse, the guildmaster's pride and joy, but that would only make things worse for Regis now. Pook would never forgive him for his treachery.

Then a more vivid recollection took Regis's legs out from under him as Entreri turned him down Rogues Circle. At the far end, around the cul-de-sac and facing back toward the entrance to the lane, stood a plain-looking wooden building with a single, unremarkable door. But Regis knew the splendors hidden within that unpretentious facade.

And the horrors.

Entreri grabbed him by the collar and dragged him along, never slowing the pace.

"Now, Drizzt, now," Regis whispered, praying that his friends were about and ready to make a desperate, last minute rescue.

But Regis knew that his prayers would not be answered this time. He had finally gotten himself stuck in the mud too deeply to escape.

Two guards disguised as bums moved in front of the pair as they approached the door. Entreri said nothing but shot them a murderous stare.

Apparently the guards recognized the assassin. One of them stumbled out of the way, tripping over his own feet, while the other rushed to the door and rapped loudly. A peephole opened, and the guard whispered something to the doorman inside. A split second later, the door swung wide.

Looking in on the thieves' guild proved too much for the half-ling. Blackness swirled about him, and he fell limp in the assassin's iron grasp. Showing neither emotion nor surprise, Entreri scooped Regis up over his shoulder and carried him like a sack into the guildhouse, and down the flight of stairs beyond the door.

Two more guards moved in to escort him, but Entreri pushed his way past them. It had been three long years since Pook had sent him on the road after Regis, but the assassin knew the way. He passed through several rooms, down another level, and then started up a long, spiral staircase. Soon he was up to street level again and still climbing to the highest chambers of the structure.

Regis regained consciousness in a dizzy blur. He glanced about desperately as the images came clearer and he remembered where he was. Entreri had him by the ankles, the halfling's head dangling halfway down the assassin's back and his hand just inches from the jeweled dagger. But even if he could have gotten to the weapon quickly enough, Regis knew that he had no chance of escape—not with Entreri holding him, two armed guards following, and curious eyes glaring at them from every doorway.

The whispers had traveled through the guild faster than Entreri.

Regis hooked his chin around Entreri's side and managed to catch a glimpse of what lay ahead. They came up onto a landing, where four more guards parted without question, opening the way down a short corridor that ended in an ornate, ironbound door.

Pasha Pook's door.

The blackness swirled over Regis once again.

⚔ ⚔ ⚔ ⚔

When he entered the chamber, Entreri found that he had been expected. Pook sat comfortably on his throne, LaValle by his side and his favorite leopard at his feet, and none of them flinched at the sudden appearance of the two long-lost associates.

The assassin and the guildmaster stared silently at each other for a long time. Entreri studied the man carefully. He hadn't expected so formal a meeting.

Something was wrong.

Entreri pulled Regis off his shoulder and held him out—still upside down—at arm's length, as if presenting a trophy. Convinced that the halfling was oblivious to the world at that moment, Entreri released his hold, letting Regis drop heavily to the floor.

That drew a chuckle from Pook. "It has been a long three years," the guildmaster said, breaking the tension.

Entreri nodded. "I told you at the outset that this one might take time. The little thief ran to the corners of the world."

"But not beyond your grasp, eh?" Pook said, somewhat sarcastically. "You have performed your task excellently, as always, Master Entreri. Your reward shall be as promised." Pook sat back on his throne again and resumed his distant posture, rubbing a finger over his lips and eyeing Entreri suspiciously.

Entreri didn't have any idea why Pook, after so many difficult years and a successful completion of the mission, would treat him so badly. Regis had eluded the guildmaster's grip for more than half a decade before Pook finally sent Entreri on the chase. With that record preceding him, Entreri did not think three years such a long time to complete the mission.

And the assassin refused to play such cryptic games. "If there is a problem, speak it," he said bluntly.

"There was a problem," Pook replied mysteriously, emphasizing the past tense of his statement.

Entreri rocked back a step, now fully at a loss—one of the very few times in his life.

Regis stirred at that moment and managed to sit up, but the two men, engaged in the important conversation, paid him no notice.

"You were being followed," Pook explained, knowing better than to play a teasing game for too long with the killer. "Friends of the halfling?"

Regis's ears perked up.

Entreri took a long moment to consider his response. He guessed what Pook was getting at, and it was easy for him to figure out that Oberon must have informed the guildmaster of more than his return with Regis. He made a mental note to visit the wizard the next time he was in Baldur's Gate, to explain to Oberon the proper limits of spying and the proper restraints of loyalty. No one ever crossed Artemis Entreri twice.

"It does not matter," Pook said, seeing no answer forthcoming. "They will bother us no more."

Regis felt sick. This was the southland, the home of Pasha Pook. If Pook had learned of his friends' pursuit, he certainly could have eliminated them.

Entreri understood that, too. He fought to maintain his calm while a burning rage reared up inside him. "I tend to my own affairs," he growled at Pook, his tone confirming to the guildmaster that he had indeed been playing a private game with his pursuers.

"And I to mine!" Pook shot back, straightening in his chair. "I know not what connection this elf and barbarian hold to you, Entreri, but they have nothing to do with my pendant!" He collected himself quickly and sat back, realizing that the confrontation was getting too dangerous to continue. "I could not take the risk."

The tension eased out of Entreri's taut muscles. He did not wish a war with Pook and he could not change what was past. "How?" he asked.

"Pirates," Pook replied. "Pinochet owed me a favor."

"It is confirmed?"

"Why do you care?" Pook asked. "You are here. The halfling is here. My pen—" He stopped suddenly, realizing that he hadn't yet seen the ruby pendant.

Now it was Pook's turn to sweat and wonder. "It is confirmed?" Entreri asked again, making no move toward the magical pendant that hung, concealed, about his neck.

"Not yet," Pook stammered, "but three ships were sent after the one. There can be no doubt."

Entreri hid his smile. He knew the powerful drow and barbarian well enough to consider them alive until their bodies had been paraded before him. "Yes, there can indeed be doubt," he whispered under his breath as he pulled the ruby pendant over his head and tossed it to the guildmaster.

Pook caught it in trembling hands, knowing immediately from its familiar tingle that it was the true gem. What power he would wield now! With the magical ruby in his hands, Artemis

Entreri returned to his side, and Rassiter's wererats under his command, he would be unstoppable!

LaValle put a steadying hand on the guildmaster's shoulder. Pook, beaming in anticipation of his growing power, looked up at him.

"Your reward shall be as promised," Pook said again to Entreri as soon as he had caught his breath. "And more!"

Entreri bowed. "Well met, then, Pasha Pook," he replied. "It is good to be home."

"Concerning the elf and barbarian," Pook said, suddenly entertaining second thoughts about ever mistrusting the assassin.

Entreri stopped him with outstretched palms. "A watery grave serves them as well as Calimport's sewers," he said "Let us not worry about what is behind us."

Pook's smile engulfed his round face. "Agreed, and well met, then," he beamed. "Especially when there is such pleasurable business ahead of us." He turned an evil eye upon Regis, but the halfling, sitting stooped over on the floor beside Entreri, didn't notice.

Regis was still trying to digest the news about his friends. At that moment, he didn't care how their deaths might affect his own future—or lack of one. He only cared that they were gone. First Bruenor in Mithral Hall, then Drizzt and Wulfgar, and possibly Catti-brie, as well. Next to that, Pasha Pook's threats seemed hollow indeed. What could Pook ever do to him that would hurt as much as those losses?

"Many sleepless nights I have spent fretting over the disappointment you have caused me," Pook said to Regis. "And many more I have spent considering how I would repay you!"

The door swung open, interrupting Pook's train of thought. The guildmaster did not have to look up to know who had dared to enter without permission. Only one man in the guild would have such nerve.

Rassiter swept into the room and cut an uncomfortably close circle as he inspected the newcomers. "Greetings, Pook," he said offhandedly, his eyes locking onto the assassin's stern gaze.

Pook said nothing but dropped his chin into his hand to watch. He had anticipated the meeting for a long time.

Rassiter stood nearly a foot taller than Entreri, a fact that only added to the wererat's already cocky attitude. Like so many simpleton bullies, Rassiter often confused size with strength, and looking down at this man who was a legend on the streets of Calimport—and thus his rival—made him think that he had already gained the upper hand. "So, you are the great Artemis Entreri," he said, contempt evident in his voice.

Entreri didn't blink. Murder was in his eyes as his gaze followed Rassiter, who still circled. Even Regis was dumbfounded at the stranger's boldness. No one ever moved so casually around Entreri.

"Greetings," Rassiter said at length, satisfied with his scan. He bowed low. "I am Rassiter, Pasha Pook's closest advisor and controller of the docks."

Still Entreri did not respond. He looked over to Pook for an explanation.

The guildmaster returned Entreri's curious gaze with a smirk and lifted his palms in a helpless gesture.

Rassiter carried his familiarity even further. "You and I," he half-whispered to Entreri, "we can do great things together." He started to place a hand on the assassin's shoulder, but Entreri turned him back with an icy glare, a look so deadly that even cocky Rassiter began to understand the peril of his course.

"You may find that I have much to offer you," Rassiter said, taking a cautious step back. Seeing no response forthcoming, he turned to Pook. "Would you like me to take care of the little thief?" he asked, grinning his yellow smile.

"That one is mine, Rassiter," Pook replied firmly. "You and yours keep your furry hands off him!"

Entreri did not miss the reference.

"Of course," Rassiter replied. "I have business, then. I will be going." He bowed quickly and spun to leave, meeting Entreri's eyes one final time. He could not hold that icy stare—could not match the sheer intensity of the assassin's gaze—with his own.

Rassiter shook his head in disbelief as he passed, convinced that Entreri still had not blinked.

"You were gone. My pendant was gone," Pook explained when the door closed again. "Rassiter has helped me retain, even expand, the strength of the guild."

"He is a wererat," Entreri remarked, as if that fact alone ended any argument.

"Head of their guild," Pook replied, "but they are loyal enough and easy to control." He held up the ruby pendant. "Easier now."

Entreri had trouble coming to terms with that, even in light of Pook's futile attempt at an explanation. He wanted time to consider the new development, to figure out just how much things had changed around the guildhouse. "My room?" he asked.

LaValle shifted uncomfortably and glanced down at Pook. "I have been using it," the wizard stammered, "but quarters are being built for me." He looked to the door newly cut into the wall between the harem and Entreri's old room. "They should be completed any day. I can be out of your room in minutes."

"No need," Entreri replied, thinking the arrangements better as they were. He wanted some space from Pook for a while, anyway, to better assess the situation before him and plan his next moves. "I will find a room below, where I might better understand the new ways of the guild."

LaValle relaxed with an audible sigh.

Entreri picked Regis up by the collar. "What am I to do with this one?"

Pook crossed his arms over his chest and cocked his head. "I have thought of a million tortures befitting your crime," he said to Regis. "Too many, I see, for truly, I have no idea of how to properly repay you for what you have done to me." He looked back to Entreri. "No matter," he chuckled. "It will come to me. Put him in the Cells of Nine."

Regis went limp again at the mention of the infamous dungeon. Pook's favorite holding cell, it was a horror chamber normally reserved for thieves who killed other members of the guild. Entreri smiled to see the halfling so terrified at the mere mention of the place. He easily lifted Regis off the floor and carried him out of the room.

"That did not go well," LaValle said when Entreri had left.

"It went splendidly!" Pook disagreed. "I have never seen Rassiter so unnerved, and the sight of it proved infinitely more pleasurable than I ever imagined!"

"Entreri will kill him if he is not careful," LaValle observed grimly.

Pook seemed amused by the thought. "Then we should learn who is likely to succeed Rassiter." He looked up at LaValle. "Fear not, my friend. Rassiter is a survivor. He has called the street his home for his entire life and knows when to scurry into the safety of shadows. He will learn his place around Entreri, and he will show the assassin proper respect."

But LaValle wasn't thinking of Rassiter's safety—he had often entertained thoughts of disposing of the wretched wererat himself. What concerned the wizard was the possibility of a deeper rift in the guild. "What if Rassiter turns the power of his allies against Entreri?" he asked in a tone even more grim. "The street war that would ensue would split the guild in half."

Pook dismissed the possibility with a wave of his hand. "Even Rassiter is not that stupid," he answered, fingering the ruby pendant, an insurance policy he might just need.

LaValle relaxed, satisfied with his master's assurances and with Pook's ability to handle the delicate situation. As usual, Pook was right, LaValle realized. Entreri had unnerved the wererat with a simple stare, to the possible benefit of all involved. Perhaps now, Rassiter would act more appropriately for his rank in the guild. And with Entreri soon to be quartered on this very level, perhaps the intrusions of the filthy wererat would come less often.

Yes, it was good to have Entreri back.

⚔ ⚔ ⚔ ⚔ ⚔

The Cells of Nine were so named because of the nine cells cut into the center of a chamber's floor, three abreast and three long. Only the center cell was ever unoccupied; the other eight held Pasha Pook's most treasured collection: great hunting cats from every corner of the Realms.

Entreri handed Regis over to the jailor, a masked giant of a man, then stood back to watch the show. Around the halfling the jailor tied one end of a heavy rope, which made its way over a pulley in the ceiling above the center cell then back to a crank off to the side.

"Untie it when you are in," the jailor grunted at Regis. He pushed Regis forward. "Pick your path."

Regis walked gingerly along the border of the outer cells. They all were roughly ten feet square with caves cut into the walls, where the cats could go to rest. But none of the beasts rested now, and all seemed equally hungry.

They were always hungry.

Regis chose the plank between a white lion and a heavy tiger, thinking those two giants the least likely to scale the twenty-foot wall and claw his ankle out from under him as he crossed. He slipped one foot onto the wall—which was barely four inches wide—separating the cells and then hesitated, terrified.

The jailor gave a prompting tug on the rope that nearly toppled Regis in with the lion.

Reluctantly he started out, concentrating on placing one foot in front of the other and trying to ignore the growls and claws below. He had nearly made the center cell when the tiger launched its full weight against the wall, shaking it violently. Regis overbalanced and tumbled in with a shriek.

The jailor pulled the crank and caught him in midfall, hoisting him just out of the leaping tiger's reach. Regis swung into the far wall, bruising his ribs but not even feeling the injury at that desperate moment. He scrambled over the wall and swung free, eventually stopping over the middle of the center cell, where the jailor let him down.

He put his feet to the floor tentatively and clutched the rope as his only possible salvation, refusing to believe that he must stay in the nightmarish place.

"Untie it!" the jailor demanded, and Regis knew by the man's tone that to disobey was to suffer unspeakable pain. He slipped the rope free.

"Sleep well," the jailor laughed, pulling the rope high out of the halfling's reach. The hooded man left with Entreri, extinguishing all the room's torches and slamming the iron door behind him, leaving Regis alone in the dark with the eight hungry cats.

The walls separating the cats' cells were solid, preventing the animals from harming each other, but the center cell was lined with wide bars—wide enough for a cat to put its paws through. And this torture chamber was circular, providing easy and equal access from all eight of the other cells.

Regis did not dare to move. The rope had placed him in the exact center of the cell, the only spot that kept him out of reach of all eight cats. He glanced around at the feline eyes, gleaming wickedly in the dim light. He heard the scraping of lunging claws and even felt a swish of air whenever one of them managed to squeeze enough leg through the bars to get a close swipe.

And each time a huge paw slammed into the floor beside him, Regis had to remind himself not to jump back—where another cat waited.

Five minutes seemed like an hour, and Regis shuddered to think of how many days Pook would keep him there. Maybe it would be better just to get it over with, Regis thought, a notion that many shared when placed in the chamber.

Looking at the cats, though, the halfling dismissed that possibility. Even if he could convince himself that a quick death in a tiger's jaws would be better than the fate he no doubt faced, he would never have found the courage to carry it through. He was a survivor—had always been—and he couldn't deny that stubborn side of his character that refused to yield no matter how bleak his future seemed.

He stood now, as still as a statue, and consciously worked to fill his mind with thoughts of his recent past, of the ten years he had spent outside Calimport. Many adventures he had seen on his travels, many perils he had come through. Regis replayed those battles and escapes over and over in his mind, trying to recapture the sheer excitement he had experienced—active thoughts that would help to keep him awake.

For if weariness overtook him and he fell to the floor, some part of him might get too close to one of the cats.

More than one prisoner had been clawed in the foot and dragged to the side to be ripped apart.

And even those who survived the Cells of Nine would never forget the ravenous stares of those sixteen gleaming eyes.

14

DANCING SNAKES

Luck was with the damaged *Sea Sprite* and the captured pirate vessel, for the sea held calm and the wind blew steadily but gently. Still, the journey around the Tethyr Peninsula proved tedious and all too slow for the four anxious friends, for every time the two ships seemed to be making headway, one or the other would develop a new problem.

South of the peninsula, Deudermont took his ships through a wide stretch of water called the Race, so named for the common spectacle there of merchant vessels running from pirate pursuit. No other pirates bothered Deudermont or his crew, however. Even Pinochet's third ship never again showed its sails.

"Our journey nears its end," Deudermont told the four friends when the high coastline of the Purple Hills came into view early on the third morning. "Where the hills end, Calimshan begins."

Drizzt leaned over the forward rail and looked into the pale blue waters of the southern seas. He wondered again if they would get to Regis in time.

"There is a colony of your people farther inland," Deudermont said to him, drawing him out of his private thoughts, "in a dark wood called Mir." An involuntary shudder shook the captain. "The drow are not liked in this region; I would advise you to don your mask."

Without thinking, Drizzt drew the magical mask over his face, instantly assuming the features of a surface elf. The act bothered the drow less than it shook his three friends, who looked on in resigned disdain. Drizzt was only doing what he had to do, they reminded themselves, carrying on with the same uncomplaining stoicism that had guided his life since the day he had forsaken his people.

The drow's new identity did not fit in the eyes of Wulfgar and Catti-brie. Bruenor spat into the water, disgusted at a world too blinded by a cover to read the book inside.

By early afternoon, a hundred sails dotted the southern horizon and a vast line of docks appeared along the coast, with a sprawling city of low clay shacks and brightly colored tents rolling out behind them. But as vast as Memnon's docks were, the number of fishing and merchant vessels and warships of the growing Calimshan navy was greater still. The *Sea Sprite* and its captured ship were forced to drop anchor offshore and wait for appropriate landings to open—a wait, the harbormaster soon informed Deudermont, of possibly a tenday.

"We shall next be visited by Calimshan's navy," Deudermont explained as the harbormaster's launch headed away, "coming to inspect the pirate ship and interrogate Pinochet."

"They'll take care o' the dog?" Bruenor asked.

Deudermont shook his head. "Not likely. Pinochet and his men are my prisoners and my trouble. Calimshan desires an end to the pirate activities and is making bold strides toward that goal, but I doubt that it would yet dare to become entangled with one as powerful as Pinochet."

"What's for him, then?" Bruenor grumbled, trying to find some measure of backbone in all the political double talk.

"He will sail away to trouble another ship on another day," Deudermont replied.

"And to warn that rat, Entreri, that we've slipped the noose," Bruenor snapped back.

Understanding Deudermont's sensitive position, Drizzt put in a reasonable request. "How long can you give us?"

"Pinochet cannot get his ship in for a tenday, and" the captain added with a sly wink, "I have already seen to it that it is no longer seaworthy. I should be able to stretch that tenday out to two. By the time the pirate finds the wheel of his ship again, you will have told this Entreri of your escape personally."

Wulfgar still did not understand. "What have you gained?" he asked Deudermont. "You have defeated the pirates, but they are to sail free, tasting vengeance on their lips. They will strike at the *Sea Sprite* on your next passage. Will they show as much mercy if they win the next encounter?"

"It is a strange game we play," Deudermont agreed with a helpless smile. "But, in truth, I have strengthened my position on the waters by sparing Pinochet and his men. In exchange for his freedom, the pirate captain will swear off vengeance. None of Pinochet's associates shall ever bother the *Sea Sprite* again, and that group includes most of the pirates sailing Asavir's Channel!"

"And ye're to trust that dog's word?" Bruenor balked.

"They are honorable enough," replied Deudermont, "in their own way. The codes have been drawn and are held to by the pirates; to break them would be to invite open warfare with the southern kingdoms."

Bruenor spat into the water again. It was the same in every city and kingdom and even on the open water: organizations of thieves tolerated within limits of behavior. Bruenor was of a different mind. Back in Mithral Hall, his clan had custom-built a closet with shelving especially designed to hold severed hands that had been caught in pockets where they didn't belong.

"It is settled, then," Drizzt remarked, seeing it time to change the subject. "Our journey by sea is at an end."

Deudermont, expecting the announcement, tossed him the pouch of gold. "A wise choice," the captain said. "You will make Calimport a full tenday and more more before the *Sea Sprite* finds her docks. But come to us when you have completed your business. We shall put back for Waterdeep before the last of the winter's snows have melted in the North. By all of my reckoning, you have earned your passage."

"We're for leaving long afore that," replied Bruenor, "but thanks for yer offer!"

Wulfgar stepped forward and clasped the captain's wrist. "It was good to serve and fight beside you," he said. "I look forward to the day when next we will meet."

"As do we all," Drizzt added. He held the pouch high "And this shall be repaid."

Deudermont waved the notion away and mumbled, "A pittance." Knowing the friends' desire for haste, he motioned for two of his crewmen to drop a rowboat.

"Farewell!" he called as the friends pulled away from the *Sea Sprite*. "Look for me in Calimport!

⚔ ⚔ ⚔ ⚔ ⚔

Of all the places the companions had visited, of all the lands they had walked through and fought through, none had seemed as foreign to them as Memnon in the kingdom of Calimshan. Even Drizzt, who had come from the strange world of the drow elves, stared in amazement as he made his way through the city's open lanes and marketplaces. Strange music, shrill and mournful—as often resembling wails of pain as harmony—surrounded them and carried them on.

People flocked everywhere. Most wore sand-colored robes, but others were brightly dressed, and all had some sort of head covering: a turban or a veiled hat. The friends could not guess at the population of the city, which seemed to go on forever, and doubted that anyone had ever bothered to count. But Drizzt and his companions could envision that if all the people of the cities along the northern stretches of the Sword Coast, Waterdeep included, gathered in one vast refugee camp, it would resemble Memnon.

A strange combination of odors wafted through Memnon's hot air: that of a sewer that ran through a perfume market, mixed with the pungent sweat and malodorous breath of the ever-pressing crowd. Shacks were thrown up randomly, it seemed, giving Memnon no apparent design or structure. Streets were any way that was not blocked by homes, though the four friends had all come to the conclusion that the streets themselves served as homes for many people.

At the center of all the bustle were the merchants. They lined every lane, selling weapons, foodstuffs, exotic pipe weeds—even slaves—shamelessly displaying their goods in whatever manner would attract a crowd. On one corner, potential buyers test-fired a large crossbow by shooting down a boxed-in range, complete with live slave targets. On another, a woman showing more skin than clothing—and that being no more than translucent veils—twisted and writhed in a synchronous dance with a gigantic snake, wrapping herself within the huge reptilian coils and then slipping teasingly back out again.

Wide-eyed and with his mouth hanging open, Wulfgar stopped, mesmerized by the strange and seductive dance, drawing a slap across the back of his head from Catti-brie and amused chuckles from his other two companions.

"Never have I so longed for home," the huge barbarian sighed, truly overwhelmed.

"It is another adventure, nothing more," Drizzt reminded him. "Nowhere might you learn more than in a land unlike your own."

"True enough," said Catti-brie. "But by me eyes, these folk be making decadence into society."

"They live by different rules," Drizzt replied. "They would, perhaps, be equally offended by the ways of the North."

The others had no response to that, and Bruenor, never surprised but always amazed by eccentric human ways, just wagged his red beard.

Outfitted for adventure, the friends were far from a novelty in the trading city. but being foreigners, they attracted a crowd, mostly naked, black-tanned children begging for tokens and coins. The merchants eyed the adventurers, too—foreigners usually brought in wealth—and one particularly lascivious set of eyes settled onto them firmly.

"Well, well?" the weaseling merchant asked his hunchbacked companion.

"Magic, magic everywhere, my master," the broken little goblin lisped hungrily, absorbing the sensations his magical wand imparted to him. He replaced the wand on his belt. "Strongest on the weapons—elf's swords, both, dwarf's axe, girl's bow, and especially the big one's hammer!" He thought of mentioning the odd sensations his wand had imparted about the elf's face, but decided not to make his excitable master any more nervous than was necessary.

"Ha ha ha ha ha," cackled the merchant, waggling his fingers. He slipped out to intercept the strangers.

Bruenor, leading the troupe, stopped short at the sight of the wiry man dressed in yellow-and-red striped robes and a flaming pink turban with a huge diamond set in its front.

"Ha ha ha ha ha. Greetings!" the man spouted at them, his fingers drumming on his own chest and his ear-to-ear smile showing every other tooth to be golden and those in between to be ivory. "I be Sali Dalib, I do be, I do be! You buy, I sell. Good deal, good deal!" His words came out too fast to be immediately sorted, and the friends looked at each other, shrugged, and started away.

"Ha ha ha ha ha," the merchant pressed, wiggling back in their path. "What you need, Sali Dalib got. In plenty, too, many. Tookie, nookie, bookie."

"Smoke weed, women, and tomes in every language known to the world," the lisping little goblin translated. "My master is a merchant of anything and everything!"

"Bestest o' de bestest!" Sali Dalib asserted. "What you need—"

"Sali Dalib got," Bruenor finished for him. The dwarf looked to Drizzt, confident that they were thinking the same thing: The sooner they were out of Memnon, the better. One weird merchant would serve as well as another.

"Horses," the dwarf told the merchant.

"We wish to get to Calimport," Drizzt explained.

"Horses, horses? Ha ha ha ha ha," replied Sali Dalib without missing a beat. "Not for long ride, no. Too hot, too dry. Camels de thing!"

"Camels. . . desert horses," the goblin explained, seeing the dumbfounded expressions. He pointed to a large dromedary being led down the street by its tan-robed master. "Much better for ride across the desert."

"Camels, then," snorted Bruenor, eyeing the massive beast tentatively. "Or whatever'll do!"

Sali Dalib rubbed his hands together eagerly. "What you need—"

Bruenor threw his hand out to stop the excited merchant. "We know, we know."

Sali Dahb sent his assistant away with some private instructions and led the friends through the maze of Memnon at great speed, though he never seemed to lift his feet from the ground as he shuffled along. All the while, the merchant held his hands out in front of him, his fingers twiddling and tap-tapping. But he seemed harmless enough, and the friends were more amused than worried.

Sali Dalib pulled up short before a large tent on the western end of the city, a poorer section even by Memnon's paupers' standards. Around the back, the merchant found what he was looking for. "Camels!" he proclaimed proudly.

"How much for four?" Bruenor huffed, anxious to get the dealings over with and get back on the road. Sali Dalib seemed not to understand.

"The price?" the dwarf asked.

"De price?"

"He wants an offer," Catti-brie observed.

Drizzt understood as well. Back in Menzoberranzan, the city of drow, merchants used the same technique. By getting the buyer—especially a buyer not familiar with the goods for sale—to make the first mention of price, they often received many times the value of their goods. And if the bid came in too low, the merchant could always hold out for the proper market value.

"Five hundred gold pieces for the four," Drizzt offered, guessing the beasts to be at least twice that value.

Sali Dalib's fingers began their tap dance again, and a sparkle came into his pale gray eyes. Drizzt expected a tirade and then an outlandish counter, but Sali Dalib suddenly calmed and flashed his gold-and-ivory smile.

"Agreed!" he replied.

Drizzt caught his tongue before his planned retort left his mouth in a meaningless gurgle. He cast a curious look at the merchant, then turned to count out the gold from the sack Deudermont had given him.

"Fifty more for ye if ye can get us hooked with a caravan for Calimport," Bruenor offered.

Sali Dalib assumed a contemplative stance, tapping his fingers against the dark bristles on his chin. "But there is one out dis very now," he replied. "You can catch it with little trouble. But you should. Last one to Calimport for de tenday."

"To the south!" the dwarf cried happily to his companions.

"De south? Ha ha ha ha ha!" Sali Dalib blurted. "Not de south. De south is for thief bait!"

"Calimport is south," Bruenor retorted suspiciously. "And so's the road, by me guessing."

"De road to Calimport is south," Sali Dalib agreed, "but those who be smart start to de west, on de bestest road."

Drizzt handed a pouch of gold to the merchant. "How do we catch the caravan?"

"De west," Sali Dalib replied, dropping the pouch into a deep pocket without even inspecting the contents. "Only out one hour. Easy catch, dis. Follow de signposts on de horizon. No problem."

"We'll need supplies," Catti-brie remarked.

"Caravan is well-stocked," answered Sali Dalib. "Bestest place to buy. Now be going. Catch dem before dey turn south to de Trade Way!" He moved to help them select their mounts: a large dromedary for Wulfgar, a two-humper for Drizzt, and smaller ones for Catti-brie and Bruenor.

"Remember, good friends," the merchant said to them when they were perched upon their mounts. "What you need—"

"Sali Dalib got!" they all answered in unison. With one final flash of his gold-and-ivory smile, the merchant shuffled into the tent.

"He was more to bargaining, by me guess," Catti-brie remarked as they headed tentatively on the stiff-legged camels toward the first signpost. "He could've gotten more for the beasts."

"Stolen, o' course!" Bruenor laughed, stating what he considered the obvious.

But Drizzt wasn't so certain. "A merchant such as he would have sought the best price even for stolen goods," he replied, "and by all my knowledge of the rules of bargaining, he most certainly should have counted the gold."

"Bah!" Bruenor snorted, fighting to keep his mount moving straight. "Ye probably gave him more than the things are worth!"

"What, then?" Catti-brie asked Drizzt, agreeing more with his reasoning.

"Where?" Wulfgar answered and asked all at once. "He sent his goblin sneak away with a message."

"Ambush," said Catti-brie.

Drizzt and Wulfgar nodded. "It would seem," said the barbarian.

Bruenor considered the possibility. "Bah!" He snorted at the notion. "He didn't have enough wits in his head to pull it off."

"That observation might only make him more dangerous,"

Drizzt remarked, looking back a final time toward Memnon.

"Turn back?" the dwarf asked, not so quick to dismiss the drow's apparently serious concerns.

"If our suspicions prove wrong and we miss the caravan . . ." Wulfgar reminded them ominously.

"Can Regis wait?" asked Catti-brie.

Bruenor and Drizzt looked to each other.

"Onward," Drizzt said at length. "Let us learn what we may."

"Nowhere might you learn more than in a land unlike your own," Wulfgar remarked, echoing Drizzt's thoughts of that morning.

When they had passed the first signpost, their suspicions did not diminish. A large board nailed to the post named their route in twenty languages, all reading the same way: "De bestest road." Once again, the friends considered their options, and once again they found themselves trapped by the lack of time. They would continue on, they decided, for one hour. If they had found no signs of the caravan by then, they would return to Memnon and "discuss" the matter with Sali Dalib.

The next signpost read the same way, as did the one after that. By the time they passed the fifth, sweat drenched their clothes and stung their eyes, and the city was no longer in sight, lost somewhere in the dusty heat of the rising dunes. Their mounts didn't make the journey any better. Camels were nasty beasts, and nastier still when driven by an inexperienced rider. Wulfgar's, in particular, had a bad opinion of its rider, for camels preferred to pick their own route, and the barbarian, with his powerful legs and arms, kept forcing his mount through the motions he chose. Twice, the camel had arched its head back and launched a slobbery wad of spittle at Wulfgar's face.

Wulfgar took it all in stride, but he spent more than a passing moment fantasizing of flattening the camel's hump with his hammer.

"Hold!" Drizzt commanded as they moved down into a bowl between dunes. The drow extended his arm, leading the surprised glances skyward, where several buzzards had taken up a lazy, circular flight.

"There's carrion about," Bruenor noted.

"Or there is soon to be," Drizzt replied grimly.

Even as he spoke, the lines of the dunes encircling them transformed suddenly from the hazy flat brown of hot sands to the ominous silhouettes of horsemen, curved swords raised and gleaming in the bright sunlight.

"Ambush," Wulfgar stated flatly.

Not too surprised, Bruenor glanced around to take a quick measure of the odds. "Five to one," he whispered to Drizzt.

"It always seems to be," Drizzt answered. He slowly slid his bow from his shoulder and strung it.

The horsemen held their position for a long while, surveying their intended prey.

"Ye think they be wantin' to talk?" Bruenor asked, trying to find some humor in the bleak situation.

"Nah," the dwarf answered himself when none of the other three cracked a smile.

The leader of the horsemen barked a command, and the thunderous charge was on.

"Blast and bebother the whole damned world," Catti-brie grumbled, pulling Taulmaril from her shoulder as she slid from her mount. "Everyone wants a fight.

"Come on, then!" she shouted at the horsemen. "But let's get the fight a bit fairer!" She set the magical bow into action, sending one silver arrow after another streaking up the dunes into the horde, blasting rider after rider out of his saddle.

Bruenor gawked at his daughter, suddenly so grim-faced and savage. "The girl's got it right!" he proclaimed, sliding down from his camel. "Can't be fightin' up on one of them things!" As soon as he hit the ground, the dwarf grabbed at his pack and pulled out two flasks of oil.

Wulfgar followed his mentor's lead, using the side of his camel as a barricade. But the barbarian found his mount to be his first foe, for the ill-tempered beast turned back on him and clamped its flat teeth onto his forearm.

Drizzt's bow joined in on Taulmaril's deadly song, but as the horsemen closed in, the drow decided upon a different course of action. Playing on the terror of the reputation of his people, Drizzt tore off his mask and pulled back the cowl of his cloak, leaping to his feet atop the camel and straddling the beast with one foot on each hump. Those riders closing in on Drizzt pulled up short at the unnerving appearance of a drow elf.

The other three flanks collapsed quickly, though, as the horsemen closed in, still outnumbering the friends.

Wulfgar stared at his camel in disbelief, then slammed his huge fist between the wretched beast's eyes. The dazed camel promptly let go of its hold and turned its woozy head away.

Wulfgar wasn't finished with the treacherous beast. He noticed three riders bearing down on him, so he decided to pit one enemy against another. He stepped under the camel and lifted it clear off the ground, his muscles rippling as he heaved the thing into the charging pack. He just managed to dodge the tumbling mass of horses, riders, camels, and sand.

Then he had Aegis-fang in his hands, and he leaped into the jumble, crushing the bandits before they ever realized what had hit them.

Two riders found a channel through the riderless camels to

get at Bruenor, but it was Drizzt, standing alone, who got in the first strike. Summoning his magical ability, the drow conjured a globe of darkness in front of the charging bandits. They tried to pull up short, but plunged in headlong.

That gave Bruenor all the time he needed. He struck a spark off his tinderbox onto the rags he had stuffed into the oil flasks, then tossed the flaming grenades into the ball of darkness.

Even the fiery lights of the ensuing explosions could not be seen within the globe of Drizzt's spell, but from the screams that erupted inside, Bruenor knew he had hit the mark.

"Me thanks, elf!" the dwarf cried. "Glad to be with ye again!"

"Behind you!" was Drizzt's reply, for even as Bruenor spoke, a third rider cut around the globe and galloped at the dwarf. Bruenor instinctively dropped into a ball, throwing his golden shield above him.

The horse trampled right over Bruenor and stumbled into the soft sand, throwing its rider.

The tough dwarf sprang to his feet and shook the sand out of his ears. That stomping would surely hurt when the adrenaline of battle died away, but right now, all Bruenor felt was rage. He charged the rider—now also rising to his feet—with his mithral axe raised above his head.

Just as Bruenor got there and started his overhead chop, a line of silver flashed by his shoulder, dropping the bandit dead. Unable to stop his momentum, the dwarf went head-long over the suddenly prostrate body and flopped facedown onto the ground.

"Next time, tell me, girl!" Bruenor roared at Catti-brie and spitting sand with every word.

Catti-brie had her own troubles. She had dropped low, hearing a horse thundering up behind her as she loosed the arrow. A curved sword swooshed past the side of her head, nicking her ear, and the rider went past.

Catti-brie meant to send out another arrow to follow the man, but while she was stooped, she saw yet another bandit bearing down on her from behind, this one with a poised spear and heavy shield leading the way.

Catti-brie and Taulmaril proved the swifter. In an instant, another arrow was on the magical bow's string and sent away. It exploded into the bandit's heavy shield and tore through, tossing the helpless man off the back of his mount and into the realm of death.

The riderless horse broke stride. Catti-brie caught its reins as it trotted by and swung up into the saddle to pursue the bandit who had cut her.

Drizzt still stood atop his camel, towering above his foes and deftly dancing away from the strikes of riders rushing by, all the while weaving his two magical scimitars into a dance of mesmerizing death. Again and again, bandits thought they had an easy shot at the standing elf, only to find their swords or spears catching nothing but air, and then to suddenly discover Twinkle or the other magical scimitar slicing a clean line across their throats as they started to gallop away.

Then two came in together, broadside to the camel and behind Drizzt. The agile drow leaped about, still comfortably holding his perch. Within mere seconds, he had both of his foes on the defensive.

Wulfgar finished the last of the three he had dropped, then sprang away from the mess, only to find his stubborn camel rising in front of him again. He slammed the nasty thing again, this time with Aegis-fang, and it dropped to the ground beside the bandits.

With that battle at an undeniable end, the first thing the

barbarian noticed was Drizzt. He marveled at the magnificent dance of the drow's blades, snapping down to deflect a curved sword or to keep one of the drow's two opponents off balance. Drizzt would dispose of both of them in a matter of seconds.

Then Wulfgar looked past the drow, to where another rider quietly trotted in, his spearhead angled to catch Drizzt in the back.

"Drizzt!" the barbarian screamed as he heaved Aegis-fang at his friend.

At the sound of the shout, Drizzt thought Wulfgar was in trouble, but when he looked and saw the warhammer spinning toward his knees, he understood immediately. Without hesitation, he leaped out and over his foes in a twisting somersault.

The charging spearman didn't even have time to lament his victim's escape, for the mighty warhammer spun in over the camel's humps and smashed his face flat.

Drizzt's dive proved beneficial in his fight up front as well, for he had caught both swordsmen by surprise. In the split second of their hesitation, the drow, though he was upside down in midair, struck hard, thrusting his blades downward.

Twinkle dug deeply into a chest. The other bandit managed to dodge the second scimitar, but it came close enough for Drizzt to lock its hilt under the man's arm. Both riders came tumbling down with the drow, and only Drizzt landed on his feet. His blades crossed twice and dived again, this time ending the struggle.

Seeing the huge barbarian unarmed, another rider went after him. Wulfgar saw the man coming and poised himself for a desperate strike. As the horse charged in, the barbarian feinted to his right, away from the rider's sword arm and as the rider had expected. Then Wulfgar reversed direction, throwing himself squarely in the horse's path.

Wulfgar accepted the stunning impact and locked his arms

about the horse's neck and his legs onto the beast's front legs, rolling backward with the momentum and causing the horse to stumble. Then the mighty barbarian yanked with all his might, bringing horse and rider right over him.

The shocked bandit could not react, though he did manage to scream as the horse drove him into the ground. When the horse finally rolled away, the bandit remained, buried upside down to the waist in the sand, his legs lolling grotesquely to one side.

His boots and beard filled with sand, Bruenor eagerly looked for someone to fight. Among the tall mounts, the short dwarf had been overlooked by all but a handful of the bandits. Now, most of them were already dead!

Bruenor rushed away from the protection of the riderless camels, banging his axe on his shield to draw attention to himself. He saw one rider turning to flee from the disastrous scene.

"Hey!" Bruenor barked at him. "Yer mother's an ore-kissin' harlot!

Thinking he had every advantage over the standing dwarf, the bandit couldn't pass up the opportunity to answer the insult. He rushed over to Bruenor and chopped down with his sword.

Bruenor brought his golden shield up to block the blow, then stepped around the front of the horse. The rider swung about to meet the dwarf on the other side, but Bruenor used his shortness to his advantage. Barely bending, he slipped under the horse's belly, back to the original side, and thrust his axe up over his head, catching the confused man on the hip. As the bandit lurched over in pain, Bruenor brought his shield arm up, caught turban and hair in his gnarled fingers, and tore the man from his seat. With a satisfied grunt, the dwarf chopped into the bandit's neck

"Too easy!" the dwarf grumbled, dropping the body to the

ground. He looked for another victim, but the battle was over. No more bandits remained in the bowl, and Wulfgar, Aegis-fang back in his hands, and Drizzt were standing easily.

"Where's me girl?" Bruenor cried.

Drizzt calmed him with a look and a pointing finger.

On the top of a dune to the side, Catti-brie sat atop the horse she had commandeered, Taulmaril taut in her hands as she looked out over the desert.

Several riders galloped across the sand in full flight and another lay dead on the other side of the dune. Catti-brie put one of them in her sights, then realized that the fighting had ended behind her.

"Enough," she whispered, moving the bow an inch to the side and sending the arrow over the fleeing bandit's shoulder.

There has been enough killing this day, she thought.

Catti-brie looked at the carnage of the battle scene and at the hungry buzzards circling patiently overhead. She dropped Taulmaril to her side. The firm set of her grim visage melted away.

THE GUIDE

S ee the pleasure it promises," the guildmaster teased, scraping his hand over the barbed tip of a single spike sticking out of a block of wood on the center of the room's little table.

Regis purposely curled his lips into a stupid smile, pretending to see the obvious logic of Pook's words.

"Just drop your palm onto it," Pook coaxed, "then you will know the joy and will again be part of our family."

Regis searched for a way out of the trap. Once before he had used the ruse, the lie within a lie, pretending to be caught under the magical charm's influence. He had worked his act to perfection then, convincing an evil wizard of his loyalty, then turning on the man at a critical moment to aid his friends.

This time, though, Regis had even surprised himself, escaping the ruby pendant's insistent, hypnotizing pull. Now, though, he was caught: A person truly duped by the gem would gladly impale his hand on the barbed spike.

Regis brought his hand above his head and closed his eyes, trying to keep his visage blank enough to carry out the dupe. He swung his arm down, meaning to follow through on Pook's suggestion.

At the last moment, his hand swerved away and banged harmlessly on the table.

Pook roared in rage, suspecting all along that Regis had somehow escaped the pendant's influence. He grabbed the halfling by the wrist and smashed his little hand onto the spike, wiggling it as the spike went through. Regis's scream multiplied tenfold when Pook tore his hand back up the barbed instrument.

Then Pook let him go and slapped him across the face as Regis clutched his wounded hand to his chest.

"Deceiving dog!" the guildmaster shouted, more angry with the pendant's failure than with Regis's façade. He lined up for another slap but calmed himself and decided to twist the halfling's stubborn will back on Regis.

"A pity," he teased, "for if the pendant had brought you back under control, I might have found a place for you in the guild. Surely you deserve to die, little thief, but I have not forgotten your value to me in the past. You were the finest thief in Calimport, a position I might have offered you once again."

"Then no pity for the failure of the gem," Regis dared to retort, guessing the teasing game that Pook was playing, "for no pain outweighs the disgust I would feel at playing lackey to Pasha Pook!"

Pook's response was a heavy slug that knocked Regis off his chair and onto the floor. The halfling lay curled up, trying to stem the blood from both his hand and his nose.

Pook rested back in his chair and clasped his hands behind his head. He looked at the pendant, resting on the table in front of him. Only once before had it failed him, when he had tried it on a will that would not be captured. Luckily, Artemis Entreri had not realized the attempt that day, and Pook had been wise enough not to try the pendant on the assassin again.

Pook shifted his gaze to Regis, now passed out from the pain. He had to give the little halfling credit. Even if Regis's familiarity with the pendant had given him an edge in his battle, only an iron will could resist the tempting pull.

"But it will not help you," Pook whispered at the unconscious form. He sat back in his chair again and closed his eyes, trying to envision still another torture for Regis.

✕ ✕ ✕ ✕ ✕

The tan-robed arm slipped in through the tent's flap and held the limp body of the red-bearded dwarf upside down by the ankle. Sali Dalib's fingers started their customary twiddle, and he flashed the gold-and-ivory smile so wide that it seemed as if it would take in his ears. His little goblin assistant jumped up and down at his side, squealing, "Magic, magic, magic!"

Bruenor opened one eye and lifted an arm to push his long beard out of his face. "Ye be likin' what ye're seeing?" the dwarf asked slyly.

Sali Dalib's smile disappeared, and his fingers got all tangled together.

Bruenor's bearer—Wulfgar, wearing the robe of one of the bandits—walked into the tent. Catti-brie came in behind him.

"So 'twas yerself that set the bandits upon us," the young woman growled.

Sali Dalib's exclamation of shock came out as so much gibberish, and the wily merchant spun away to flee. . . only to find a neat hole sliced into the back of his tent and Drizzt Do'Urden standing within it, leaning on one scimitar while the other rested easily on his shoulder. Just to heighten the merchant's terror, Drizzt had again taken off the magical mask.

"Uh . . . um, de bestest road?" the merchant stammered

"Bestest for yerself and yer friends!" Bruenor growled.

"So they thought," Catti-brie was quick to put in.

Sali Dalib curled his smile sheepishly, but he had been in tight spots a hundred times before and had always weaseled his way out. He lifted his palms, as if to say, "You caught me," but then jerked into a dizzying maneuver, pulling several small ceramic globes out of one of his robe's many pockets. He slammed them to the floor at his feet. Explosions of multicolored light left a thick, blinding smoke in their wake, and the merchant dashed for the side of the tent.

Instinctively Wulfgar dropped Bruenor and jumped ahead, catching an armful of emptiness. The dwarf plopped onto the floor headfirst and rolled to a sitting position, his one-horned helm tilted to the side of his head. As the smoke thinned, the embarrassed barbarian looked back to the dwarf, who just shook his head in disbelief and mumbled, "Suren to be a long adventure."

Only Drizzt, ever alert, had not been caught unawares. The drow had shielded his eyes from the bursts, then watched the smoky silhouette of the merchant darting to the left. Drizzt would have had him before he got out of the hidden flap in the tent, but Sali Dalib's assistant stumbled into the drow's way. Barely slowing, Drizzt slammed Twinkle's hilt into the little goblin's forehead, dropping the creature into unconsciousness, then slipped the mask back on his face and jumped out to the streets of Memnon.

Catti-brie rushed by to follow Drizzt, and Bruenor leaped to his feet. "After 'im, boy!" the dwarf shouted at Wulfgar. The chase was on.

Drizzt caught sight of the merchant slipping into the throng of the streets. Even Sali Dalib's loud robe would blend well in the city's myriad of colors, so Drizzt added a touch of his own. As he had done to the invisible mage on the deck of the pirate ship, the drow sent a purplish glowing outline of dancing flames over the merchant.

Drizzt sped off in pursuit, weaving in and out of the crowd with amazing ease and watching for the bobbing line of purple ahead.

Bruenor was less graceful. The dwarf cut ahead of Catti-brie and plunged headlong into the throng, stomping toes and using his shield to bounce bodies out of his way. Wulfgar, right behind, cut an even wider swath, and Catti-brie had an easy time following in their wake.

They passed a dozen lanes and crashed through an open market, Wulfgar accidentally overturning a cart of huge yellow melons. Shouts of protest erupted behind them as they passed, but they kept their eyes ahead, each watching the person in front and trying not to get lost in the overwhelming bustle.

Sali Dalib knew at once that he was too conspicuous with the fiery outline to ever escape in the open streets. To add to his disadvantage, the eyes and pointing fingers of a hundred curious onlookers greeted him at every turn, signposts for his pursuers. Grabbing at the single chance before him, the merchant cut down one lane and scrambled through the doors of a large stone building.

Drizzt turned to make certain that his friends were still behind, then rushed through the doors, skidding to a stop on the steam-slicked marble floor of a public bathhouse. Two huge eunuchs moved to block the clothed elf, but as with the merchant who had come in just before, the agile Drizzt regained his momentum too quickly to be hindered. He skated through the short entry corridor and into the main room, a large open bath, thick with steam and smelling of sweat and perfumed soaps. Naked bodies crossed his path at every step, and Drizzt had to he careful where he placed his hands as he slipped through.

Bruenor nearly fell as he entered the slippery chamber, and the eunuchs, already out of their positions, got in front of him.

"No clothes!" one of them demanded, but Bruenor had no time for idle discussions. He stamped a heavy boot onto one of the giant's bare feet, then crunched the other foot for good measure. Wulfgar came in then and heaved the remaining eunuch aside.

The barbarian, leaning forward to gain speed, had no chance to stop or turn on the slippery floor, and as Bruenor turned to make his way along the perimeter of the bath, Wulfgar slammed into him, knocking them both to the floor and into a slide they could not brake.

They bounced over the rim of the bath and plunged into the water, Wulfgar coming up, waist deep, between two voluptuous and naked, giggling women.

The barbarian stammered an apology, finding his tongue twisted within the confines of his mouth. A slap across the back of his head shook him back to his senses.

"Ye're looking for the merchant, ye remember?" Catti-brie reminded him.

I am looking!" Wulfgar assured her.

"Then be lookin' for the one lined in purple!" Catti-brie shot back.

Wulfgar, his eyes freed with the expectation of another smack, noticed the single horn of a helmet poking out of the water at his side. Frantically he plunged his hand under, catching Bruenor by the scruff of the neck and hoisting him out of the bath. The not-too-happy dwarf came up with his arms crossed over his chest and shaking his head in disbelief once again.

Drizzt got out the back door of the bathhouse and found himself in an empty alley, the only unpopulated stretch he had seen since entering Memnon. Seeking a better vantage, the drow scaled the side of the bathhouse and jogged along the roof.

Sali Dalib slowed his pace, thinking he had slipped the pursuit. The drow's purple fire died away, further adding to the merchant's sense of security. He wound his way through the back-alley maze. Not even the usual drunks leaned against the walls to inform his pursuers. He moved a hundred twisting yards, then two, and finally down an alley that he knew would turn onto the largest marketplace in Memnon, where anyone could become invisible in the blink of an eye.

As Sali Dalib approached the end of the alley, however, an elven form dropped in front of him and two scimitars flashed out of their sheaths, crossing before the stunned merchant, coming to rest on his collarbones, then drawing lines on either side of his neck.

When the four friends returned to the merchant's tent with their prisoner, they found, to their relief, the little goblin lying where Drizzt had bopped him. Bruenor none too gently pulled the unfortunate creature up behind Sali Dalib and tied the two back to back. Wulfgar moved to help and wound up hooking a loop of the rope over Bruenor's forearm. The dwarf wiggled free and pushed the barbarian away.

"Should've stayed in Mithral Hall," Bruenor grumbled. "Safer with the gray ones than beside yerself and the girl!"

Wulfgar and Catti-brie looked to Drizzt for support, but the drow just smiled and moved to the side of the tent.

"Ha ha ha ha ha," Sali Dalib giggled nervously "No problem here. We deal? Many riches, I have. What you need—"

"Shut yer mouth!" Bruenor snapped at him. The dwarf

winked at Drizzt, indicating that he meant to play the bad guy role in the encounter.

"I don't be lookin' for riches from one what's tricked me," Bruenor growled. "Me heart's for revenge!" He looked around at his friends. "Ye all saw his face when he thought me dead. Suren was him that put the riding bandits on us."

"Sali Dalib never—" the merchant stammered.

"I said, 'Shut yer mouth!' " Bruenor shouted in his face, cowing him. The dwarf brought his axe up and ready on his shoulder.

The merchant looked to Drizzt, confused, for the drow had replaced the mask and now appeared as a surface elf once again. Sali Dalib guessed the truth of Drizzt's identity, figuring the black skin to be more fitting on the deadly elf, and he did not even think of begging for mercy from Drizzt.

"Wait on it, then," Catti-brie said suddenly, grabbing the handle of Bruenor's weapon. "May that there be a way for this dog to save his neck."

"Bah! What would we want o' him?" Bruenor shot back, winking at Catti-brie for playing her part to perfection.

"He'll get us to Calimport," Catti-brie replied. She cast a steely gaze at Sali Dalib, warning him that her mercy was not easily gotten. "Suren this time he'll take us down the true bestest road."

"Yes, yes, ha ha ha ha ha," Sali Dalib blurted. "Sali Dalib show you de way!"

"Show?" balked Wulfgar, not to be left out. "You will lead us all the way to Calimport."

"Very long way," grumbled the merchant. "Five days or more. Sali Dalib cannot—"

Bruenor raised his axe.

"Yes, yes, of course," the merchant erupted. "Sali Dalib take you there. Take you right to de gate . . . through de gate," he corrected quickly. "Sali Dalib even get de water. We must catch de caravan."

"No caravan," Drizzt interrupted, surprising even his friends. "We will travel alone."

"Dangerous," Sali Dalib replied. "Very, very. De Calim Desert be very full of monsters. Dragons and bandits."

"No caravan," Drizzt said again in a tone that none of them dared question. "Untie them, and let them get things ready."

Bruenor nodded, then put his face barely an inch from Sali Dalib's. "And I mean to be watchin' them meself," he said to Drizzt, though he sent the message more pointedly to Sali Dalib and the little goblin. "One trick and I'll cut 'em in half!"

Less than an hour later, five camels moved out of southern Memnon and into the Calim Desert with ceramic water jugs clunking on their sides. Drizzt and Bruenor led the way, following the signposts of the Trade Way. The drow wore his mask, but kept the cowl of his cloak as low as he could, for the sizzling sunlight on the white sands burned at his eyes, which had once been accustomed to the absolute blackness of the underworld.

Sali Dalib, his assistant sitting on the camel in front of him, came in the middle, with Wulfgar and Catti-brie bringing up the rear. Catti-brie kept Taulmaril across her lap, a silver arrow notched as a continual reminder to the sneaky merchant.

The day grew hotter than anything the friends had ever experienced, except for Drizzt, who had lived in the very bowels of the world. Not a cloud hindered the sun's brutal rays, and not a wisp of a breeze came to offer any relief. Sali Dalib, more used to the heat, knew the lack of wind to be a blessing, for wind in the desert meant blowing and blinding sand, the most dangerous killer of the Calim.

The night was better, with the temperature dropping comfortably and a full moon turning the endless line of dunes into a silvery dreamscape, like the rolling waves of the ocean. The friends set a camp for a few hours, taking turns watching over their reluctant guides.

Catti-brie awoke sometime after midnight. She sat and stretched, figuring it to be her turn on watch. She saw Drizzt, standing on the edge of the firelight, staring into the starry heavens.

Hadn't Drizzt taken the first watch? she wondered.

Catti-brie studied the moon's position to make certain of the hour. There could be no doubt; the night grew long.

"Trouble?" she asked softly, going to Drizzt's side. A loud snore from Bruenor answered the question for Drizzt.

"Might I spell ye, then?" she asked. "Even a drow elf needs to sleep."

"I can find my rest under the cowl of my cloak," Drizzt replied, turning to meet her concerned gaze with his lavender eyes, "when the sun is high."

"Might I join ye, then?" Catti-brie asked. "Suren a wondrous night."

Drizzt smiled and turned his gaze back to the heavens, to the allure of the evening sky with a mystical longing in his heart as profound as any surface elf had ever experienced.

Catti-brie slipped her slender fingers around his and stood quietly by his side, not wanting to disturb his enchantment further, sharing more than mere words with her dearest of friends.

✖ ✖ ✖ ✖ ✖

The heat was worse the next day, and even worse the following, but the camels plodded on effortlessly, and the four friends, who had come through so many hardships, accepted the brutal trek as just one more obstacle on the journey they had to complete.

They saw no other signs of life and considered that a blessing, for anything living in that desolate region could only be hostile. The heat was enemy enough, and they felt as if their skin would simply shrivel and crack away.

Whenever one of them felt like quitting, like the relentless sun and burning sand and heat were simply too much to bear, he or she just thought of Regis.

What terrible tortures was the halfling now enduring at the hands of his former master?

EPILOGUE

F rom the shadows of a doorway, Entreri watched Pasha Pook make his way up the staircase to the exit of the guildhouse. It had been less than an hour since Pook had regained his ruby pendant and already he was off to put it to use. Entreri had to give the guildmaster credit; he was never late for the dinner bell.

The assassin waited for Pook to clear the house altogether, then made his way stealthily back to the top level. The guards outside the final door made no move to stop him, though Entreri did not remember them from his earlier days in the guild. Pook must have prudently put out the word of Entreri's station in the guild, according him all the privileges he used to enjoy.

Never late for the dinner bell.

Entreri moved to the door to his old room, where LaValle now resided, and knocked softly.

"Come in, come in," the wizard greeted him, hardly surprised that the assassin had returned.

"It is good to be back," Entreri said.

"And good to have you back," replied the wizard sincerely. "Things have not been the same since you left us, and they have only become worse in recent months."

Entreri understood the wizard's point. "Rassiter?"

LaValle grimaced. "Keep your back to the wall when that one is about." A shudder shook through him, but he composed himself quickly. "But with you back at Pook's side, Rassiter will learn his place."

"Perhaps," replied Entreri, "though I am not so certain that Pook was as glad to see me."

"You understand Pook," LaValle chuckled. "Ever thinking as a guildmaster! He desired to set the rules for your meeting with him to assert his authority. But that incident is far behind us already."

Entreri's look gave the wizard the impression that he was not so certain.

"Pook will forget it," LaValle assured him.

"Those who pursued me should not so easily be forgotten," Entreri replied.

"Pook called upon Pinochet to complete the task," said LaValle. "The pirate has never failed."

"The pirate has never faced such foes," Entreri answered. He looked to the table and LaValle's crystal ball. "We should be certain."

LaValle thought for a moment, then nodded his accord. He had intended to do some scrying anyway. "Watch the ball," he instructed Entreri. "I shall see if I can summon the image of Pinochet."

The crystal ball remained dark for a few moments, then filled with smoke. LaValle had not dealt often with Pinochet, but he knew enough of the pirate for a simple scrying. A few seconds later, the image of a docked ship came into view—not a pirate vessel, but a merchant ship. Immediately Entreri suspected something amiss.

Then the crystal probed deeper, beyond the hull of the ship, and the assassin's guess was confirmed, for in a sectioned corner of the hold sat the proud pirate captain, his elbows on his knees and his head in his hands, shackled to the wall.

LaValle, stunned, looked to Entreri, but the assassin was too intent on the image to offer any explanations. A rare smile had found its way onto Entreri's face.

LaValle cast an enhancing spell at the crystal ball. "Pinochet," he called softly.

The pirate lifted his head and looked around.

"Where are you?" LaValle asked.

"Oberon?" Pinochet asked. "Is that you, wizard?"

"Nay, I am LaValle, Pook's sorcerer in Calimport. Where are you?"

"Memnon," the pirate answered. "Can you get me out?"

"What of the elf and the barbarian?" Entreri asked LaValle, but Pinochet heard the question directly.

"I had them!" the pirate hissed. "Trapped in a channel with no escape. But then a dwarf appeared, driving the reins of a flying chariot of fire, and with him a woman archer—a deadly archer." He paused, fighting off his distaste as he remembered the encounter.

"To what outcome?" LaValle prompted, amazed at the development.

"One ship went running, one ship—my ship—sank, and the third was captured," groaned Pinochet. He locked his face into a grimace and asked again, more emphatically, "Can you get me out?"

LaValle looked helplessly to Entreri, who now stood tall over the crystal hall, absorbing every word. "Where are they?" the assassin growled, his patience worn away.

"Gone," answered Pinochet. "Gone with the girl and the dwarf into Memnon."

"How long?"

"Three days."

Entreri signaled to LaValle that he had heard enough.

"I will have Pasha Pook send word to Memnon immediately," LaValle assured the pirate. "You shall be released."

Pinochet sank into his original, despondent position. Of course he would be released; that had already been arranged. He had hoped that LaValle could somehow magically get him out of the *Sea Sprite*'s hold, thereby releasing him from any pledges he would be forced to make to Deudermont when the captain set him free.

"Three days," LaValle said to Entreri as the crystal darkened. "They could be halfway here by now."

Entreri seemed amused at the notion. "Pasha Pook is to know nothing of this," he said suddenly.

LaValle sank back in his chair. "He must be told."

"No!" Entreri snapped. "This is none of his affair."

"The guild may be in danger," LaValle replied.

"You do not trust that I am capable of handling this?" Entreri asked in a low, grim tone. LaValle felt the assassin's callous eyes looking through him, as though he had suddenly become just another barrier to be overcome.

But Entreri softened his glare and grinned. "You know of Pasha Pook's weakness for hunting cats," he said, reaching into his pouch. "Give him this. Tell him you made it for him." He tossed a small black object across the table to the wizard. LaValle caught it, his eyes widening as soon as he realized what it was.

Guenhwyvar.

✕ ✕ ✕ ✕ ✕

On a distant plane, the great cat stirred at the wizard's touch upon the statuette and wondered if its master meant to summon it, finally, to his side.

But, after a moment, the sensation faded, and the cat put its head down to rest.

So much time had gone by.

✕ ✕ ✕ ✕ ✕

"It holds an entity," the wizard gasped, sensing the strength in the onyx statuette.

"A powerful entity," Entreri assured him. "When you learn to control it, you will have brought a new ally to the guild."

"How can I thank—" LaValle began, but he stopped as he realized that he had already been told the price of the panther. "Why trouble Pook with details that do not concern him?" The wizard laughed, tossing a cloth over his crystal ball.

Entreri clapped LaValle on the shoulder as he passed toward the door. Three years had done nothing to diminish the understanding the two men had shared.

But with Drizzt and his friends approaching, Entreri had more pressing business. He had to go to the Cells of Nine and pay a visit to Regis.

The assassin needed another gift.

PART THREE

I t is like looking into a mirror that paints the world with opposing colors: white hair to black; black skin to white, light eyes to dark. What an intricate

DESERT EMPIRES

mirror it is to replace a smile with a frown, and an expression of friendship with a seemingly perpetual scowl.

For that is how I view Artemis Entreri, this warrior who can compliment every movement I make with similar precision and grace, the warrior who, in every way but one, I would regard as my equal.

How difficult it was for me to stand with him in the depths of Mithral Hall, fighting side by side for both our lives! Strangely, it was not any moral imperative that bothered me about fighting in that situation. It was no belief that Entreri should die, had to die, and that I, if I was not such a coward, would have killed him then and there, even if the action cost me my own life as I tried to escape the inhospitable depths. No, nothing like that.

What made it all so difficult for me was watching that man, that human assassin, and knowing, without the slightest shred of doubt, that I very well might have been looking at myself.

Is that who I would have become had I not found Zaknafein in those early years in Menzoberranzan? Had I not discovered the example of one who so validated my own beliefs that the ways of the drow were not right, morally and practically? Is that cold-hearted killer who I would have become had it been my vicious sister Briza training me instead of the more gentle Vierna?

I fear that it is, that I, despite all that I know to be true within the depths of my very heart, would have been overwhelmed by the situation about me, would have succumbed to the despair to a point where there remained little of compassion and justice. I would have become an assassin, holding strong within my own code of ethics, but with that code so horribly warped that I could no longer understand the truth of my actions, that I could justify them with the sheerest cynicism.

I saw all of that when I looked upon Entreri, and thanked Mielikki profoundly for those in my life, for Zaknafein, for Belwar Dissengulp and for Montolio, who helped me to steer the correct course. And if I saw a potential for myself within Entreri, then I must admit that there once was a potential for Entreri to become as I have become, to know compassion and community, to know friends, good friends, and to know love.

I think about him a lot, as he, no doubt, thinks about me. While his obsession is based in pride, in the challenge of overcoming me in battle, mine own is wrought of curiosity, of seeking answers within myself by observing the actions of who I might have become.

Do I hate him?

Strangely, I do not. That lack of hatred is not based on the respect that I give the man for his fighting prowess, for that measure of respect ends right there, at the edge of the battlefield. No, I do not hate Artemis Entreri because I pity him, the events that led to the wrong decisions he has made. There is true strength within him, and there is, or once was, a substantial potential to do good in a world so in need of heroes. For, despite his actions, I have come to understand that Entreri operates within a very strict code. In his own warped view of the world, I believe that Entreri honestly believes that he never killed anyone who did not deserve it. He held Catti-brie captive but did not rape her.

As for his actions concerning Regis . . . well, Regis was, in reality, a thief, and though he stole from another thief that does not excuse that crime. In Luskan, as in most cities in the Realms, thieves lose their hands, or worse, and certainly a bounty hunter sent to retrieve a stolen item, and the person who stole it, is well within the law to kill that person, and anyone else who hinders his task.

In Calimport, Artemis Entreri operates among thieves and thugs, among the very edge of civilization. In that capacity, he deals death, as did Zaknafein in the alleys of Menzoberranzan. There is a difference—certainly!—between the two, and I do not in any way mean to excuse Entreri from his crimes. Neither will I consider him the simple killing monster that was, say, Errtu.

No, there was once potential there, I

know, though I fear he is far gone from that road, for when I look upon Artemis Entreri, I see myself, I see the capacity to love, and also the capacity to lose all of that and become cold.

So very cold.

Perhaps we will meet again and do battle, and if I kill him, I will shed no tears for him. Not for who he is, at least, but quite possibly, I will cry for who this marvelous warrior might have become.

If I kill him, I will be crying for myself.

—Drizzt Do'Urden

16
NEVER A FOULER PLACE

E ntreri slipped through the shadows of Calimport's bowels as quietly as an owl glided through a forest at twilight. This was his home, the place he knew best, and all the street people of the city would mark the day when Artemis Entreri again walked beside them—or behind them.

Entreri couldn't help but smile slightly whenever the hushed whispers commenced in his wake—the more experienced rogues telling the newcomers that the king had returned. Entreri never let the legend of his reputation—no matter how well earned—interfere with the constant state of readiness that had kept him alive through the years. In the streets, a reputation of power only marked a man as a target for ambitious second-rates seeking, reputations of their own.

Thus, Entreri's first task in the city, outside of his responsibilities to Pasha Pook, was to reestablish the network of informants and associates that entrenched him in his station.

He already had an important job for one of them, with Drizzt and company fast approaching, and he knew which one.

"I had heard you were back," squeaked a diminutive chap appearing as a human boy not yet into adolescence when Entreri ducked and entered his abode. "I guess most have."

Entreri took the compliment with a nod. "What has changed, my halfling friend?"

"Little," replied Dondon, "and lots." He moved to the table in the darkest corner of his small quarters, the side room, facing the ally, in a cheap inn called the Coiled Snake. "The rules of the street do not change, but the players do." Dondon looked up from the table's unlit lamp to catch Entreri's eyes with his own.

"Artemis Entreri was gone, after all," the halfling explained, wanting to make sure that Entreri fully understood his previous statement. "The royal suite had a vacancy."

Entreri nodded his accord, causing the halfling to relax and sigh audibly.

"Pook still controls the merchants and the docks," said Entreri. "Who owns the streets?"

"Pook, still," replied Dondon, "at least in name. He found another agent in your stead. A whole horde of agents." Dondon paused for a moment to think. Again he had to be careful to weigh every word before he spoke it. "Perhaps it would be more accurate to say that Pasha Pook does not control the streets, but rather that he still has the streets controlled."

Entreri knew, even before asking, what the little halfling was leading to. "Rassiter," he said grimly.

"There is much to be said about that one and his crew," Dondon chuckled, resuming his efforts to light the lantern.

"Pook loosens his reins on the wererats, and the ruffians of the street take care to stay out of the guild's way," Entreri reasoned.

"Rassiter and his kind play hard."

"And fall hard."

The chill of Entreri's tone brought Dondon's eyes back up from the lantern, and for the first time, the halfling truly recognized the old Artemis Entreri, the human street fighter who had built his shadowy empire one ally at a time. An involuntary shudder rippled up Dondon's spine, and he shifted uncomfortably on his feet.

Entreri saw the effect and quickly switched the subject. "Enough of this," he said. "Let it not concern you, little one. I have a job for you that is more in line with your talents."

Dondon finally got the lantern's wick to take, and he pulled up a chair, eager to please his old boss.

They talked for more than an hour, until the lantern became a solitary defense against the insistent blackness of the night. Then Entreri took his leave, through the window and into the ally. He didn't believe that Rassiter would be so foolish as to strike before taking full measure of the assassin, before the wererat could even begin to understand the dimensions of his enemy.

Then again, Entreri didn't mark Rassiter high on any intelligence scale.

Perhaps it was Entreri, though, who didn't truly understand his enemy, or how completely Rassiter and his wretched minions had come to dominate the streets over the last three years. Less than five minutes after Entreri had gone, Dondon's door swung open again.

And Rassiter stepped through.

"What did he want?" the swaggering fighter asked, plopping comfortably into a chair at the table.

Dondon moved away uneasily, noticing two more of Rassiter's cronies standing guard in the hall. After more than a year, the halfling still felt uncomfortable around Rassiter.

"Come, come now," Rassiter prompted. He asked again, his tone more grim, "What did he want?"

The last thing Dondon wanted was to get caught in a crossfire between the wererats and the assassin, but he had little choice but to answer Rassiter. If Entreri ever learned of the double-cross, Dondon knew that his days would swiftly end.

Yet, if he didn't spill out to Rassiter, his demise would be no less certain, and the method less swift.

He sighed at the lack of options and spilled his story, detail by detail, to Rassiter.

Rassiter gave no countermand to Entreri's instructions. He would let Dondon play out the scenario exactly as Entreri had devised it. Apparently, the wererat believed he could twist it into his own gains. He sat quietly for a long moment, scratching his hairless chin and savoring the anticipation of the easy victory, his broken teeth gleaming even a deeper yellow in the lamplight.

"You will run with us this night?" he asked the halfling, satisfied that the assassin business was completed. "The moon will be bright." He squeezed one of Dondon's cherublike cheeks. "The fur will be thick, eh?"

Dondon pulled away from the grasp. "Not this night," he replied, a bit too sharply.

Rassiter cocked his head, studying Dondon curiously. He always had suspected that the halfling was not comfortable with his new station. Might this defiance be linked to the return of his old boss? Rassiter wondered.

"Tease him and die," Dondon replied, drawing an even more curious look from the wererat.

"You have not begun to understand this man you face," Dondon continued, unshaken. "Artemis Entreri is not to be toyed with—not by the wise. He knows everything. If a half-sized rat is seen running with the pack, then my life is forfeit and your plans are ruined." He moved right up, in spite of his revulsion for the man, and set a grave visage barely an inch from Rassiter's nose.

"Forfeit," he reiterated, "at the least."

Rassiter spun out of the chair, sending it bouncing across the room. He had heard too much about Artemis Entreri in a single day for his liking. Everywhere he turned, trembling lips uttered the assassin's name.

Don't they know? he told himself once again as he strode angrily to the door. It is Rassiter they should fear!

He felt the telltale itching on his chin, then the crawling sensation of tingling growth swept through his body. Dondon backed away and averted his eyes, never comfortable with the spectacle.

Rassiter kicked off his boots and loosened his shirt and pants. The hair was visible now, rushing out of his skin in scraggly patches and clumps. He fell back against the wall as the fever took him completely. His skin bubbled and bulged, particularly around his face. He sublimated his scream as his snout elongated, though the wash of agony was no less intense this time—perhaps the thousandth time—than it had been during his very first transformation.

He stood then before Dondon on two legs, as a man, but whiskered and furred and with a long pink tail that ran out the back of his trousers, as a rodent.

"Join me?" he asked the halfling.

Hiding his revulsion, Dondon quickly declined. Looking at the ratman, the halfling wondered how he had ever allowed Rassiter to bite him, infecting him with his lycanthropic nightmare. "It will bring you power!" Rassiter had promised.

But at what cost? Dondon thought. To look and smell like a rat? No blessing this, but a disease.

Rassiter guessed at the halfling's distaste, and he curled his rat snout back in a threatening hiss, then turned for the door.

He spun back on Dondon before exiting the room. "Keep away from this!" he warned the halfling. "Do as you were bid and hide away!"

"No doubt to that," Dondon whispered as the door slammed shut.

⚔ ⚔ ⚔ ⚔ ⚔

The aura that distinguished Calimport as home to so very many Calishites came across as foul to the strangers from the North. Truly, Drizzt, Wulfgar, Bruenor, and Catti-brie were weary of the Calim Desert when their five-day trek came to an end, but looking down on the city of Calimport made them want to turn around and take to the sands once again.

It was wretched Memnon on a grander scale, with the divisions of wealth so blatantly obvious that Calimport cried out as ultimately perverted to the four friends. Elaborate houses, monuments to excess and hinting at wealth beyond imagination, dotted the cityscape. Yet, right beside those palaces loomed lane after lane of decrepit shanties of crumbling clay or ragged skins. The friends couldn't guess how many people roamed the place—certainly more than Waterdeep and Memnon combined!—and they knew at once that in Calimport, as in Memnon, no one had ever bothered to count.

Sali Dalib dismounted, bidding the others do likewise, and led them down a final hill and into the unwalled city. The friends found the sights of Calimport no better up close. Naked children, their bellies bloated from lack of food, scrambled out of the way or were simply trampled as gilded, slave-drawn carts rushed through the streets. Worse still were the sides of those avenues, ditches mostly, serving as open sewers in the city's poorest sections. There were thrown the bodies of the impoverished, who had fallen to the roadside at the end of their miserable days.

"Suren Rumblebelly never told of such sights when he spoke of home," Bruenor grumbled, pulling his cloak over his face to deflect the awful stench. "Past me guessing why he'd long for this place!"

"De greatest city in de world, dis be!" Sali Dalib spouted, lifting his arms to enhance his praise.

Wulfgar, Bruenor, and Catti-brie shot him incredulous stares. Hordes of people begging and starving was not their idea of greatness. Drizzt paid the merchant no heed, though. He was busy making the inevitable comparison between Calimport and another city he had known, Menzoberranzan. Truly there were similarities, and death was no less common in Menzoberranzan, but Calimport somehow seemed fouler than the city of the drow. Even the weakest of the dark elves had the means to protect himself, with strong family ties and deadly innate abilities. The pitiful peasants of Calimport, though, and more so their children, seemed helpless and hopeless indeed.

In Menzoberranzan, those on the lowest rungs of the power ladder could fight their way to a better standing. For the majority of Calimport's multitude, though, there would only be poverty, a day-to-day squalid existence until they landed on the piles of buzzard-pecked bodies in the ditches.

"Take us to the guildhouse of Pasha Pook," Drizzt said, getting to the point, wanting to be done with his business and out of Calimport, "then you are dismissed."

Sali Dalib paled at the request. "Pasha Poop?" he stammered. "Who is dis?"

"Bah!" Bruenor snorted, moving dangerously close to the merchant. "He knows him."

"Suren he does," Catti-brie observed, "and fears him."

"Sali Dalib not—" the merchant began.

Twinkle came out of its sheath and slipped to a stop under the merchant's chin, silencing the man instantly. Drizzt let his mask slip a bit, reminding Sali Dalib of the drow's heritage. Once again, his suddenly grim demeanor unnerved even his own friends. "I think of my friend," Drizzt said in a calm, low tone, his lavender eyes absently staring into the city, "tortured even as we delay."

He snapped his scowl at Sali Dalib. "As you delay! You will take us to the guildhouse of Pasha Pook," he reiterated, more insistently, "and then you are dismissed."

"Pook? Oh, Pook," the merchant beamed. "Sali Dalib know dis man, yes, yes. Everybody know Pook. Yes, yes, I take you dere, den I go."

Drizzt replaced the mask but kept the stern visage. "If you or your little companion try to flee," he promised so calmly that neither the merchant nor his assistant doubted his words for a moment, "I will hunt you down and kill you."

The drow's three friends exchanged confused shrugs and concerned glances. They felt confident that they knew Drizzt to his soul, but so grim was his tone that even they wondered how much of his promise was an idle threat.

⚔ ⚔ ⚔ ⚔ ⚔

It took more than an hour for them to twist and wind their way through the maze that was Calimport, to the dismay of the friends, who wanted nothing more than to be off the streets and away from the fetid stench. Finally, to their relief, Sali Dalib turned a final corner, to Rogues Circle, and pointed to the unremarkable wooden structure at its end: Pasha Pook's guildhouse.

"Dere be de Pook," Sali Dalib said. "Now, Sali Dalib take his camels and be gone, back to Memnon."

The friends were not so quick to be rid of the wily merchant. "More to me guessin' that Sali Dalib be heading for Pook to sell some tales o' four friends," Bruenor growled.

"Well, we've a way beyond that," said Catti-brie. She shot Drizzt a sly wink, then moved up to the curious and frightened merchant, reaching into her pack as she went.

Her look went suddenly grim, so wickedly intense that Sali Dalib jerked back when her hand came up to his forehead. "Hold yer place!" Catti-brie snapped at him harshly, and he had no resistance to the power of her tone. She had a powder, a flourlike substance, in her pack. Reciting some gibberish that sounded like an arcane chant, she traced a scimitar on Sali Dalib's forehead. The merchant tried to protest but couldn't find his tongue for his terror.

"Now for the little one," Catti-brie said, turning to Sali Dalib's goblin assistant. The goblin squeaked and tried to dash away, but Wulfgar caught it in one hand and held it out to Catti-brie, squeezing tighter and tighter until the thing stopped wiggling.

Catti-brie performed the ceremony again then turned to Drizzt. "They be linked to yer spirit now," she said. "Do ye feel them?"

Drizzt, understanding the bluff, nodded grimly and slowly drew his two scimitars.

Sali Dalib paled and nearly toppled over, but Bruenor, moving closer to watch his daughter's games, was quick to prop the terrified man up.

"Ah, let them go, then. Me witchin's through," Catti-brie told both Wulfgar and Bruenor. "The drow'll feel yer presence now," she hissed at Sali Dalib and his goblin. "He'll know when ye're about and when ye've gone. If ye stay in the city, and if ye've thoughts o' going to Pook, the drow'll know, and he'll follow yer feel—hunt ye down." She paused a moment, wanting the two to fully comprehend the horror they faced.

"And he'll kill ye slow."

"Take yer lumpy horses, then, and be gone!" Bruenor roared. "If I be seein' yer stinkin' faces again, the drow'll have to get in line for his cuts!"

Before the dwarf had even finished, Sali Dalib and the goblin had collected their camels and were off, away from Rogues Circle and back toward the northern end of the city.

"Them two're for the desert," Bruenor laughed when they had gone. "Fine tricks, me girl."

Drizzt pointed to the sign of an inn, the Spitting Camel, half-way down the lane. "Get us rooms," he told his friends. "I will follow them to make certain they do indeed leave the city."

"Wastin' yer time," Bruenor called after him. "The girl's got 'em running, or I'm a bearded gnome!"

Drizzt had already started padding silently into the maze of Calimport's streets.

Wulfgar, caught unawares by her uncharacteristic trickery and still not quite sure what had just happened, eyed Catti-brie carefully. Bruenor didn't miss his apprehensive look.

"Take note, boy," the dwarf taunted. "Suren the girl's got herself a nasty streak ye'll not want turned on yerself!"

Playing through for the sake of Bruenor's enjoyment, Catti-brie glared at the big barbarian and narrowed her eyes, causing Wulfgar to back off a cautious step. "Witchin' magic," she cackled. "Tells me when yer eyes be filled with the likings of another woman!" She turned slowly, not releasing him from her stare until she had taken three steps down the lane toward the inn Drizzt had indicated.

Bruenor reached high and slapped Wulfgar on the back as he started after Catti-brie. "Fine lass," he remarked to Wulfgar. "Just don't be gettin' her mad!"

Wulfgar shook the confusion out of his head and forced out a laugh, reminding himself that Catti-brie's "magic" had been only a dupe to frighten the merchant.

But Catti-brie's glare as she had carried out the deception, and the sheer strength of her intensity, followed him as he walked down Rogues Circle. Both a shudder and a sweet tingle spread down his spine.

✖ ✖ ✖ ✖ ✖

Half the sun had fallen below the western horizon before Drizzt returned to Rogues Circle. He had followed Sali Dalib and his assistant far out into the Calim Desert, though the merchant's frantic pace gave no indications that he had any intentions of turning back to Calimport. Drizzt simply wouldn't take the chance; they were too close to finding Regis and too close to Entreri.

Masked as an elf—Drizzt was beginning to realize how easily the disguise now came to him—he made his way into the Spitting Camel and to the innkeeper's desk. An incredibly skinny, leather-skinned man, who kept his back always to a wall and his head darting nervously in every direction, met him.

"Three friends," Drizzt said gruffly. "A dwarf, a woman, and a golden-haired giant."

"Up the stairs," the man told him. "To the left. Two gold if you mean to stay the night." He held out his bony hand.

"The dwarf already paid you," Drizzt said grimly, starting away.

"For himself, the girl, and the big the innkeeper started,

grabbing Drizzt by the shoulder. The look in Drizzt's lavender eyes, though, stopped the innkeeper cold.

"He paid," the frightened man stuttered. "I remember. He paid."

Drizzt walked away without another word.

He found the two rooms on opposite sides of the corridor at the far end of the structure. He had meant to go straight in with Wulfgar and Bruenor and grab a short rest, hoping to be out on the street when night fully fell, when Entreri would likely be about. Drizzt found, instead, Catti-brie in her doorway, apparently waiting for him. She motioned him into her chamber and closed the door behind him.

Drizzt settled on the very edge of one of the two chairs in the center of the room, his foot tapping the floor in front of him.

Catti-brie studied him as she walked around to the other chair. She had known Drizzt for years but never had seen him so agitated.

"Ye seem as though ye mean to tear yerself into pieces," she said.

Drizzt gave her a cold look, but Catti-brie laughed it away. "Do ye mean to strike me, then?"

That prompted the drow to settle back in his chair.

"And don't ye be wearing that silly mask," Catti-brie scolded.

Drizzt reached for the mask but hesitated.

"Take it off!" Catti-brie ordered, and the drow complied before he had time to reconsider

"Ye came a bit grim in the street afore ye left," Catti-brie remarked, her voice softening.

"We had to make certain," Drizzt replied coldly. I do not trust Sali Dalib."

"Nor meself," Catti-brie agreed, "but ye're still grim, by me seeing."

"You were the one with the witching magic," Drizzt shotback, his tone defensive. "It was Catti-brie who showed herself grim then."

Catti-brie shrugged. "A needed act," she said. "An act I dropped when the merchant had gone. But yerself," she said pointedly, leaning forward and placing a comforting hand on Drizzt's knee. "Ye're up for a fight."

Drizzt started to jerk away but realized the truth of her observations and forced himself to relax under her friendly touch. He looked away, for he found that he could not soften the sternness of his visage.

"What's it about?" Catti-brie whispered.

Drizzt looked back to her then and remembered all the times he and she had shared back in Icewind Dale. In her sincere concern for him now, Drizzt recalled the first time they had met, when the smile of the girl—for she was then but a girl—had given the displaced and disheartened drow a renewed hope for his life among the surface dwellers.

Catti-brie knew more about him than anyone alive, about those things that were important to him, and made his stoic existence bearable. She alone recognized the fears that lay beneath his black skin, the insecurity masked by the skill of his sword arm.

"Entreri," he answered softly.

"Ye mean to kill him?"

"I have to."

Catti-brie sat back to consider the words. "If ye be killing Entreri to free Regis," she said at length, "and to stop him from hurting anyone else, then me heart says it's a good thing." She leaned forward again, bringing her face close to Drizzt's, "but if ye're meaning to kill him to prove yerself or to deny what he is, then me heart cries."

She could have slapped Drizzt and had the same effect. He sat up straight and cocked his head, his features twisted in angry denial. He let Catti-brie continue but he could not dismiss the importance of the observant woman's perceptions.

"Suren the world's not fair, me friend. Suren by the measure of hearts, ye been wronged. But are ye after the assassin for yer own anger? Will killing Entreri cure the wrong?

Drizzt did not answer, but his look turned stubbornly grim again.

"Look in the mirror, Drizzt Do'Urden," Catti-brie said, "without the mask. Killin' Entreri won't change the color of his skin—or the color of yer own."

Again Drizzt had been slapped, and this time it brought an undeniable ring of truth with it. He fell back in his chair, looking upon Catti-brie as he had never looked upon her before. Where had Bruenor's little girl gone? Before him loomed a woman, beautiful and sensitive and laying bare his soul with a few words. They had shared much, it was true, but how could she know him so very well? And why had she taken the time?

"Ye've truer friends than ever ye'll know," Catti-brie said, "and not for the way ye twirl a sword. Ye've others who would call themselves friend if only they could get inside the length of yer arm—if only ye'd learn to look."

Drizzt considered the words. He remembered the *Sea Sprite* and Captain Deudermont and the crew, standing behind him even when they knew his heritage.

"And if only ye'd ever learned to love," Catti-brie continued, her voice barely audible. "Suren ye've let things slip past, Drizzt Do'Urden."

Drizzt studied her intently, weighing the glimmer in her dark, saucerlike eyes. He tried to fathom what she was getting at, what personal message she was sending to him.

The door burst open suddenly, and Wulfgar bounded into the room, a smile stretching the length of his face and the eager look of adventure gleaming in his pale blue eyes. "Good that you are back," he said to Drizzt. He moved behind Catti-brie and dropped an arm comfortably across her shoulders. "The night has come, and a bright moon peeks over the eastern rim. Time for the hunt!"

Catti-brie put her hand on Wulfgar's and flashed him an adoring smile. Drizzt was glad they had found each other. They would grow together in a blessed and joyful life, rearing children that would no doubt be the envy of all the northland.

Catti-brie looked back to Drizzt. "Just for yer thoughts, me friend," she said quietly, calmly. "Are ye more trapped by the way the world sees ye or by the way ye see the world seein' ye?"

The tension eased out of Drizzt's muscles. If Catti-brie was right in her observations, he would have a lot of thinking to do.

"Time to hunt!" Catti-brie cried, satisfied that she had gotten her point across. She rose beside Wulfgar and headed for the door, but she turned her head over her shoulder to face Drizzt one final time, giving him a look that told him that perhaps he should have asked for more from Catti-brie back in Icewind Dale, before Wulfgar had entered her life.

Drizzt sighed as they left the room and instinctively reached for the magical mask.

Instinctively? he wondered.

Drizzt dropped the thing suddenly and fell back in the chair in thought, clasping his hands behind his head. He glanced around, hoping, but the room had no mirror.

17
IMPOSSIBLE LOYALTIES

LaValle held his hand within the pouch for a long moment, teasing Pook. They were alone with the eunuchs, who didn't count, in the central chamber of the top level. LaValle had promised his master a gift beyond even the news of the ruby pendant's return, and Pook knew that the wizard would offer such a promise with great care. It was not wise to disappoint the guildmaster.

LaValle had great confidence in his gift and had no trepidations about his grand claims. He slid it out and presented it to Pook, smiling broadly as he did so.

Pook lost his breath, and sweat thickened on his palms at the onyx statuette's touch. "Magnificent," he muttered, overwhelmed. "Never have I seen such craftsmanship, such detail. One could almost pet the thing!"

"One can," LaValle whispered under his breath. The wizard did not want to let on to all of the gift's properties at once, however, so he replied, "I am pleased that you are pleased."

"Where did you get it?"

LaValle shifted uneasily. "That is not important," he answered. "It is for you, Master, given with all of my loyalty." He quickly moved the conversation along to prevent Pook from pressing the point. "The workmanship of the statuette is but a fraction of its value," he teased, drawing a curious look from Pook.

"You have heard of such figurines," LaValle went on, satisfied that the time to overwhelm the guildmaster had come once again. "They can be magical companions to their owners."

Pook's hands verily trembled at the thought. "This," he stammered excitedly, "this might bring the panther to life?"

LaValle's sly smile answered the question.

"How? When might I—"

"Whenever you desire," LaValle answered.

"Should we prepare a cage?" Pook asked.

"No need."

"But at least until the panther understands who its master—"

"You possess the figurine," LaValle interrupted. "The creature you summon is wholly yours. It will follow your every command exactly as you desire."

Pook clutched the statuette close to his chest. He could hardly believe his fortune. The great cats were his first and foremost love, and to have in his possession one with such obedience, an extension of his own will, thrilled him as he had never been thrilled before.

"Now," he said. "I want to call the cat now. Tell me the words."

LaValle took the statue and placed it on the floor, then whispered into Pook's ear, taking care that his own uttering of the cat's name didn't summon Guenhwyvar and ruin the moment for Pook.

"Guenhwyvar," Pook called softly. Nothing happened at first, but both Pook and LaValle could sense the link being completed to the distant entity.

"Come to me, Guenhwyvar!" Pook commanded.

His voice rolled through the tunnel gate in the Planes of existence, down the dark corridor to the Astral Plane, the home of the entity of the panther. Guenhwyvar awakened to the summons. Cautiously the cat found the path.

"Guenhwyvar," the call came again, but the cat did not recognize the voice. It had been many tendays since its master had brought it to the Prime Material Plane, and the panther had had a well-deserved and much-needed rest, but one that had brought with it a cautious trepidation. Now, with an unknown voice summoning it, Guenhwyvar understood that something had definitely changed.

Tentatively, but unable to resist the summons, the great cat padded off down the corridor.

Pook and LaValle watched, mesmerized, as a gray smoke appeared, shrouding the floor around the figurine. It swirled lazily for a few moments then took definite shape, solidifying into Guenhwyvar. The cat stood perfectly still, seeking some recognition of its surroundings.

"What do I do?" Pook asked LaValle. The cat tensed at the sound of the voice—its master's voice.

"Whatever pleases you," LaValle answered. "The cat will sit by you, hunt for you, walk at your heel—kill for you."

Some ideas popped into the guildmaster's head at the last comment. "What are its limits?"

LaValle shrugged. "Most magic of this kind will fade after a length of time, though you can summon the cat again once it has rested," he quickly added, seeing Pook's disheartened look. "It cannot be killed; to do so would only return it to its

plane, though the statue could be broken."

Again Pook's look soured. The item had already become too precious for him to consider losing it.

"I assure you that destroying the statue would not prove an easy task," LaValle continued. "Its magic is quite potent. The mightiest smith in all the Realms could not scratch it with his heaviest hammer!"

Pook was satisfied. "Come to me," he ordered the cat, extending his hand.

Guenhwyvar obeyed and flattened its ears as Pook gently stroked the soft black coat.

"I have a task," Pook announced suddenly, turning an excited glance at LaValle, "a memorable and marvelous task! The first task for Guenhwyvar."

LaValle's eyes lit up at the pure pleasure stamped across Pook's face.

"Fetch me Regis," Pook told LaValle. "Let Guenhwyvar's first kill be the halfling I most despise!"

⚔ ⚔ ⚔ ⚔ ⚔

Exhausted from his ordeal in the Cells of Nine, and from the various tortures Pook had put him through, Regis was easily shoved flat to his face before Pook's throne. The halfling struggled to his feet, determined to accept the next torture—even if it meant death—with dignity.

Pook waved the guards out of the room. "Have you enoyed your stay with us?" he teased Regis.

Regis brushed the mop of hair back from his face. "Acceptable," he replied. "The neighbors are noisy, though, growling and purring all the night through."

"Silence!" Pook snapped He looked at LaValle, standing

beside the great chair. "He will find little humor here," the guildmaster said with a venomous chuckle.

Regis had passed beyond fear, though, into resignation. "You have won," he said calmly, hoping to steal some of the pleasure from Pook. "I took your pendant and was caught. If you believe that crime is deserving of death, then kill me."

"Oh, I shall!" Pook hissed. "I had planned that from the start, but I knew not the appropriate method."

Regis rocked back on his heels. Perhaps he wasn't as composed as he had hoped.

"Guenhwyvar," Pook called.

"Guenhwyvar?" Regis echoed under his breath.

"Come to me, my pet."

The halfling's jaw dropped to his chest when the magical cat slipped out of the half-opened door to LaValle's room.

"Wh-where did you get him?" Regis stuttered.

"Magnificent, is he not?" Pook replied. "But do not worry, little thief. You shall get a closer look." He turned to the cat.

"Guenhwyvar, dear Guenhwyvar," Pook purred, "this little thief wronged your master. Kill him, my pet, but kill him slowly. I want to hear his screams."

Regis stared into the panther's wide eyes. "Calm, Guenhwyvar," he said as the cat took a slow, hesitant stride his way. Truly it pained Regis to see the wondrous panther under the command of one as vile as Pook. Guenhwyvar belonged with Drizzt.

But Regis couldn't spend much time considering the implications of the cat's appearance. His own future became his primary concern.

"He is the one," Regis cried to Guenhwyvar, pointing at Pook. "He commands the evil one who took us from your true master, the evil one your true master seeks!"

"Excellent!" Pook laughed, thinking Regis to be grasping at

a desperate lie to confuse the animal. "This show may yet be worth the agony I have endured at your hands, thief Regis!

LaValle shifted uneasily, understanding more of the truth to Regis's words.

"Now, my pet!" Pook commanded. "Bring him pain!"

Guenhwyvar growled lowly, eyes narrowed.

"Guenhwyvar," Regis said again, backing away a step. "Guenhwyvar, you know me."

The cat showed no indication that it recognized the halfling. Compelled by its master's voice, it crouched and inched across the floor toward Regis.

"Guenhwyvar!" Regis cried, feeling along the wall for an escape.

"That is the cat's name," Pook laughed, still not realizing the halfling's honest recognition of the beast. "Good-bye, Regis. Take comfort in knowing that I shall remember this moment for the rest of my life!"

The panther flattened its ears and crouched lower, tamping down its back paws for better balance. Regis rushed to the door, though he had no doubt that it was locked, and Guenhwyvar leaped, impossibly quick and accurate. Regis barely realized that the cat was upon him.

Pasha Pook's ecstasy, though, proved short-lived. He jumped from his chair, hoping for a better view of the action, as Guenhwyvar buried Regis. Then the cat vanished, slowly fading away.

The halfling, too, was gone.

"What?" Pook cried. "That is it? No blood?" He spun on LaValle. "Is that how the thing kills?"

The wizard's horrified expression told Pook a different tale. Suddenly the guildmaster recognized the truth of Regis's banterings with the cat. "It took him away!" Pook roared. He rushed around the side of the chair and pushed his face into LaValle's. "Where? Tell me!"

LaValle nearly fell from his trembling. "Not possible." He gasped. "The cat must obey its master, the possessor."

"Regis knew the cat!" Pook cried.

"Impossible loyalties," LaValle replied, truly dumbfounded.

Pook composed himself and settled back in his chair. "Where did you get it?" he asked LaValle.

"Entreri," the wizard replied immediately, not daring to hesitate.

Pook scratched his chin. "Entreri," he echoed. The pieces started falling into place. Pook understood Entreri well enough to know that the assassin would not give away so valuable an item without getting something in return. "It belonged to one of the halfling's friends," Pook reasoned, remembering Regis's references to the cat's true master.

"I did not ask," replied LaValle.

"You did not have to ask!" Pook shot back. "It belonged to one of the halfling's friends—perhaps one of those Oberon spoke of. Yes. And Entreri gave it to you in exchange for . . ." He tossed a wicked look LaValle's way.

"Where is the pirate, Pinochet?" he asked slyly.

LaValle nearly fainted, caught in a web that promised death wherever he turned.

"Enough said," said Pook, understanding everything from the wizard's paled expression "Ah, Entreri," he mused, "ever you prove a headache, however well you serve me. And you," he breathed at LaValle. "Where have they gone?"

LaValle shook his head. "The cat's plane," he blurted, "the only possibility."

"And can the cat return to this world?"

"Only if summoned by the possessor of the statue."

Pook pointed to the statue lying on the floor in front of the door. "Get that cat back," he ordered. LaValle rushed for the figurine.

"No, wait." Pook reconsidered. "Let me first have a cage built for it. Guenhwyvar will be mine in time. She will learn discipline."

LaValle continued over and picked up the statue, not really knowing where to begin. Pook grabbed him as he passed the throne.

"But the halfling," Pook growled, pressing his nose flat against LaValle's. "On your life, wizard, get that halfling back to me!"

Pook shoved LaValle back and headed for the door to the lower levels. He would have to open some eyes in the streets, to learn what Artemis Entreri was up to and to learn more about those friends of the halfling, whether they still lived or had died in Asavir's Channel.

If it had been anyone other than Entreri, Pook would have put his ruby pendant to use, but that option was not feasible with the dangerous assassin.

Pook growled to himself as he exited the chamber. He had hoped, on Entreri's return, that he would never have to take this route again, but with LaValle so obviously tied into the assassin's games, Pook's only option was Rassiter.

✕ ✕ ✕ ✕ ✕

"You want him removed?" the wererat asked, liking the beginnings of this assignment as well as any that Pook had ever given him.

"Do not flatter yourself," Pook shot back. "Entreri is none of your affair, Rassiter, and beyond your power."

"You underestimate the strength of my guild."

"You underestimate the assassin's network—probably

numbering many of those you errantly call comrades," Pook warned. "I want no war within my guild."

"Then what?" the wererat snapped in obvious disappointment.

At Rassiter's antagonistic tone, Pook began to finger the ruby pendant hanging around his neck. He could put Rassiter under its enchantment, he knew, but he preferred not to. Charmed individuals never performed as well as those acting of their own desires, and if Regis's friends had truly escaped Pinochet, Rassiter and his cronies would have to be at their very best to defeat them.

"Entreri may have been followed to Calimport," Pook explained. "Friends of the halfling, I believe, and dangerous to our guild."

Rassiter leaned forward, feigning surprise. Of course, the wererat had already learned from Dondon of the Northerners' approach.

"They will be in the city soon," Pook continued. "You haven't much time."

They are already here, Rassiter answered silently, trying to hide his smile. "You want them captured?"

"Eliminated," Pook corrected. "This group is too mighty. No chances."

"Eliminated," Rassiter echoed. "Ever my preference."

Pook couldn't help but shudder. "Inform me when the task is complete," he said, heading for the door.

Rassiter silently laughed at his master's back. "Ah, Pook," he whispered as the guildmaster left, "how little you know of my influences." The wererat rubbed his hands together in anticipation. The night grew long, and the Northerners would soon be on the streets—where Dondon would find them.

18
DOUBLE TALKER

Perched in his favorite corner, across Rogues Circle from the Spitting Camel, Dondon watched as the elf, the last of the four, moved into the inn to join his friends. The halfling pulled out a little pocket mirror to check his disguise—all the dirt and scruff marks seemed in the right places; his clothes were far too large, like those a waif would pull off an unconscious drunk in an ally; and his hair was appropriately tousled and snarled, as if it hadn't been combed in years.

Dondon looked longingly to the moon and inspected his chin with his fingers. Still hairless but tingling, he thought. The halfling took a deep breath, and then another, and fought back the lycanthropic urges. In the year he had joined Rassiter's ranks, he had learned to sublimate those fiendish urges fairly well, but he hoped that he could finish his business quickly this night. The moon was especially bright.

People of the street, locals, gave an approving wink as they passed the halfling, knowing the master con artist to be on the prowl once more. With his reputation, Dondon had long become ineffective against the regulars of Calimport's streets, but those characters knew enough to keep their mouths shut about the halfling to strangers. Dondon always managed to surround himself with the toughest rogues of the city, and blowing his cover to an intended victim was a serious crime indeed!

The halfling leaned back against the corner of a building to observe as the four friends emerged from the Spitting Camel a short time later.

For Drizzt and his companions, Calimport's night proved as unnatural as the sights they had witnessed during the day. Unlike the northern cities, where nighttime activities were usually relegated to the many taverns, the bustle of Calimport's streets only increased after the sun went down. Even the lowly peasants took on a different demeanor, suddenly mysterious and sinister.

The only section of the lane that remained uncluttered by the hordes was the area in front of the unmarked structure on the back side of the circle: the guildhouse. As in the daylight, bums sat against the building's walls on either side of its single door, but now there were two more guards farther off to either side.

"If Regis is in that place, we've got to find our way in," Catti-brie observed.

"No doubt that Regis is in there," Drizzt replied. "Our hunt should start with Entreri."

"We've come to find Regis," Catti-brie reminded him, casting a disappointed glance his way. Drizzt quickly clarified his answer to her satisfaction.

"The road to Regis lies through the assassin," he said. "Entreri has seen to that. You heard his words at the chasm of Garumn's Gorge. Entreri will not allow us to find Regis until we have dealt with him."

Catti-brie could not deny the drow's logic. When Entreri had snatched Regis from them back in Mithral Hall, he had gone to great pains to bait Drizzt into the chase, as though his capture of Regis was merely part of a game he was playing against Drizzt.

"Where to begin?" Bruenor huffed in frustration. He had expected the street to be quieter, offering them a better opportunity to scope out the task before them. He had hoped that they might even complete their business that very night.

"Right where we are," Drizzt replied, to Bruenor's amazement. "Learn the smell of the street," the drow explained. "Watch the moves of its people and hear their sounds. Prepare your mind for what is to come."

"Time, elf!" Bruenor growled back. "Me heart tells me that Rumblebelly's liken to have a whip at his back as we stand here smelling the stinkin' street!"

"We need not seek Entreri," Wulfgar cut in, following Drizzt's line of thinking. "The assassin will find us."

Almost on cue, as if Wulfgar's statement had reminded them all of their dangerous surroundings, the four of them turned their eyes outward from their little huddle and watched the bustle of the street around them. Dark eyes peered at them from every corner; each person that ambled past cast them a sidelong glance. Calimport was not unaccustomed to strangers—it was a trading port, after all—but these four would stand out clearly on the streets of any city in the Realms. Recognizing their vulnerability, Drizzt decided to get them moving. He started off down Rogues Circle, motioning for the others to follow.

Before Wulfgar, at the tail of the forming line, had even taken a step, however, a childish voice called out to him from the shadows of the Spitting Camel.

"Hey," it beckoned, "are you looking for a hit?"

Wulfgar, not understanding, moved a bit closer and peered

into the gloom. There stood Dondon, seeming a young, disheveled human boy.

"What're yer fer?" Bruenor asked, moving beside Wulfgar.

Wulfgar pointed to the corner.

"What're yer fer?" Bruenor asked again, now targeting the diminutive, shadowy figure.

"Looking for a hit?" Dondon reiterated, moving out from the gloom.

"Bah!" Bruenor snorted, waving his hand "Just a boy. Get ye gone, little one. We've no time for play!" He grabbed Wulfgar's arm and turned away.

"I can set you up," Dondon said after them.

Bruenor kept right on walking, Wulfgar beside him, but now Drizzt had stopped, noticing his companions' delay, and had heard the boy's last statement.

"Just a boy!" Bruenor explained to the drow as he approached.

"A street boy," Drizzt corrected, stepping around Bruenor and Wulfgar and starting back, "with eyes and ears that miss little."

"How can you set us up?" Drizzt whispered to Dondon while moving close to the building, out of sight of the too curious hordes.

Dondon shrugged. "There is plenty to steal; a whole bunch of merchants came in today. What are you looking for?"

Bruenor, Wulfgar, and Catti-brie took up defensive positions around Drizzt and the boy, their eyes outward to the streets but their ears trained on the suddenly interesting conversation.

Drizzt crouched low and led Dondon's gaze with his own toward the building at the end of the circle.

"Pook's house," Dondon remarked offhandedly. "Toughest house in Calimport."

"But it has a weakness," Drizzt prompted.

"They all do," Dondon replied calmly, playing perfectly the role of a cocky street survivor.

"Have you ever been in there?"

"Maybe I have."

"Have you ever seen a hundred gold pieces?"

Dondon let his eyes light up, and he purposely and pointedly shifted his weight from one foot to the other.

"Get him back in the rooms," Catti-brie said. "Ye be drawing too many looks out here."

Dondon readily agreed, but he shot Drizzt a warning in the form of an icy stare and proclaimed, "I can count to a hundred!"

When they got back to the room, Drizzt and Bruenor fed Dondon a steady stream of coins while the halfling laid out the way to a secret back entrance to the guildhouse. "Even the thieves," Dondon proclaimed, "do not know of it!"

The friends gathered closely, eager for the details.

Dondon made the whole operation sound easy.

Too easy.

Drizzt rose and turned away, hiding his chuckle from the informant. Hadn't they just been talking about Entreri making contact? Barely minutes before this enlightening boy so conveniently arrived to guide them.

"Wulfgar, take off his shoes," Drizzt said. His three friends turned to him curiously. Dondon squirmed in his chair.

"His shoes," Drizzt said again, turning back and pointing to Dondon's feet. Bruenor, so long a friend of a halfling, caught the drow's reasoning and didn't wait for Wulfgar to respond. The dwarf grabbed at Dondon's left boot and pulled it off, revealing a thick patch of foot hair—the foot of a halfling.

Dondon shrugged helplessly and sank back in his chair. The meeting was taking the exact course that Entreri had predicted.

"He said he could set us up," Catti-brie remarked sarcastically, twisting Dondon's words into a more sinister light.

"Who sent ye?" Bruenor growled.

"Entreri," Wulfgar answered for Dondon. "He works for Entreri, sent here to lead us into a trap." Wulfgar leaned over Dondon, blocking out the candlelight with his huge frame.

Bruenor pushed the barbarian aside and took his place. With his boyish looks, Wulfgar simply could not be as imposing as the pointy-nosed, red-bearded, fire-eyed dwarven fighter with the battered helm. "So, ye little sneakster," Bruenor growled into Dondon's face. "Now we deal for yer stinkin' tongue! Wag it the wrong way, and I'll be cutting it out!"

Dondon paled—he had that act down pat—and began to tremble visibly.

"Calm yerself," Catti-brie said to Bruenor, playing out a lighter role this time. "Suren ye've scared the little one enough."

Bruenor shoved her back, turning enough away from Dondon to toss her a wink. "Scared him?" the dwarf balked. He brought his axe up to his shoulder. "More than scarin' him's in me plans!"

"Wait! Wait!" Dondon begged, groveling as only a halfling could. "I was just doing what the assassin made me do, and paid me to do."

"You know Entreri?" Wulfgar asked.

"Everybody knows Entreri," Dondon replied. "And in Calimport, everybody heeds Entreri's commands!"

"Forget Entreri!" Bruenor growled in his face. "Me axe'll stop that one from hurting yerself."

"You think you can kill Entreri?" Dondon shot back, though he knew the true meaning of Bruenor's claim.

"Entreri can't hurt a corpse," Bruenor replied grimly. "Me axe'll beat him to yer head!"

"It is you he wants," Dondon said to Drizzt, seeking a calmer situation.

Drizzt nodded, but remained silent. Something came across as out of place in this out of place meeting.

"I choose no sides," Dondon pleaded to Bruenor, seeing no relief forthcoming from Drizzt. "I only do what I must to survive."

"And to survive now, ye're going to tell us the way in," Bruenor said. "The safe way in."

"The place is a fortress," Dondon shrugged. "No way is safe." Bruenor started slipping closer, his scowl deepening.

"But, if I had to try," the halfling blurted, "I would try through the sewers."

Bruenor looked around at his friends.

"It seems correct," Wulfgar remarked.

Drizzt studied the halfling a moment longer, searching for some clue in Dondon's darting eyes. "It is correct," the drow said at length.

"So he saved his neck," said Catti-brie, "but what are we to do with him? Take him along?"

"Ayuh," said Bruenor with a sly look. "He'll be leading!"

"No," replied Drizzt, to the amazement of his companions. "The halfling did as we bade. Let him leave."

"And go straight off to tell Entreri what has happened?" Wulfgar said.

"Entreri would not understand," Drizzt replied. He looked Dondon in the eye, giving no indication to the halfling that he had figured out his little ploy within a ploy. "Nor would he forgive."

"Me heart says we take him," Bruenor remarked.

"Let him go," Drizzt said calmly. "Trust me."

Bruenor snorted and dropped his axe to his side, grumbling

as he moved to open the door. Wulfgar and Catti-brie exchanged concerned glances but stepped out of the way.

Dondon didn't hesitate, but Bruenor stepped in front of him as he reached the door. "If I see yer face again," the dwarf threatened, "or any face ye might be wearin', I'll chop ye down!"

Dondon slipped around and backed into the hall, never taking his eyes off the dangerous dwarf, then he darted down the hall, shaking his head at how perfectly Entreri had described the encounter, at how well the assassin knew those friends, particularly the drow.

Suspecting the truth about the entire encounter, Drizzt understood that Bruenor's final threat carried little weight to the wily halfling. Dondon had faced them down through both lies without the slightest hint of a slip.

But Drizzt nodded approvingly as Bruenor, still scowling, turned back into the room, for the drow also knew that the threat, if nothing else, had made Bruenor feel more secure.

On Drizzt's suggestion, they all settled down for some sleep. With the clamor of the streets, they would never be able to slip unnoticed into one of the sewer grates. But the crowds would likely thin out as the night waned and the guard changed from the dangerous rogues of evening to the peasants of the hot day.

Drizzt alone did not find sleep. He sat propped by the door of the room, listening for sounds of any approach and lulled into meditations by the rhythmic breathing of his companions. He looked down at the mask hanging around his neck. So simple a lie, and he could walk freely throughout the world.

But would he then be trapped within the web of his own deception? What freedom could he find in denying the truth about himself?

Drizzt looked over at Catti-brie, peacefully slumped in the

room's single bed, and smiled. There was indeed wisdom in innocence, a vein of truth in the idealism of untainted perceptions.

He could not disappoint her.

Drizzt sensed a deepening of the outside gloom. The moon had set. He moved to the room's window and peeked out into the street. Still the night people wandered, but they were fewer now, and the night neared its end. Drizzt roused his companions; they could not afford any more delays. They stretched away their weariness, checked their gear, and moved back down to the street.

Rogues Circle was lined with several iron sewer grates that looked as though they were designed more to keep the filthy things of the sewers underground than as drains for the sudden waters of the rare but violent rainstorms that hit the city. The friends chose one in the alley beside their inn, out of the main way of the street but close enough to the guildhouse that they could probably find their underground way without too much trouble.

"The boy can lift it," Bruenor remarked, waving Wulfgar to the spot. Wulfgar bent low and grasped the iron.

"Not yet," Drizzt whispered, glancing around for suspicious eyes. He motioned Catti-brie to the end of the ally, back along Rogues Circle, and he darted off down the darker side. When he was satisfied that all was clear, he waved back to Bruenor. The dwarf looked to Catti-brie, who nodded her approval.

"Lift it, boy," Bruenor said, "and be quiet about it!"

Wulfgar grasped the iron tightly and sucked in a deep draft of air for balance. His huge arms pumped red with blood as he heaved, and a grunt escaped his lips. Even so, the grate resisted his tugging.

Wulfgar looked at Bruenor in disbelief, then redoubled his efforts, his face now flushing red. The grate groaned in protest, but came up only a few inches from the ground.

"Suren somethings holdin' it down," Bruenor said, leaning over to inspect it.

A "clink" of snapping chain was the dwarf's only warning as the grate broke free, sending Wulfgar sprawling backward. The lifting iron clipped Bruenor's forehead, knocking his helmet off and dropping him on the seat of his pants. Wulfgar, still clutching the grate, crashed heavily and loudly into the wall of the inn.

"Ye blasted, foolheaded . . ." Bruenor started to grumble, but Drizzt and Catti-brie, rushing to his aid, quickly reminded him of the secrecy of their mission.

"Why would they chain a sewer grate?" Catti-brie asked.

Wulfgar dusted himself off. "From the inside," he added. "It seems that something down there wants to keep the city out."

"We shall know soon enough," Drizzt remarked. He dropped down beside the open hole, slipping his legs in. "Prepare a torch," he said. "I will summon you if all is clear."

Catti-brie caught the eager gleam in the drow's eyes and looked at him with concern.

"For Regis," Drizzt assured her, "and only for Regis." Then he was gone, into the blackness. Black like the lightless tunnels of his homeland.

The other three heard a slight splash as he touched down, then all was quiet.

Many anxious moments passed. "Put a light to the torch," Bruenor whispered to Wulfgar.

Catti-brie caught Wulfgar's arm to stop him. "Faith," she said to Bruenor.

"Too long," the dwarf muttered. "Too quiet."

Catti-brie held on to Wulfgar's arm for another second, until Drizzt's soft voice drifted up to them. "Clear," the drow said. "Come down quickly."

Bruenor took the torch from Wulfgar. "Come last," he said, "and slide the grate back behind ye. No need in tellin' the world where we went!"

⚔ ⚔ ⚔ ⚔ ⚔

The first thing the companions noticed when the torchlight entered the sewer was the chain that had held the grate down. It was fairly new, without doubt, and fastened to a locking box constructed on the sewer's wall.

"Me thinking's that we're not alone," Bruenor whispered.

Drizzt glanced around, sharing the dwarf's uneasiness. He dropped the mask from his face, a drow again in an environ suited for a drow. "I will lead," he said, "at the edge of the light. Keep ready." He padded away, picking his silent steps along the edge of the murky stream of water that rolled slowly down the center of the tunnel.

Bruenor came next with the torch, then Catti-brie and Wulfgar. The barbarian had to stoop low to keep his head clear of the slimy ceiling. Rats squeaked and scuttled away from the strange light, and darker things took silent refuge under the shield of the water. The tunnel meandered this way and that, and a maze of side passages opened up every few feet. Sounds of trickling water only worsened the confusion, leading the friends for a moment, then coming louder at their side, then louder still from across the way.

Bruenor shook the diversions clear of his thoughts, ignored the muck and the fetid stench, and concentrated on keeping his track straight behind the shadowy figure that darted in and out at the front edge of his torchlight. He turned a confusing, multicornered intersection and caught sight of the figure suddenly off to his side.

Even as he turned to follow, he realized that Drizzt still had to be up front.

"Ready!" Bruenor called, tossing the torch to a dry spot beside him and taking up his axe and shield. His alertness saved them all, for only a split second later, not one, but two cloaked forms emerged from the side tunnel, swords raised and sharp teeth gleaming under twitching whiskers.

They were man-sized, wearing the clothes of men and holding swords. In their other form, they were indeed humans and not always vile, but on the nights of the bright moon they took on their darker form, the lycanthrope side. They moved like men but were mantled with the trappings—elongated snout, bristled brown fur, and pink tail—of sewer rats.

Lining them up over the top of Bruenor's helm, Catti-brie launched the first strike. The silvery flash of her killing arrow illuminated the side tunnel like a lightning bolt, showing many more sinister figures making their way toward the friends.

A splash from behind caused Wulfgar to spin about to face a rushing gang of the ratmen. He dug his heels into the mud as well as he could and slapped Aegis-fang to a ready position.

"They was layin' on us, elf!" Bruenor shouted.

Drizzt had already come to that conclusion. At the dwarf's first shout, he had slipped farther from the torch to use the advantage of darkness. Turning a bend brought him face to face with two figures, and he guessed their sinister nature before he ever got the blue light of Twinkle high enough to see their furry brows.

The wererats, though, certainly did not expect what they found standing ready before them. Perhaps it was because they believed that their enemies were solely in the area with the torchlight, but more likely it was the black skin of a drow elf that sent them back on their heels.

Drizzt didn't miss the opportunity, slicing them down in a single flurry before they ever recovered from their shock. The drow then melted again into the blackness, seeking a back route to ambush the ambushers.

Wulfgar kept his attackers at bay with long sweeps of Aegis-fang. The hammer blew aside any wererat that ventured too near, and smashed away chunks of the muck on the sewer walls every time it completed an arc. But as the wererats came to understand the power of the mighty barbarian, and came in at him with less enthusiasm, the best that Wulfgar could accomplish was a stalemate—a deadlock that would only last as long as the energy in his huge arms.

Behind Wulfgar, Bruenor and Catti-brie fared better. Catti-brie's magical bow—loosing arrows over the dwarf's head—decimated the ranks of the approaching wererats, and those few that reached Bruenor, off-balance and ducking the deadly arrows of the woman behind him, proved easy prey for the dwarf. But the odds were fully against the friends, and they knew that one mistake would cost them dearly.

The wererats, hissing and spitting, backed away from Wulfgar. Realizing that he had to initiate more decisive fighting, the barbarian strode forward.

The ratmen parted ranks suddenly, and down the tunnel, at the very edge of the torchlight, Wulfgar saw one of them level a heavy crossbow and fire.

Instinctively the big man flattened against the wall, and he was agile enough to get out of the missile's path, but Catti-brie, behind him and facing the other way, never saw the bolt coming.

She felt a sudden searing burst of pain, then the warmth of her blood pouring down the side of her head. Blackness swirled about the edges of her vision, and she crumbled against the wall.

⋈ ⋈ ⋈ ⋈ ⋈

Drizzt slipped through the dark passages as silently as death. He kept Twinkle sheathed, fearing its revealing light, and led the way with his other magical blade. He was in a maze, but figured that he could pick his route well enough to rejoin his friends. Every tunnel he picked, though, lit up at its other end with torchlight as still more wererats made their way to the fighting.

The darkness was certainly ample for the stealthy drow to remain concealed, but Drizzt got the uneasy feeling that his moves were being monitored, even anticipated. Dozens of passages opened up all around him, but his options came fewer and fewer as wererats appeared at every turn. The circuit to his friends was growing wider with each step, but Drizzt quickly realized that he had no choice but to go forward. Wererats had filled the main tunnel behind him, following his route.

Drizzt stopped in the shadows of one dark nook and surveyed the area about him, recounting the distance he had covered and noting the passages behind him that now flickered in torchlight. Apparently there weren't as many wererats as he had originally figured; those appearing at every turn were probably the same groups from the previous tunnels, running parallel to Drizzt and turning into each new passage as Drizzt came upon it at the other end.

But the revelation of wererat numbers came as little comfort to Drizzt. He had no doubts to his suspicions now. He was being herded.

⋈ ⋈ ⋈ ⋈ ⋈

Wulfgar turned and started toward his fallen love, his Catti-brie, but the wererats came in on him immediately. Fury now drove the mighty barbarian. He tore into his attackers' ranks, smashing and squashing them with bone-splitting chops of his warhammer or reaching out with a bare hand to twist the neck of any who had slipped in beside him. The ratmen managed a few retreating stabs, but nicks and little wounds wouldn't slow the enraged barbarian.

He stomped on the fallen as he passed, grinding his booted heels into their dying bodies. Other wererats scrambled in terror to get out of his way.

At the end of their line, the crossbowman struggled to reload his weapon, a job made more difficult by his inability to keep his eyes off the spectacle of the approaching barbarian and made doubly difficult by his knowledge that he was the focus of the powerful man's rage.

Bruenor, with the wererat ranks dissipated in front of him, had more time to tend to Catti-brie. He bent over the young woman, his face ashen as he pulled her thick mane of auburn hair, thicker now with the wetness of her blood, from her fair face.

Catti-brie looked up at him through stunned eyes. "But an inch more, and me life'd be at its end," she said with a wink and a smile.

Bruenor scrambled to inspect the wound, and found, to his relief, that his daughter was correct in her observations. The quarrel had gouged her wickedly, but it was only a grazing shot.

"I'm all right," Catti-brie insisted, starting to rise.

Bruenor held her down. "Not yet," he whispered.

The fight's not done," Catti-brie replied, still trying to plant her feet under her. Bruenor led her gaze down the tunnel, to Wulfgar and the bodies piling all about him.

"There's our chance," he chuckled "Let the boy think ye're down."

Catti-brie bit her lip in astonishment of the scene. A dozen ratmen were down and still Wulfgar pounded through, his hammer tearing away those unfortunates who couldn't flee out of his way.

Then a noise from the other direction turned Catti-brie away. With her bow down, the wererats from the front had returned.

"They're mine," Bruenor told her. "Keep yerself down!"

"If ye get into trouble—"

"If I need ye, then be there," Bruenor agreed, "but for now, keep yerself down! Give the boy something to fight for!"

⚔ ⚔ ⚔ ⚔ ⚔

Drizzt tried to double back along his route, but the ratmen quickly closed off all of the tunnels. Soon his options had been cut down to one, a wide, dry side passage moving in the opposite direction from where he had hoped to go.

The ratmen were closing on him fast, and in the main tunnel he would have to fight them off from several different directions. He slipped into the passage and flattened against the wall.

Two ratmen shuffled up to the tunnel entrance and peered into the gloom, calling a third, with a torch, to join them. The light they found was not the yellow flicker of a torch, but a sudden line of blue as Twinkle came free of its scabbard. Drizzt was upon them before they could raise their weapons in defense, thrusting a blade clean through one wererat's chest and spinning his second blade in an arc across the other's neck.

The torchlight enveloped them as they fell, leaving the drow standing there, revealed both his blades dripping blood. The nearest wererats shrieked; some even dropped their weapons and ran, but more of them came up, blocking all of the tunnel entrances in the area, and the advantage of sheer numbers soon gave the ratmen a measure of confidence. Slowly, looking to each other for support with every step, they closed in on Drizzt.

Drizzt considered rushing a single, group, hoping to cut through their ranks and be out of the ring of the trap, but the ratmen were at least two deep at every passage, three or even four deep at some. Even with his, skill and agility, Drizzt could never get through them fast enough to avoid attacks at his back.

He darted back into the side passage and summoned a globe of darkness inside its entrance, then he sprinted beyond the area of the globe to take up a ready position just behind it.

The ratmen, quickening their charge as Drizzt disappeared back into the tunnel, stopped short when they turned into the area of unbreakable darkness. At first, they thought that their torches must have gone out, but so deep was the gloom that they soon realized the truth of the drow's spell. They regrouped out in the main tunnel, then came back in, cautiously.

Even Drizzt, with his night eyes, could not see into the pitch blackness of his spell, but positioned clear of the other side, he did make out a sword tip, and then another, leading the two front ratmen down the passage. They hadn't even broken from the darkness when the drow struck, slapping their swords away and reversing the angle of his cuts to drive his scimitars up the lengths of their arms and into their bodies. Their agonized screams sent the other ratmen scrambling back out into the main corridor, and gave Drizzt another moment to consider his position.

⚔ ⚔ ⚔ ⚔ ⚔

The crossbowman knew his time was up when the last two of his companions shoved him aside in their desperate flight from the enraged giant. He at last fumbled the quarrel back into position and brought his bow to bear.

But Wulfgar was too close. The barbarian grabbed the crossbow as it swung about and tore it from the wererat's hands with such ferocity that it broke apart when it slammed into the wall. The wererat meant to flee, but the sheer intensity of Wulfgar's glare froze him in place. He watched, horrified, as Wulfgar clasped Aegis-fang in both hands.

Wulfgar's strike was impossibly fast. The wererat never comprehended that the death blow had even begun. He only felt a sudden explosion on top of his head.

The ground rushed up to meet him; he was dead before he ever splatted into the muck. Wulfgar, his eyes rimmed with tears, hammered on the wretched creature viciously until its body was no more than a lump of undefinable waste.

Spattered with blood and muck and black water, Wulfgar finally slumped back against the wall. As he released himself from the consuming rage, he heard the fighting behind and spun to find Bruenor beating back two of the ratmen, with several more lined up behind them.

And behind the dwarf, Catti-brie lay still against the wall. The sight refueled Wulfgar's fire. "Tempus!" he roared to his god of battle, and he pounded through the muck, back down the tunnel. The wererats facing Bruenor tripped over themselves trying to get away, giving the dwarf the opportunity to cut down two more of them—he was happy to oblige. They fled back into the maze of tunnels.

Wulfgar meant to pursue them, to hunt each of them down and vent his vengeance, but Catti-brie rose to intercept him. She leaped into his chest as he skidded in surprise, wrapped her arms around his neck, and kissed him more passionately than he had ever imagined he could be kissed.

He held her at arm's length, gawking and stuttering in confusion until a joyful smile spread wide and took all other emotions out of his face. Then he hugged her back for another kiss.

Bruenor pulled them apart. "The elf?" he reminded them. He scooped up the torch, now halfcovered with mud and burning low, and led them off down the tunnel.

They didn't dare turn into one of the many side passages, for fear of getting lost. The main corridor was the swiftest route, wherever it might take them, and they could only hope to catch a glimpse or hear a sound that would direct them to Drizzt.

Instead they found a door.

"The guild?" Catti-brie whispered.

"What else could it be?" Wulfgar replied." Only a thieves' house would keep a door to the sewers."

Above the door, in a secret cubby, Entreri eyed the three friends curiously. He had known that something was amiss when the wererats had begun to gather in the sewers earlier that night. Entreri had hoped they would move out into the city, but it had soon become apparent that the wererats meant to stay.

Then these three showed up at the door without the drow.

Entreri put his chin in his palm and considered his next course of action.

Bruenor studied the door curiously. On it, at about eye level for a human, was nailed a small wooden box. Having no time to play with riddles, the dwarf boldly reached up and tore the box free, bringing it down and peeking over its rim.

The dwarf's face twisted with even more confusion when he saw inside. He shrugged and held the box out to Wulfgar and Catti-brie.

Wulfgar was not so confused. He had seen a similar item before, back on the docks of Baldur's Gate. Another gift from Artemis Entreri—another halfling's finger.

"Assassin!" he roared, and he slammed his shoulder into the door. It broke free of its hinges, and Wulfgar stumbled into the room beyond, holding the door out in front of him. Before he could even toss it aside, he heard the crash behind him and realized how foolish the move had been. He had fallen right into Entreri's trap.

A portcullis had dropped in the entranceway, separating him from Bruenor and Catti-brie.

⚔ ⚔ ⚔ ⚔ ⚔

The tips of long spears led the wererats back through Drizzt's globe of darkness. The drow still managed to take one of the lead ratmen down, but he was backed up by the press of the group that followed. He gave ground freely, fighting off their thrusts and jabs with defensive swordwork. Whenever he saw an opening, he was quick enough to strike a blade home.

Then a singular odor overwhelmed even the stench of the sewer. A syrupy sweet smell that rekindled distant memories in the drow. The ratmen pressed him on even harder, as if the scent had renewed their desire to fight.

Drizzt remembered. In Menzoberranzan, the city of his birth, some drow elves had kept as pets creatures that exuded such an odor. Sundews, these monstrous beasts were called, lumpy masses of raglike, sticky tendrils that simply engulfed and dissolved anything that came too near.

Now Drizzt fought for every step. He had indeed been herded, to face a horrid death or perhaps to be captured, for the sundew devoured its victims so very slowly, and certain liquids could break its hold.

Drizzt felt a flutter and glanced back over his shoulder. The sundew was barely ten feet away, already reaching out with a hundred sticky fingers.

Drizzt's scimitars weaved and dived, spun and cut, in as

magnificent a dance as he had ever fought. One wererat was hit fifteen times before it even realized that the first blow had struck home.

But there were simply too many of the ratmen for Drizzt to hold his ground, and the sight of the sundew urged them on bravely.

Drizzt felt the tickle of the flicking tendrils only inches from his back. He had no room to maneuver now; the spears would surely drive him into the monster.

Drizzt smiled, and the eager fires burned brighter in his eyes. "Is this how it ends?" he whispered aloud. The sudden burst of his laughter startled the wererats.

With Twinkle leading the way, Drizzt spun on his heels and dived at the heart of the sundew.

19

TRICKS AND TRAPS

Wulfgar found himself in a square, unadorned room of worked stone. Two torches burned low in wall sconces, revealing another door before him, across from the portcullis. He tossed aside the broken door and turned back to his friends. "Guard my back," he told Catti-brie, but she had already figured her part out and had brought her bow up level with the door across the room.

Wulfgar rubbed his hands together in preparation for his attempt to lift the portcullis. It was a massive piece indeed, but the barbarian did not think it beyond his strength. He grasped the iron, then fell back, dismayed, even before he had attempted to lift.

The bars had been greased.

"Entreri, or I'm a bearded gnome," Bruenor grumbled. "Ye put yer face in deep, boy."

"How are we to get him out?" Catti-brie asked.

Wulfgar looked back over his shoulder at the unopened door. He knew that they could accomplish nothing by standing there, and he feared that the noise of the dropping portcullis must have attracted some attention—attention that could only mean danger for his friends.

"Ye can't be thinking to go deeper," Catti-brie protested.

"What choice have I?" Wulfgar replied. "Perhaps there is a crank in there."

"More likely an assassin," Bruenor retorted, "but ye have to try it."

Catti-brie pulled her bowstring tight as Wulfgar moved to the door. He tried the handle but found it locked. He looked back to his friends and shrugged, then spun and kicked with his heavy boot. The wood shivered and split apart, revealing yet another room, this one dark.

"Get a torch," Bruenor told him.

Wulfgar hesitated. Something didn't feel right, or smell right. His sixth sense, that warrior instinct, told him he would not find the second room as empty as the first, but with no other place to go, he moved for one of the torches.

Intent on the situation within the room, Bruenor and Catti-brie did not notice the dark figure drop from the concealed cubby on the wall a short distance down the tunnel. Entreri considered the two of them for a moment. He could take them out easily, and perhaps quietly, but the assassin turned away and disappeared into the darkness.

He had already picked his target.

⚔ ⚔ ⚔ ⚔ ⚔

Rassiter stooped over the two bodies lying in front of the side passage. Reverting halfway through the transformation between rat and human, they had died in the excruciating agony that only a lycanthrope could know. Just like the ones farther back down the main tunnel, these had been slashed and nipped with expert precision, and if the line of bodies didn't mark the path clearly enough, the globe of darkness hanging in the side passage certainly did. It appeared to Rassiter that his trap had worked, though the price had certainly been high.

He dropped to the lower corner of the wall and crept along, nearly tripping over still more bodies of his guildmates as he came through the other side.

The wererat shook his head in disbelief as he moved down the tunnel, stepping over a wererat corpse every few feet. How many had the master swordsman killed?

"A drow!" Rassiter balked in sudden understanding as he turned the final bend. Bodies of his comrades were piled deep there, but Rassiter looked beyond them. He would willingly pay such a price for the prize he saw before him, for now he had the dark warrior in hand, a drow elf for a prisoner! He would gain Pasha Pook's favor and rise above Artemis Entreri once and for all.

At the end of the passage, Drizzt leaned silently against the sundew, draped by a thousand tendrils. He still held his two scimitars, but his arms hung limply at his sides and his head drooped down, his lavender eyes closed.

The wererat moved down the passage cautiously, hoping the drow was not already dead. He inspected his waterskin, filled with vinegar, and hoped he had brought enough to dissolve the sundew's hold and free the drow. Rassiter dearly wanted this trophy alive.

Pook would appreciate the present more that way.

The wererat reached out with his sword to prod at the drow, but recoiled in pain as a dagger flashed by, slicing across his arm. He spun back around to see Artemis Entreri, his saber drawn and a murderous look in his dark eyes.

Rassiter found himself caught in his own trap; there was no other escape from the passage. He fell flat against the wall, clutching his bleeding arm, and started inching his way back up the passage.

Entreri followed the ratman's progress without a blink.

"Pook would never forgive you," Rassiter warned.

"Pook would never know," Entreri hissed back.

Terrified, Rassiter darted past the assassin, expecting a sword in his side as he passed. But Entreri cared nothing about Rassiter; his eyes had shifted down the passage to the specter of Drizzt Do'Urden, helpless and defeated.

Entreri moved to recover his jeweled dagger, undecided as to whether to cut the drow free or let him die a slow death in the sundew's clutches.

"And so you die," he whispered at length, wiping the slime from his dagger.

⚔ ⚔ ⚔ ⚔ ⚔

With a torch out before him, Wulfgar gingerly stepped into the second room. Like the first, it was square and unadorned, but one side was blocked halfway across by a floor-to-ceiling screen. Wulfgar knew that danger lurked behind the screen, knew it to be a part of the trap Entreri had set out and into which he had blindly rushed.

He didn't have the time to berate himself for his lack of judgment. He positioned himself in the center of the room, still in sight of his friends, and laid the torch at his feet, clutching Aegis-fang in both hands.

But when the thing rushed out, the barbarian still found himself gawking, amazed.

Eight serpentlike heads interwove in a tantalizing dance, like the needles of frenzied women knitting at a single garment. Wulfgar saw no humor in the moment, though, for each mouth was filled with row upon row of razor-sharp teeth.

Catti-brie and Bruenor understood that Wulfgar was in trouble when they saw him shuffle back a step. They expected Entreri, or a host of soldiers, to confront him. Then the hydra crossed the open doorway.

"Wulfgar!" Catti-brie cried in dismay, loosing an arrow. The silver bolt blasted a deep hole into a serpentine neck, and the hydra roared in pain and turned one head to consider the stinging attackers from the side.

Seven other heads struck out at Wulfgar.

⚔ ⚔ ⚔ ⚔ ⚔

"You disappoint me, drow," Entreri continued. I had thought you my equal, or nearly so. The bother, and risks, I took to guide you here so we could decide whose life was the lie! To prove to you that those emotions you cling to so dearly have no place in the heart of a true warrior.

"But now I see that I have wasted my efforts," the assassin lamented. "The question has already been decided, if it ever was a question. Never would I have fallen into such a trap!"

Drizzt peeked out from one half-opened eye and raised his head to meet Entreri's gaze. "Nor would I," he said, shrugging off the limp tendrils of the dead sundew. "Nor would I!"

The wound became apparent in the monster when Drizzt moved out. With a single thrust, the drow had killed the sundew.

A smile burst across Entreri's face. "Well done!" he cried, readying his blades. "Magnificent!"

"Where is the halfling?" Drizzt snarled.

"This does not concern the halfling," Entreri replied, "or your silly toy, the panther."

Drizzt quickly sublimated the anger that twisted his face.

"Oh, they are alive," Entreri taunted, hoping to distract his enemy with anger. "Perhaps, though perhaps not."

Unbridled rage often aided warriors against lesser foes, but in an equal battle of skilled swordsmen, thrusts had to be measured and defenses could not be let down.

Drizzt came in with both blades thrusting. Entreri deflected them aside with his saber and countered with a jab of his dagger.

Drizzt twirled out of danger's way, coming around a full circle and slicing down with Twinkle. Entreri caught the weapon with his saber, so that the blades locked hilt to hilt and brought the combatants close.

"Did you receive my gift in Baldur's Gate?" the assassin chuckled.

Drizzt did not flinch. Regis and Guenhwyvar were out of his thoughts now. His focus was Artemis Entreri.

Only Artemis Entreri.

The assassin pressed on. "A mask?" he questioned with a wide smirk. "Put it on, drow. Pretend you are what you are not!"

Drizzt heaved suddenly, throwing Entreri back.

The assassin went with the move, just as happy to continue the battle from a distance. But when Entreri tried to catch himself, his foot hit a mud-slicked depression in the tunnel floor and he slipped to one knee.

Drizzt was on him in a flash, both scimitars wailing away. Entreri's hands moved equally fast, dagger and saber twisting and turning to parry and deflect. His head and shoulders bobbed wildly, and remarkably, he worked his foot back under him.

Drizzt knew that he had lost the advantage. Worse, the assault had left him in an awkward position with one shoulder too close to the wall. As Entreri started to rise, Drizzt jumped back.

"So easy?" Entreri asked him as they squared off again. "Do you think that I sought this fight for so long, only to die in its opening exchanges?"

"I do not figure anything where Artemis Entreri is concerned," Drizzt came back. "You are too foreign to me, assassin. I do not pretend to understand your motives, nor do I have any desire to learn of them."

"Motives?" Entreri balked. "I am a fighter—purely a fighter. I do not mix the calling of my life with lies of gentleness and love!" He held the saber and dagger out before him. "These are my only friends, and with them—"

"You are nothing," Drizzt cut in. "Your life is a wasted lie."

"A lie?" Entreri shot back. "You are the one who wears the mask, drow. You are the one who must hide."

Drizzt accepted the words with a smile. Only a few days before, they might have stung him, but now, after the insight Catti-brie had given him, they rang hollowly in Drizzt's ears. "You are the lie, Entreri," he replied calmly. "You are no more than a loaded crossbow, an unfeeling weapon, that will never know life." He started walking toward the assassin, jaw firm in the knowledge of what he must do.

Entreri strode in with equal confidence.

"Come and die, drow," he spat.

⚔ ⚔ ⚔ ⚔ ⚔

Wulfgar backed quickly, snapping his warhammer back and forth in front of him to parry the hydra's dizzying attacks. He knew that he couldn't hold the incessant thing off for long. He had to find a way to strike back against its offensive fury.

But against the seven snapping maws, weaving a hypnotic dance and lunging out singly or all together, Wulfgar had no time to prepare an attack sequence.

With her bow, beyond the range of the heads, Catti-brie had more success. Tears rimmed her eyes in fear for Wulfgar, but she held them back with a grim determination not to surrender. Another arrow blasted into the lone head that had turned her way, scorching a hole right between the eyes. The head shuddered and jerked back, then dropped to the floor with a thud, quite dead.

The attack, or the pain from it, seemed to paralyze the rest of the hydra for just a second, and the desperate barbarian did not miss the opportunity. He rushed forward a step and slammed Aegis-fang with all of his might into the snout of another head, snapping it back. It, too, dropped lifelessly to the floor.

"Keep it in front of the door!" Bruenor called. "And don't ye be coming through without a shout. Suren the girl'd cut' ye down!"

If the hydra was a stupid beast, it at least understood hunting tactics. It turned its body at an angle to the open door, preventing any chance for Wulfgar to get by. Two heads were down, and another silver arrow, and then another, sizzled in, this time catching the bulk of the hydra's body. Wulfgar, working frantically and just finished with the furious battle against the wererats, was beginning to tire.

He missed the parry as one head came in, and powerful jaws closed around his arm, cutting gashes just below his shoulder.

The hydra attempted to shake its neck and tear the man's arm off, its usual tactic, but it had never encountered one of Wulfgar's strength before. The barbarian locked his arm tight against his side, grimacing away the pain, and held the hydra in place. With his free hand Wulfgar grasped Aegis-fang just under the hammer's head and jabbed the butt end into the hydra's eye. The beast loosened its grip and Wulfgar tore himself free and fell back, just in time to avoid five other snapping attacks.

He could still fight, but the wound would slow him even more.

"Wulfgar!" Catti-brie cried again, hearing his groan.

"Get out o' there, boy!" Bruenor yelled.

Wulfgar was already moving. He dived toward the back wall and rolled around the hydra. The two closest heads followed his movement and dipped in to snap him up.

Wulfgar rolled right to his feet and reversed his momentum, splitting one jaw wide open with a mighty chop. Catti-brie, witnessing Wulfgar's desperate flight, put an arrow into the other head's eye.

The hydra roared in agony and rage and spun about, now having four lifeless heads bouncing across the floor.

Wulfgar, backing across to the other side of the room, got an angle to see what lay behind the screen. "Another door!" he cried to his friends.

Catti-brie got in one more shot as the hydra crossed over to pursue Wulfgar. She and Bruenor heard the crack as the door split free of its hinges, then a sliding bang as yet another portcullis dropped behind the big man.

⚔ ⚔ ⚔ ⚔ ⚔

Entreri carried the latest attack, whipping his saber across at Drizzt's neck while simultaneously thrusting low with his dagger. A daring move, and if the assassin had not been so skilled with his weapons, Drizzt would surely have found an opening to drive a blade through Entreri's heart. The drow had all he could handle, though, just raising one scimitar to block the saber and lowering the other to push the dagger aside.

Entreri went through a series of similar double attack routines, and Drizzt turned him away each, time, showing only one small cut on the shoulder before Entreri finally was forced to back away.

"First blood is mine," the assassin crowed. He ran a finger down the blade of his saber, pointedly showing the drow the red stain.

"Last blood counts for more," Drizzt retorted as he came in with blades leading. The scimitars cut at the assassin from impossible angles, one dipping at a shoulder, the other rising to find the ridge under the rib cage.

Entreri, like Drizzt, foiled the attacks with perfect parries.

⚔ ⚔ ⚔ ⚔ ⚔

"Are ye alive, boy?" Bruenor called. The dwarf heard the renewed fighting back behind him in the corridors, to his relief, for the sound told him that Drizzt was still alive.

"I am safe," Wulfgar replied, looking around the new room he had entered. It was furnished with several chairs and one table which had been recently used, it appeared, for gambling. Wulfgar had no doubt now that he was under a building, most probably the thieves' guildhouse.

"The path is closed behind me," he called to his friends. "Find Drizzt and get back to the street. I will find my way to meet you there!"

"I'll not leave ye!" Catti-brie replied.

"I shall leave you," Wulfgar shot back.

Catti-brie glared at Bruenor. "Help him," she begged.

Bruenor's look was equally stern.

"We have no hope in staying where we are," Wulfgar called. "Surely I could not retrace my steps, even if I managed to lift this portcullis and defeat the hydra. Go, my love, and take heart that we shall meet again!"

"Listen to the boy," Bruenor said. "Yer heart's telling ye to stay, but ye'll be doing no favors for Wulfgar if ye follow that course. Ye have to trust in him."

Grease mixed with the blood on Catti-brie's head as she leaned heavily on the bars before her. Another demolished door sounded from deeper within the complex of rooms, like a hammer driving a stake into her heart. Bruenor grabbed her elbow gently. "Come, girl," he whispered. "The drow's afoot and needin' our help. Trust in Wulfgar."

Catti-brie pulled herself away and followed Bruenor down the tunnel.

⚔ ⚔ ⚔ ⚔ ⚔

Drizzt pressed the attack, studying the assassin's face as he went. He had succeeded in sublimating his hatred of the assassin, heeding Catti-brie's words and remembering the priorities of the adventure. Entreri became to him just another obstacle in the path to freeing Regis. With a cool head, Drizzt focused on the business at hand, reacting to his opponent's thrusts and counters as calmly as if he were in a practice gym in Menzoberranzan.

The visage of Entreri, the man who proclaimed superiority as a fighter because of his lack demotions, often twisted violently, bordering on explosive rage. Truly Entreri hated Drizzt. For all of the warmth and friendships the drow had found in his life, he had attained perfection with his weapons. Every time Drizzt foiled Entreri's attack routine and countered with an equally skilled sequence, he exposed the emptiness of the assassin's existence.

Drizzt recognized the boiling anger in Entreri and sought a way to exploit it. He launched another deceptive sequence but was again deterred.

Then he came in a straight double-thrust, his scimitars side by side and only an inch apart.

Entreri blew them both off to the side with a sweeping saber parry, grinning at Drizzt's apparent mistake. Growling wickedly, Entreri launched his dagger arm through the opening, toward the drow's heart.

But Drizzt had anticipated the move—had even set the assassin up. He dipped and angled his front scimitar even as the saber came in to parry it, sliding it under Entreri's blade and cutting back a reverse swipe. Entreri's dagger arm came thrusting out right in the scimitar's path, and before the assassin could poke his blade into Drizzt's heart, Drizzt's scimitar gashed into the back of his elbow.

The dagger dropped to the muck. Entreri grabbed his wounded arm, grimaced in pain, and rushed back from the battle. His eyes narrowed on Drizzt, angry and confused.

"Your hunger blurs your ability," Drizzt said to him, taking a step forward. "We have both looked into a mirror this night. Perhaps you did not I enjoy the sight it showed to you."

Entreri fumed but had no retort. "You have not won yet," he spat defiantly, but he knew that the drow had gained an overwhelming advantage.

"Perhaps not," Drizzt shrugged, "but you lost many years ago."

Entreri smiled evilly and bowed low, then took flight back through the passage.

Drizzt was quick to pursue, stopping short, though, when he

reached the edge of the globe of blackness. He heard shuffling on the other side and braced himself. Too loud for Entreri, he reasoned, and he suspected that some wererat had returned.

"Are ye there, elf?" came a familiar voice.

Drizzt dashed through the blackness and side-stepped his astonished friends. "Entreri?" he asked, hoping that the wounded assassin had not escaped unseen.

Bruenor and Catti-brie shrugged curiously and turned to follow as Drizzt ran off into the darkness.

20

BLACK AND WHITE

W ulfgar, nearly overcome by exhaustion and by the pain in his arm, leaned heavily against the smooth wall of an upward-sloping passage. He clutched the wound tightly, hoping to stem the flow of his lifeblood.

How alone he felt.

He knew that he had been right in sending his friends away. They could have done little to help him, and standing there, in the open of the main corridor right in front of the very spot Entreri had chosen for his trap, left them too vulnerable. Wulfgar now had to move along by himself, probably into the heart of the infamous thieves' guild.

He released his grip on his biceps and examined the wound. The hydra had bitten him deeply, but he found that he could still move his arm. Gingerly he took a few swings with Aegis-fang.

He then leaned back against the wall once more, trying to figure a course of action in a cause that seemed truly hopeless.

⚔ ⚔ ⚔ ⚔ ⚔

Drizzt slipped from tunnel to tunnel, sometimes slowing his pace to listen for faint sounds that would aid his pursuit. He didn't really expect to hear anything; Entreri could move as silently as he. And the assassin, like Drizzt, moved along without a torch, or even a candle.

But Drizzt felt confident in the turns he took, as if he were being led along by the same reasoning that guided Entreri. He felt the assassin's presence, knew the man better than he cared to admit, and Entreri could no more escape him than he could Entreri. Their battle had begun in Mithral Hall months before—or perhaps theirs was only the present embodiment in the continuation of a greater struggle that was spawned at the dawn of time—but, for Drizzt and Entreri, two pawns in the timeless struggle of principles, this chapter of the war could not end until one claimed victory.

Drizzt noted a glimmer down to the side—not the flickering yellow of a torch, but a constant silvery stream. He moved cautiously and found an open grate, with the moonlight streaming in and highlighting the wet iron rungs of a ladder bolted into the sewer wall. Drizzt glanced around quickly—too quickly—and rushed to the ladder.

The shadows to his left exploded into motion, and Drizzt caught the telltale shine of a blade just in time to turn his back from the angle of the blow. He staggered forward, feeling a burning across his shoulder blades and then the wetness of his blood rolling down under his cloak.

Drizzt ignored the pain, knowing that any hesitation would surely result in his death, and spun around, slamming his back into the wall and sending the curved blades of both his scimitars into a defensive spin before him.

Entreri issued no taunts this time. He came in furiously, cutting and slicing with his saber, knowing that he had to finish Drizzt before the shock of the ambush wore off. Viciousness replaced finesse, engulfing the injured assassin in a frenzy of hatred.

He leaped into Drizzt, locking one of the drow's arms under his own wounded limb and trying to use brute strength to drive his saber into his opponent's neck.

Drizzt steadied himself quickly enough to control the initial assault. He surrendered his one arm to the assassin's hold, concentrating solely on getting his free scimitar up to block the strike. The blade's hilt again locked with that of Entreri's saber, holding it motionless in midswing halfway between the combatants.

Behind their respective blades, Drizzt and Entreri eye-balled each other with open hatred, their grimaces only inches apart.

"How many crimes shall I punish you for, assassin?" Drizzt growled. Reinforced by his own proclamation, Drizzt pushed the saber back an inch, shifting the angle of his own deadly blade down more threateningly toward Entreri.

Entreri did not answer, nor did he seem alarmed at the slight shift in the blades' momentum. A wild, exhilarated look came into his eyes, and his thin lips widened into an evil grin.

Drizzt knew that the killer had another trick to play.

Before the drow could figure the game, Entreri spat a mouthful of filthy sewer water into his lavender eyes.

✕ ✕ ✕ ✕ ✕

The sound of renewed fighting led Bruenor and Catti-brie along the tunnels. They caught sight of the moonlit forms struggling just as Entreri played his wicked card.

"Drizzt!" Catti-brie shouted, knowing that she couldn't get

to him, even get her bow up, in time to stop Entreri.

Bruenor growled and bolted forward with only one thought on his mind: If Entreri killed Drizzt, he would cut the dog in half!

⚔ ⚔ ⚔ ⚔ ⚔

The sting and shock of the water broke Drizzt's concentration, and his strength, for only a split second, but he knew that even a split second was too long against Artemis Entreri. He jerked his head to the side desperately.

Entreri snapped his saber down, slicing a gash across Drizzt's forehead and crushing the drow's thumb between the twisting hilts. "I have you!" he squealed, hardly believing the sudden turn of events.

At that horrible moment, Drizzt could not disagree with the observation, but the drow's next move came more on instinct than on any calculations, and with agility that surprised even Drizzt. In the instant of a single, tiny hop, Drizzt snapped one foot behind Entreri's ankle and tucked the other under him against the wall. He pushed away and twisted as he went. On the slick floor, Entreri had no chance to dodge the trip, and he toppled backward into the murky stream, Drizzt splashing down on top of him.

The weight of Drizzt's heavy fall jammed the crosspiece of his scimitar into Entreri's eye. Drizzt recovered from the surprise of his own movement faster than Entreri, and he did not miss the opportunity. He spun his hand over on the hilt and reversed the flow of the blade, pulling it free of Entreri's and swinging a short cut back and down, with the tip of the scimitar diving in at the assassin's ribs. In grim satisfaction, Drizzt felt it begin to cut in.

It was Entreri's turn for a move wrought of desperation. Having no time to bring his saber to bear, the assassin punched straight out, slamming Drizzt's face with the butt of his weapon. Drizzt's nose splattered onto his cheek, flashes of color exploded before his eyes, and he felt himself lifted and dropped off to the side before his scimitar could finish its work.

Entreri scrambled out of reach and pulled himself from the murky water. Drizzt, too, rolled away, struggling against the dizziness to regain his feet. When he did, he found himself facing Entreri once again, the assassin even worse off than he.

Entreri looked over the drow's shoulder, to the tunnel and the charging dwarf and to Catti-brie and her killer bow, coming up level with his face. He jumped to the side, to the iron rungs, and started up to the street.

Catti-brie followed his motion in a fluid movement, keeping him dead in her sights. No one, not even Artemis Entreri, could escape once she had him cleanly targeted.

"Get him, girl!" Bruenor yelled.

Drizzt had been so involved in the battle that he hadn't even noticed the arrival of his friends. He spun around to see Bruenor rolling in, and Catti-brie just about to loose her arrow.

"Hold!" Drizzt growled in a tone that froze Bruenor in his tracks and sent a shiver through Catti-brie's spine. They both gawked, open-mouthed, at Drizzt.

"He is mine!" the drow told them.

Entreri didn't hesitate to consider his good fortune. Out in the open streets, his streets, he might find his sanctuary.

With no retort forthcoming from either of his unnerved friends, Drizzt slapped the magical mask up over his face and was just as quick to follow.

✕ ✕ ✕ ✕ ✕

The realization that his delay might bring danger to his friends—for they had gone rushing off to search for some way to meet him back on the street—spurred Wulfgar to action. He clasped Aegis-fang tightly in the hand of his wounded arm, forcing injured muscles to respond to his commands.

Then he thought of Drizzt, of that quality his friend possessed to completely sublimate fear in the face of impossible odds and replace it with pointed fury.

This time, it was Wulfgar's eyes that burned with an inner fire. He stood wide-legged in the corridor, his breath rasping out as low growls, and his muscles flexing and relaxing in a rhythmic pattern that honed them to fighting perfection.

The thieves' guild, the strongest house in Calimport, he thought.

A smile spread over the barbarian's face. The pain was gone now, and the weariness had flown from his bones. His smile became a heartfelt laugh as he rushed off.

Time to fight.

He took note of the ascending slope of the tunnel as he jogged along and knew the next door he went through would be at or near street level. He soon came upon, not one, but three doors: one at the end of the tunnel and one on either side. Wulfgar hardly slowed, figuring the direction he was traveling to be as good as any, and barreled through the door at the corridor's end, crashing into an octagonal-shaped guard room complete with four very surprised guards.

"Hey!" the one in the middle of the room blurted as Wulfgar's huge fist slammed him to the floor. The barbarian spotted another door directly across from the one he had entered, and cut a beeline for it, hoping to get through the room without a drawn-out fight.

One of the guards, a puny, dark-haired little rogue, proved

the quickest. He darted to the door, inserted a key, and flipped the lock, then he turned to face Wulfgar, holding the key out before him and grinning a broken-toothed smile.

"Key," he whispered, tossing the device to one of his comrades to the side.

Wulfgar's huge hand grabbed his shirt, taking out more than a few chest hairs, and the little rogue felt his feet leave the floor.

With one arm, Wulfgar threw him through the door.

"Key," the barbarian said, stepping over the kindling—and thief pile.

Wulfgar hadn't nearly outrun the danger, though. The next room was a great meeting hall, with dozens of chambers directly off it. Cries of alarm followed the barbarian as he sprinted through, and a well-rehearsed defense plan went into execution all around him. The human thieves, Pook's original guild members, fled for the shadows and the safety of their rooms, for they had been relieved of the responsibilities of dealing with intruders more than a year before—since Rassiter and his crew had joined the guild.

Wulfgar rushed to a short flight of stairs and leaped up them in a single bound, smashing through the door at the top. A maze of corridors and open chambers loomed before him, a treasury of artworks—statues, paintings, and tapestries—beyond any collection the barbarian had ever imagined. Wulfgar had little time to appreciate the artwork. He saw the forms chasing him. He saw them off to the side and gathering down the corridors before him to cut him off. He knew what they were; he had just been in their sewers.

He knew the smell of wererats.

✕ ✕ ✕ ✕ ✕

Entreri had his feet firmly planted, ready for Drizzt as he came up through the open grate. When the drow's form began to exit onto the street, the assassin cut down viciously with his saber.

Drizzt, running up the iron rungs in perfect balance, had his hands free, however. Expecting such a move, he had crossed his scimitars up over his head as he came through. He caught Entreri's saber in he wedge and pushed it harmlessly aside.

Then they were faced off on the open street.

The first hints of dawn cracked over the eastern horizon, the temperature had already begun to soar, and the lazy city awakened around them.

Entreri came in with a rush, and Drizzt fought him back with wicked counters and sheer strength. The drow did not blink, his features locked in a determined grimace. Methodically he moved at the assassin, both scimitars cutting with even, solid strokes.

His left arm useless and his left eye seeing no more than a blur, Entreri knew that he could not hope to win. Drizzt saw it, too, and he picked up the tempo, slapping again and again at the slowing saber in an effort to further weary Entreri's only defense.

But as Drizzt pressed into the battle, his magical mask once again loosened and dropped from his face.

Entreri smirked, knowing that he had once again dodged certain death. He saw his out.

"Caught in a lie?" he whispered wickedly.

Drizzt understood.

"A drow!" Entreri shrieked to the multitude of people he knew to be watching the battle from nearby shadows. "From the Forest of Mir! A scout, a prelude to an army! A drow!"

Curiosity now pulled a throng from their concealments. The

battle had been interesting enough before, but now the street people had to come closer to verify Entreri's claims. Gradually a circle began to form around the combatants, and Drizzt and Entreri heard the ring of swords coming free of scabbards.

"Good-bye, Drizzt Do'Urden," Entreri whispered under the growing tumult and the cries of "drow!" springing up throughout the area. Drizzt could not deny the effectiveness of the assassin's ploy. He glanced around nervously, expecting an attack from behind at any moment.

Entreri had the distraction he needed. As Drizzt looked to the side again, he broke away and stumbled off through the crowd, shouting, "Kill the drow! Kill him!"

Drizzt swung around, blades ready, as the anxious mob cautiously moved in. Catti-brie and Bruenor came up onto the street then and saw at once what had happened, and what was about to happen. Bruenor rushed to Drizzt's side and Catti-brie notched an arrow.

"Back away!" the dwarf grumbled. "Suren there be no evil here, except for the one ye fools just let get away!"

One man approached boldly, his spear leading the way.

A silver explosion caught the weapon's shaft, severing its tip. Horrified, the man dropped the broken spear and looked to the side, to where Catti-brie had already notched another arrow.

"Get away," she growled at him. "Leave the elf in peace, or me next shot won't be lookin' for yer weapon!"

The man backed away, and the crowd seemed to lose its heart for the fight as quickly as it had found it. None of them ever really wanted to tangle with a drow elf anyway, and they were more than happy now to believe the dwarf's words, that this one wasn't evil.

Then a commotion down the lane turned all heads. Two of the guards posing as bums outside the thieves' guild pulled open the door—to the sound of fighting—and charged inside, slamming the door behind them.

"Wulfgar!" shouted Bruenor, roaring down the road. Catti-brie started to follow but turned back to consider Drizzt.

The drow stood as if torn, looking one way, to the guild, and the other, to where the assassin had run. He had Entreri beaten; the injured man could not possibly stand up against him.

How could he just let Entreri go?

"Yer friends need ye," Catti-brie reminded him. "If not for Regis, then for Wulfgar."

Drizzt shook his head in self-reproach. How could he even have considered abandoning his friends at that critical moment? He rushed past Catti-brie, chasing Bruenor down the road.

⚔ ⚔ ⚔ ⚔ ⚔

Above Rogues Circle, the dawn's light had already found Pasha Pook's lavish chambers. LaValle moved cautiously toward the curtain at the side of his room and pushed it aside. Even he, a practiced wizard, would not dare to approach the device of unspeakable evil before the sun had risen, the Taros Hoop, his most powerful—and frightening—device.

He grasped its iron frame and slid it out of the tiny closet. On its stand and rollers, it was taller than he, with the worked hoop, large enough for a man to walk through, fully a foot off the floor. Pook had remarked that it was similar to the hoop the trainer of his great cats had used.

But any lion jumping through the Taros Hoop would hardly land safely on the other side.

LaValle turned the hoop to the side and faced it fully, examining the symmetrical spider web that filled its interior. So fragile the webbing appeared, but LaValle knew the strength in its strands, a magical power that transcended the very planes of existence.

LaValle slipped the instrument's trigger, a thin scepter capped with an enormous black pearl, into his belt and wheeled the Taros Hoop out into the central room of the level. He wished that he had the time to test his plan, for he certainly didn't want to disappoint his master again, but the sun was nearly full in the eastern sky and Pook would not be pleased with any delay.

Still in his nightshirt, Pook dragged himself out into the central chamber at LaValle's call. The guildmaster's eyes lit up at the sight of the Taros Hoop, which he, not a wizard and not understanding the dangers involved with such an item, thought a simply wonderful toy.

LaValle, holding the scepter in one hand and the onyx figurine of Guenhwyvar in the other, stood before the device. "Hold this," he said to Pook, tossing him the statuette. "We can get the cat later; I'll not need the beast for the task at hand."

Pook absently dropped the statuette into a pocket.

"I have scoured the planes of existence," the wizard explained. I knew the cat to be of the Astral Plane, but I wasn't certain that the halfling would remain there—if he could find his way out. and of course, the Astral Plane is very extensive."

"Enough!" ordered Pook. "Be on with it! What have you to show me?"

"Only this," LaValle replied, waving the scepter in front of the Taros Hoop. The webbing tingled with power and lit up in tiny flashes of lightning. Gradually the light became more constant, filling in the area between strands, and the image of the webbing disappeared into the background of cloudy blue.

LaValle spoke a command word, and the hoop focused in on a bright, well-lit grayness, a scene in the Astral Plane. There sat

Regis, leaning comfortably against the limned image of a tree, a starlight sketch of an oak, with his hands tucked behind his head and his feet crossed out in front of him.

Pook shook the grogginess from his head. "Get him," he coughed. "How can we get him?"

Before LaValle could answer, the door burst open and Rassiter stumbled into the room. "Fighting, Pook," he gasped, out of breath, "in the lower levels. A giant barbarian."

"You promised me that you would handle it," Pook growled at him.

"The assassin's friends—" Rassiter began, but Pook had no time for explanations. Not now.

"Shut the door," he said to Rassiter.

Rassiter quieted and did as he was told. Pook was going to be angry enough with him when he learned of the disaster in the sewers—no need to press the point.

The guildmaster turned back to LaValle, this time not asking. "Get him," he said.

LaValle chanted softly and waved the scepter in front of the Taros Hoop again, then he reached through the glassy curtain separating the planes and caught the sleepy Regis by the hair.

"Guenhwyvar!" Regis managed to shout, but then LaValle tugged him through the portal and he tumbled on the floor, rolling right up to the feet of Pasha Pook.

"Uh . . . hello," he stammered, looking up at Pook apologetically. "Can we talk about this?"

Pook kicked him hard in the ribs and planted the butt of his walking stick on Regis's chest. "You will cry out for death a thousand times before I release you from this world," the guildmaster promised.

Regis did not doubt a word of it.

21
WHERE NO SUN SHINES

Wulfgar dodged and ducked, slipping into the midst of lines of statues or behind heavy tapestries as he went. There were simply too many of the wererats, closing in all about him, for him to even hope to escape.

He passed one corridor and saw a group of three ratmen rushing down toward him. Feigning terror, the barbarian sprinted beyond the opening, then pulled up short and put his back tight against the corner. When the ratmen rushed into the room, Wulfgar smashed them down with quick chops of Aegis-fang.

He then retraced their steps back down the passage, hoping that he might confuse the rest of his pursuers.

He came into a wide room with rows of chairs and a high ceiling—a stage area for Pook's private showings by performing troupes. A massive chandelier, thousands of candles burning within its sconces, hung above the center of the room, and marble pillars, delicately carved into the likenesses of famed

heroes and exotic monsters, lined the walls. Again Wulfgar had
no time to admire the decorations. He noticed only one feature
in the chamber: a short staircase along one side that led up to
a balcony.

Ratmen poured in from the room's numerous entrances.
Wulfgar looked back over his shoulder, down the passage, but
saw that it, too, was blocked. He shrugged and sprinted up the
stairs, figuring that that route would at least allow him to fight
off his attackers in a line rather than a crowd.

Two wererats rushed up right on his heels, but when Wulfgar
made the landing and turned on them, they realized their disadvantage. The barbarian would have towered over them on
even footing. Now, three steps up, his knees ran level with their
eyes.

It wasn't such a bad position for offense; the wererats could
poke at Wulfgar's unprotected legs. But when Aegis-fang
descended in that tremendous arc, neither of the ratmen could
possibly slow its momentum. And on the stairs, they didn't have
much room to move out of the way.

The warhammer cracked onto the skull of one ratman with
enough force to break his ankles, and the other, blanching under
his brown fur, leaped over the side of the staircase.

Wulfgar nearly laughed aloud.

Then he saw the spears being readied.

He rushed into the balcony for the cover the railings and the
chairs might provide and hoping for another exit. The wererats
flooded onto the staircase in pursuit.

Wulfgar found no other doors. He shook his head, realizing
that he was trapped, and slapped Aegis-fang to the ready.

What was it that Drizzt had told him about luck? That a true
warrior always seemed to find the proper route—the one open
path that casual observers might consider lucky?

Now Wulfgar did laugh out loud. He had killed a dragon once by dislodging an icicle above its back. He wondered what a huge chandelier with a thousand burning candles might do to a room full of ratmen.

"Tempus!" the barbarian roared to his battle god, seeking a measure of deity-inspired luck to aid his way—Drizzt did not know everything, after all! He launched Aegis-fang with all his strength, breaking into a dead run after the warhammer.

Aegis-fang twirled across the room as precisely as every throw Wulfgar had ever made with it. It blasted through the chandelier's supports, bringing a fair measure of the ceiling down with it. Ratmen scrambled and dived off to the side as the massive ball of crystal and flames exploded onto the floor.

Wulfgar, still in stride, planted a foot atop the balcony railing and leaped.

⚔ ⚔ ⚔ ⚔

Bruenor growled and brought his axe up over his head, meaning to chop the door to the guildhouse down in a single stroke, but as the dwarf pounded through the final strides to the place, an arrow whistled over his shoulder, scorching a hole around the latch, and the door swung free.

Unable to break his momentum, Bruenor barreled through the opening and tumbled head over heels down the stairs inside, taking the two surprised guards along with him.

Dazed, Bruenor pulled himself to his knees and looked back up the stairs, to see Drizzt sprinting down five steps at a stride and Catti-brie just cresting the top to follow.

"Durn ye, girl!'" the dwarf roared. "I told ye to tell me when ye was meaning to do that!"

"No time," Drizzt interrupted. He leaped the last seven

steps—and clear over the kneeling dwarf—to intercept two wererats coming in on Bruenor's back.

Bruenor scooped up his helmet, plopped it back in place, and turned to join the fun, but the two wererats were long dead before the dwarf ever got back to his feet, and Drizzt was rushing away to the sounds of a larger battle farther in the complex. Bruenor offered Catti-brie his arm as she came charging past, so that he could profit from her momentum in the pursuit.

⚔ ⚔ ⚔ ⚔ ⚔

Wulfgar's huge legs brought him clear over the mess of the chandelier, and he tucked his head under his arms as he dropped into a group of ratmen, knocking them every which way. Dazed but still coherent enough to mark his direction, Wulfgar barreled through a door and stumbled into another wide chamber. An open door loomed before him, leading into yet another maze of chambers and corridors.

But Wulfgar couldn't hope to get there with a score of wererats blocking his way. He slipped over to the side of the room and put his back to a wall.

Thinking him unarmed, the ratmen rushed in, shrieking in glee. Then Aegis-fang magically returned to Wulfgar's hands and he swatted the first two aside. He looked around, searching for another dose of luck.

Not this time.

Wererats hissed at him from every side, nipping with their ravaging teeth. They didn't need Rassiter to explain the power such a giant—a wererat giant—could add to their guild.

The barbarian suddenly felt naked in his sleeveless tunic as each bite narrowly missed its mark. Wulfgar had heard enough legends concerning such creatures to understand the horrid implications of a lycanthrope's bite, and he fought with every ounce of strength he could muster.

Even with his adrenaline pumping in his terror, the big man had spent half the night in battle and had suffered many wounds, most notably the gash on his arm from the hydra, opened again by his leap from the balcony. His swipes were beginning to slow.

Normally Wulfgar would have fought to the end with a song on his lips as he racked up a pile of dead enemies at his feet and smiled in the knowledge that he had died a true warrior. But now, knowing his cause to be hopeless, with implications much worse than death, he scanned the room for a certain method of killing himself.

Escape was impossible. Victory even more so. Wulfgar's only thought and desire at that moment was to be spared the indignity and anguish of lycanthropy.

Then Drizzt entered the room.

He came in on the back of the wererat ranks like a sudden tornado dropping onto an unprepared village. His scimitars flashed blood red in seconds; and patches of fur flew about the room. Those few ratmen in his path who managed to escape put their tails between themselves and the killer drow and fled from the room.

One wererat turned and got his sword up to parry, but Drizzt lopped off his arm at the elbow and drove a second blade through the beast's chest. Then the drow was beside his giant friend, and his appearance gave Wulfgar renewed courage and strength. Wulfgar grunted in exhilaration, catching one attacker full in the chest with Aegis-fang and driving the wretched beast right through a wall. The ratman lay, quite dead, on his back in one room, but his legs, looped at the knees through the room's newest window, twitched grotesquely for his comrades to witness.

The ratmen glanced nervously at each other for support and came at the two warriors tentatively.

If their morale was sinking, it flew away altogether a moment later, when the roaring dwarf pounded into the room, led by a volley of silver-streaking arrows that cut the rats down with unerring accuracy. For the ratmen, it was the sewer scenario all over again, where they had lost more than two dozen of their comrades earlier that same night. They had no heart to face the four friends united, and those that could flee, did.

Those that remained had a difficult choice: hammer, blade, axe, or arrow.

⚔ ⚔ ⚔ ⚔ ⚔

Pook sat back in his great chair, watching the destruction through an image in the Taros Hoop. It did not pain the guild-master to see wererats dying—a few well-placed bites out in the streets could replenish the supply of the wretched things—but Pook knew that the heroes cutting their way through his guild would eventually wind up in his face.

Regis, held off the ground by the seat of his pants by one of Pook's hill giant eunuchs, watched, too. The mere sight of Bruenor, whom Regis had believed killed in Mithral Hall, brought tears to the halfling's eyes. And the thought that his dearest friends had traveled the breadth of the Realms to rescue him and were now fighting for his sake as mightily as he had ever witnessed, overwhelmed him. All of them bore wounds, particularly Catti-brie and Drizzt, but all of them ignored the pain as they tore into Pook's militia. Watching them felling foes with every cut and thrust, Regis had little doubt that they would win through to get to him.

Then the halfling looked to the side of the Taros Hoop, where LaValle stood, unconcerned, his arms crossed over his chest and his pearl-tipped scepter tapping on one shoulder.

"Your followers do not fare so well, Rassiter," the guildmaster remarked. "One might even note their cowardice."

Rassiter shuffled uneasily from one foot to the other.

"Is it that you cannot hold to your part of our arrangement?"

"My guild fights mighty enemies this night," Rassiter stammered. "They . . . we have not been able . . . the fight is not yet lost!"

"Perhaps you should see to it that your rats fare better," Pook said calmly, and Rassiter did not miss the command's—the threat's—tone. He bowed low and rushed out of the chamber, slamming the door behind him.

Even the demanding guildmaster could not hold the wererats wholly responsible for the disaster at hand.

"Magnificent," he muttered as Drizzt fought off two simultaneous thrusts and sliced down both wererats with individual, yet mystically intertwined counters. "Never have I seen such grace with a blade." He paused for a moment to consider that thought. "Perhaps once!"

Surprised at the revelation, Pook looked at LaValle, who nodded in accord.

"Entreri," LaValle inferred. "The resemblance is unmistakable. We know now why the assassin coaxed this group to the south."

"To fight the drow?" Pook mused. "At last, a challenge for the man without peer?"

"So it would seem."

"But, where is he, then? Why has he not made his appearance?"

"Perhaps he already has," LaValle replied grimly.

Pook paused to consider the words for a long moment; they

were too unconscionable for him to believe. "Entreri beaten?" He gasped. "Entreri dead?"

The words rang like sweet music to Regis, who had watched the rivalry between the assassin and Drizzt with horror from its inception. All along, Regis had suspected that those two would fall into a duel that only one could survive. And all along, the halfling had feared for his drow friend.

The thought of Entreri gone put a new perspective on the battle at hand for Pasha Pook. Suddenly he needed Rassiter and his cohorts again; suddenly the carnage he watched through the Taros Hoop had a more direct impact on his guild's immediate power.

He leaped from his seat and ambled over to the evil device. "We must stop this," he snarled at LaValle. "Send them away to a dark place!"

The wizard grinned wickedly and shuffled off to retrieve a huge book, bound in black leather. Opening it to a marked page, LaValle walked before the Taros Hoop and began the initial chantings of an ominous incantation.

⚔ ⚔ ⚔ ⚔ ⚔

Bruenor was first out of the room, searching for a likely route to Regis—and for more wererats to chop down. He stormed along a short corridor and kicked open a door, finding, not wererats, but two very surprised human thieves. Holding a measure of mercy in his battle-hardened heart—after all, he was the invader—Bruenor held back his twitching axe hand and shield-slammed the two rogues to the ground. He then rushed back out into the corridor and fell in line with the rest of his friends.

"Watch yer right!" Catti-brie cried out, noting some movement behind a tapestry near the front of the line, beside Wulfgar. The barbarian pulled the heavy tapestry down with a single heave, revealing a tiny man, barely more than a halfling, crouched and poised to spring. Exposed, the little thief quickly lost his heart for the fight and just shrugged apologetically as Wulfgar slapped his puny dagger away.

Wulfgar caught him up by the back of the neck, hoisting the little man into the air and putting his nose to the thief's. "What manner are you?" Wulfgar scowled. "Man or rat?"

"Not a rat!" the terrified thief shrieked. He spat on the ground to emphasize his point. "Not a rat!"

"Regis?" Wulfgar demanded. "You know of him?"

The thief nodded eagerly.

"Where can I find Regis?" Wulfgar roared, his bellow draining the blood from the thief's face.

"Up," the little man squeaked. "Pook's rooms. All the way up." Acting solely on instinct for survival, and having no real intentions to do anything but get away from the monstrous barbarian, the thief slipped one hand to a hidden dagger tucked in the back of his belt.

Bad judgment.

Drizzt slapped a scimitar against the thief's arm, exposing the move to Wulfgar.

Wulfgar used the little man to open the next door.

Again the chase was on. Wererats darted in and out of the shadows to the sides of the four companions, but few stood to face them. Those that did wound up in their path more often by accident than design!

More doors splintered and more rooms emptied, and a few minutes later, a stairway came into view. Broad and lavishly carpeted, with ornate banisters of shining hardwood, it could only be the ascent to the chambers of Pasha Pook.

Bruenor roared in glee and charged on. Wulfgar and Catti-brie eagerly followed. Drizzt hesitated and looked around, suddenly fearful.

Drow elves were magical creatures by nature, and Drizzt now sensed a strange and dangerous tingle, the beginnings of a spell aimed at him. He saw the walls and floor around him waver suddenly, as if they had become somehow less tangible.

Then he understood. He had traveled the Planes before, as companion to Guenhwyvar, his magical cat, and he knew now that someone, or something, was pulling him from his place on the Prime Material Plane. He looked ahead to see Bruenor and the others now similarly confused.

"Join hands!" the drow cried, rushing to get to his friends before the dweomer banished them all.

✄ ✄ ✄ ✄ ✄

In hopeless horror, Regis watched his friends huddle together. Then the scene in the Taros hoop shifted from the lower levels of the guildhouse to a darker place, a place of smoke and shadows, of ghouls and demons.

A place where no sun shone.

"No!" the halfling cried out, realizing the wizard's intent. LaValle paid him no heed, and Pook only snickered at him. Seconds later, Regis saw his friends in their huddle again, this time in the swirling smoke of the dark plane.

Pook leaned heavily on his walking stick and laughed. "How I love to foil hopes!" he said to his wizard. "Once more you prove your inestimable worth to me, my precious LaValle!"

Regis watched as his friends turned back to back in a pitiful attempt at defense. Already, dark shapes swooped about them or hovered over them—beings of great power and great evil.

Regis dropped his eyes, unable to watch.

"Oh, do not look away, little thief," Pook laughed at him. "Watch their deaths and be happy for them, for I assure you that the pain they are about to suffer will not compare to the torments I have planned for you."

Regis, hating the man and hating himself for putting his friends in such a predicament, snapped a vile glare at Pook. They had come for him. They had crossed the world for him. They had battled Artemis Entreri and a host of wererats, and most probably many other adversaries. All of it had been for him.

"Damn you," Regis spat, suddenly no longer afraid. He swung himself down and bit the eunuch hard on the inner thigh. The giant shrieked in pain and loosened his grip, dropping Regis to the floor.

The halfling hit the ground running. He crossed before Pook, kicking out the walking stick the guildmaster was using for support, while very deftly slipping a hand into Pook's pocket to retrieve a certain statuette. He then went on to LaValle.

The wizard had more time to react and had already begun a quick spell when Regis came at him, but the halfling proved the quicker. He leaped up, putting two fingers into LaValle's eyes, disrupting the spell, and sending the wizard stumbling backward.

As the wizard struggled to hold his balance, Regis jerked the pearl-tipped scepter away and ran up to the front of the Taros Hoop. He glanced around at the room a final time, wondering if he might find an easier way.

Pook dominated the vision. His face blood red and locked into a grimace, the guildmaster had recovered from the attack and now twirled his walking stick as a weapon, which Regis knew from experience to be deadly.

"Please give me this one," Regis whispered to whatever god

might be listening. He gritted his teeth and ducked his head, lurching forward and letting the scepter lead him into the Taros Hoop.

22

THE RIFT

Smoke, emanating from the very ground they stood upon, wafted by drearily and rolled around their feet. By the angle of its roll, the way it fell away below them only a foot or two off to either side, only to rise again in another cloud, the friends saw that they were on a narrow ledge, a bridge across some endless chasm.

Similar bridges, none more than a few feet wide, crisscrossed above and below them, and for what they could see, those were the only walkways in the entire plane. No solid land mass showed itself in any direction, only the twisting, spiraling bridges.

The friends' movements were slow, dreamlike, fighting against the weight of the air. The place itself, a dim, oppressive world of foul smells and anguished cries, exuded evil. Vile, misshapen monsters swooped over their heads and around the gloomy emptiness, crying out in glee at the unexpected appearance of such tasty morsels. The four friends, so indomitable against the perils of their own world, found themselves without courage.

"The Nine Hells?" Catti-brie whispered in a tiny voice, afraid that her words might shatter the temporary inaction of the multitudes gathering in the ever-present shadows.

"Hades," Drizzt guessed, more schooled in the known planes. "The domain of Chaos." Though he was standing right beside his friends, his words rang out as distant as had Catti-brie's.

Bruenor started to growl out a retort, but his voice faded away when he looked at Catti-brie and Wulfgar, his children, or so he considered them. Now there was nothing he could possibly do to help them.

Wulfgar looked to Drizzt for answers. "How can we escape?" he pressed bluntly. "Is there a door? A window back to our own world?"

Drizzt shook his head. He wanted to reassure them, to keep their spirits up in the face of the danger. This time, though, the drow had no answers for them. He could see no escape, no hope.

A bat-winged creature, doglike, but with a face grotesquely and unmistakably human, dived at Wulfgar, putting a filthy talon in line with the barbarian's shoulder.

"Drop!" Catti-brie yelled to Wulfgar at the last possible second. The barbarian didn't question the command. He fell to his face, and the creature missed its mark. It swerved around in a loop and hung in midair for a split second as it made a tight turn, then it came back again, hungry for living flesh.

Catti-brie was ready for it this time, though, and as it neared the group, she loosed an arrow. It reached out lazily toward the monster, cutting a dull gray streak instead of the usual silver. The magic arrow blasted in with the customary strength, though, scorching a wicked hole in the dog fur and unbalancing the monster's flight. It rolled in just above them, trying to right itself, and Bruenor chopped it down, dropping it in a spiraling descent into the gloom below them.

The friends could hardly be pleased with the minor victory. A hundred similar beasts flitted in and out of their vision above, below, and to the sides, many of them ten times larger than the one Bruenor and Catti-brie had felled.

"We can't be staying here," Bruenor muttered. "Where do we go, elf?"

Drizzt would have been just as content staying where they were, but he knew that marching out a course would comfort his friends and give them at least some feeling that they were making progress against their dilemma. Only the drow understood the depth of the horror they now faced. Only Drizzt knew that wherever they might travel on the dark plane, the situation would prove to be the same: no escape.

"This way," he said after a moment of mock contemplation. "If there is a door, I sense that it is this way." He took a step down the narrow bridge but stopped abruptly as the smoke heaved and swirled before him.

Then it rose in front of him.

Humanoid in shape, it was tall and slender, with a bulbous, froglike head and long, three-fingered hands that ended in claws. Taller even than Wulfgar, it towered over Drizzt. "Chaos, dark elf?" it lisped in a guttural, foreign voice. "Hades?"

Twinkle glowed eagerly in Drizzt's hand, but his other blade, the one forged with ice-magic, nearly leaped out at the monster.

"Err, you do," the creature croaked.

Bruenor rushed up beside Drizzt. "Get yerself back, demon," he growled.

"Not demon," said Drizzt, understanding the creature's references and remembering more of the many lessons he had been taught about the Planes during his years in the city of drow. "Demodand."

Bruenor looked up at him curiously.

"And not Hades," Drizzt explained. "Tarterus."

"Good, dark elf," croaked the demodand. "Knowing of the lower planes are your people."

"Then you understand of the power of my people," Drizzt bluffed, "and you know how we repay even demon lords who cross us."

The demodand laughed, if that's what it was, for it sounded more like the dying gurgle of a drowning man. "Dead drow avenge do not. Far from home are you!" It reached a lazy hand toward Drizzt.

Bruenor rushed by his friend. "Moradin!" he cried, and he swiped at the demodand with his mithral axe. The demodand was faster than the dwarf had expected, though, and it easily dodged the blow, countering with a clubbing blow of its arm that sent Bruenor skidding on his face farther down the bridge.

The demodand reached down at the passing dwarf with its wicked claws.

Twinkle cut the hand in half before it ever reached Bruenor.

The demodand turned on Drizzt in amazement. "Hurt me you did, dark elf," it croaked, though no hint of pain rang out in its voice, "but better you must do!" It snapped the wounded hand out at Drizzt, and as he reflexively dodged it, the demodand sent its second hand out to finish the task of the first, cutting a triple line of gashes down the sprawled dwarf's shoulder.

"Blast and bebother!" Bruenor roared, getting back to his knees. "Ye filthy, slime-covered . . ." he grumbled, launching a second unsuccessful attack.

Behind Drizzt, Catti-brie bobbed and ducked, trying to get

a clear shot with Taulmaril. Beside her, Wulfgar stood at the ready, having no room on the narrow bridge to move up beside the drow.

Drizzt moved sluggishly, his scimitars awkwardly twisting through an uneven sequence. Perhaps it was because of the weariness of a long night of fighting or the unusual weight of the air in the plane, but Catti-brie, looking on curiously, had never seen the drow so lackluster in his efforts.

Still on his knees farther down the bridge, Bruenor swiped more with frustration than his customary lust for battle.

Catti-brie understood. It wasn't weariness or the heavy air. Hopelessness had befallen the friends.

She looked to Wulfgar, to beg him to intervene, but the sight of the barbarian beside her gave her no comfort. His wounded arm hung limply at his side, and the heavy head of Aegis-fang dipped below the low-riding smoke. How many more battles could he fight? How many of these wretched demodand would he be able to put down before he met his end?

And what end would a victory bring in a plane of unending battles? she wondered.

Drizzt felt the despair most keenly. For all the trials of his hard life, the drow had held faith for ultimate justice. He had believed, though he never dared to admit it, that his unyielding faith in his precious principles would bring him the reward he deserved. Now, there was this, a struggle that could only end in death, where one victory brought only more conflict.

"Damn ye all!" Catti-brie cried. She didn't have a safe shot, but she fired anyway. Her arrow razed a line of blood across Drizzt's arm, but then exploded into the demodand, rocking it back and giving Bruenor the chance to scramble back to Drizzt's side.

"Have ye lost yer fight, then?" Catti-brie scolded them.

"Easy, girl," Bruenor replied somberly, cutting low at the demodand's knees. The creature hopped over the blade gingerly and started another attack, which Drizzt deflected.

"Easy yerself, Bruenor Battlehammer!" Catti-brie shouted. "Ye've the gall to call yerself king o' yer clan. Ha! Garumn'd be tossin' in his grave to see ye fightin' so!"

Bruenor turned a wicked glare on Catti-brie, his throat too choked for him to spit out a reply.

Drizzt tried to smile. He knew what the young woman, that wonderful young woman, was up to. His lavender eyes lit up with the inner fire. "Go to Wulfgar," he told Bruenor. "Secure our backs and watch for attacks from above."

Drizzt eyed the demodand, who had noted his sudden change in demeanor.

"Come, farastu," the drow said evenly, remembering the name given to that particular type of creature. "Farastu," he taunted, "the least of the demodand kind. Come and feel the cut of a drow's blade."

Bruenor backed away from Drizzt, almost laughing. Part of him wanted to say, "What's the point?" but a bigger part, the side of him that Catti-brie had awakened with her biting references to his proud history, had a different message to speak. "Come on and fight, then!" he roared into the shadows of the endless chasm. "We've enough for the whole damn world of ye!"

In seconds, Drizzt was fully in command. His movements remained slowed with the heaviness of the plane, but they were no less magnificent. He feinted and cut, sliced and parried, in harmony to offset every move the demodand made.

Instinctively Wulfgar and Bruenor started in to help him, but stopped to watch the display.

Catti-brie turned her gaze outward, plucking off a bowshot whenever a foul form flew from the hanging smoke. She took a quick bead on one body as it dropped from the darkness high above.

She pulled Taulmaril away at the last second in absolute shock.

"Regis!" she cried.

The halfling ended his half-speed plummet, plopping with a soft puff into the smoke of a second bridge a dozen yards across the emptiness from friends. He stood and managed to hold his ground against a wave of dizziness and disorientation.

"Regis!" Catti-brie cried again. "How did ye get yerself here?"

"I saw you in that awful hoop,'" the halfling explained. "Thought you might need my help."

"Bah! More that ye got yerself thrown here, Rumblebelly," Bruenor replied.

"Good to see you, too," Regis shot back, "but this time you are mistaken. I came of my own choice." He held the pearl-tipped scepter up for them to see. "To bring you this."

Truly Bruenor had been glad to see his little friend even before Regis had refuted his suspicion. He admitted his error by bowing low to Regis, his beard dipping under the smoky swirl.

Another demodand rose up, this one across the way, on the same bridge as Regis. The halfling showed his friends the scepter again. "Catch it," he begged, winding up to throw. "This is your only chance to get out of here!" He mustered up his nerve— there would only be one chance—and heaved the scepter as powerfully as he could. It spun end over end, tantalizingly slow in its journey toward the three sets of outstretched hands.

It could not cut a swift enough path through the heavy air, though, and it lost its speed short of the bridge.

"No!" Bruenor cried, seeing their hopes falling away.

Catti-brie growled in denial, unhitching her laden belt and dropping Taulmaril in a single movement.

She dived for the scepter.

Bruenor dropped flat to his chest desperately to grab her ankles, but she was too far out. A contented look came over her as she caught the scepter. She twisted about in midair and threw it back to Bruenor's waiting hands, then she plummeted from sight without a word of complaint.

⚔ ⚔ ⚔ ⚔ ⚔

LaValle studied the mirror with trembling hands. The image of the friends and the plane of Tarterus had faded into a dark blur when Regis had jumped through with the scepter. But that was the least of the wizard's concerns now. A thin crack, detectable only at close inspection, slowly etched its way down the center of the Taros Hoop.

LaValle spun on Pook, charging his master and grabbing at the walking stick. Too surprised to fight the wizard off, Pook surrendered the cane and stepped back curiously.

LaValle rushed back to the mirror. "We must destroy its magic!" he screamed and he smashed the cane into the glassy image.

The wooden stick, sundered by the device's power, splintered in his hands, and LaValle was thrown across the room. "Break it! Break it!" he begged Pook, his voice a pitiful whine.

"Get the halfling back!" Pook retorted, still more concerned with Regis and the statuette.

"You do not understand!" LaValle cried. "The halfling has the scepter! The portal cannot be closed from the other side!"

Pook's expression shifted from curiosity to concern as the gravity of his wizard's fears descended over him. "My dear

LaValle," he began calmly, "are you saying that we have an open door to Tarterus in my living quarters?"

LaValle nodded meekly.

"Break it! Break it!" Pook screamed at the eunuchs standing beside him. "Heed the wizard's words! Smash that infernal hoop to pieces!"

Pook picked up the broken end of his walking stick, the silver-shod, meticulously crafted cane he had been given personally by the Pasha of Calimshan.

The morning sun was still low in the eastern sky, but already the guildmaster knew that it would not be a good day.

⚔ ⚔ ⚔ ⚔ ⚔

Drizzt, trembling with anguish and anger, roared toward the demodand, his every thrust aimed at a critical spot. The creature, agile and experienced, dodged the initial assault, but it could not stay the enraged drow. Twinkle cut a blocking arm off at the elbow, and the other blade dived into the demodand's heart. Drizzt felt a surge of power run through his arm as his scimitar sucked the life-force out of the wretched creature, but the drow contained the strength, burying it within his own rage, and held on stubbornly.

When the thing lay lifeless, Drizzt turned to his companions.

"I did not . . ." Regis stammered from across the chasm. "She . . . I . . ."

Neither Bruenor nor Wulfgar could answer him. They stood frozen, staring into the empty darkness below.

"Run!" Drizzt called, seeing a demodand closing in behind the halfling. "We shall get to you!"

Regis tore his eyes from the chasm and surveyed the situation. "No need!" he shouted back. He pulled out the statuette and held it up for Drizzt to see. "Guenhwyvar will get me out of here, or perhaps the cat could aid—"

"No!" Drizzt cut him short, knowing what he was about to suggest. "Summon the panther and be gone!"

"We will meet again in a better place," Regis offered, his voice breaking in sniffles. He placed the statuette down before him and called out softly.

Drizzt took the scepter from Bruenor and put a comforting hand on his friend's shoulder. He then held the magic item to his chest, attuning his thoughts to its magical emanations.

His guess was confirmed; the scepter was indeed the key to the portal back to their own plane, a gate that Drizzt sensed was still open. He scooped up Taulmaril and Catti-brie's belt. "Come," he told his two friends, still staring at the darkness. He pushed them along the bridge, gently but firmly.

⚔ ⚔ ⚔ ⚔ ⚔

Guenhwyvar sensed the presence of Drizzt Do'Urden as soon as it came into the plane of Tarterus. The great cat moved with hesitancy when Regis asked it to take him away, but the halfling now possessed the statuette and Guenhwyvar had always known Regis as a friend. Soon Regis found himself in the swirling tunnel of blackness, drifting toward the distant light that marked Guenhwyvar's home plane.

Then the halfling knew his error.

The onyx statuette, the link to Guenhwyvar, still lay on the smoky bridge in Tarterus.

Regis turned himself about, struggling against the pull of the planar tunnel's currents. He saw the darkness at the back end of the tunnel and could guess the risks of reaching through. He could not leave the statuette, not only for fear of losing his magnificent feline friend, but in revulsion at the thought of some foul beast of the lower planes gaining control over Guenhwyvar. Bravely he poked his three-fingered hand through the closing portal.

All of his senses jumbled. Overwhelming bursts of signals and images from two planes rushed at him in a nauseating wave. He blocked them away, using his hand as a focal point and concentrating all of his thoughts and energies on the sensations of that hand.

Then his hand dropped upon something hard, something vividly tangible. It resisted his tug, as though it were not meant to pass through such a gate.

Regis was fully stretched now, his feet held straight down the tunnel by the incessant pull, and his hand stubbornly latched to the statuette he would not leave behind. With a final heave, with all the strength the little halfling had ever summoned—and just a tiny bit more—he pulled the statuette through the gate.

The smooth ride of the planar tunnel transformed into a nightmarish bounce and skip, with Regis hurtling head over heels and deflecting off the walls, which twisted suddenly, as if to deny him passage. Through it all, Regis clutched at only one thought: keep the statuette in his grasp.

He felt he would surely die. He could not survive the beating, the dizzying swirl.

Then it died away as abruptly as it had begun, and Regis, still holding the statuette, found himself sitting beside Guenhwyvar with his back to an astral tree. He blinked and looked around, hardly believing his fortune.

"Do not worry," he told the panther. "Your master and the others will get back to their world." He looked down at the statuette, his only link to the Prime Material Plane. "But how shall I?"

While Regis floundered in despair, Guenhwyvar reacted

differently. The panther spun about in a complete circuit and roared mightily into the starry vastness of the plane. Regis watched the cat's actions in amazement as Guenhwyvar leaped about and roared again, then bounded away into the astral nothingness.

Regis, more confused than ever, looked down at the statuette. One thought, one hope overrode all others at that moment.

Guenhwyvar knew something.

⚔ ⚔ ⚔ ⚔ ⚔

With Drizzt taking a ferocious lead, the three friends charged along, cutting down everything that dared to rise in their path. Bruenor and Wulfgar fought wildly, thinking that the drow was leading them to Catti-brie.

The bridge wound along a curving and rising route, and when Bruenor realized its ascending grade, he grew concerned. He was about to protest, to remind the drow that Catti-brie had fallen below them, but when he looked back, he saw that the area they had started from was clearly above them. Bruenor was a dwarf accustomed to lightless tunnels, and he could detect the slightest grade unerringly.

They were going up, more steeply now than before, and the area they had left continued to rise above them.

"How, elf?" he cried. "Up and up we go, but down by what me eyes be telling me."

Drizzt looked back and quickly understood what Bruenor was talking about. The drow didn't have time for philosophical inquiries; he was merely following the emanations of the scepter that would surely lead them to a gate. Drizzt did pause, though, to consider one possible quirk of the directionless, and apparently circular, plane.

Another demodand rose up before them, but Wulfgar swatted it from the bridge before it could even ready a strike. Blind rage drove the barbarian now, a third burst of adrenaline that denied his wounds and his weariness. He paused every few steps to look about, searching for something vile to hit, then he rushed back to the front, beside Drizzt, to get the first whack at anything trying to block their path.

The swirling smoke parted before them suddenly, and they faced a lighted image, blurry, but clearly of their own plane.

"The gate," Drizzt said. "The scepter has kept it open. Bruenor will pass through first."

Bruenor looked at Drizzt in blank amazement. "Leave?" he asked breathlessly. "How can ye ask me to leave, elf? Me girl's here."

"She is gone, my friend," Drizzt said softly.

"Bah!" Bruenor snorted, though it sounded as more of a sniffle. "Don't ye be so quick to make such a claim!"

Drizzt looked upon him with sincere sympathy, but refused to relinquish the point or change his course.

"And if she were gone, I'd stay as well," Bruenor proclaimed, "to find her body and carry it from this eternal hell!"

Drizzt grabbed the dwarf by the shoulders and squared up to face him. "Go, Bruenor, back to where we all belong," he said. "Do not diminish the sacrifice that Catti-brie has made for us. Do not steal the meaning from her fall."

"How can ye ask me to leave?" Bruenor said with a sniffle that he did not mask. Wetness glistened the edges of his gray eyes. "How can ye—"

"Think not of what has passed!" Drizzt said sharply. "Beyond that gate is the wizard that sent us here, the wizard that sent Catti-brie here!"

It was all Bruenor Battlehammer needed to hear. Fire

replaced the tears in his eyes, and with a roar of anger he dived through the portal, his axe leading the way.

"Now—" Drizzt began, but Wulfgar cut him short.

"You go, Drizzt," the barbarian replied. "Avenge Catti-brie and Regis. Finish the quest we undertook together. For myself, there will be no rest. My emptiness will not fade."

"She is gone," Drizzt said again.

Wulfgar nodded. "As am I," he said quietly.

Drizzt searched for some way to refute the argument, but truly Wulfgar's grief seemed too profound for him to ever recover.

Then Wulfgar's gaze shot up, and his mouth gaped in horrified—and elated—disbelief. Drizzt spun about, not as surprised, but still overwhelmed, by the sight before him.

Catti-brie fell limply and slowly from the dark sky above them.

It was a circular plane.

Wulfgar and Drizzt leaned together for support. They could not determine if Catti-brie was alive or dead. She was wounded gravely, at the least, and even as they watched, a winged demodand swooped down and grabbed at her leg with its huge talons.

Before a conscious thought had time to register in Wulfgar's mind, Drizzt had Taulmaril bent and sent a silver arrow into flight. It thundered into the side of the demodand's head just as the creature took hold of the young woman, blasting the thing from life.

"Go!" Wulfgar yelled at Drizzt, taking one stride. "I see my quest now! I know what I must do!"

Drizzt had other ideas. He slipped a foot through Wulfgar's legs and dropped in a spin, driving his other leg into the back of the barbarian's knees and tripping Wulfgar down to the side, toward the portal. Wulfgar understood the drow's intentions at once, and he scrambled to regain his balance.

Again Drizzt was the quicker. The point of a scimitar nicked in under Wulfgar's cheekbone, keeping him moving in the desired direction. As he neared the portal, just when Drizzt expected him to try some desperate maneuver, the drow drove a boot under his shoulder and kicked him hard.

Betrayed, Wulfgar tumbled into Pasha Pook's central chamber. He ignored his surroundings, grabbed at the Taros Hoop and shook it with all his strength.

"Traitor!" he yelled. "Never will I forget this, cursed drow!"

"Take your place!" Drizzt yelled back at him from across the planes. "Only Wulfgar has the strength to hold the gate open and secure. Only Wulfgar! Hold it, son of Beornegar. If you care for Drizzt Do'Urden, and if ever you loved Catti-brie, hold the gate!"

Drizzt could only pray that he had appealed to the small part of rationale accessible in the enraged barbarian. The drow turned from the portal, tucking the scepter into his belt and slinging Taulmaril over his shoulder. Catti-brie was below him now, still falling, still unmoving.

Drizzt drew out both his scimitars. How long would it take him to pull Catti-brie to a bridge and find his way back to the portal? he wondered. Or would he, too, be caught in an endless, doomed, fall?

And how long could Wulfgar hold the gate open?

He brushed away the questions. He had no time to speculate on their answers.

The fires gleamed in his lavender eyes, Twinkle glowed in one hand, and he felt the urgings of his other blade, pleading for a demodand's heart to bite.

With all the courage that had marked Drizzt Do'Urden's

existence coursing through his veins, and with all the fury of his perceptions of injustice focused on the fate of that beautiful and broken woman failing endlessly in a hopeless void, he dived into the gloom.

23

IF EVER YOU LOVED CATTI-BRIE

B ruenor had come into Pook's chambers cursing and swinging, and by the time his initial momentum had worn away,
he was far across the room from the Taros Hoop and from the
two hill giant eunuchs that Pook had on guard. The guildmaster
was closest to the raging dwarf, looking at him more in curiosity
than terror.

Bruenor paid Pook no mind whatsoever. He looked beyond
the plump man, to a robed form sitting against a wall: the wizard
who had banished Catti-brie to Tarterus.

Recognizing the murderous hate in the red-bearded dwarf's
eyes, LaValle rolled to his feet and scrambled through the door
to his own room. His racing heart calmed when he heard the
click of the door behind him, for it was a magic doorway with
several holding and warding spells in place. He was safe—or so
he thought.

Often wizards were blinded by their own considerable

strength to other—less sophisticated, perhaps, but equally strong—forms of power. LaValle could not know the boiling cauldron that was Bruenor Battlehammer, and could not anticipate the brutality of the dwarf's rage.

His surprise was complete when a mithral axe, like a bolt of his own lightning, sundered his magically barred door to kindling and the wild dwarf stormed in.

⚔ ⚔ ⚔ ⚔ ⚔

Wulfgar, oblivious to the surroundings and wanting only to return to Tarterus and Catti-brie, came through the Taros Hoop just as Bruenor exited the room. Drizzt's call from across the planes, though, begging him to hold the portal open, could not be ignored. However the barbarian felt at that moment, for Catti-brie or Drizzt, he could not deny that his place was in guarding the mirror.

Still, the image of Catti-brie falling through the eternal gloom of that horrid place burned at his heart, and he wanted to spring right back through the Taros Hoop to rush to her aid.

Before the barbarian could decide whether to follow his heart or his thoughts, a huge fist slammed into the side of his head, dropping him to the floor. He flopped facedown between the tree trunk legs of two of Pook's hill giants. It was a difficult way to enter a fight, but Wulfgar's rage was every bit as intense as Bruenor's.

The giants tried to drop their heavy feet on Wulfgar, but he was too agile for such a clumsy maneuver. He sprang up between them and slammed one square in the face with a huge fist. The giant stared blankly at Wulfgar for a long moment, disbelieving that a human could deliver such a punch, then it hopped backward weirdly and dropped limply to the floor.

Wulfgar spun on the other, shattering its nose with the butt end of Aegis-fang. The giant clutched its face in both hands and reeled. For it, the fight was already over.

Wulfgar couldn't take the time to ask. He kicked the giant in the chest, launching it halfway across the room.

"Now, there is only me," came a voice. Wulfgar looked across the room to the huge chair that served as the guildmaster's throne, and to Pasha Pook, standing behind it.

Pook reached down behind the chair and pulled out a neatly concealed heavy crossbow, loaded and ready. "And I may be fat like those two," Pook chuckled, "but I am not stupid." He leveled the crossbow on the back of the chair.

Wulfgar glanced around. He was caught, fully, with no chance to dodge away.

But maybe he didn't have to.

Wulfgar firmed his jaw and puffed out his chest. "Right here, then," he said without flinching, tapping his finger over his heart. "Shoot me down." He cast a glance over his shoulder, to where the image in the Taros Hoop now showed the shadows of gathering demodands. "And you defend the entrance to the plane of Tarterus."

Pook eased his finger off the trigger.

If Wulfgar's point had made an impression, it was driven home a second later when the clawed hand of a demodand reached through the portal and latched onto Wulfgar's shoulder.

✖ ✖ ✖ ✖ ✖

Drizzt moved as if swimming in his descent through the gloom, the pumping actions gaining him ground on Catti-brie. He was vulnerable, though, and he knew it.

So did a winged demodand watching him fall by.

The wretched creature hopped off its perch as soon as Drizzt had passed, flapping its wings at an awkward angle to gain momentum in its dive. Soon it was overtaking the drow, and it reached out its razor-sharp claws to tear at him as it passed.

Drizzt noticed the beast at the last moment. He twisted over wildly and spun about, trying to get out of the diving thing's path and struggling to ready his scimitars.

He should have had no chance. It was the demodand's environment, and it was a winged creature, more at home in flight than on the ground.

But Drizzt Do'Urden never played the odds.

The demodand strafed past, its wicked talons ripping yet another tear in Drizzt's fine cloak. Twinkle, as steady as ever even in midfall, lopped off one of the creature's wings. The demodand fluttered helplessly to the side and continued down in a tumble. It had no heart left for battle against the drow elf, and no wing left to catch him anyway.

Drizzt paid it no heed. His goal was in reach.

He caught Catti-brie in his arms, locking her tightly against his chest. She was cold, he noted grimly, but he knew that he had too far to go to even think about that. He wasn't certain if the planar gate was still open, and he had no idea of how he could stop his eternal fall.

A solution came to him in the form of another winged demodand, one that cut an intercepting path at him and Catti-brie. The creature did not mean to attack yet, Drizzt could see; its route seemed more of a flyby, where it would pass under them to better inspect its foe.

Drizzt didn't let the chance go. As the creature passed under, the dark elf snapped himself downward, extending to his limit with one blade-wielding hand. Not aimed to kill, the scimitar found its mark, digging into the creature's backside. The demodand shrieked and dived away, pulling free of the blade.

Its momentum, though, had tugged Drizzt and Catti-brie along, angling their descent enough to line them up with one of the intersecting smoky bridges.

Drizzt twisted and turned to keep them in line, holding out his cloak with his free arm to catch a draft, or tucking it in tightly to lessen the drag. At the last moment, he spun himself under Catti-brie to shield her from the impact. With a heavy thud and a whoosh of smoke, they landed.

Drizzt crawled out and forced himself to his knees, trying to find his breath.

Catti-brie lay below him, pale and torn, a dozen wounds visible, most vividly the gash from the wererat's quarrel. Blood soaked much of her clothing and matted her hair, but Drizzt's heart did not drop at the gruesome sight, for he had noted one other event when they had plopped down.

Catti-brie had groaned.

⚔ ⚔ ⚔ ⚔ ⚔

LaValle scrambled behind his little table. "Keep you back, dwarf," he warned, "I am a wizard of great powers."

Bruenor's terror was not apparent. He drove his axe through the table, and a blinding explosion of smoke and sparks filled the room.

When LaValle recovered his sight a moment later, he found himself facing Bruenor, the dwarf's hands and beard trailing wisps of gray smoke, the little table broken flat, and his crystal ball severed clean in half.

"That the best ye got?" Bruenor asked.

LaValle couldn't get any words past the lump in his throat.

Bruenor wanted to cut him down, to drive his axe right between the man's bushy eyebrows, but it was Catti-brie, his beautiful daughter, who truly abhorred killing with all of her heart, whom he meant to avenge. Bruenor would not dishonor her memory.

"Drats!" he groaned, slamming his forehead into LaValle's face. The wizard thumped up against the wall and stayed there, dazed and motionless, until Bruenor closed a hand on his chest, tearing out a few hairs for good measure, and threw him facedown on the floor. "Me friends might be needin' yer help, wizard," the dwarf growled, "so crawl! And know in yer heart that if ye make one turn I don't be liking, me axe'll cleave yer head down the middle!"

In his semiconscious state, LaValle hardly heard the words, but he fathomed the dwarf's meaning well enough and forced himself to his hands and knees.

⚔ ⚔ ⚔ ⚔ ⚔

Wulfgar braced his feet against the iron stand of the Taros Hoop and locked his own iron grip onto the demodand's elbow, matching the creature's mighty pull. In his other hand the barbarian held Aegis-fang ready, not wanting to swing through the planar portal but hoping for something more vulnerable than an arm to come through to his world.

The demodand's claws cut deep wounds in his shoulder, filthy wounds that would be long in healing, but Wulfgar shrugged away the pain. Drizzt had told him to hold the gate if ever he had loved Catti-brie.

He would hold the gate.

Another second passed and Wulfgar saw his hand slipping dangerously close to the portal. He could match the demodand's strength, but the demodand's power was magical, not physical, and Wulfgar would grow weary long before his foe.

Another inch, and his hand would cross through to Tarterus, where other hungry demodands no doubt waited.

A memory flashed in Wulfgar's mind, the final image of Catti-brie, torn and falling. "No!" he growled, and he forced his hand back, pulling savagely until he and the demodand were back to where they had started. Then Wulfgar dropped his shoulder suddenly, tugging the demodand down instead of out.

The gamble worked. The demodand lost its momentum altogether and stumbled down, its head poking through the Taros Hoop and into the Prime Material Plane for just a second, long enough for Aegis-fang to shatter its skull.

Wulfgar jumped back a step and slapped his warhammer into both hands. Another demodand started through, but the barbarian blasted it back into Tarterus with a powerful swipe.

Pook watched it all from behind his throne, his crossbow still aimed to kill. Even the guildmaster found himself mesmerized by the sheer strength of the giant man, and when one of his eunuchs recovered and stood up, Pook waved it away from Wulfgar, not wanting to disturb the spectacle before him.

A shuffle off to the side forced him to look away, though, as LaValle came crawling out of his room, the axe-wielding dwarf walking right behind.

Bruenor saw at once the perilous predicament that Wulfgar faced and knew that the wizard would only complicate things. He grabbed LaValle by the hair and pulled him up to his knees, walking around to face the man.

"Good day for sleepin'," the dwarf commented, and he slammed his forehead again into the wizard's, knocking LaValle into blackness. He heard a click behind him as the wizard slumped, and he reflexively swung his shield between himself and the noise, just in time to catch Pook's crossbow quarrel. The wicked dart drove a hole through the foaming mug standard and barely missed Bruenor's arm as it poked through the other side.

Bruenor peeked over the rim of his treasured shield, stared at the bolt, and then looked dangerously at Pook. "Ye shouldn't be hurtin' me shield!" he growled, and he started forward.

The hill giant was quick to intercept.

Wulfgar caught the action out of the corner of his eye, and would have loved to join in—especially with Pook busy reloading his heavy crossbow—but the barbarian had troubles of his own. A winged demodand swooped through the gate in a sudden rush and flashed by Wulfgar.

Fine-tuned reflexes saved the barbarian, for he snapped a hand out and caught the demodand by a leg. The monster's momentum staggered Wulfgar backward, but he managed to hold on. He slammed the demodand down beside him and drove it into the floor with a single chop of his warhammer.

Several arms reached through the Taros Hoop, shoulders and heads poked through, and Wulfgar, swinging Aegis-fang furiously, had all he could handle simply keeping the wretched things at bay.

❌ ❌ ❌ ❌ ❌

Drizzt ran along the smoky bridge, Catti-brie draped limply over one shoulder. He met no further resistance for many minutes and understood why when he at last reached the planar gate.

Huddled around it, and blocking his passage, was a score of demodands.

The drow, dismayed, dropped to one knee and laid Catti-brie gently beside him. He considered putting Taulmaril to use, but realized that if he missed, if an arrow somehow found its way through the horde, it would pass through the gate and into the room where Wulfgar stood. He couldn't take that chance.

"So close," he whispered helplessly, looking down to Catti-brie. He held her tightly in his arms and brushed a slender hand across her face. How cool she seemed. Drizzt leaned low over her, meaning only to discern the rhythm of her breathing, but he found himself too close to her, and before he even realized his actions, his lips were to hers in a tender kiss. Catti-brie stirred but did not open her eyes.

Her movement brought new courage to Drizzt. "Too close," he muttered grimly, "and you'll not die in this foul place!" He scooped Catti-brie up over his shoulder, wrapping his cloak tightly around her to secure her to him. Then he took up his scimitars in tight grips, rubbing his sensitive fingers across the intricate craftings of their hilts, becoming one with his weapons, making them the killing extensions of his black arms. He took a deep breath and set his visage.

He charged, as silently as only a drow elf could be, at the back of the wretched horde.

⚔ ⚔ ⚔ ⚔ ⚔

Regis rose uncomfortably as the black silhouettes of hunting cats darted in and out of the starlight surrounding him. They did not seem to threaten him—not yet—but they were gathering. He knew beyond doubt that he was their focal point.

Then Guenhwyvar bounded up and stood before him, the great cat's head level with his own.

"You know something," Regis said, reading the excitement in the panther's dark eyes. Regis held up the statuette and examined it, noting the cat's tenseness at the sight of the figurine.

"We can get back with this," the halfling said in sudden revelation. "This is the key to the journey, and with it, we can go wherever we desire!" He glanced around and considered some very interesting possibilities. "All of us?"

If cats could smile, Guenhwyvar did.

24

INTERPLANAR GOO

Outta me way, ye overstuffed bag o' blubber!" Bruenor roared.

The giant eunuch planted its legs wide apart and reached down at the dwarf with a huge hand—which Bruenor promptly bit.

"They never listen," he grumbled, He stooped low and dashed between the giant's legs, then straightened quickly, the single horn on his helmet putting the poor eunuch up on its toes. For the second time that day, its eyes crossed and it tumbled, this time its hands low to hold its newest wound.

A killing rage evident in his gray eyes, Bruenor turned back to Pook. The guildmaster, though, seemed unconcerned, and in truth, the dwarf hardly, noticed the man. He concentrated instead on the crossbow again, which was loaded and leveled at him.

⚔ ⚔ ⚔ ⚔ ⚔

Drizzt's single emotion as he came in was anger, anger at the pain the wretched creatures of Tarterus had caused to Catti-brie.

His goal, too, was singular: the little patch of light in the gloom, the planar gate back to his own world.

His scimitars led the way, and Drizzt grinned at the thought of tearing through the demodand flesh, but the drow slowed as he came in, his anger tempered by the sight of his goal. He could whirl in on the demodand horde in an attacking frenzy and probably manage to slip through the gate, but could Catti-brie take the punishment the mighty creatures would surely inflict before Drizzt got her through?

The drow saw another way. As he inched in on the back of the demodand line, he reached out wide to either side with his blades, tapping the back two demodands on their outside shoulders. As the creatures reflexively turned to look back over their shoulders, Drizzt darted between them.

The drow's blades became a whirring prow, nicking away the hands of any other demodands that tried to catch him. He felt a tug on Catti-brie and whirled quickly, his rage doubled. He couldn't see his target, but he knew that he had connected on something when he brought Twinkle down and heard a demodand shriek.

A heavy arm clubbed him on the side of the head, a blow that should have felled him, but Drizzt spun back again and saw the light of the gate only a few feet ahead—and the silhouette of a single demodand, standing to block his passage.

The dark tunnel of demodand flesh began to close about him. Another large arm wheeled in, but Drizzt was able to duck beneath its arc.

If the demodand delayed him a single second, he would be caught and slaughtered.

Again it was instinct, faster than thought, that carried Drizzt through. He slapped the demodand's arms wide apart with his scimitars and ducked his head, slamming into the demodand's chest, his momentum forcing the creature backward through the gate.

✕ ✕ ✕ ✕ ✕

The dark head and shoulders came through into Wulfgar's sights, and he hammered Aegis-fang home. The mighty blow snapped the demodand's backbone and jolted Drizzt, who pushed from the other side.

The demodand fell dead, half in and half out of the Taros Hoop, and the stunned drow rolled limply to the side and out, tumbling into Pook's room, beneath Catti-brie.

Wulfgar paled at the sight and hesitated, but Drizzt, realizing that more creatures would soon rush through, managed to lift his weary head from the floor. "Close the gate," he gasped.

Wulfgar had already discerned that he could not shatter the glassy image within the hoop—striking at it only sent his warhammer's head into Tarterus. Wulfgar started to drop Aegis-fang to his side.

Then he noticed the action across the room.

✕ ✕ ✕ ✕ ✕

"Are you quick enough with that shield?" Pook teased, wiggling the crossbow.

Intent on the weapon, Bruenor hadn't even noticed Drizzt and Catti-brie's grand entrance. "So ye've one shot to kill me, dog," he spat back, unafraid of death, "and one alone." He took a determined step forward.

Pook shrugged. He was an expert marksman, and his crossbow was as enchanted as any weapon in the Realms. One shot would be enough.

But he never got it off.

A twirling warhammer exploded into the throne, knocking the huge chair over into the guildmaster and sending him sprawling heavily into the wall.

Bruenor turned with a grim smile to thank his barbarian friend, but his smile washed away and the words died in his throat when he saw Drizzt and Catti-brie lying beside the Taros Hoop.

The dwarf stood as if turned to stone, his eyes not blinking, his lungs not drawing breath. The strength went out of his legs, and he fell to his knees. He dropped his axe and shield and scrambled, on all fours, to his daughter's side.

Wulfgar clasped the iron edges of the Taros Hoop in his hands and tried to force them together. His entire upper body flushed red, and the veins and sinewy muscles stood out like iron cords in his huge arms. But if there was any movement in the gate, it was slight.

A demodand arm reached through the portal to prevent the closing, but the sight of it only spurred Wulfgar on. He roared to Tempus and pushed with all his strength, driving his hands together, bending the edges of hoop in to meet each other.

The glassy image bowed with the planar shift, and the demodand's arm dropped to the floor, cleanly severed. Likewise, the demodand that lay dead at Wulfgar's feet, with half its body still inside the gate, twitched and turned.

Wulfgar averted his eyes at the horrid spectacle of a winged demodand caught within the warping planar tunnel, bent and bowed until its skin began to rip apart.

The magic of the Taros Hoop was strong, and Wulfgar, for all of his strength, could not hope to bend the thing far enough to complete the job. He had the gate warped and blocked, but for how long? When he tired, and the Taros Hoop returned to its normal shape, the portal would open once again. Stubbornly the barbarian roared and drove on, turning his head to the side in anticipation of the shattering of the glassy surface.

⚔ ⚔ ⚔ ⚔ ⚔

How pale she seemed, her lips almost blue and her skin dry and chill. Her wounds were vicious, Bruenor saw, but the dwarf sensed that the most telling injury was neither cut nor bruise. Rather, his precious girl seemed to have lost her spirit, as though she'd given up her desire for life when she had fallen into the darkness.

She now lay limp, cold, and pale in his arms. On the floor, Drizzt instinctively recognized the dangers. He lolled over to the side, pulling his cloak out wide, shielding Bruenor, who was quite oblivious to his surroundings, and Catti-brie with his own body.

Across the room, LaValle stirred, shaking the grogginess out of his head. He rose to his knees and surveyed the room, immediately recognizing Wulfgar's attempt to close the gate.

"Kill them," Pook whispered to the wizard but not daring to crawl out from under the overturned chair.

LaValle wasn't listening; he had already begun a spell.

⚔ ⚔ ⚔ ⚔ ⚔

For the first time in his life, Wulfgar found his strength inadequate. "I cannot!" he grunted in dismay, looking to

Drizzt—as he always looked to Drizzt—for an answer.

The wounded drow was barely coherent.

Wulfgar wanted to surrender. His arm burned from the gashes of the hydra bite; his legs seemed barely able to hold him; his friends were helpless on the floor.

And his strength was not enough!

He shot his gaze to and fro, searching for some alternate method. The hoop, however powerful, had to have a weakness. Or, at least, to hold out any hope, Wulfgar had to believe that it did.

Regis had gotten through it, had found a way to circumvent its power.

Regis.

Wulfgar found his answer.

He gave a final heave on the Taros Hoop, then released it quickly, sending the portal into a momentary wobble. Wulfgar didn't hesitate to watch the eerie spectacle. He dived down and snatched the pearl-tipped scepter from Drizzt's belt, then leaped up straight and slammed the fragile device onto the top of the Taros Hoop, shattering the black pearl into a thousand tiny shards.

At that same moment, LaValle uttered the last syllable of his spell, releasing a mighty bolt of energy. It ripped past Wulfgar, searing the hairs on his arm, and blasted into the center of the Taros Hoop. The glassy image, cracked into the circular design of a spider's web by Wulfgar's cunning strike, broke apart altogether.

The ensuing explosion rocked the foundations of the guildhouse.

Thick patches of darkness swirled about the room; the onlookers perceived the whole place to be spinning, and a sudden wind whistled and howled in their ears, as though they had all been caught in the tumult of a rift in the very planes of existence. Black smoke and fumes rushed in upon them. The darkness became total.

Then, as quickly as it had begun, it passed away and daylight returned to the battered room. Drizzt and Bruenor were the first to their feet, studying the damage and the survivors.

The Taros Hoop lay twisted and shattered, a bent frame of worthless iron with a sticky, weblike substance clinging stubbornly in torn patches. A winged demodand lay dead on the floor, the severed arm of another creature beside it, and half the body of yet another beside that, still twitching in death, with thick, dark fluids spilling onto the floor.

A dozen feet back sat Wulfgar, propped up on his elbows and looking perplexed, one arm bright red from LaValle's energy bolt, his face blackened by the rush of smoke, and his entire frame matted in the gooey webbing. A hundred little dots of blood dotted the barbarian's body. Apparently the glassy image of the planar portal had been more than just an image.

Wulfgar looked at his friends distantly, blinked his eyes a few times, and dropped flat on his back.

LaValle groaned, catching the notice of Drizzt and Bruenor. The wizard started to struggle back to his knees, but realized that he would only be exposing himself to the victorious invaders. He slumped back to the floor and lay very still.

Drizzt and Bruenor looked at each other, wondering what to do next.

"Fine to see the light again," came a soft voice below them. They looked down to meet the gaze of Catti-brie, her deep blue eyes opened once again.

Bruenor, in tears, dropped to his knees and huddled over her. Drizzt started to follow the dwarf's lead, but sensed that theirs should be a private moment. He gave a comforting pat on

Bruenor's shoulder and walked away to make sure that Wulfgar was all right.

A sudden burst of movement interrupted him as he knelt over his barbarian friend. The great throne, torn and scorched against the wall, toppled forward. Drizzt held it away easily, but while he was engaged, he saw Pasha Pook dart out from behind the object and bolt for the room's main door.

"Bruenor!" Drizzt called, but he knew even as he said it that the dwarf was too caught up with his daughter to be bothered. Drizzt pushed the great chair away and pulled Taulmaril off his back, stringing it as he started in pursuit.

Pook rushed through the door, swinging around to slam it behind him. "Rassit—" he started to yell as he turned back toward the stairs, but the word stuck in his throat when he saw Regis, arms crossed, standing before him at the top of the stairway.

"You!" Pook roared, his face twisting and his hands clenching in rage.

"No, him," Regis corrected, pointing a finger above as a sleek black form leaped over him.

To the stunned Pook, Guenhwyvar appeared as no more than a flying ball of big teeth and claws.

By the time Drizzt got through the door, Pook's reign as guildmaster had come to a crashing end.

"Guenhwyvar!" the drow called, within reach of his treasured companion for the first time in many tendays. The big panther loped over to Drizzt and nuzzled him warmly, every bit as happy with the reunion.

Other sights and sounds kept the meeting short, however. First there was Regis, reclining comfortably on the decorated banister, his hands locked behind his head and his furry feet crossed. Drizzt was glad to see Regis again, as well, but more disturbing to the drow were the sounds echoing up the stairs: screams of terror and throaty growls.

Bruenor heard them, too, and he came out of the room to investigate. "Rumblebelly!" he hailed Regis, following Drizzt to the halfling's side.

They looked down the great stairway at the battles below. Every now and then, a wererat crossed by, pursued by a panther. One group of ratmen formed a defensive circle, their blades flashing about to deter Guenhwyvar's feline friends, right below the friends, but a wave of black fur and gleaming teeth buried them where they stood.

"Cats?" Bruenor gawked at Regis. "Ye brought cats?"

Regis smiled and shifted his head in his hands. "You know a better way to get rid of mice?"

Bruenor shook his head and couldn't hide his own smile. He looked back at the body of the man who had fled the room. "Dead, too," he remarked grimly.

"That was Pook," Regis told them, though they had already guessed the guildmaster's identity. "Now he is gone, and so, I believe, will his wererats associates be."

Regis looked at Drizzt, knowing an explanation to be necessary. "Guenhwyvar's friends are only hunting the ratmen," he said. "And him, of course" He pointed to Pook. "The regular thieves are hiding in their rooms—if they're smart—but the panthers wouldn't hurt them anyway."

Drizzt nodded his approval at the discretion Regis and Guenhwyvar had chosen. Guenhwyvar was not a vigilante.

"We all came through the statue," Regis continued. "I kept it with me when I went out of Tarterus with Guenhwyvar. The cats can go back through it to their own plane when their work is done." He tossed the figurine back to its rightful owner.

A curious look came over the halfling's face. He snapped his fingers and hopped down from the banister, as if his last action had given him an idea. He ran to Pook, rolled the former guild-master's head to the side—trying to ignore the very conspicuous wound in Pook's neck—and lifted off the ruby pendant that had started the whole adventure. Satisfied, Regis turned to the very curious stares of his two friends.

"Time to make some allies," the haffling explained, and he darted off down the stairs.

Bruenor and Drizzt looked at each other in disbelief.

"He'll own the guild," Bruenor assured the drow.

Drizzt didn't argue the point.

⚔ ⚔ ⚔ ⚔ ⚔

From an alley on Rogues Circle, Rassiter, again in his human form, heard the dying screams of his fellow ratmen. He had been smart enough to understand that the guild was overmatched by the heroes from the North, and when Pook sent him down to rally the fight, he had slipped instead back into the protection of the sewers.

Now he could only listen to the cries and wonder how many of his lycanthrope kin would survive the dark day. "I will build a new guild," he vowed to himself, though he fully understood the enormity of the task, especially now that he had achieved such notoriety in Calimport. Perhaps he could travel to another city—Memnon or Baldur's Gate—farther up the coast.

His ponderings came to an abrupt end as the flat of a curving blade came to rest on his shoulder, the razor edge cutting a tiny line across the side of his neck.

Rassiter held up a jeweled dagger. "This is yours, I believe," he said, trying to sound calm. The saber slipped away and Rassiter turned to face Artemis Entreri.

Entreri reached out with a bandaged arm to pull the dagger away, at the same time slipping the saber back into its scabbard.

"I knew you had been beaten," Rassiter said boldly. "I feared you dead."

"Feared?" Entreri grinned. "Or hoped?"

"It is true that you and I started as rivals," Rassiter began.

Entreri laughed again. He had never figured the ratman worthy enough to be considered a rival.

Rassiter took the insult in stride. "But we then served the same master." He looked to the guildhouse, where the screaming had finally begun to fade. "I think Pook is dead, or at least thrown from power."

"If he faced the drow, he is dead," Entreri spat, the mere thought of Drizzt Do'Urden filling his throat with bile.

"Then the streets are open," Rassiter reasoned. He gave Entreri a sly wink. "For the taking."

"You and I?" Entreri mused.

Rassiter shrugged. "Few in Calimport would oppose you," the wererat said, "and with my infectious bite, I can breed a host of loyal followers in mere tendays. Certainly none would dare stand against us in the night."

Entreri moved beside him, joining him in his scan of the guildhouse. "Yes, my ravenous friend," he said quietly, "but there remain two problems."

"Two?"

"Two," Entreri reiterated. "First, I work alone."

Rassiter's body jolted straight as a dagger blade cut into his spine.

"And second," Entreri continued, without missing a breath, "You are dead." He jerked the bloody dagger out and held it vertical, to wipe the blade on Rassiter's cloak as the wererat fell lifeless to the ground.

Entreri surveyed his handiwork and the bandages on his wounded elbow. "Stronger already," he muttered to himself, and he slipped away to find a dark hole. The morning was full and bright now, and the assassin, still with much healing to do, was not ready to face the challenges he might come across on the daytime streets.

25

A WALK IN THE SUN

B ruenor knocked lightly on the door, not expecting a
response. As usual, no reply came back. This time, though,
the stubborn dwarf did not walk away. He turned the latch and
entered the darkened room.

Stripped to the waist and running his slender fingers through
his thick mane of white hair, Drizzt sat on his bed with his back
to Bruenor. Even in the dimness, Bruenor could clearly see the
scab line sliced across the drow's back. The dwarf shuddered,
never imagining in those wild hours of battle that Drizzt had
been so viciously wounded by Artemis Entreri.

"Five days, elf," Bruenor said quietly. "Do ye mean to live yer
life in here?"

Drizzt turned slowly to face his dwarven friend. "Where else
would I go?" he replied.

Bruenor studied the lavender eyes, twinkling to reflect the
light of the hallway beyond the open door. The left one had

opened again, the dwarf noted hopefully. Bruenor had feared that the demodand's blow had forever closed Drizzt's eye.

Clearly it was healing, but still those marvelous orbs worried Bruenor. They seemed to him to have lost a good bit of their luster.

"How is Catti-brie?" Drizzt asked, sincerely concerned about the young woman, but also wanting to change the subject.

Bruenor smiled. "Not for walkin' yet," he replied, "but her fighting's back and she's not caring for lyin' quiet in a bed!" He chuckled, recalling the scene earlier in the day, when one attendant had tried to primp his daughter's pillow. Catti-brie's glare alone had drained the blood from the man's face. "Cuts her servants down with her blade of a tongue when they fuss over her."

Drizzt's smile seemed strained. "And Wulfgar?"

"The boy's better," Bruenor replied. "Took four hours scraping the spider gook off him, and he'll be wearin' wrappings on his arm for a month to come, but more'n that's needed to bring that boy down! Tough as a mountain, and nearen as big!"

They watched each other until the smiles faded and the silence grew uncomfortable. "The halfling's feast is about to begin," Bruenor said. "Ye going? With a belly so round, me guess is that Rumblebelly will set a fine table."

Drizzt shrugged noncommittally.

"Bah!" Bruenor snorted. "Ye can't be living yer life between dark walls!" He paused as a thought suddenly popped into his head. "Or are ye out at night?" he asked slyly.

"Out?"

"Hunting," explained Bruenor. "Are ye out hunting Entreri?"

Now, Drizzt did laugh—at the notion that Bruenor linked his desire for solitude to some obsession with the assassin.

"Ye're burning for him," Bruenor reasoned, "and he for yerself if he's still for drawing breath."

"Come," Drizzt said, pulling a loose shirt over his head. He picked up the magical mask as he started around the bed, but stopped to consider the item. He rolled it over in his hands, then dropped it back to the dressing table. "Let us not be late for the feast."

Bruenor's guess about Regis had not missed the mark; the table awaiting the two friends was splendidly adorned with shining silver and porcelain, and the aromas of delicacies had them unconsciously licking their lips as they moved to their appointed seats.

Regis sat at the long table's head, the thousand gemstones he had sewn into his tunic catching the candlelight in a glittering burst every time he shifted in his seat. Behind him stood the two hill giant eunuchs who had guarded Pook at the bitter end, their faces bruised and bandaged

At the halfling's right sat LaValle, to Bruenor's distaste, and at his left, a narrow-eyed halfling and a chubby young man, the chief lieutenants in the new guild.

Farther down the table sat Wulfgar and Catti-brie, side by side, their hands clasped between them, which, Drizzt guessed—by the pale and weary looks of the two—was as much for mutual support as genuine affection.

As weary as they were, though, their faces lit with smiles, as did Regis's, when they saw Drizzt enter the room, the first time any of them had seen the drow in nearly a tenday.

"Welcome, welcome!" Regis said happily. "It would have been a shallow feast if you could not join us!"

Drizzt slid into the chair beside LaValle, drawing a concerned look from the timid wizard. The guild's lieutenants, too, shifted uneasily at the thought of dining with a drow elf.

Drizzt smiled away the weight of their discomfort; it was their problem, not his. "I have been busy," he told Regis.

"Brooding," Bruenor wanted to say as he sat next to Drizzt, but he tactfully held his tongue.

Wulfgar and Catti-brie stared at their black friend from across the table.

"You swore to kill me," the drow said calmly to Wulfgar, causing the big man to sag back in his chair.

Wulfgar flushed a deep red and tightened his grip on Catti-brie's hand.

"Only the strength of Wulfgar could have held that gate," Drizzt explained. The edges of his mouth turned up in a wistful smile.

"But, I—" Wulfgar began, but Catti-brie cut him short.

"Enough said about it, then," the young woman insisted, banging her fist into Wulfgar's thigh. "Let us not be talking about troubles we've past. Too much remains before us!"

"Me girl's right," spouted Bruenor. "The days walk by us as we sit and heal! Another tenday, and we might be missing a war."

"I am ready to go," declared Wulfgar.

"Ye're not," retorted Catti-brie. "Nor am I. The desert'd stop us afore we ever got on the long road beyond."

"Ahem," Regis began, drawing their attention. "About your departure . . ." He stopped to consider their stares, nervous about presenting his offer in just the right way. "I . . . uh . . . thought that . . . I mean . . ."

"Spit it," demanded Bruenor, guessing what his little friend had in mind.

"Well, I have built a place for myself here," Regis continued.

"And ye're to stay," reasoned Catti-brie. "We'll not blame ye, though we're sure to be missing ye!"

"Yes," said Regis, "and no. There is room here, and wealth. With the four of you by my side . . ."

Bruenor halted him with an upraised hand. "A fine offer," he said, "but me home's in the North."

"We've armies waiting on our return," added Catti-brie.

Regis realized the finality of Bruenor's refusal, and he knew that Wulfgar would certainly follow Catti-brie back to Tarterus if she so chose. So the halfling turned his sights on Drizzt, who had become an unreadable puzzle to them all in the last few days.

Drizzt sat back and considered the proposition, his hesitancy to deny the offer drawing concerned stares from Bruenor, Wulfgar, and particularly, Catti-brie. Perhaps life in Calimport would not be so bad, and certainly the drow had the tools to thrive in the shadowy realm Regis planned to operate within. He looked Regis square in the eye.

"No," he said. He turned at the audible sigh from Catti-brie across the table, and their eyes locked. "I have walked through too many shadows already," he explained. "A noble quest stands before me, and a noble throne awaits its rightful king."

Regis relaxed back in his chair and shrugged. He had expected as much. "If you are all so determined to go back to a war, then I would be a sorry friend if I did not aid your quest."

The others eyed him curiously, never amazed at the surprises the little one could pull.

"To that end," Regis continued, "one of my agents reported the arrival of an important person—from the tales Bruenor has told me of your journey south—in Calimport this morning." He snapped his fingers, and a young attendant entered from a side curtain, leading Captain Deudermont.

The captain bowed low to Regis, and lower still to the dear friends he had made on the perilous journey from Waterdeep. "The wind was at our backs," he explained, "and the *Sea Sprite* runs swifter than ever. We can depart on the morrow's dawn;

surely the gentle rock of a boat is a fine place to mend weary bones!"

"But the trade," said Drizzt. "The market is here in Calimport. And the season. You did not plan to leave before spring."

"I may not be able to get you all the way to Waterdeep," said Deudermont. "The winds and ice will tell. But you surely will find yourself closer to your goal when you take to land once again." He looked over at Regis, then back to Drizzt. "For my losses in trade, accommodations have been made."

Regis tucked his thumbs into his jeweled belt. "I owed you that, at the least!"

"Bah!" snorted Bruenor, an adventurous gleam in his eye. "Ten times more, Rumblebelly, ten times more!"

⚔ ⚔ ⚔ ⚔ ⚔

Drizzt looked out of his room's single window at the dark streets of Calimport. They seemed quieter this night, hushed in suspicion and intrigue, anticipating the power struggle that would inevitably follow the downfall of a guildmaster as powerful as Pasha Pook.

Drizzt knew that there were other eyes out there, looking back at him, at the guildhouse, waiting for word of the drow elf—waiting for a second chance to battle Drizzt Do'Urden.

The night passed lazily, and Drizzt, unmoving from his window, watched it drift into dawn. Again, Bruenor was the first to his room.

"Ye ready, elf?" the eager dwarf asked, closing the door behind him as he entered.

"Patience, good dwarf," Drizzt replied. "We cannot leave until the tide is right, and Captain Deudermont assured me that we had the bulk of the morning to wait."

Bruenor plopped down on the bed. "Better," he said at length. "Gives me more time to speak with the little one."

"You fear for Regis," observed Drizzt.

"Ayuh," Bruenor admitted. "The little one's done well by me." He pointed to the onyx statuette on the dressing table. "And by yerself. Rumblebelly said it himself: There's wealth to be taken here. Pook's gone, and it's to be grab-as-grab-can. And that Entreri's about—that's not to me likin'. And more of them ratmen, not to doubt, looking to pay the little one back for their pain. And that wizard! Rumblebelly says he's got him by the gemstones, if ye get me meaning, but it seems off to me that a wizard's caught by such a charm."

"To me, as well," Drizzt agreed.

"I don't like him, and I don't trust him!" Bruenor declared. "Rumblebelly's got him standing right by his side."

"Perhaps you and I should pay LaValle a visit this morning," Drizzt offered, "that we might judge where he stands."

⚔ ⚔ ⚔ ⚔ ⚔

Bruenor's knocking technique shifted subtly when they arrived at the wizard's door, from the gentle tapping he had laid on Drizzt's door, to a battering-ram crescendo of heavy slugs. LaValle jumped from his bed and rushed to see what was the matter, and who was beating upon his brand new door.

"Morning, wizard," Bruenor grumbled, pushing into the room as soon as the door cracked open.

"So I guessed," muttered LaValle, looking to the hearth and beside it to the pile of kindling that was once his old door.

"Greetings, good dwarf," he said as politely as he could muster. "And Master Do'Urden," he added quickly when he noticed Drizzt slipping in behind. "Were you not to be gone by this late hour?"

"We have time," said Drizzt.

"And we're not for leaving till we've seen to the safety of Rumblebelly," Bruenor explained.

"Rumblebelly?" echoed LaValle.

"The halfling!" roared Bruenor. "Yer master."

"Ah, yes, Master Regis," said LaValle wistfully, his hands going together over his chest and his eyes taking on a distant, glossy look.

Drizzt shut the door and glared, suspicious, at him.

LaValle's faraway trance faded back to normal when he considered the unblinking drow. He scratched his chin, looking for somewhere to run. He couldn't fool the drow, he realized. The dwarf, perhaps, the halfling, certainly, but not this one. Those lavender eyes burned holes right through his facade. "You do not believe that your little friend has cast his enchantment over me," he said.

"Wizards avoid wizards' traps," Drizzt replied.

"Fair enough," said LaValle, slipping into a chair.

"Bah! Then ye're a liar, too!" growled Bruenor, his hand going to the axe on his belt. Drizzt stopped him.

"If you doubt the enchantment," said LaValle, "do not doubt my loyalty. I am a practical man who has served many masters in my long life. Pook was the greatest of these, but Pook is gone. LaValle lives on to serve again."

"Or mighten be that he sees a chance to make the top," Bruenor remarked, expecting an angry response from LaValle.

Instead, the wizard laughed heartily. "I have my craft," he said. "It is all that I care for. I live in comfort and am free to go as I please. I need not the challenges and dangers of a guildmaster." He looked to Drizzt as the more reasonable of the two. "I will serve the halfling, and if Regis is thrown down, I will serve he that takes the halfling's place."

The logic satisfied Drizzt, and convinced him of the wizard's loyalty beyond any enchantment the ruby could have induced. "Let us take our leave," he said to Bruenor, and he started out the door.

Bruenor could trust Drizzt's judgment, but he couldn't resist one final threat. "Ye crossed me, wizard," he growled from the doorway. "Ye nearen killed me girl. If me friend comes to a bad end, ye'll pay with yer head."

LaValle nodded but said nothing.

"Keep him well," the dwarf finished with a wink, and he slammed the door with a bang.

"He hates my door," the wizard lamented.

The troupe gathered inside the guildhouse's main entrance an hour later, Drizzt, Bruenor, Wulfgar, and Catti-brie outfitted again in their adventuring gear, and Drizzt with the magical mask hanging loose around his neck.

Regis, with attendants in tow, joined them. He would make the trip to the *Sea Sprite* beside his formidable friends. Let his enemies see his allies in all their splendor, the sly new guildmaster figured, particularly a drow elf.

"A final offer before we go," Regis proclaimed.

"We're not for staying," Bruenor retorted.

"Not to you," Regis said. He turned squarely to Drizzt. "To you."

Drizzt waited patiently for the pitch as the halfling rubbed his eager hands together.

"Fifty thousand gold pieces," Regis said at length, "for your cat."

Drizzt's eyes widened to double their size.

"Guenhwyvar will be well cared for, I assure—"

Catti-brie slapped Regis on the back of the head. "Find yer shame," she scolded. "Ye know the drow better than that!"

Drizzt calmed her with a smile. "A treasure for a treasure?" he said to Regis. "You know I must decline. Guenhwyvar cannot be bought, however good your intentions may be."

"Fifty thousand," Bruenor huffed. "If we wanted it, we'd take it afore we left!"

Regis then realized the absurdity of the offer, and he blushed in embarrassment.

"Are you so certain that we came across the world to your aid?" Wulfgar asked him. Regis looked at the barbarian, confused.

"Perhaps 'twas the cat we came after," Wulfgar continued seriously.

The stunned look on Regis's face proved more than any of them could bear, and a burst of laughter like none of them had enjoyed in many months erupted, infecting even Regis.

"Here," Drizzt offered when things had quieted once again. "Take this instead." He pulled the magical mask off his head and tossed it to the halfling.

"Should ye keep it until we get to the boat?" Bruenor asked.

Drizzt looked to Catti-brie for an answer, and her smile of approval and admiration cast away any remaining doubts he might have had.

"No," he said. "Let the Calishites judge me for what they will." He swung open the doors, allowing the morning sun to sparkle in his lavender eyes.

"Let the wide world judge me for what it will," he said, his look one of genuine contentment as he dropped his gaze alternately into the eyes of each of his four friends.

"You know who I am."

EPILOGUE

The *Sea Sprite* cut a difficult course northward up the Sword Coast, into the wintry winds, but Captain Deudermont and his grateful crew were determined to see the four friends safely and swiftly back to Waterdeep.

Stunned expressions from every face on the docks greeted the resilient vessel as it put into Waterdeep Harbor, dodging the breakers and the ice floes as it went. Mustering all the skill he had gained through years of experience, Deudermont docked the *Sea Sprite* safely.

The four friends had recovered much of their health, and their humor, during those two months at sea, despite the rough voyage. All had turned out well in the end—even Catti-brie's wounds appeared as if they would fully heal.

But if the sea voyage back to the North was difficult, the trek across the frozen lands was even worse. Winter was on the wane but still thick in the land, and the friends could not afford to wait for the snows to melt. They said their good-byes to Deudermont and the men of the *Sea Sprite*, tightened heavy cloaks and boots, and trudged off through Waterdeep's gate along the Trade Way on the northeastern course to Longsaddle.

Blizzards and wolves reared up to stop them. The path of the road, its plentiful markings buried under a year's worth of snow, became no more than the guess of a drow elf reading the stars and the sun.

Somehow they made it, though, and they stormed into Longsaddle, ready to retake Mithral Hall. Bruenor's kin from Icewind Dale were there to greet them, along with five hundred of Wulfgar's people. Less than two tendays later, General Dagnabit of Citadel Adbar led his eight thousand dwarven troops to Bruenor's side.

Battle plans were drawn and redrawn. Drizzt and Bruenor put their memories of the undercity and mine caverns together to create models of the place and estimate the number of duergar the army would face.

Then, with spring defeating the last blows of winter, and only a few days before the army was to set out to the mountains, two more groups of allies came in, quite unexpectedly: contingents of archers from Silverymoon and Nesme. Bruenor at first wanted to turn the warriors from Nesme away, remembering the treatment he and his friends had received at the hands of a Nesme patrol on their initial journey to Mithral Hall, and also because the dwarf wondered how much of the show of allegiance was motivated in the hopes of friendship, and how much in the hopes of profit!

But, as usual, Bruenor's friends kept him on a wise course. The dwarves would have to deal extensively with Nesme, the closest settlement to Mithral Hall, once the mines were reopened, and a smart leader would patch the bad feelings there and then.

✠ ✠ ✠ ✠

Their numbers were overwhelming, their determination unrivaled, and their leaders magnificent. Bruenor and Dagnabit led the main assault force of battle-hardened dwarves and wild barbarians, sweeping out room after room of the duergar scum. Catti-brie, with her bow, the few Harpells who had made the journey, and the archers from the two cities, cleared the side passages along the main force's thrust.

Drizzt, Wulfgar, and Guenhwyvar, as they had so often in the past, forged out alone, scouting the areas ahead of and below the army, taking out more than their share of duergar along the way.

In three days, the top level was cleared. In two tendays, the undercity. By the time spring had settled fully onto the northland, less than a month after the army had set out from Longsaddle, the hammers of Clan Battlehammer began their smithing song in the ancient halls once again.

And the rightful king took his throne.

✠ ✠ ✠ ✠

Drizzt looked down from the mountains to the distant lights of the enchanted city of Silverymoon. He had been turned away from that city once before—a painful rejection—but not this time.

He could walk the land as he chose, now, with his head held high and the cowl of his cloak thrown back. Most of the world did not treat him any differently; few knew the name of Drizzt Do'Urden. But Drizzt knew now that he owed no apologies, or excuses, for his black skin, and to those who placed unfair judgment upon him, he offered none.

The weight of the world's prejudice would still fall upon him heavily, but Drizzt had learned, by the insights of Catti-brie, to stand against it.

What a wonderful friend she was to him. Drizzt had watched her grow into a special young woman, and he was warmed now by the knowledge that she had found her home.

The thought of her with Wulfgar, and standing beside Bruenor, touched the dark elf, who had never experienced the closeness of family.

"How much we all have changed," the drow whispered to the empty mountain wind.

His words were not a lament.

⚔ ⚔ ⚔ ⚔ ⚔

The autumn saw the first crafted goods flow from Mithral Hall to Silverymoon, and by the time winter turned again to spring, the trade was in full force, with the barbarians from Icewind Dale working as market bearers for the dwarven goods.

That spring, too, a carving was begun in the Hall of Kings: the likeness of Bruenor Battlehammer.

To the dwarf who had wandered so far from his home and had seen so many marvelous—and horrible—sights, the reopening of the mines, and even the carving of his bust, seemed of minor importance when weighed against another event planned for that year.

"I told ye he'd be back," Bruenor said to Wulfgar and Catti-brie, who both sat beside him in his audience hall. "Th' elf'd not be missing such a thing as yer wedding!"

General Dagnabit—who, with blessings from King Harbromme of Citadel Adbar, had stayed on with two thousand other dwarves, swearing allegiance to Bruenor—entered the room, escorting a figure who had become less and less noticeable in Mithral Hall over the last few months.

"Greetings," said Drizzt, moving up to his friends

"So ye made it," Catti-brie said absently, feigning disinterest.

"We had not planned for this," added Wulfgar in the same casual tone. "I pray that there may be an extra seat at the table."

Drizzt only smiled and bowed low in apology. He had been absent quite often—for tendays at a time—lately. Personal invitations to visit the Lady of Silverymoon and her enchanted realm were not so easily refused.

"Bah!" Bruenor snorted. "I told ye he'd come back! And back to stay, this time!"

Drizzt shook his head.

Bruenor cocked his in return, wondering what was getting into his friend. "Ye hunting for that assassin, elf?" he could not help but ask.

Drizzt grinned and shook his bead again "I've no desire to meet that one again," he replied. He looked at Catti-brie—she understood—then back to Bruenor. "There are many sights in the wide world, dear dwarf, that cannot be seen from the shadows. Many sounds more pleasant than the ring of steel, and many smells preferable to the stench of death."

"Cook another feast," Bruenor grumbled. "Suren the elf has his eyes fixed on another wedding!"

Drizzt let it go at that. Maybe there was a ring of truth in Bruenor's words, for some distant date. No longer did Drizzt limit his hopes and desires. He would see the world as he could and draw his choices from his wishes, not from limitations he might impose upon himself. For now, though, Drizzt had found something too personal to be shared.

For the first time in his life, the drow had found peace.

Another dwarf entered the room and scurried up to Dagnabit. They both took their leave, but Dagnabit returned a few moments later.

"What is it?" Bruenor asked him, confused by all the bustle.

"Another guest," Dagnabit explained, but before he could launch a proper introduction, a halfling figure slipped into the room.

"Regis!" Catti-brie cried. She and Wulfgar rushed to meet their old friend.

"Rumblebelly!" Bruenor yelled. "What in the Nine Hells—"

"Did you believe that I would miss this occasion?" Regis huffed. "The wedding of two of my dearest friends?"

"How'd ye know?" Bruenor asked.

"You underestimate your fame, King Bruenor," Regis said, dropping into a graceful bow.

Drizzt studied the halfling curiously. He wore his gem-studded jacket and more jewelry, including the ruby pendant, than the drow had ever seen in one place. And the pouches hanging low on Regis's belt were sure to be filled with gold and gems.

"Might ye be staying long?" Catti-brie asked.

Regis shrugged. "I am in no hurry," he replied. Drizzt cocked an eyebrow. A master of a thieves' guild did not often leave his place of power; too many were usually ready to steal it out from under him.

Catti-brie seemed happy with the answer and happy with the timing of the halfling's return. Wulfgar's people were soon to rebuild the city of Settlestone, at the base of the mountains. She and Wulfgar, though, planned to remain in Mithral Hall, at Bruenor's side. After the wedding, they planned to do a bit of traveling they'd had in mind, maybe back to Icewind Dale, maybe along with Captain Deudermont later in the year, when the *Sea Sprite* sailed back to the southlands.

Catti-brie dreaded telling Bruenor that they would be leaving, if only for a few months. With Drizzt so often on the road, she feared that the dwarf would be miserable. But if Regis planned to stay on for a while . . .

"Might I have a room," Regis asked, "to put my things and to rest away the weariness of a long road?"

"We'll see to it," Catti-brie offered.

"And for your attendants?" Bruenor asked.

"Oh," stammered Regis, searching for a reply. "I . . . came alone. The southerners do not take well to the chill of a northern spring, you know."

"Well, off with ye, then," said Bruenor. "Suren it be me turn to set out a feast for the pleasure of yer belly."

Regis rubbed his hands together eagerly and left with Wulfgar and Catti-brie, the three of them breaking into tales of their latest adventures before they had even left the room.

"Suren few folk in Calimport have ever heared o' me name, elf," Bruenor said to Drizzt after the others had gone. "And who south o' Longsaddle would be knowing of the wedding?" He turned a sly eye on his dark friend. "Suren the little one brings a bit of his treasure along with him, eh?"

Drizzt had come to the same conclusion the moment Regis had entered the room. "He is running."

"Got himself into trouble again," Bruenor snorted, "or I'm a bearded gnome!"